RISK EVERYTHING

JANIE CROUCH

COLD CONSPIRACY

CINDI MYERS

MILLS & BOON

First Published in Great Britain 2019
by Mills & Boon, an imprint of HarperCollins*Publishers*
1 London Bridge Street, London, SE1 9GF

Risk Everything © 2019 Janie Crouch
Cold Conspiracy © 2019 Cynthia Myers

ISBN: 978-0-263-27441-7

1019

MIX
Paper from
responsible sources
FSC
www.fsc.org
FSC™ C007454

This book is produced from independently certified FSC™ paper to ensure responsible forest management.

For more information visit: www.harpercollins.co.uk/green

Printed and bound in Spain
by CPI, Barcelona

Janie Crouch has loved to read romance her whole life. This *USA TODAY* bestselling author cut her teeth on Mills & Boon novels as a preteen, then moved on to a passion for romantic suspense as an adult. Janie lives with her husband and four children overseas. She enjoys travelling, long-distance running, movie watching, knitting and adventure/obstacle racing. You can find out more about her at janiecrouch.com

Cindi Myers is the author of more than fifty novels. When she's not crafting new romance plots, she enjoys skiing, gardening, cooking, crafting and daydreaming. A lover of small-town life, she lives with her husband and two spoiled dogs in the Colorado mountains.

Also by Janie Crouch

Calculated Risk
Security Risk
Constant Risk
Daddy Defender
Protector's Instinct
Cease Fire
Special Forces Saviour
Fully Committed
Armoured Attraction
Man of Action

Also by Cindi Myers

Ice Cold Killer
Snowbound Suspicion
Saved by the Sheriff
Avalanche of Trouble
Deputy Defender
Danger on Dakota Ridge
Murder in Black Canyon
Undercover Husband
Manhunt on Mystic Mesa
Soldier's Promise

Discover more at millsandboon.co.uk

RISK EVERYTHING

JANIE CROUCH

This book is dedicated to Marci Mathers.
Thank you for the years of support and friendship.
You mean the world to me.

Chapter One

In the past year Bree Daniels had been chased across the country, shot at, kidnapped, almost blown up, strangled and had watched the man she loved almost bleed to death right in front of her.

But she could honestly say none of that was as treacherous as what she was going through now.

Planning her wedding.

Seriously. When a bad guy with a gun or a knife came at you, you knew you were in trouble. But nobody suspected that agreeing to get married and giving the ladies of the small town where you'd made your home free rein in planning said nuptials was also just as dangerous.

If they were ever arrested, wedding planners would need their own special section in prison. In isolation. Because otherwise they would take over and rule the place, for sure.

For the past seven months the women of Risk Peak—mostly Cassandra, her good friend and future sister-in-law, and Cheryl, owner of the Sunrise Diner and surrogate mother to Bree—had tracked Bree down, no matter where she'd tried to hide, demanding answers to impossible questions of all types.

Like what kinds of flower arrangements Bree wanted.

And whether she wanted a custard cream, buttercream or whipped cream to go along with the raspberry ganache in the cake.

When Bree had finally had a chance to look up what a ganache was, she wanted to throw her computer across the room. Why the heck hadn't they just said raspberry *filling*?

The ladies were so enthusiastic about the event that Bree wasn't even sure they would notice if she fled the state.

The thought had crossed her mind.

But she was trying to be more *normal*. Normal women were excited about all this wedding planning, right? Cassandra had shown her the scrapbook she'd made from the ages of seven to eighteen. That thing had roughly four million pages of pictures of wedding gowns, color schemes, flower types and bridesmaids' dresses.

Bree had mentioned there were much better ways to organize the information electronically, but Cassandra had just rolled her eyes and said that wasn't the point.

Bree wasn't exactly sure what was the point, but she knew that most women were a lot more excited about this whole planning process than she was.

Bree just wanted to be Mrs. Tanner Dempsey. She wished she could go back in time and punch her past self in the face for not taking him up on his offer/threat to drag her in front of the nearest county judge and get married right away after they'd gotten engaged.

Well, the *second* time they'd gotten engaged.

The first time he'd asked her it had been right after a monster from her past had almost blown them both up. They'd been covered in smoke, bleeding and a little shaky on their feet. But Tanner had dropped to one knee right there and asked her to marry him, not wanting to wait a second longer.

The second time, a few weeks later on Valentine's Day, Tanner had taken her deep into the land of the ranch they both loved and asked her again—so romantically—at sunset, the gorgeous Rocky Mountains in the distance.

He'd explained that when she told their grandkids about how he'd asked her to marry him, he wanted this to be the story she would tell.

She planned to tell *both*.

But the next day when Tanner had threatened to drag her to get married *right then*, she should've taken him up on it.

Maybe then she wouldn't be going through the most vicious of wedding planning torture: the gown fittings. The gown *everything*. She'd almost rather be on the run for her life than be twisted, pulled on, poked and prodded and, worst of all, *oohed* over.

"My brother is going to lose his…*stuff* when he sees you in this wedding gown."

Cassandra Dempsey Martin was the only person Bree knew who could out curse a seasoned sailor yet still be in tears at the sight of the wedding gown.

Cheryl grabbed Cassandra's hand that was fluttering emotionally in midair and nodded. "Oh, honey, it really does look more gorgeous every time you put it on."

Bree grimaced. "It's just so much money to spend on a dress that I'm only going to wear once. That's just so impractical. Why would I do this?"

It went against every instinct Bree had to be impractical. She was nothing if not logical, orderly and pragmatic.

Cassandra rolled her eyes. "It's your *wedding dress*.

It's supposed to be impractical. Because if you do it right, you only do it once. Because you deserve to wear a beautiful gown walking down the aisle. And besides, it's really not that much for a wedding dress. Most gowns cost five times that much."

Bree just stared at herself in the three-way mirror. She had to admit, it was a beautiful, elaborate dress. It made her waist seem trimmer, and her hips, which had filled out to a much more feminine shape over the last few months since she was eating regularly and not on the run for her life, flared nicely under the material.

But it was too fancy. Too much lace. Too many sequins. Too much of that itchy white stuff. It was a gorgeous gown, but it just wasn't *her*. She shouldn't have let herself be talked into it, but Cheryl and Dan—the people who had taken her in when she first arrived in Risk Peak basically living out of her car—had insisted on buying her a gown. Then Bree had made the mistake of taking Cassandra and a group of their friends shopping with her for one.

She'd put this gown on in the dressing room with the associate's help and then almost taken it back off again. It was too fancy. But the damned associate had talked her into showing it to her friends.

There was so much crying and cursing from her friends when they saw the dress, Bree figured they must know something she didn't. And when it came to dresses, that was a lot. So she'd gotten it.

And it was still just as beautiful. She couldn't deny that.

Plus, if she was honest, she could admit it wasn't really even the dress that had her in such a tizzy. It was the fact that in two weeks she was going to have to stand up in front of over five hundred people—that was more people than she'd ever talked to in her entire life *combined*—and say her vows to Tanner. Vows they'd agreed to personalize and write themselves.

If Bree speaking in front of a huge group of people about her emotions wasn't a recipe for disaster, she didn't know what was. The elegant bride in the beautiful dress looking back at her from the mirror broke out into a sweat at the thought.

She'd been engaged to Tanner for seven months. In love with him since almost the first moment she'd met him months before that. But she was only just now getting to the point where she could make coherent sentences about her emotions directly to him *alone*. He didn't seem to mind when she stuttered over words or blurted out often socially inappropriate declarations. He took it in stride and had learned how to "speak Bree fluently," as he called it.

But it wouldn't be just Tanner at the wedding in two weeks. It would be a bunch of people who *didn't* speak Bree fluently. She was going to make a complete fool out of herself and embarrass him. She already knew it. And didn't see any way to get around it.

"Hey, do you really not like it that much? You look gorgeous." Cassandra made eye contact with Bree in the mirror as she peeked over her shoulder.

"No, it's not the dress." Not *just* the dress, although the dress was pretty much an icon for the fraud Bree felt like. "It's the whole wedding. I'm just not good at this stuff, you know that."

Cassandra grinned. "You're not giving yourself enough credit for how far you've come in the last few months. Think about what we've done with New Journeys."

Cheryl smiled her encouragement too. "A far cry

from that exhausted woman who fell asleep at the diner table over a year ago."

The seamstress came in and positioned Bree's arms to do the pinnings for the final fitting. Cassandra was right in a lot of ways. When Bree moved here a year ago, she'd barely known how to talk to anyone. Now she was helping run a very successful women's shelter program. It had grown so big that a few months ago they'd had to move into a larger facility.

"New Journeys still doesn't mean I'm not going to make a complete idiot out of myself in front of the town during the ceremony." Bree spun in the opposite direction when the seamstress motioned for her to do so. "Good thing we're not going to split the aisles between the bride's side and the groom's side. My side would be so empty we might tip over the whole church."

Bree's only family was her cousin Melissa. She and her husband, Chris, and their twin nineteen-month-olds were coming, and Bree was so thrilled to see the babies that had first brought her and Tanner together. But it still didn't make up for the fact that Tanner had been born and raised in Risk Peak and knew half the residents of Grand County personally.

Cassandra shook her head. "You know people here love you. Mom would probably sit on your side. I definitely would. We both like you better than Tanner anyway."

Bree laughed as the seamstress finished her pinning and began to carefully take off the lovely gown. Cassandra was right—the people in Risk Peak cared about her. She needed to remember that.

And try to live through her own wedding.

An hour later, Bree and Cassandra were pulling up to the three-story office building on the outskirts of

Risk Peak that had been converted into apartments and bedrooms for the shelter. The stress from the wedding planning and dress fitting melted away when Bree saw it. This place gave her purpose. This place made a difference in women's lives.

Bree knew what it was like to live in fear and feel like she had no options. If she could help take that same heavy sense of despair from another woman, she would gladly do it. She'd been teaching computer skills to the women at New Journeys for the past seven months; Cassandra offered training in basic cosmetology for those interested in that route.

Cassandra and Bree walked in the main front door that opened into the hallway and expansive living room of New Journeys. The living room was giant—they'd deliberately knocked out a number of walls when they remodeled the place to give the room a wide-open feel. A television sat in one corner with a couch and a couple of chairs around it. A second corner had been turned into a giant reading nook, with books of every kind and for every age. The other end of the room held a table with a half-completed jigsaw puzzle and board games stacked on a corner shelf.

This was the family room, even for the people here, many of whom struggled to understand what a family was supposed to feel like. Family was another concept Bree hadn't understood very well before meeting Tanner and coming to live in Risk Peak.

She hung her lightweight jacket on a wall hook and looked around. Even May in Colorado could be cool. Everything was as it should be—loud and relaxed. Women talking, kids laughing, the TV on in the background, the dog running around in circles after its own tail. Late afternoon tended to be a boisterous time around here.

"Bree Cheese!"

Bree smiled at the sound of the two small voices calling her name from the table and chairs over in the corner. It was one of her favorite sounds in the entire world.

Sam and Eva, seven and five years old respectively, were the two children of Marilyn Ellis. They'd lived here for four months with their mom.

Marilyn had been Bree's best computer student to date. Even though the woman hadn't graduated from high school, nor gone to college, she picked up the computer classes Bree taught with the ease of a natural.

And had also become one of Bree's good friends to the point that she was even going to be a bridesmaid in her wedding. Little Eva was going to be the flower girl.

"You guys should let Miss Bree get in the door before you start screaming your heads off for her," Marilyn admonished softly. Marilyn did everything softly. In the four months Bree had known her, she had never once heard the other woman raise her voice.

Bree didn't know everything about Marilyn's situation before she arrived in Risk Peak, but she knew her husband had put her in the hospital and was now awaiting trial. Marilyn and the kids had been some of the first residents at New Journeys. And when they'd opened the new facility, Marilyn had agreed to take a full-time job as the building facilitator and sort of den mom.

She excelled at it.

"Of course I want to see these two as soon as I come in the door." Bree pulled the kids in for a hug. "Who wouldn't want a squad of rug rats chanting their name first thing?"

And it was true. To see how Eva and Sam were blossoming made it worth any possible crazy name the kids might call her. Including Bree Cheese, which had been the compromise between them calling her Bree the way she had wanted, and Miss Daniels, the way Marilyn wanted.

"Schoolwork, you two. Got to make sure you're ready for next week's camping trip." Marilyn pointed back to the table. The kids moaned and tromped forward like they were headed to the guillotine.

Bree laughed at their dramatics, delighting in it. Just a few months ago they would've never acted that way. "Their teacher must be pretty mean."

Marilyn gave a small smile. She was their teacher since she'd decided to teach them at home for the rest of this school year rather than add the trauma of a new school to an already traumatic year. "They're so excited about the camping, I can hardly get an hour's worth of work out of them."

"Understandable." Bree smiled once more.

"Everything okay here while we were gone?" Cassandra asked.

"Nothing of particular interest. That pipe in the hall bath is still leaking a little."

"And no word about Jared?" Bree asked softly.

Marilyn flinched at the sound of her estranged husband's name before smoothing her features. "Nothing either way."

Jared's lawyer was trying to get him out on bail, something Marilyn definitely didn't want happening.

"Okay, good." Bree nodded. "Keep us posted."

"I will. Although finding out details isn't easy. Ironically, because of privacy issues." Marilyn sighed softly and looked over at Eva and Sam. "The kids are sad that Chandler is gone."

Bree met Cassandra's eyes and then looked at Marilyn, all of them giving resigned nods. Chandler's mother, Angel, had been here three weeks. Two days ago, she'd decided to move back in with her boyfriend, despite the violent situation that had originally caused her to leave in the first place.

Angel said her boyfriend had changed. Had made promises.

Bree didn't know which was harder: seeing the hope in the other woman's eyes or knowing that the chances her boyfriend had changed after multiple years of abuse were pretty nonexistent.

And poor Chandler was caught in the middle of it all.

It wasn't the first time someone from New Journeys had decided to return to a less than optimal situation. It had taken both Bree and Cassandra quite a bit of time to come to grips with the fact that not everyone could make the permanent break from their abusive situations. For some, the unknown was harder to deal with than the pain.

But it still sometimes broke Bree's heart.

All they could do was provide what they could: a safe place and a new set of skills so that these women could support themselves, get back up on their feet and move on with their lives.

People like Marilyn were a prime example of why places like New Journeys was needed. She had made a huge difference in her own life once she had just a little help. But it was also needed for people like Angel who found the steps so much more difficult to take.

Bree and Cassandra grabbed cups of coffee, and they all came back into the family room to chat about all the daily things that needed tending to here. Half the building still hadn't been renovated yet. New Journeys had quite a bit of private funding thanks to the Matarazzo family, who worked with some law enforcement group named Omega Sector in Colorado Springs, but renovating everything at once would have been too much to handle on multiple levels.

They currently had sixteen residents in the building, about three-quarters of its current capacity, and roughly one-third of what the building would be able to house once all the renovations were finished.

New Journeys had gone out of their way to make themselves particularly welcoming to women with children, so over half of the residents now had children with them—babies up through middle-school age.

Which explained the noise level in the room right now. None of the three women paid much attention to it. Cassandra and Marilyn were used to it since they had their own kids, and Bree just loved the chaos of it all.

But when the room fell almost completely silent a few moments later she sadly knew what had happened. A man had walked into the room. Bree forced herself not to tense or turn around to see who it was. How she reacted would influence how everyone else reacted.

Cassandra winked at her—able to see who was in the doorway—and a half smile pulled at Bree's face as she heard giggles a few moments later. She knew exactly what man had walked into the room.

Hers.

Chapter Two

Tanner kept his stance neutral, his posture relaxed as he made his way into the silent room. Susan, one of the residents here, knew him and had let him in the side kitchen door when he'd knocked.

Nobody got into New Journeys who wasn't invited. Every door had double reinforced locks and a security code. Nobody could just wander in from the streets and enter the building. With all the time Bree spent here, and with as many violent offenders the residents of New Journeys had contact with, Tanner had personally made sure of it.

Tanner knew the code, of course, and had a key to let himself in if there was an emergency, but he'd never done so. The women and children who lived here needed to know they were safe from both danger and from uninvited men just wandering around, even those who didn't mean harm.

Case in point, the silence that fell over the large living room when he entered. Every child stopped what they were doing—playing, homework, talking—and stared at him.

He wasn't sure if his Grand County Sheriff's Office uniform helped or hindered his attempt to set a positive example of what a man should be. Some of these women and children had received no help from law enforcement when they'd needed it most.

He stood in the doorway for a long moment, a smile on his face, arms resting loosely at his sides as everyone processed who he was and that he meant no one here any harm. It didn't take them more than a couple of seconds to get past their instinctive fear.

He grinned as big as he could, then brought his finger up to his lips, telling all the kids to keep quiet. Using exaggerated motions, he pretended to sneak up behind Bree. The kids began to giggle, knowing both Cassandra and Marilyn could see him and weren't concerned, so they didn't have to be either.

"You can't escape the kissing monster," he said in a deep, Muppet-sounding voice. He began pecking at the top of her head, her cheeks, her shoulders, from where she sat in the chair at the table.

Bree played along, like he'd known she would. "Oh, no, not the kissing monster."

Giggles broke out all over the room, then turned into laughing noises of disgust as Bree finally turned her head up and Tanner kissed her—very chastely— on the lips.

It was their routine. It had started out in jest, but when they'd realized how much some of these children, and their moms, needed to see men in a more easygoing, positive light, it had become a regular part of their day as Tanner picked her up to escort her home.

The noise in the room fell back to its dull roar, everyone returning to their activities now that the show was over, as Bree stood up and smiled at him.

Those green eyes still gutted him just as much now as they had the first time he saw her shoplifting in the drugstore over a year ago.

"Hi," she whispered.

He looped an arm around her waist and pulled her close, but he didn't kiss her the way he wanted to, mindful of the audience who might not be actively watching but were still aware of their every move. "Hi, yourself. Good day?"

He knew she'd had a wedding dress fitting today, and that that event tended to stress her out.

But he was also a man and knew better than to try to offer any advice or help. That would probably just get him killed. Not by Bree, but definitely by Cassandra or one of the other women in the throes of wedding planning bliss.

"Let's just say I'll be happy two weeks from now when all this is over and I never have to be the center of attention again."

He trailed a finger down her cheek and leaned closer to make sure no one could hear them. "You may not be the center of the town's attention, but I can promise you that once you are Mrs. Dempsey, you very definitely will be the center of my attention."

He loved how her breath hitched and her mouth formed a little O shape.

"Hey, you two," Cassandra's voice rang out. "There are little eyes everywhere."

Tanner was well aware of that. It was the only reason he didn't have Bree pushed up against the wall kissing the life out of her.

He forced himself to take a step back. "I'll behave."

The look of disappointment on Bree's face was almost the death of him. Whoever's idea it had been not to have sex for the last two months before their wedding was a complete idiot.

Oh, yeah, that was him.

He forced himself to step away and sat down to talk about New Journeys and any issues. What happened here affected him on multiple levels. Personally, because of his tie to Bree and Cassandra. Professionally, because he was the captain of the sheriff's department for this section of the county. Whatever he could do to help keep these women safe and secure, he was more than willing to do.

Sometimes that meant grabbing a hammer and drill and helping hang some pictures or adjust some light fixtures. Tanner didn't mind. As a matter of fact, he and his brother, Noah, had been spending quite a few hours here during their time off. Both of them also realized that they were doing a lot more than some random honey-do list items by showing up week after week. They were trying, in some small way, to reclaim part of what had been lost by the years of violence perpetrated against the residents here.

It wasn't enough. Wouldn't ever be enough. But at least it was something.

Bree was talking schedules with Cassandra and Marilyn when Tanner felt a tug on his sleeve. He knew who it was before he even looked by how Marilyn's eyes tracked the entire situation.

"Why, hello there, princess."

Eva smiled up at him. "Hi, Captain Lips."

Tanner managed not to grimace at his nickname. Bree had made the mistake of calling him by her private nickname for him—Captain Hot Lips—in front of Cassandra. His sister, never one to let a humiliating situation die naturally, started calling him that all the time. But at least the kids had overheard only part of it, and thus the nickname Captain Lips.

But this sweet child could call him anything she

wanted if it meant she felt free enough to come talk to him.

Sam was standing next to her silently, not making eye contact with Tanner, but prepared to step in as best he could to protect his sister if needed. Tanner had nothing but respect for that.

"You ready for the camping trip next week?" he asked Eva. "You're going to have a great time."

Eva nodded vehemently, but her little face scrunched up as she pointed at the dog standing between her and Sam. "Mom says Tromso can't go."

Tanner reached down and petted the oversize pup named after the city in Norway where thousands of people flock every year to see the northern lights. Since the pup's mom was named Corfu, after an island in Greece, the name sort of fit.

"Yeah, Tromso's not quite ready for that type of adventure yet. He might get into something poisonous or run off before we could grab him. Better let him stay here where he'll be nice and safe."

Eva considered him soberly. "That's probably true. Mom says Tromso can find trouble faster than anyone she's ever seen."

As if to make her point, the dog began pushing at Eva with his nose, wanting her to play. Eva giggled—a beautiful sound. Even Sam looked up and smiled when Tromso put his wet nose against the boy's stomach.

Eva let out a sigh. "Mom also says we've got to get all our schoolwork done or we can't go."

Tanner couldn't imagine any circumstances under which Marilyn wasn't going to allow her children to go on this beloved camping trip, but he didn't let that cat out of the bag. "You guys better work hard then. It would be a shame to miss it."

"Do you think Mr. Noah will come back this Saturday?" Sam asked softly, staring down and rubbing at some invisible stain in the carpet with his foot. "He and I were supposed to finish hanging the shower rod in the new bathroom."

"I'm sure he will," Tanner said, knowing that even if his brother had to break plans, he would be here if it meant Sam wouldn't be disappointed. Kid had already been let down too many times in his life.

Tanner's words seemed to be all the encouragement the children needed. They made a beeline back to the table with their work. Marilyn mouthed the words *thank you* to him. He just smiled.

Tanner waited as Bree finished her discussions with the other women, listening and commenting when they asked for his opinion. He loved how confident Bree had become since starting her position here. He could still remember the first night Cassandra had mentioned the possibility and how Bree had scoffed at the thought of being able to teach others. But now she was much more easily able to speak her mind and share her opinions, at least with small groups. She'd battled through her fears and had come out on the other side stronger for it.

He couldn't wait to make this woman his wife.

Holding her hand after dinner at the Sunrise Diner, Tanner walked her to her apartment on the outskirts of town. Most of her stuff was already at his ranch house—soon to be their house—on the land he shared with Noah. But neither of them trusted themselves to keep the no-sex agreement if they were both sleeping under the same roof. So Bree had been staying back at her apartment for the last two months.

He was definitely an idiot to have suggested the no-sex plan.

Bree sighed softly as they walked into her apartment. Tanner pulled her up against him.

"Please tell me that sigh means you're going to call me a moron for suggesting we not have sex until the wedding." He reached down and began nibbling at her lips. "Because I feel like that was the most stupid thing I've ever said in my entire life."

He rubbed up against her like a damned teenager. Bree smiled and wrapped her arms around his neck.

"No, this particular sigh was concerning Marilyn."

Tanner took a breath and forced himself to step back.

"About her position at New Journeys? I thought she was doing a good job."

She shook her head. "No, she's doing a wonderful job. Cassandra and I both know that neither of us could do as good a job as Marilyn is doing. She just mentioned that her husband might get out on bail. She's concerned for her and the kids."

Tanner couldn't blame the woman for that. "Because of the restraining order and the violence against her, she should be notified right away if her husband makes bail." He reached over and slid both his hands under Bree's hair on either side of her neck. "I've seen the police report for what happened to Marilyn. No judge is going to let him out on bail knowing what he tried to do."

"I just don't want anything to happen to her or the kids."

He pulled her closer and kissed her forehead. He loved her protectiveness of her friend. "Have I mentioned how excited I am to be marrying you in just a couple more weeks? Cass said you had some wedding stuff to deal with today. Did it go okay?"

"Yeah. Wedding dress fitting." She didn't sound too thrilled.

"I can't wait to see you in it." Bree's taste in clothing leaned toward casual. And as much as he loved it when she stole one of his shirts to tie at her waist and wear with her jeans—or even better, wore only his shirt and *nothing* else—he was truly looking forward to that first glance at her walking down the aisle.

She sighed. "Are you sure I can't talk you into dragging me in front of the nearest judge like you once threatened?"

"I'm pretty sure the women of this town, led by my sister, would string up you and me both by our toes if we eloped."

Bree laughed. The sound was soft and simple and genuinely happy. He was looking forward to hearing that sound for the next fifty years or so.

She chewed on her lip for just a moment, then stepped a little closer, trailing one finger up his chest. "Are you sure I can't talk you into going before a judge tomorrow morning? You can outrun a bunch of women. You're Captain Hot Lips."

Her own little hot lips pressed against his, her tongue running against the seam of his mouth, before biting down gently with her teeth. "If we knew we were getting married in front of the judge tomorrow," she continued, "there would be no reason for us not to make love right here, right now, against this wall. Doesn't that sound like the best plan ever?"

He could feel her smiling against his mouth as he reached under her thighs and picked her up, trapping her body between the wall and his torso. They both let out a groan as her legs came around his hips and brought them flush up against one another.

"There's nothing I want more than to peel you out of those clothes and spend the rest of the night making love to you on every available surface in this apartment," he growled into her mouth.

She let out a gasp as his lips found the side of her neck. It may have been two months since he'd last seen her naked, but he definitely remembered every single spot on her body that could drive her crazy.

"Then do it," she said. "I won't let the meanie town ladies hurt you. I just want to be married to you tomorrow."

Using every ounce of self-control he had, Tanner forced himself to ease Bree back down onto her feet and step away from her.

Two more weeks. He wanted to do this right. Wanted the next time they made love to be as husband and wife.

"We will get married. But in the church in front of all our family and friends, the way it should be. The way you deserve. I want everyone in this county—hell, the entire state—to know that you are who I very proudly choose as my wife. I don't want there to be any mistake about that, no rumored whispers that might accompany a quick trip to the judge."

She genuinely looked disappointed. "Fine."

He chuckled. "The wedding won't be as bad as you think."

"For you, maybe. You don't have to wear the scratchy white netting stuff."

"Tulle?"

"Damn it, how does everyone know the name of that material except me?"

He reached over and kissed her again. "You wear tulle for me for just a few hours and then you never have to wear it again."

"Promise?" she whispered.

"Absolutely. As a matter of fact, after we're married, I'm going to do my best to make sure you spend as much time as possible wearing nothing at all."

Chapter Three

Damn Tanner and his smooth talking. Five hours after he left, Bree still couldn't sleep.

Part of it was being wound up from their heavy make-out session against the wall. The other part was the fact that she hadn't been able to talk him into going before the judge, so those damn vows were still coming up and she had no idea what she was going to say.

I will love you forever and always my whole life, you and no one else.

Yeah, that was perfect.

If she was looking for complete stupidity meets *Braveheart*.

Bree punched the pillow beside her. Why were emotions so hard for her? Why did there seem to be so many variables that she had to take into consideration when writing these vows?

And why couldn't she get any sleep?

A few minutes later she finally just gave up and decided to go work in her office at the New Journeys building. Sitting at her own desk with her computer would at least be more familiar. And it had to be more useful than lying here tossing and turning in bed.

Twenty minutes later, dressed in a sweatshirt and yoga pants, she discovered that staring at a blank screen on her computer in her office was, in fact, just as bad as tossing and turning in bed.

She had nothing.

What the hell was she supposed to say to explain to the man she loved that she loved him?

Wasn't actually *getting married* enough of a declaration?

And the *tulle*? Wasn't tulle enough of a declaration of love, for heaven's sake? A solemn description of what agonies she was willing to bear for him?

When no other words or ideas came to her, she did the only thing she knew how to do: she opened her browser and began coding. Within fifteen minutes she had a program written that would automatically filter every mention of wedding vows from the internet and into a folder. She may not be able to write these vows herself but she could at least research—

She froze, head spinning to the side as something caught her peripheral vision on one of the black-and-white monitors on the table in the corner. What the heck was that?

Those monitors were set to the cameras recording the section of the building that hadn't been remodeled yet. Bree and Cassandra had installed them after some town teenagers were caught having a little rowdy fun back there. Bree had written a quick program that caused the cameras only to record if motion was detected.

Evidently motion had been detected.

Bree's fingers flew across the keyboard so she could bring up the footage on her computer monitor, which provided a much larger and clearer picture of the un-inhabited area. Except the picture wasn't much clearer. It took her a moment to realize it wasn't because of a problem with her computer, but because the room was full of smoke.

The building was on fire.

Bree grabbed the phone on her desk and dialed 911.

"Grand County emergency services. You've reached 911. What's your emergency?"

"Debbie, it's Bree Daniels." Recognizing the 911 operator was definitely one of the perks of living in a small town. "There's a fire at New Journeys. Not in the main section, thank God, but it might spread. Send the fire trucks around to the back to the section that hasn't been renovated yet. I'm going to see if I can get it under control with the fire extinguisher."

"Now wait a minute, Bree. You need to stay on the line with me so we can direct the first responder—"

Bree didn't wait for Debbie to finish her sentence. The woman had lived in Risk Peak her whole life. She knew exactly where to send the first responders.

Bree grabbed the fire extinguisher in the corner of her office and dashed out into the hall, yanking down the fire alarm. Her office was on the opposite end of the housing area—uniquely situated between the residential space and the area that hadn't been renovated. Pulling the alarm would be the quickest way to get everyone out without having to run down to the living quarters herself.

Because maybe she could stop this whole thing before it got out of hand.

Once the alarm was blaring, she dashed back into her office and out the door on the other side that took her into the section of the building where the fire was located. She started in a sprint down the hall to the room where the motion had triggered the camera, but soon slowed. Already smoke was starting to fill the hallway.

The farther down the hall Bree went, the thicker the smoke became. Would she be able to put out a blaze making this much smoke with a single fire extinguisher? She had to try.

She heard some sort of screeching noise ahead of her and started to run again, coughing as she took in more smoke. Was somebody trapped back here? Teenagers fooling around again who accidentally started a fire and got trapped?

She turned the corner and dropped low in the thick smoke, crawling forward now. It almost sounded like someone was calling her name, but she couldn't tell from where. The smoke and her own coughing had her disoriented already, and that screeching noise was growing louder.

Someone had to be trapped in there. She pushed forward faster.

Extinguisher in one hand, she reached for the door handle with the other and let out a shriek when an arm wrapped around her waist and lifted her off her knees, spinning her around.

"Oh, no you don't," a voice said in her ear. "You're not getting out of the tulle that easily."

"Tanner." His name came out in a relieved cough. "There's a fire. I heard a noise and I think someone was calling my name. It's behind that door."

"That was *me* calling your name. We've got to go."

She gestured toward the door. "But what about the noise? There may be someone trapped in there."

The screeching noise got higher and louder and Tanner muttered a curse under his breath, tucking his arm around her and launching her toward the corner. They just made it around and she was about to argue her case again when a thundering explosion roared from where they'd just been standing. Smoke encased the hall from top to bottom.

"What—" Bree stuttered.

"Too many accelerants in a construction area. It was like a pressure cooker."

A pressure cooker that would've killed her if Tanner hadn't been there to stop her from opening that door and get her out of the hallway.

Taking the fire extinguisher, he tucked her under his arm again and propelled them both back toward her office. Once there she was at least able to breathe again.

"You're going to have to let the firefighters go after that blaze, freckles. There's nothing you can do. Let's just get everybody out of the front of the building."

She nodded, sucking in huge gulps of air. "You saved my life. I just called 911 a couple minutes ago. How did you get here so fast?"

"I was already here when you pulled the alarm."

They rushed together toward the housing units.

"You were? Why?"

He stopped for the briefest of seconds and gave her a hard kiss, before taking her arm and spurring her down the hall once again. "I went by your apartment to tell you I wanted *both*. We could go before the judge tomorrow *and* have the church wedding in two weeks. All I knew was I had to have you in bed with me tonight. When you weren't there, I came over here to plead my case."

"Holy hell," she whispered, then coughed again. "If you hadn't needed a booty call…"

She would've been dead.

He gave a short bark of laughter and shook his head grimly at the same time. "Yeah. Thank God I'm addicted to you."

A few moments later they were in the housing area.

"Bree!" Marilyn said. "What's going on? Is this some sort of drill?"

Bree was still coughing from the smoke she'd taken in and her run down both hallways.

"No," Tanner answered for her. "Not a drill. Everybody needs to get out. There's a fire in the other section of the building."

The panic was almost instantaneous. Mothers began calling for their children and some of the other women yelled for anyone who might still be asleep. Most of the kids were crying and Eva and Sam were looking up at Bree and Tanner, eyes huge in their pale faces, Tromso's leash in their hand.

Bree couldn't stop coughing. It paired horribly with the dog's whining.

Tanner put both hands on her shoulders. "You need to get outside and stop exerting yourself." He turned to Marilyn. "Can she take the kids outside and you and I will get everyone else out?"

Marilyn nodded.

Bree started to argue but another coughing fit overtook her. Tanner was right—he and Marilyn would get everyone out. The most she could do to help right now would be to get out of the way. She nodded and offered Eva and Sam her hands. They took them and she led them quickly outside, some of the other residents along with them.

Outside was pure chaos. Lights from fire trucks, police cars and ambulances lit up their block like it was some sort of disco rave party. Half the town was frantically pacing back and forth, and everyone seemed to be talking all at once.

Eva and Sam were looking even more traumatized,

so Bree pulled them back toward the outer edge of the action. She wanted to reassure them, but every time she started talking she was besieged by coughs. So she just crouched beside them and put an arm around each small, shivering body.

It wasn't long before a paramedic came up to her.

"Miss, I think we ought to get your cough checked out. Can you come with me?"

She shook her head. She wasn't leaving Sam and Eva alone in this craziness. "I'll stay with them," she managed to get out.

The paramedic smiled at the kids. "Yeah, this is pretty nuts, isn't it?"

They both nodded solemnly.

He gave Bree a kind smile. "This sort of situation can be pretty overwhelming for folks their age, especially in the middle of the night. But you really ought to get that cough checked out. How about if I escort you over to the ambulance, and I'll personally stay with the kiddos to make sure they're not scared."

"I don't know—"

"I can keep them over at the side, out of harm's way and where it's not so chaotic. Probably best for everyone that way." He gave her a smile.

Bree was about to agree, but then she looked down at Sam and Eva, who still hadn't said a word. One silent tear rolled down Sam's cheek and he was clutching Tromso's leash with shaking fingers.

No. She wasn't leaving them. She didn't care if she had to hack up a lung until Tanner and Marilyn arrived.

"I'm fine. I'll stay with them," she whispered.

The paramedic looked like he was going to argue, but then there was some yelling closer to the building, so he shrugged and took off. Bree sat watching the burning building, clutching two tiny hands in hers, trying to establish the extent of the damage in the dark. And offering up constant prayers that no one had been hurt.

When Tanner jogged over to her a couple minutes later, she didn't resist at all as he pulled her against his chest. He smelled like smoke, but she was sure she smelled the same. "Everybody's out and accounted for. Doesn't look like anyone was hurt or that there was much damage to the living quarters."

Marilyn clutched her kids to her and they all watched the firefighters attack the blaze in the back of the building. It looked like most of it was contained back there, not the living quarters, but it was impossible to tell.

More townspeople continued to gather around. Tanner had to step up into his role of law enforcement when some teenagers kept trying to get too close to record for social media what was mostly now just smoke.

The blaze was completely out before Bree let Tanner lead her over to one of the ambulances so she could be examined. The younger, female paramedic was quite a bit less friendly than the guy Bree had met outside, stuffing an oxygen mask over Bree's face and suggesting she go to the hospital for follow-up. Bree didn't want to go but knew from the determined look in Tanner's eyes there would be a trip to get her lungs checked out in the next few hours. She might as well get it out of the way tonight.

Because it looked like there was going to be a whole lot of stuff requiring her attention tomorrow.

Chapter Four

Tanner had almost lost Bree.

Two days later that knowledge still wasn't ever very far out of his mind. If he'd gotten there one minute later, if he hadn't been thinking with his libido rather than his brain, she would've opened that door and provided the fire somewhere to escape.

And the escape would've been straight through her.

She hadn't been aware that the screeching noise they heard from inside the room was from the fire building in intensity. Opening the door would've provided more oxygen to the flames and caused them to engulf her.

If she'd opened that door, they would've been planning the final details of a funeral today rather than a wedding. Fear still clawed inside his gut at the thought, as he sat staring at the charred remains of the doorway.

"Pretty jarring to look at, isn't it?" Grand County fire inspector Randall Abrahams said from behind Tanner.

It would take a couple of days before the official report would be filed and Tanner could act on it, so Randall had agreed to meet Tanner out here as a personal favor in order to try to get this wrapped up before the wedding.

"You have no idea. Bree almost opened that door."

Randall whistled through his teeth. "If she had, this

definitely would've been a homicide investigation rather than plain old arson."

Tanner turned. "You're sure it was arson? There were a lot of building supplies and leftover stuff from the construction. Maybe not stored properly or something. An accident could've lit it on fire."

Randall walked around Tanner and entered the room where the blaze had started. "That was our initial thought."

"But something changed your mind." It wasn't a question.

"When we talked to your fiancée, we found out that she had put a security camera in here. That's how she realized the building was on fire so quickly—the camera turned on when the smoke and blaze got big enough to trigger the motion detector."

"Yes, that's right."

"Did you help rig that camera? Know anything about it?"

Tanner shook his head. "Not a whole lot. Cassandra and Bree wanted to do it themselves. I gave them a couple good camera suggestions and then looked it over once they had it hung. Seemed fine to me."

"But someone could've sneaked by the camera?"

"Yeah, definitely." Tanner shrugged, looking around. "They were just trying to keep teenagers out of trouble, not provide full-fledged security for an empty section of the building."

"Camera was up in that corner, right?"

"Yes." Tanner took a step farther into the room with the older man, stepping carefully around the debris left by the fire and the hoses. "Do you think someone sneaked in around the camera and lit the fire? I checked the footage first thing and there was nothing. Just the blaze itself."

"Did you go back any further than the night of the fire?"

Tanner nodded, still looking around at the mess. "Yeah, just in case someone had been hiding in here. Nothing had triggered the camera in the forty-eight hours before the fire. The footage doesn't keep more than that."

"Let me show you what we found."

Randall and Tanner stepped carefully through the debris until they were standing in the corner of the room directly under where the camera had been located before it was destroyed in the fire.

"You're gonna have to tell me what you want me to see, because it all looks like the bottom of my fire pit to me," Tanner told him.

Randall pulled out a plastic evidence bag from his pocket. "This is what I want you to see, and this corner was where we found it."

Tanner took the bag, squinting at it as he held it up. Randall didn't keep him in suspense.

"It's a timer. We found parts of it and a pretty sophisticated detonation device in this corner. Somebody very definitely set this fire."

Tanner let out a low curse. "A sophisticated detonator goes well beyond some kids playing a prank or a firebug who wanted to watch a building burn."

"I agree. This was set with deliberate intent to go off exactly when it did. And I think someone broke in here ahead of time and planted the device and timer. It could've been a while ago, but every day it sat here, it risked detection."

Tanner ran a hand through his hair. "So it was probably in the last couple of days. And if there's no re-cord of it in the footage, that means whoever sneaked in here knew where that camera was located and how to avoid it."

This had just become much more serious than any of them had counted on.

Tanner studied the evidence bag and its contents. "But to what end? Were they trying to blow up the whole building? Kill everyone?"

Randall shook his head. "No. If anything, the op-posite. I know Bree was here and called the fire de-partment much more quickly than would've occurred on any other night. But the way this fire was set up, it would've burned itself out before it ever got to the in-habited side of the building. I don't think it was meant to harm anyone."

"Well, it damn nearly harmed Bree."

Randall gave an apologetic shrug. "That's true, but on any other given night she wouldn't have been here."

"So, we are looking at some sort of explosives ex-pert?"

What the hell would one be doing at a women's shel-ter? Especially if they weren't trying to blow the build-ing up? This didn't make a lot of sense.

"Not necessarily. Yes, an explosives expert would know how to do all of this and it's definitely beyond what your normal amateur pyromaniac is involved with. But there are certain jobs—military, construction, even some welding jobs—that would also provide that sort of knowledge. Or it could be hired out."

"I liked this much better when I thought it might be a run-of-the-mill arsonist just trying to burn the place down. Now we're talking about someone with a specific skill set who also has studied New Journeys enough to know the basics about their security and what would or wouldn't happen in a fire."

"I don't blame you there. A pyro may be a pain in the ass, but they're also predictable. Their endgame is to watch the world burn."

Tanner looked around, trying to put himself in the arsonist's mind. "What was this guy's endgame? No one was hurt. Nothing was stolen, as far as we know."

Randall walked over and slapped him on the shoulder. "That, my friend, is your job and thankfully not mine."

Randall showed Tanner a few more things, including where the fire would've burned out on its own if the fire department hadn't stopped it before that. And he was right—it definitely wouldn't have hurt anyone, unless, like Bree, they just happened to be wandering in that section of the building.

As Tanner walked back to his office, he kept trying to figure out what the motive was.

What was the purpose? That was the ultimate question. All this had really served to do was shake everyone up.

He let out a low curse. Maybe that was the purpose—getting everyone shaken up. Thanks to the fire, everyone was back in the old building where there was much less security and no set routine.

Ronnie Kitchens, the other deputy in their office, met Tanner as soon as he walked in the door. "That face doesn't look good. Problems?"

Tanner explained about the detonator and everything else Randall had told him.

Ronnie let out a low whistle. "That's not good."

"The only people I can think that might have something to gain from pulling a stunt like this would be the men involved in these women's lives."

"Definitely. Although I would think they'd want to do as much damage as possible, not set a blaze that would burn out on its own. The residents will be able to move back in in just a couple more days."

They walked toward Tanner's office. "Maybe the plan is to make the women not feel safe at New Journeys so they'll be more likely to return to their previous situations."

That was a common enough problem under the best of circumstances for some of these women; it wouldn't take much to encourage them to leave.

"Pull the files we started on all the men connected to the current residents at New Journeys. We need to cross-reference them with their backgrounds and professions. We're looking for anyone with a military background or who has worked in construction, demolition or anything that would provide training in explosives."

Ronnie began the cross-referencing while Tanner put a call in to Cassandra. He didn't want to cause any undue panic, but he wanted his sister and Bree to be aware of the situation. He promised to call them back if he had any solid suspects.

Three frustrating hours later, despite working through lunch, they hadn't found any promising suspects. The two men who seemed most *qualified* to have set the fire both lived out of state. Phone calls to their current places of employment had provided solid alibis. There was no way they could've been at work all week across the country and then made it to Risk Peak and back.

The couple of others who might have the knowledge

were in prison, including Jared Ellis, Marilyn's husband, who worked in construction.

Ronnie sat back in the chair across from Tanner's desk, two files balancing on his leg crossed at the knee. "If our perp isn't someone associated with New Journeys, could it be someone coming after Bree? She was the only one who had to be taken to the hospital. Granted, most of the Organization is behind bars, but after what happened in Atlanta—"

Ronnie was about to say something else when the phone on Tanner's desk rang.

"Hold that thought." Although there damn well better not be anyone coming after Bree again. He picked up the phone. "Tanner Dempsey speaking."

"Captain Dempsey, this is Conrad Parnam with the Denver County Warrants and Bonding Office." The man's voice was sort of distant and breathy, like the phone wasn't directly next to his mouth. Or like he was bored with the conversation before it even started.

"What can I do for you, Mr. Parnam?"

"I'm trying to reach a Mrs. Marilyn Ellis at a facility called New Journeys but I'm having difficulty. Do you have a way to get in touch with her?"

"I do." He had a sinking suspicion he knew where this was going and wasn't going to like it.

"Because of the restraining order against Mrs. Ellis's husband, Jared Ellis, we wanted to let her know that he was released on bail."

Yep, he didn't like it. This already bad day just got worse. "Earlier today?"

He could hear Parnam shuffling through papers. "Actually, no. Mr. Ellis was released three days ago."

Chapter Five

Tanner fought not to roar into the phone. Jared Ellis was released from a Denver county jail *three* days ago and no one had told Marilyn?

He forced himself to speak reasonably, even though he had a white-knuckled grip on the phone. "Three days ago? Why wasn't Mrs. Ellis notified immediately? Jared Ellis is considered to be a threat to both her and her children."

"You know how it is. Things sometimes fall through the cracks." There was no apology in Parnam's tone.

Tanner wrote the word *Noah* on the notepad and spun it around so Ronnie could see it. Ronnie nodded and Tanner tapped the phone in his hand to indicate Ronnie needed to tell Noah about Jared Ellis's release. Ronnie already had his phone in hand as he walked out of the office.

This was definitely a police matter, but when it came to protecting Marilyn and those kids, it was a personal matter also. Noah would want to know.

"I'm going to need the details about Ellis's release," he said into the phone.

"Is there some sort of problem?" Finally something else took the place of boredom in Parnam's tone: irritation. But Tanner didn't give a damn if Parnam was perturbed that he would have to actually do his job.

"Yes, there's a problem. We have a woman in our care here who was damn near beaten to death by her husband. So finding out he's been out on bail for three days and nobody saw fit to notify either her or my office is very much a problem."

"Look, I just run the paperwork for whoever the judge tells me to and make the calls that come across my desk. Nothing more or less than that. But hang on a minute and let me see what I can find out." Irritation still painted the other man's tone, but at least Tanner could hear the clicking of his fingers on the keyboard. "Judge doesn't usually let violent offenders out on bail." More clicking. "Well, that explains it. Oscar Stobbart. He's a very high-end defense attorney—has a great record of getting people out on bail, and honestly, getting them reduced sentencing. Ellis must have a ton of money to hire someone like him."

Tanner was now frustrated with himself that he didn't know more about Jared Ellis. But he honestly hadn't thought there would be much he needed to know since the man was behind bars. Did he have money? Tanner didn't know.

But he was out. And more important, had been out of jail within the window for setting the detonator for the fire. "Do you at least have his last known address?" They would definitely be paying a visit to Jared as soon as possible.

"Actually, I can do a little better than an address. As part of Mr. Ellis's bail, he was placed on a GPS tracking monitor. That was probably why it wasn't a priority for me to call Mrs. Ellis or your office. Jared Ellis is required to stay within a two-mile radius of his listed home address, which is in downtown Denver."

An ankle monitor was good news. "So you can tell where he's been at any particular hour? What happens if he leaves the two-mile radius?"

"Yep, there's a log that keeps record of exactly where he is at any given time. And if Ellis leaves the radius for which the monitor is set, it automatically sets up an alarm with the Denver marshals. They'll be at his house in minutes. Plus, it's completely unhackable."

"So if I wanted to know where he was two nights ago, you could get that for me." If there was some sort of glitch in this "unhackable" system, Tanner wanted to know about it.

Parnam gave a long-suffering sigh. "How about if I just send you the entire log of Ellis's whereabouts since the moment he was released. That will save us a number of different calls and emails, don't you think?"

And would require a lot less work from Parnam.

"Fine. I'll expect it in an email within the next hour."

Tanner hung up without waiting for a response. The fact that Ellis had been released without notifying Marilyn would be addressed within the system.

But right now, until they could confirm *exactly* where Jared Ellis was, he needed to get security on Marilyn and her kids.

He had Ronnie start the paperwork for protective surveillance, even though Tanner knew the approval was a long shot unless a direct threat to Marilyn and the kids could be proved—which hopefully it would be as soon as they checked Ellis's whereabouts on the night of the fire.

He was also going to request the live data from Parnam's office. Knowing where Jared *had been* afterward wasn't good enough. They needed to know his current whereabouts. Not that Tanner didn't trust the Denver marshal's office to do their job. But all it would take was Jared tricking the system *one time* and he could attack Marilyn. And as long as that was a possibility—until Jared's trial when he went away long-term—Tanner wanted to be multiple steps ahead of the other man.

Right now that included making sure Marilyn knew her ex was out of jail.

His cell phone buzzed on his belt with a call from Noah before Tanner even made it out of the office.

"Ronnie said Jared Ellis was released on bail?" His brother didn't even waste time with a greeting.

Neither did Tanner. "Affirmative."

Noah's curse was foul. "Does the sheriff's office have money to put surveillance on Marilyn and the kids?"

"I've already got the process started, but I'll be honest, unless we get proof that Ellis is a threat to her or was anywhere in the area of the fire, then I don't have much of a legal leg to stand on."

"I'm on my way into town. If we can't get a uniform on her, then I'll take up watch duty myself. It's very suspicious that there was a fire at New Journeys at the same time Ellis got out on bail."

Tanner began walking down the block toward the old New Journeys building. It would be quicker than driving. "Especially since it looks like someone started it deliberately." He explained what the fire inspector had found.

Noah cursed again.

"I've spent all day trying to figure out why someone would've started a fire that wasn't trying to hurt anyone or burn down the building," Tanner said.

"It might have made a perfect opportunity for Jared to snatch Marilyn and the kids. Probably wouldn't have taken into account how much the people of Risk Peak would be surrounding them."

"Definitely true," Tanner said. "Although the fire may have nothing to do with Ellis."

"I'm not willing to take that chance," Noah said quietly. "Or take the chance that he's just going to leave Marilyn alone. She's been through enough."

They both felt that way. It was the very reason he'd had Ronnie call his brother to begin with. "I'll meet you at the old New Journeys building."

Even though there hadn't been much damage to the living quarters of the new building by the fire, they'd still moved everyone back into the old building while the initial cleaning was going on. Tanner wasn't thrilled about the change. It definitely didn't have the security upgrades the new building had.

When he arrived at New Journeys' current home, he immediately asked to talk to Marilyn. He hated to see the shadows cross the quiet woman's face when she saw him. She knew this was going to be bad news.

Bree was there and gave him a tight smile. "I'll just hang out in the office so you two can talk. Give you guys some privacy."

Tanner nodded, but Marilyn shook her head, holding her hand out to Bree. "No, stay. This is going to affect all of us. The kids are doing schoolwork, so this is a good time. Let's go into the kitchen."

Bree reached over and grabbed Tanner's hand as Marilyn put on a pot of coffee with jerky movements.

"Do you want to bring Cassandra in too?" Tanner asked.

Bree shook her head. "She's not here. She's having a

throwdown with the insurance company, trying to get us back in the other building by next week. But evidently she's having some difficulties because of what's in the fire report."

Tanner nodded. "The fire inspector thinks the blaze was deliberate." He turned back to Marilyn, who was trying to pour the coffee she'd made with shaky hands. Damn it, he didn't want to have this conversation. He tried to start but couldn't force the words out.

"Just tell me," Marilyn said softly, when she handed him his mug. "It's Jared, right? He made bail?"

Bree muttered a curse that would've made Cassandra proud.

Tanner nodded.

"Yes. Three days ago."

Nope, *this* new string of curses from Bree would've made Cassandra proud.

Marilyn blanched. "Three days ago? I thought they were going to tell me immediately if he made bail."

It was so hard to watch Marilyn's sense of safety and security be torn away with his words. The skin across her cheekbones was drawn and pale. Her shoulders hunched in as if to protect herself from a blow.

"I know. They should have told you right away. It was some sort of communication breakdown, but it was wrong and I'm very sorry."

Marilyn was clutching her coffee like a drowning victim would a lifeline.

"But there is a little bit of good news," Tanner continued. "Jared is on an ankle tracker. I've got the Denver County bonding office sending me the log for everywhere Jared has been since the moment he got out. I've also got one of my men looking into seeing if we can get direct access to the live data, so we know where he is at all times."

"I thought you said Jared wouldn't get out on bail given what he did," Bree said softly.

He grimaced. "Yeah, I'll be honest, I was shocked to hear it. Evidently he got himself one of the most expensive and well-connected lawyers in the state."

"Jared has a lot of powerful friends. His fraternity brothers," Marilyn whispered.

"Is Oscar Stobbart one of those?" Tanner asked.

If possible, Marilyn's face got even whiter. "Yes."

There was a wealth of agony in that single word. Tanner didn't press, but he could imagine that there was probably a lot more to Marilyn's abuse than she had let anyone know about.

A soft tap at the kitchen door had them all turning in that direction. It was Noah.

"I asked Noah to come by just for added security until we have a true grip on what's going on. Is that okay?" Tanner said. The last thing either he or Noah wanted was to make Marilyn more uncomfortable.

Marilyn was staring at Noah through the glass panes of the kitchen door. She nodded. "No, I'll feel better if he's here."

Noah never took his eyes from Marilyn as he walked in the door. He didn't move near her, but his focus and awareness of her were almost tangible.

"You can do this," he said softly.

Marilyn didn't look like she believed him, but she just shrugged and said, "Doesn't look like I have any choice." She rubbed a hand across her eyes. "I should probably leave. Take the kids and get farther away."

"No," Noah said. "He's not going to get to you."

His brother's volume might be soft and his tone even,

but there was no way to mistake the certainty behind the words. For the first time since Tanner arrived, Marilyn relaxed just the slightest bit. She probably didn't even know about Noah's background in Special Forces. But when Noah gave his word that he was going to protect her, he had the skills to back up that promise.

Noah Dempsey may be a rancher by trade, but that didn't change the fact that he was also a warrior in every possible way.

"If Jared got out on bail three days ago, could he have been the one who set the fire?" Marilyn asked.

Tanner glanced over at Noah, then at Marilyn. "We don't know for sure, but if Jared was involved, it would answer a lot of questions."

"Like what?" Bree asked.

Noah leaned back against the counter. The women didn't recognize the stance for what it was, but Tanner did. Noah was placing himself between Marilyn and any danger that might come through that door.

Tanner took a sip of his coffee. "It looks like the fire was set deliberately, but whoever did it wasn't trying to burn the building down completely or even hurt anyone."

"It was set to shake things up," Noah said. "Get everyone out of their routine."

"They certainly managed that," Bree muttered.

"He could've been out there," Marilyn whispered. "Waiting to get me or the kids alone. That's exactly something Jared would do."

"And none of us suspected there was any danger." Bree shook her head. "I almost left the kids with a paramedic. He wouldn't have known to look out for Jared."

Tanner rubbed the back of his neck. "We can't automatically assume it was Jared. He's got that ankle monitor, and it sends a notification if he goes out of his set range. My colleague in Denver assures me it isn't hackable."

Bree actually laughed out loud, rolling her eyes. "Okay. We'll just let them go on believing that. *Everything* is hackable."

He reached over and grabbed his little computer genius's hand. "Everything is hackable by *you*. The chances that Jared has someone with your skill in his personal list of friends—no matter how many fraternity brothers he has—is slim."

Bree nodded. "Agreed. All I'm saying is that a false sense of security that something can't be hacked might lead to laziness on law enforcement's part."

Tanner couldn't disagree with that. Not when the department already didn't have a stellar showing when it came to this situation.

A text came in on his phone from Ronnie. Finally a little good news.

"Ronnie got the log for Jared's monitor. According to the reports, he was not anywhere around Risk Peak at the time of the fire. He hasn't been out of Denver city limits since he made bail."

"Unless he did have someone who could hack the anklet for him," Bree said.

"Could you tell if it had been tampered with?" Tanner asked her. "Would you be able to see if the reports of his whereabouts were wrong?"

"From the source computer or the anklet itself, yes," she said.

"Then maybe it's time you and I took a little field trip. A nice tour of the Denver County Warrants and Bonding Office seems like a great idea."

Chapter Six

"You let me do the talking, okay?"

Bree rolled her eyes. "Remember how for as long you've known me, I've never had any sort of desire to talk to people? Still true."

It was the next morning and Bree and Tanner were on their way to the Denver County Warrants and Bonding Office. Tanner had wanted to come yesterday, but by four o'clock the person they'd needed to see was already gone, he'd found out with disgust.

But it was better they made the trip today, since it had given Bree time to research the monitoring system being used on Jared. She had to admit, this one was sophisticated—definitely high-end. Most types of ankle monitors were meant for nonviolent first-time offenders—people who needed to be scared into staying in one place and were a pretty low flight risk overall. Those units were pretty easily hackable and would've definitely been a mistake in Jared's case.

But this version of electronic monitoring was much more advanced. Had been used successfully all over the country without anyone being able to escape undetected.

Regardless, Bree wanted to check out this system for herself. Wanted to know for certain Marilyn and the kids were safe. The easiest way to do that was through official access at the bonding office.

Of course, she could've hacked the system *without* official access, but she didn't even bring that possibility up. For some absurd reason, her law enforcement husband-to-be didn't like breaking the law. Go figure.

"I'm not going to explain to them outright what we're doing unless I have to," Tanner said. "Parnam didn't seem like a bad guy, but he definitely isn't interested in adding to his workload. Nobody in the warrants and bonding office is going to like us peeking over their shoulder to double-check their work. So let's try not to inform them."

Bree let out a frustrated sigh. "And what about Marilyn and the kids? Do they care at all that if Jared has found some way to circumvent the monitoring system, he might put Marilyn back in the hospital or worse?"

"As far as the law is concerned, Marilyn is protected because she has that restraining order."

"That restraining order isn't worth the paper it's printed on if Jared decides he's willing to risk getting away with it."

Tanner's long fingers wrapped around hers where her hand rested on her legs. "I agree, and that's why we've got Noah on the lookout. Ronnie has also volunteered to do some lookout shifts during his time off, and when Richard Whitaker heard about it, he offered also."

She had to smile at Whitaker's name. "How is our old friend the jackass?"

"He's coming to the wedding, you know."

The other officer was Tanner's counterpoint in the northern section of the county. He'd accused both Bree and Tanner of murder last year, but then had helped take care of Bree when Tanner had been near death in the hospital.

"I'm glad Marilyn will have protection," she said. "But we both know these are temporary measures."

"Just because Jared's lawyer managed to convince a judge that he's not a flight risk doesn't mean that he's not going to go to jail for a long time for what he did to her. I've seen the evidence. So even if we have to take turns watching over her and the kids for the next four months until the trial, we'll do it. Everyone is willing to help her out in that way."

She squeezed his hand, her heart filling up almost painfully with the emotions she felt for him. He was such a good man. Willing to do whatever he had to do to make sure the people who depended on him were safe.

"Thank you," she whispered, wishing she was better with words. Better at expressing everything she felt inside herself for him.

He brought her hand to his lips. "Marilyn and those kids deserve a fresh start. A future that doesn't involve pain or fear. All of us want to give them that."

"I do too." And she was going to do whatever she had to do to get the information she needed from that computer. If she could prove that Jared had been around Risk Peak during the fire—hell, *anytime* since he'd been released—he'd be spending the rest of his time awaiting trial behind bars.

Where he belonged.

They pulled up at the bonding office, attached to the courthouse and Denver marshals' office.

"I'm just going to introduce you as a computer expert," Tanner said as they got out of the vehicle. "I don't think anyone around here knows either of us, so introducing you as my colleague shouldn't raise any eyebrows."

She gave a brisk nod. "IT colleague here to help make sure that data is running smoothly between two different systems. Got it. Piece of cake."

They signed in at the front desk and made their way up a single flight of stairs to Parnam's office. The door was half open and Parnam, a pudgy man in his mid-fifties, an office phone lodged between his shoulder and jaw, gestured for them to come in. His voice was a blend of boredom and exhaustion as he read a series of numbers to whoever was on the phone.

Bree and Tanner took seats across from his desk as he hung up.

"Mr. Parnam, I'm Tanner Dempsey. This is IT expert Ms. Daniels."

Bree noticed how adeptly Tanner avoided lying. Kept it just general enough to avoid telling any untruths. Bree was an IT expert, after all.

"Dempsey. Ms. Daniels." Parnam nodded his head at both of them. "I've already sent you all the reports I have on Jared Ellis. I looked into the case a little myself, and I really am sorry Mrs. Ellis wasn't notified. We had two people retire in the last six months and their positions haven't been backfilled, so, like I said, things just sometimes slip through the cracks."

Tanner raised an eyebrow. "I'm sorry to hear you're trying to work three people's jobs, because in a situation like this, Mrs. Ellis could've been hurt or worse, not even knowing there was any possible danger out there."

Parnam settled his weight back in his chair. "Well, in my defense, Ellis does have the ankle monitor on. If he had gone anywhere near his wife, it would've set off all sorts of alarms. That thing is unhackable."

Bree got straighter in her chair, trying to swallow the words bubbling up her throat at his utter faith in technology. She'd spent most of her childhood within an organization that made it their mission in life to hack information systems and use it to their advantage.

Nothing was unhackable.

Next to her, Tanner cleared his throat. His fingers, resting on his knees, made a swiping gesture over and over. She got the message: don't do anything stupid like argue with Parnam. She forced herself to relax in the chair.

"Be that as it may," Tanner said. "Ms. Daniels is here to make sure there won't be any problem with the data communicating between the Denver County and Grand County systems."

"Whatever." Parnam let out a weary sigh. "What do you need?"

"Ten minutes on the monitoring system," Bree responded. "I've already made sure our system is ready. I just need to double-check a couple of things in your system."

Parnam nodded and escorted Bree and Tanner to a separate office that contained a computer, a worktable with miscellaneous electronic equipment and sensors, and a couple of hard plastic chairs.

"This is where everything is calibrated and connected. Every offender to be fitted with a monitor comes in here, and those with the particular version being used for Jared Ellis come back once a week to make sure the calibration is still correct and the GPS system is online."

"But Ellis hasn't been back yet, right? He's not scheduled for a few more days?" Tanner asked.

"Actually, the tech should've had him in this morning. I put in the request since there was such concern from Grand County—I wanted to cover our bases. I haven't heard about any results yet, though. Those would go straight to the Denver marshals. Once I set up the initial paperwork, I'm pretty much out of the loop. If someone does go outside of their monitor's set parameters, the call goes to the Denver marshals, with a backup call to the Denver sheriff's departments. But their offices are here in the same building, so I usually hear about it."

"You don't work for the sheriff's department?" Bree asked.

"Parnam is a state employee, not law enforcement," Tanner said.

"Exactly. I'm just in charge of paperwork. I don't make the decision on who goes free or not—that's the judge. I don't chase down the people who decide to hammer off their anklet—that's the cops. I'm just trying to make sure everything gets filed correctly."

And the dude did not sound very excited about his job—not that Bree blamed him.

"So just go ahead and do what you need to do. You said it would only take a few minutes?" Parnam leaned up against the doorway.

She doubted he would know enough about computers to understand what she was going to do, but it would be a lot more complicated with him looking over her shoulder the whole time. She glanced over at Tanner, who gave her a brief nod.

Tanner put his hand on Parnam's shoulder. "Conrad, you probably don't get told this a lot, and that's a shame. But your job is very important. Just think of how long it would've taken for Mrs. Ellis to be notified that Jared had been released if it wasn't for you. I appreciate your hard work."

Bree sat down at the computer and managed not to roll her eyes. Tanner. That man could be the epitome of fierce warrior when the need called for it. She'd seen that herself when he'd fought to save their lives a few months ago. He'd been nearly dead—covered in his own blood from multiple gunshot wounds—and still managed to save them both.

But damned if he couldn't also charm his way out of most situations. He was just so *likable*. Parnam wasn't immune to Tanner's charm either.

"Thank you for saying that," the other man said. "I hear plenty if something goes wrong, but nobody ever thinks to say thank you for things going right."

Tanner made a sound of agreement and cleared his throat. "Well, we are thankful that you've done your job so well." Bree kept her eyes glued on the computer so she wouldn't snicker. "Would you mind showing me the way to the marshals' offices? I want to make sure that they understand the severity of the situation too, like you do."

"Yeah, absolutely." She wasn't surprised to hear that Parnam wanted to show Tanner, his new bestie, anything he needed to see. "Will you be okay in here by yourself, Ms. Daniels?"

Bree looked over her shoulder at them and smiled. "Absolutely. It will probably be much quicker for me without you two."

The two were chatting like pals as they walked down the hallway.

She didn't waste any time accessing the system and familiarizing herself with its particulars in just a few minutes. She immediately brought up the file on Jared's ankle monitor and pored over the data. It was identical to the report Tanner had shown her this morning, the same one that had been sent over by Parnam yesterday.

Of course, that didn't mean the anklet system hadn't been tampered with, just that Parnam probably wasn't in on it.

Closing down the tracking system, she opened a source-code editor and quickly coded a program she'd already developed in her mind, bootstrapping it so it could run immediately. The program was simple but powerful. It would determine whether any outside shells were attempting to hide the real data concerning Jared.

She was almost disappointed when it came back with nothing.

Closing that, she wrote another quick program—the coding coming easier to her than conversation would to most normal people—to look for GPS manipulation. That was pretty high-level, and she'd be impressed if Jared had somebody savvy enough to know how to re-configure data based on that.

It was how she would do it.

But after a few more minutes it became clear no one had hacked Jared's monitoring system through that method either.

She tried the half dozen other ways she could think of to infiltrate the monitoring system but was either shut down by the system itself or found no evidence that the system had been tampered with in any way.

Finally, she just sat back and stared at the screen in front of her, having to come to grips with what the data was telling her. Jared was clean.

She closed her source code and compiling windows and pulled up Jared's file again, staring at his picture. There was no doubt he was a handsome guy. Midthirties, blondish-brown hair, piercing blue eyes. A charming smirk, even in his mug shot.

"How did you do it, you bastard?"

His picture didn't respond.

She reopened her windows and wrote another program quickly to see if Jared might have just delayed the transmission of data in some way. That would've been pretty clever also. By the time the police realized they'd been fooled, he could've done all sorts of damage to Marilyn and the kids.

But that came back negative also.

Bree sat back, feeling something she didn't often at a computer: stumped.

Was it possible Jared didn't have anything to do with the fire at all? That perhaps he really had stayed within the two-mile radius he was allowed to travel in since his release? Because Bree was one of the top computer geniuses on the planet, and if he was fooling the system, then she couldn't figure out how it was being done.

The office door crashing open had her jumping in her seat. She immediately tapped the required keys to hide what she'd been doing, expecting to find Tanner returning with Parnam.

But instead it was Jared Ellis himself.

Chapter Seven

Jared was bigger than Bree would've thought. She imagined Marilyn, who was probably a good three inches shorter than Bree's own five foot five, struggling against him. It was hard to visualize a situation in which Marilyn would come out the victor.

A man stepped from behind Jared, much shorter, but still stocky. "This is pretty much harassment," the shorter man said in a booming voice. "My client has been out on bail for four days and we're already being called in here like he's done something wrong? Do not doubt I'm going to make sure the judge hears about this."

"I thought you came in earlier?" Bree said without thinking. Wasn't that what Parnam had said?

"Believe it or not, my client does not jump at the whims of this office. If the judge tells us to come in at a certain time, we will certainly comply, but this office having technical difficulties is not Mr. Ellis's problem. You're lucky he's here at all."

They didn't know who she was, of course. They thought she was a computer tech assigned to this office.

This was a gift horse. She was going to ride that sucker, not look it in the mouth.

"Of course, Mr. Stobbart." Bree forced her most sub-

dued tone. Wait—would the tech have known his name?
Too late now. "We appreciate you and Mr. Ellis coming
in so we can take a look at the hardware."

Stobbart looked slightly appeased, at least enough
to stop yelling. "Well, I certainly wasn't going to allow
my client here without representation," he huffed. "It's
not my first day being a lawyer."

He and Jared both chuckled.

"If you don't mind stepping over here, I'll evaluate
the hardware." She studied Jared's face. Stobbart may
be a loud bully, but it was the look in Jared's eye that
had her recoiling.

Jared Ellis was evil.

He hadn't said a word yet, and he didn't say a word
now; he just walked over and placed his leg on the chair
next to Bree's, exposing his ankle under his khaki pants.
She wasn't surprised to find him wearing loafers.

If wearing loafers in Colorado didn't tell you everything you needed to know about a man, she didn't
know what would.

"Have you attempted to remove the device or modify
it in any way?" she asked. "Maybe it got uncomfortable
so you did something to it?"

"Like what?" His voice was deep and low and had
almost a hiss-like quality to it.

She yanked her gaze from his face and studied the
ankle monitor. There were no scratches, no markings
whatsoever to indicate it had been tampered with.

"Just any attempt to open the device. Believe it or
not, some people could start to feel claustrophobic because they can't remove the hardware."

She had no idea if that was true, but it sounded reasonable enough.

"No. I'm not prone to claustrophobia." Icy voice once again.

There were no markings to indicate it had been overloaded with electricity, another way of attempting to dismantle it, but that would also have telltale signs.

"I'm just going to run a system diagnostics test while you're here," Bree said. "You shouldn't feel anything."

Although if she could've managed to rewrite the system so that the ankle monitor gave off a shock to Jared, she wouldn't have hesitated to do so. Unfortunately, the device didn't work that way.

She backdoored into the system, praying neither Jared nor his lawyer would understand what she was doing, and ran a full diagnostics test on everything: the monitor, the link between it and the system, the system itself.

She also made sure the GPS tracking was accurately calibrated, since she knew exactly where Jared was and could tell if it had been tampered with.

The system was perfect. The anklet was broadcasting exactly as it was meant to. Damn it.

She tried to think of any other tests she could run, but there wasn't anything. She was grasping at straws. She stared at the hardware, willing an idea to come to her.

"Are we done here? My client hasn't done anything wrong. Obviously the judge believes that to be true enough to release him on bail. I'm confident that Mr. Ellis will also be exonerated at his trial. We feel very certain of that. He'll be free of your technology soon enough."

Bree breathed past the bile pooling in her gut at the thought that this man could walk totally free. That Stobbart seemed so damn certain he would be. Jared just calmly rolled his pants leg back down, without a concern in the world.

"I hope you rot in hell." As soon as the impulsive whisper was out of her mouth, she wished she could take the words back. Then prayed she'd said it low enough that neither of them heard her.

She wasn't so lucky.

Jared's eyes narrowed into slits. "You know Marilyn, don't you?"

Bree scrambled out of her chair and backed up as Jared yanked his foot down and closed in on her. "Is she here? Where is she? I just want to talk to her."

"Jared, not here—" Stobbart grabbed his shoulder, but Jared shook him off.

"Stay the hell out of this, Oscar," Jared bit out, grabbing Bree by the upper arms and squeezing with bruising force. "You will tell me where my wife and family are. She's my *wife*. I have a right to see her. To explain my side of things."

Almost from a distance she heard the office door open and Tanner's angry roar over Jared's words. A second later Jared's painful fingers released her as he was thrown up against the wall by Tanner.

"What's going on here?" Parnam asked from the far side of the room, obviously not wanting to step in between Tanner and Jared.

"I'll tell you what's going on here…police brutality," Stobbart said.

But Tanner had already released Jared and was standing by Bree, keeping himself between her and the other man.

"Your client was manhandling and intimidating my colleague," Tanner said. "If you're looking for brutality, it was coming at the hands of your client."

"She knows where my wife is," Jared spit out. "I just want to talk to Marilyn."

"Jared, enough," Oscar said. "Think about long term."

"But she—"

"Enough!" Oscar yelled.

The room fell into silence except for Jared's breathing as he attempted to get himself under control.

"The only thing you need to know about your wife and kids is that the restraining order against you still stands. If you come anywhere near them, you're going right back to jail." Tanner looked over his shoulder at Bree. "Are you okay? Did you get what you needed?"

"Yes." She would have to give him the bad news later.

Stobbart was pulling Jared toward the door. "You can believe that this is all going to come back up in court. I'm not going to allow this to go unreported. My client has rights."

Tanner shook his head. "Your client is the worst kind of scum, and I'll look forward to making that fact known to anyone you want to bring this up with, judge included. There's nothing I'd like better."

Bree grabbed the back of his shirt, a little turned on by what a badass Tanner was. But mostly she just wanted them to get out of here.

Jared had regained his composure. "I'm okay, Oscar."

Oscar turned to Parnam. "I assume you've got all you needed for the device to be calibrated and my client won't be harassed again? We will only come in from now on if we're instructed to by the judge."

Parnam was still looking around trying to figure out exactly what was going on. "I guess so."

"Then let's go," Stobbart said to Jared, taking him by the arm.

Both men walked toward the office door, but Jared turned around just before they left. He looked straight at Bree with those icy eyes.

"I'm sure we'll be seeing each other again."

Tanner kept her body pinned all the way behind his. She wouldn't even be able to see Jared if she didn't peek her head out from around Tanner's broad shoulders. She tried to step around him, to confront Jared herself, but Tanner wouldn't let her.

That was fine. She didn't really want to be face-to-face with Jared anyway. Not because she was afraid of him, but because she wasn't sure she could stop herself from punching him in the jaw—and that would just make Stobbart giddy with all the harassment suits he could file. So she stayed behind Tanner.

Jared and Stobbart left without another word.

Tanner immediately turned around and yanked her to his chest. "Are you sure you're all right? Did he hurt you?"

"Yes, I'm fine. Do you really think he doesn't know where Marilyn is?"

"I don't know. She's not announcing where she is, but she's not hiding it either. Jared is smart. It's a good way of professing his innocence without overtly drawing attention to it. But it's possible he doesn't know, I guess."

"What exactly is going on here?" Parnam asked, studying them.

Bree pulled away and they both turned back to Parnam. "Nothing has changed," Tanner said. "We're still trying to make sure Jared Ellis is not able to get anywhere near his wife, whom he assaulted bad enough to put into the hospital a few months ago."

Parnam nodded, then looked at Bree. "But you know his wife? I thought you worked for Grand County?"

"She's an independent contractor," Tanner said. Bree just nodded.

Parnam raised an eyebrow. "Fine. I don't want to get caught in the middle of anything. Somebody my age can't be trying to look for a new job in this economy."

Tanner nodded. "You're not going to get caught in the middle of anything. Bree is definitely a computer expert. If there's any chance Jared Ellis is manipulating his tracking monitor, she's going to find it."

"He's not," she said.

Tanner looked at her, lips in a thin line. "You're sure? You were able to check everything you needed to? They didn't stop you by showing up?"

She shrugged one shoulder. "They actually *helped* by showing up. I'm not an electronics expert, but I was able to figure out the workings of the anklet pretty easily. It's transmitting exactly the way it's supposed to. All backup systems and GPS tracking are online and calibrated correctly. It wasn't Jared who started the fire."

Tanner let out a low curse. "I don't know if that's better or worse."

"Trust me, I wanted it to be him. I tried damn near everything I could think of. If he's manipulating that monitoring system, he's smarter than me."

Tanner turned to her and tucked a strand of her hair behind her ear. "Then he's not manipulating the system. Because he's definitely not smarter than you."

"If Jared isn't behind the fire, then who is?"

"That's what we've got to find out."

Chapter Eight

The image of Jared Ellis's hands on Bree was enough to send fire through Tanner's gut all the way back to Risk Peak. It had taken every ounce of control he possessed not to punch Ellis in the face, damn the consequences.

But that would've been a mistake that might have gotten the entire trial thrown out and made Jared a free man. Oscar Stobbart would've liked nothing better.

Bree was quiet on the way home. At first, he'd been worried that she'd been hurt and wasn't telling anyone, but she'd assured him that wasn't it, in a tight, almost distant voice. Bree wasn't a cranky or irritable person. If she was short with him, it was because that brilliant mind of hers was focusing intently on something else.

Most people could multitask, or at least hold a conversation with other people while thinking about something else. Not Bree. When she was focused on something, inconsequential things—like talking to people—got lost for her.

So while she was still trying to figure out how Jared might circumvent the monitoring system, Tanner knew better than to interrupt her thought process.

"I don't know how he could've done it," she finally whispered as they pulled up to the New Journeys building. "He might have paid someone else to start the fire, but I don't think there's any way he did it himself. I'm sorry."

Tanner reached over and cupped her cheek. "Don't be sorry. Eliminating a suspect is also helpful. It means we don't waste our time looking in that direction anymore."

"If he or anyone else tries to hack the ankle monitor, I've put stopgaps in place to notify me. Unless he's got someone smarter than me, there's no way he's going to get to Marilyn without us knowing."

He kissed her. "He doesn't have anyone smarter than you. I'm sure of it. So now we focus on finding who started the fire if it wasn't Jared."

He left her at New Journeys and spent the rest of the day attempting to do that and not getting very far. He and Ronnie were back to looking into the significant others of the residents of New Journeys and scouring over the fire inspector's report. Neither the timing mechanism nor the detonator matched any particulars of the fire department's list of known arsonists, so that was a dead end too.

Tanner's investigating brought him back around to Jared. Just because the man hadn't set the fire himself didn't mean he wasn't involved. The more Tanner looked into Jared's fraternity brothers, the less he liked what he saw. This was a tight-knit group. Even now, years after college, they still got together regularly. There seemed to be a group of five of them who were closest. Not all of them lived in Colorado, but most of them were here now, celebrating Jared's bail.

The preliminary background checks on all of them had come back clean. Tanner wasn't surprised. These guys were too smart to keep their dirty laundry out in the open.

But that didn't mean it wasn't there.

The trick was going to be catching them while keeping Marilyn safe.

Until Jared's trial, it looked like the protective shifts around Marilyn and her kids would need to continue. Tanner would do his part too, particularly because if danger was coming after Marilyn, it would definitely be too close to Bree for his liking.

He was ready to get married to her and have her right beside him every night. With their track record, he could pretty much guarantee trouble would still be coming, but at least he'd have her by his side where he could be sure to protect her.

Just twelve more days. Twelve more days and they'd be tied to each other forever.

He was smiling as he finally left the office at 8:00 p.m. and walked toward his car. Forever didn't scare him in the least.

"I don't even want to ask what that smile is all about." Noah was leaning against Tanner's SUV.

"Just happy to see you, brother, of course."

"Got time to hang out in Denver?"

Tanner rolled his eyes. "You know I've already been there once today, right?"

Noah pushed off from against the vehicle. "I know Bree said Ellis isn't hacking his ankle monitor—"

"He's not."

"—but I need eyes on him and his crew myself," Noah continued. "I'm going with or without you."

Tanner studied his brother. He didn't like the look in his eyes. "Then I'm going."

Noah gave him a surprised nod, like he had more arguments he could pull out if he needed to. He didn't need to. Tanner wasn't letting him go alone. After what happened this morning, things were already too delicate.

Tanner threw his bag into the back seat, then got in the driver's side. Noah got in on the passenger's side.

"I'm a little surprised you even told me you were going," Tanner said once they were a few miles down the road. Noah was more than capable of handling any sort of surveillance by himself.

He was capable of a hell of a lot more by himself too.

Noah shrugged. "I respect you, little brother. I respect that you chose the same route as Dad and choose to help uphold the law. And, even though I don't spend much time hanging out in the town itself, Risk Peak is my home."

"None of which actually explains why you invited me on this little adventure."

Noah stared straight out the windshield. "I needed someone I could trust."

"Trust to do what?"

"Trust to keep me from killing these bastards if the opportunity presents itself."

Those words coming from anyone else would've had Tanner shifting straight into law-enforcement mode. But this was his brother. So Tanner kept himself relaxed, even if he didn't really feel that way. "You know we have absolutely no proof that Jared or any of his cronies were involved with the fire."

Noah didn't say anything for a long time. "Ellis doesn't realize how lucky he is just to be still breathing after what he did to Marilyn."

Tanner's hands gripped the steering wheel more tightly. "Noah, you're going to have to let the system be his judge and jury. Not you." He glanced over at his brother. "Make no mistake, I will lock you up until after the trial to keep you from doing something stupid."

"It's why I've got you here," Noah muttered. He stared out the passenger window for a long time.

"I've seen stuff, Tanner. You know that. In special ops, I saw all sorts of violence against men, women and children that is the stuff nightmares are made of. But nothing I ever saw there puts me anywhere near the killing rage I feel when I think about Ellis hurting Marilyn."

Tanner wasn't sure his brother was aware of the reality of his own feelings. "You do know that's got more to do with Marilyn than it does Ellis, right?"

Noah's eyes, so much like Tanner's own, pinned him with a glare. "I know you're not trying to say what Ellis did was okay."

"Not at all. What I'm saying is that killing rage you feel isn't just because of his actions. It's because of him doing it to *her*." Tanner held a hand out to stop Noah's argument before it could go any further. "I'm not saying the bastard doesn't deserve to rot in jail. I'm just saying that rage you're talking about is because of her, not because of him."

Tanner returned his eyes to the road. Noah didn't say anything further as he processed it all. It may take Noah a while to recognize the truth, but he didn't lie to himself.

"I've been working with Marilyn," Noah finally said softly, still looking out the window. "Self-defense stuff, even before we knew Ellis's release was a possibility. She's so damn little. Doesn't seem to have any sort of warrior instinct. She's not like Bree, who survived on her own for so long. Marilyn is the type of woman who is meant to be cared for. She's not someone who should have to fight tooth and nail just to exist."

"Marilyn is stronger than you think. She has to be to have survived what she's survived."

Noah rubbed the top of his black hair—still cut military short even though he'd been out of the army for nearly five years now. "Oh, believe me, I know she's strong. I have never mistaken her quietness for weakness."

"You're doing the right thing, teaching her what you can. Whatever she doesn't have as natural intuition can be made up for with other skills. She may not have the attack instinct…"

"But she can be taught other ways to make up for that."

They were silent for long minutes.

"I want to fight her battles for her," Noah said. "But I know that in the long run I'm doing a disservice to her by feeling that way. The best thing I can do for her is teach her how to fight the monsters herself."

Tanner waited for him to say more, but evidently, he was done talking about it. It was the most he'd heard his brother talk about anything personal in the five years he'd been home.

Noah might be teaching Marilyn some things, but it seemed she was teaching him some things, as well.

It wasn't long before they were pulling up at the downtown Denver town house where Jared was staying. Neither of them said what both of them were thinking: that something was definitely not right when Ellis currently resided in a million-dollar home while his wife and children lived in a shelter designed for people without a home at all.

Tanner had researched this property earlier today. "Town house is owned by a guy named Marius Nixon. He's the same one who put the money up for Jared's bail. Of all this little posse, Nixon is the cleanest. I've got confirmation that he's not even in the country right now."

Noah nodded, staring at the building. The window shades were open, allowing them to see inside to parts of the living room and dining room.

"The rest of Ellis's clan includes investment banker George Pearson, Paul Wyn, owner of a chain of restaurants, and of course his lawyer, Oscar Stobbart. None of them have ever been arrested or in any trouble with the law besides Ellis."

Noah grimaced. "Completely clean. Convenient."

"Almost squeakily so."

"Any of the rest of them married?"

"This is where it gets more interesting," Tanner said. "Both Pearson and Wyn had wives who died within the last five years."

"Isn't that an interesting coincidence?" Noah said. "No other wives around to ask if Jared's friends had been abusive also."

Tanner nodded. "Unfortunately, according to the coroner's reports, in both cases there was nothing suspicious about the deaths. One was a car accident. One was a skiing accident."

"If you had said cancer, I might have agreed it wasn't suspicious," Noah grunted. "But we both know a death that didn't get labeled as suspicious by the coroner's office could still be murder. But on paper they look like tragic characters who lost their loved ones and have never broken the law. Nice."

It was a tricky situation. Pearson and Wyn were both upstanding businessmen. They'd never done anything wrong in the eyes of the law. Accusing them of anything when their only questionable action was their association with Ellis—and he hadn't even been found guilty yet—would be career suicide for Tanner.

Tanner pulled out his laptop and ran the program Bree had created. "According to the ankle monitor, Jared is definitely inside the town house."

Noah pulled some binoculars out of his bag and trained them toward the building.

"Affirmative," he said after a few minutes. "I've spotted him inside. Pearson and Wyn are with him. Looks like they're having some sort of business meeting. Papers spread out all over the table. Maybe building plans or maps or something."

"I don't think any of them are in business with each other, but I haven't searched definitively. It's possible. None of them have business ties with Jared that we've found."

Noah put the binoculars back up to his eyes. "Well, whatever's happening here, Jared's definitely in charge. Now I wish I hadn't brought you."

"Why? You going to go in there and take them all out for looking over business plans?"

"No," Noah said. "If I wasn't with you, I'd already have surveillance equipment that would allow me to hear what they're talking about in there. No need to get a warrant."

Tanner let out a low curse, both because it would be so helpful to have that information, and also because it was so risky. "You have to be careful, Noah. Between me bringing in Bree to the bonding office today, and getting caught, if Ellis or Stobbart catch either of us nearby, it could affect the case. They might really have an argument for harassment."

"I'm not going to get caught. I don't want anything to jeopardize Ellis spending a good solid chunk of his life behind bars. But I'd still like to know what they're talking about and if it affects Marilyn."

"If it's maps and plans, it probably doesn't have anything to do with her. It's more likely business plans," Tanner said.

"Ellis seems pretty involved with those for someone who'll likely be going to prison soon."

They watched for another hour, passing the binoculars back and forth, as the men continued to discuss and argue over their plans inside the town house.

"Okay, they're on the move, putting on jackets." Noah put down his binoculars and both of them sank a little lower in their seats.

Jared and his friends came out the front door a few minutes later and entered an Uber that pulled up outside the door. Tanner handed Noah his tablet as he started the car.

"Make sure the updates about Jared's location coming to the computer are accurate and timely."

Staying far enough back not to be noticed, Tanner followed along behind the car.

"So far, pretty damn accurate," Noah muttered after a few minutes. "It's providing updates every thirty seconds and they seem to be very close to Jared's physical location."

Just further confirmation that the tracker was working.

They followed the car to a restaurant just within Jared's range, waited while they ate, then followed them to a strip club. Tanner barely refrained from rolling his eyes.

It really was like a group of overgrown frat boys getting together.

They stayed outside the strip club for another few

hours until Ellis and his buddies stumbled out and back into another car to take them home.

Tanner didn't bother keeping as much distance from the vehicle this time. Ellis and his friends weren't doing anything suspicious, so they probably wouldn't be checking to see if they were followed, even if they were sober enough to do so.

"I guess this was a bust," Noah said as they parked across the street and watched Jared and company stumble back inside the town house. "I'm sorry I dragged you out half the night after you worked all day."

"You did the right thing. Better to have me with you if you're not sure you're going to be able to control yourself around Ellis. And at least we've got further confirmation that the tracker is calibrated correctly." Not that Tanner had much doubt after the work Bree had done.

Noah wiped a weary hand down his face as Tanner started the SUV. There wasn't any point in staying. "Do you really think Jared didn't have anything to do with the fire?"

"Him personally? No. I think the ankle monitor is solid. Hell, to be honest, I'm not even sure he paid someone to do it. And just because we don't like his buddies, it doesn't necessarily mean they're guilty of actual crimes, so we've got to be careful with this." Noah couldn't start throwing out accusations.

"I will be. After tonight I'm not even sure Jared had anything to do with it, eith—" Noah's head jerked forward. "What the actual hell?"

Tanner spun his head to see what Noah was talking about and spotted Jared Ellis standing across the street, motioning with a finger for them to come closer.

Noah was out the car door and rushing toward Jared before Tanner knew what was happening. Noah was going to attack the man. Maybe not kill him, but definitely punch him.

It was exactly what Jared wanted.

"Noah!" Tanner ran—ignoring the honking horn and car that had to slam on its brakes to not hit him as he darted out in front of it. Noah was picking up speed and was almost to Jared.

Tanner ran, coming at his brother from the side in a flying tackle just before he reached out and landed a punch on Jared's jaw.

"Get off me, Tanner," Noah said through gritted teeth.

Tanner wrapped his arms around him in a bear hug. Strength for strength he and his brother were pretty evenly matched.

"It's what he wants, Noah." Tanner grunted as Noah's elbow caught him in the ribs. "Somebody's probably got a camera on us right now. You hit him and the whole case against him becomes shaky."

Jared was smiling at the both of them from just a few feet away. There wasn't much Tanner would like more than to let Noah go so he could pound on the smug son of a bitch.

"The case is shaky anyway, Captain Dempsey. No matter what you or your brother do."

Noah stopped struggling. "How do you know who we are?"

Jared's cold smile got bigger. "I met Tanner earlier today when he had a non-law-enforcement employee impersonate a lab technician to harass me. But you, I understand, have been spending quite a bit of time with my wife."

"Soon to be ex-wife, you bastard," Noah spit out. He tapped Tanner on the arm. "I'm okay."

"You sure?"

"Yeah."

Tanner let his brother go, ready to tackle him again, if needed. But Noah had found his control, even if fury seemed to crackle off his body. Tanner got up and offered Noah a hand.

"You stay away from Marilyn and those kids." Noah's every word was clipped. "You want to get to them, you're going to have to go through me."

Jared tilted his head. "Marilyn will always be mine. All I need is a little time to persuade her of that."

Noah's eyes narrowed into slits. "Soon you'll be rotting away in prison, where you belong. You'll never be coming near Marilyn again."

"My lawyer had enough to get me out on bail. Believe me when I say he has more than enough to keep me out of prison for good."

Now it was Tanner who took a step forward. "I don't think so, Ellis. I've seen the evidence. So enjoy your last few weeks of freedom. Or as much as you can in a two-mile radius. Because if you step one foot outside of that we're going to nail your ass."

Jared looked like he was going to charge Tanner, get violent, but stopped himself. Instead, he backed away slowly, holding his hands out in front of him. "I guess we'll see what happens at the trial. But if I was a betting man, I'd bet I walk out of the court a free man that day."

He winked at them and Tanner threw out an arm to catch Noah in case he lunged. But Noah had himself under control. Maybe more so than Tanner.

"And after the trial," Jared continued, backing up step-by-step. "I'll have as much time as I need to woo my wife back."

He turned and walked away. "See you at the trial, gentlemen," Jared called out over his shoulder. "I trust it won't be again before that."

Chapter Nine

They were able to move back into the New Journeys building three days later. The residents and townspeople worked together to get everything cleaned up and all their belongings transferred from the old building back to the new one.

Bree was still triple-checking Jared's ankle monitor every day, making sure her results matched what was being sent to the Denver marshals' office. She'd also spent at least a couple hours every day still trying to come up with a way Jared might try to outthink the system. She'd gone as far as to hack into the company itself to make sure everything was on the up-and-up.

It was.

Based on the conversation he and Noah had with the man, Tanner didn't think Jared was behind the fire. It was worse than that, if possible. Tanner was afraid Jared had something up his sleeve when it came to the trial. He told Bree about the brief conversation he and Noah had with Jared—how secure he'd felt that the trial was going to go his way.

Tanner had been poring over every piece of evidence he could find, determined to make sure there was nothing that had been missed that the prosecuting attorney might need.

And all of it weighed pretty heavily on Marilyn.

There hadn't been a peep from Jared or his ankle monitor. Bree had written a program so that if the monitor went off for any reason, it would send a notification to her computer and damn near everyone's phone. They wouldn't have to wait for anyone from Denver to notify them this time. They would know *instantly*.

But just the knowledge that Jared wasn't behind bars, that he was so confident about his upcoming trial, ate at Marilyn. She'd been barely keeping it together over the past few days since the fire.

Everyone was glad to be moving back into the new building with its heightened security and the general feeling of being back in their home. The fire would mean that the renovations scheduled for the next few months would have to be pushed back, but ultimately it wouldn't affect much now.

Cassandra was sitting in her office in the New Journeys building when Bree plopped down in a chair across from her after a day of carrying boxes up and down stairs.

"It's good to be home," Bree said.

"Yeah." Cassandra smiled, but it wasn't nearly as big as Bree would've thought.

"What's going on?"

"I'm going to have to cancel the camping trip. There's still too much going on with the insurance company and I just can't go. I can't be out of contact for three days right now, and there's zero cell phone coverage in that section of the wilderness."

Bree's heart sank. Eva and Sam had been looking forward to this trip so much. They would be devastated.

But maybe they didn't have to be.

"What about Tanner? He could lead the trip and do

the teaching, right? I know he knows these woods well and as long as there's nothing going on in his office, he'd be willing to do it." She was sure of it. Nobody wanted to see these kids be disappointed.

Cassandra nodded. "Absolutely, he does. Dad used to take all three of us out all over these woods, and then they kept hunting and hiking even as they got older. That's not the issue."

"What is?"

"For insurance purposes, either you or I, as the directors of New Journeys, need to be there. Not to mention we can't send Tanner alone with three women, given their histories, no matter how upstanding of a guy he is."

Bree shrugged. "I'll go. A chance to watch my fiancé out in the wilderness he loves? I wouldn't mind witnessing that."

Cassandra tilted her head to the side and gave Bree a look that all but screamed that the other woman thought she was crazy. "You do know we're nine days from your wedding, right? What bride wants to go tromping off into the wilderness for three days a little more than a week before her wedding?"

"This bride right here." The more she thought about it, the more perfect the idea became. Nothing sounded better to Bree than getting away from all the wedding craziness. Maybe some relaxing in nature would help her brain come up with her vows, because she hadn't made one iota of progress on that.

And no amount of Jareds, ankle monitors or fires was going to stop the fact that she was getting married in nine days.

"I'll tell you what." Bree grinned at her future sister-in-law. "If you, Cheryl and Judy will handle all the wedding details for the next three days, I will talk Tanner into this camping trip slash rafting slash wilderness excursion. Believe me, I'm getting the better end of the deal."

Cassandra reached over her desk and they shook on it. "I'm already making most of the wedding decisions anyway, since you're hopeless at making decisions, so this will work out for both of us. The camping trip is officially back on."

When two little cheers and a round of giggles rang out in the hallway, Bree and Cassandra met each other's eyes and smiled.

The camping trip was back on.

THE BACKPACK ON Tanner's shoulders was a familiar and comfortable weight. Every step he took deeper into these woods made something inside him loosen and relax. How many times had Dad taken him, Noah and Cassandra out here over the years? Too many to count. Long after most teenagers weren't interested in hanging out with their parents anymore, he and Noah had still loved to come out here with their dad.

He loved the diversity of this area most of all. There were deep sections of forests and wilderness, then large patches of meadows that would open up out of nowhere, providing breathtaking views of the surrounding Rocky Mountains. There were thousands of square acres to lose yourself—or find yourself—in. And the Colorado River ran straight through it, at times gentle, but more often massive and majestic.

He'd been a little surprised when Bree called him up yesterday and asked him to lead the trip. He'd known how excited Eva and Sam were about it and would've agreed immediately as soon as he'd made sure there was nothing going on with the office.

But he was no dummy. When his bride-to-be started promising certain, *quite explicit*, sexual favors if Tanner would make time to do this, he'd pretended like his calendar was much fuller than it actually was. And he intended to collect on every last sweet, sexy and surprisingly dirty thing she'd offered to trade on their wedding night.

Although the temptation to go pick her up right then and get started had been very difficult to resist.

But looking at the faces surrounding him now, he was doubly glad he'd been able to take the time to lead this little expedition.

Sam and Eva, both carrying appropriately sized backpacks, were beaming from ear to ear. The two other children who were supposed to have come on the trip had to cancel, but that had not dampened the kids' spirits. Marilyn didn't beam, but at least for once she didn't look like the weight of the world was crashing down on her shoulders as she walked forward carrying a backpack not much bigger than Sam's. Tanner had made sure that was the case. The woman just needed to relax and enjoy herself rather than worry about the heavy lifting. She had done the heavy lifting for long enough.

The other two women, Barb and Francis, he didn't know very well, but they seemed to be enjoying themselves as they chatted quietly and walked.

Maybe most surprising was who brought up the rear of their group: Noah. His brother had shown up this morning at the place where they'd be leaving the cars, backpack ready.

If Tanner thought Sam had been happy before, the sight of his hero showing up to go on the camping trip nearly put him over the moon. The little boy hadn't been more than ten feet from Noah all day.

Tanner didn't press his brother for details about why he was here. He'd spent more time in Risk Peak in the last five days than he had since he'd gotten out of the army. Noah trusted Bree's research on the ankle monitor but wanted to be nearby Marilyn just in case.

Tanner didn't care why his brother was here. It was good to have a second person he could count on 100 percent in wilderness situations.

He knew he could count on Bree also. His computer genius had become quite the outdoors woman over the past few months. But this wilderness—as beautiful as it was—could turn deadly in a dozen ways before you could even blink.

"Everything good?" Bree's hand slid into his and she smiled up at him.

"Perfect. We're right on track and right on schedule. Not that we have anything too aggressive planned, since our group is made up of quite a few novices."

"Excited novices."

He smiled and took a sip of water out of his canteen before offering it to her. "Those are the best kind." He leaned closer so only she could hear him. "You know I would've done this without all those special…*favors* you offered."

She smiled as she sipped the water. "That's okay. I didn't even get to the really good stuff I was going to offer if I thought you wouldn't say yes."

Tanner couldn't keep in his bark of laughter. This woman. He'd created a monster when he'd taken her to bed nearly a year ago. The very best, most sexy kind of monster. And he got to keep her as his own personal monster for the rest of his life.

"I can't wait to get married to you," he whispered, reaching closer to nuzzle behind her ear with his nose.

"I'm just glad to leave all the wedding planning to your sister and the other gals. This will allow them to do what they've wanted to do for a while—get rid of the feet-dragging, decision-phobic bride. They'll be able to get stuff done a lot quicker without me there. Plus, they can't force me to try on my wedding dress again if I'm off hiking with you."

"Are you sure you're okay being gone this close to the wedding?"

She grabbed his shirt and pulled him close, rising up on her tiptoes to give him a kiss. "More than sure. Believe me, there's nowhere else I'd rather be."

They turned to look at Noah, who was crouched down, showing Sam and Eva something in the wildlife behind them.

"You didn't tell me Noah was coming," Bree said. "I was surprised."

"I didn't know he was coming. I haven't talked to him since we paid Jared our little visit. I know Noah's been around, keeping tabs on Marilyn and the kids as often as possible."

"Anything new regarding Jared?"

He rubbed his eyes with his thumb and fingers. "No. I'm still poring over the files. Still trying to find anything that might prove he was connected to the fire. Ronnie and I even went out and questioned Paul Wyn and George Pearson, to see if they had alibis for the night of the fire."

"And let me guess, they did."

"Yes. Each other, and Jared."

She let out a sigh. "Convenient. I just feel so frustrated that I can't do more."

He wrapped an arm around her shoulder as Noah began leading the group forward again. "How about no

thinking about Jared today. No thinking about the case
or the ankle monitor. No tulle. Only thinking about the
majestic beauty surrounding us and making this trip as
memorable for the kids as possible."

She leaned into his side. "You had me at the words
no tulle."

Chapter Ten

The tents were set up and everyone was settled in for the night when Tanner came out to sit next to Noah at the fire.

They made it to the camping site with no problem and had caught fish in the stream tributary of the Colorado River they'd be coasting on tomorrow. By the time they'd finished making the s'mores with the ingredients Tanner had sneaked in as a special surprise, the smile on everyone's face had been near giddy.

Except Noah's.

Not that his brother was ever going to be much of a talker or smiler, but he was definitely tenser now than he had been when they first started the hike.

"What's going on?" Tanner asked softly. He didn't want anyone else to hear this conversation.

"Nothing I can put my finger on."

Tanner sat down on the log across from his brother. "But you're thinking there might be trouble?"

"I don't have concrete evidence of anything." Noah looked around into what anyone else would consider to be peaceful darkness.

Tanner rolled his eyes. "I'll take your gut feeling over 99 percent of the population's concrete evidence any day."

Noah was quiet for a long minute. "I'm not sure I can trust my gut too much either, to be honest. But there's nobody around us right now, that much I know for sure. I set up a few observation traps that would let me know if anybody had been surveilling us. When I checked them a few minutes ago there was no evidence of anybody else around."

"Could be stress wearing on you. That talk with Jared definitely didn't put me at ease."

"That's for damn sure. Bastard was way too confident he wouldn't be convicted at the trial. Like he knows something we don't."

Tanner nodded, lips tight. Oscar Stobbart already put a call in to Sheriff Duggan, Tanner's boss. Nothing formal, just a verbal complaint and concern about harassment against his client. Fortunately, they didn't have an ID for Bree, so there was nothing official Oscar could do. But Tanner had no doubt this would come up again at the trial if Stobbart could possibly work it in.

"Have you been following Jared more? We don't want to do anything that gives Stobbart any reason to try to have the case dismissed outright."

"I've got a colleague who's gone into Denver a couple of times for me, with instructions to stay far from Jared. I do know they've still got those building plans and maps out everywhere. Stobbart has joined them most nights. Another man joined them last night."

"That's probably Marius Nixon, the guy who provided money for Jared's bail. He arrived back in the country yesterday."

Noah rolled his shoulders. "They're planning something, Tanner."

"Do you know that for sure? Has your guy been using the surveillance equipment you talked about?"

Anything the man heard wouldn't be allowable in court, but at this point, Tanner would be glad just to have information. Once they knew what was going on, they'd figure out a plan later.

"I know there's something going on because my man couldn't hear anything with his surveillance equipment. They're using counter surveillance equipment."

Tanner let out a low curse.

Noah nodded. "That's how I felt too. It's high-end stuff. Took my man a night to figure out the info he was receiving wasn't legit. He happened to hear a loop in the recording their equipment was spitting out. Most people wouldn't have caught it at all."

"What do you think they're planning?" Tanner leaned closer to the fire, trying to process all of this.

"Honestly, I think they have something up their sleeves for the trial, then are planning to take Marilyn and the kids somewhere. I'm not going to let that happen, Tanner."

Tanner nodded. "*We're* not going to let that happen. Not you, not me, not Bree, not anyone else at New Journeys or in Risk Peak. Marilyn and those kids are one of ours now. You're not alone in this. Neither is she."

Noah shrugged. "It's hard for me not to work alone."

"We've got almost four months until the trial. We know the ankle monitor is working, so we focus on figuring out their plan. In this case, the best offense is a good defense. But we've got to let the law handle this. We cannot go after them just because they're doing suspicious stuff."

"Roger that."

"So let's try to enjoy this camping trip and make it something memorable for Marilyn and the kids. Unless you think there's actual danger here."

Noah ran a hand through his thick black hair that looked so much like Tanner's own. "Honestly, I don't know. I feel like something is off, but my neutrality is definitely compromised when it comes to that woman and those kids. Maybe I want Jared to be here so that I have an excuse to take him out and make sure they're safe for the rest of their lives."

"As an officer of the law, I'm afraid I'd probably have to let you do exactly that if Jared showed up here." Tanner gave his brother a wide grin.

"I have the emergency radio," Tanner said after a few minutes. "If there's any change in Jared's status, Ronnie will let us know right away."

"Good. There's probably nothing out there right now except my own feelings of inadequacy haunting me."

"Well, you better let those die out in the cold, because we're going to need your help protecting Marilyn if Jared really is found innocent by some miracle. And I need you on this trip because those kids certainly look up to you. Especially Sam."

Noah shrugged. "That's good, because I look up to them too. And especially their mom."

That was about as gushing and flowery as Noah got. Tanner swallowed his chuckle, but not quickly enough.

"Stuff it, jackass," Noah muttered.

"Yes, sir. How about I take first shift on lookout, just in case? We've got a long day of hiking and rafting ahead of us tomorrow."

None of it would be very rough—nobody wanted to take young children on rapids they couldn't handle—but it would be a full and exciting day.

"Wake me up in a couple hours and I'll relieve you."

Tanner settled into his place by the fire, listening for changes in the night noises around him. That would be his first indication that danger was nearby. He looked up at the moon, barely visible through the trees. Standing guard was no hardship for him. Maybe Noah was right, and his gut feelings were just a manifestation of the frustration inside him for not being able to do anything about the abuse Marilyn had suffered.

But either way, Tanner would be ready in case danger came.

BEING OUT HERE in the woods was so much better than wedding planning, but it didn't take Bree long to recognize tension in both Noah and Tanner the next day.

It wasn't overt—they were both still teaching and smiling, at least as much as Noah ever smiled, and they seemed to be having a good time. But there was a tension in Tanner—an awareness—that hadn't been there yesterday when they'd started their trip.

"What's going on?" she asked when they stopped for water. She'd been watching him all morning and all through their lunch break. Watching him watch the area around them, looking for threats.

"Nothing's going on. Why do you ask?"

She narrowed her eyes at him. "I don't know. Maybe because I've seen you around enough dangerous situations to recognize the I'm-about-to-turn-into-supercop look? What aren't you telling me?"

He pulled her against him and kissed her temple. "Nothing. I promise. Nothing concrete. Noah just got a little spooked—although it ended up being nothing—and both of us just want to be diligent."

"But nothing happened besides Noah's Spidey senses tingling?"

He smiled and kissed her. "Nothing. I promise I'll tell you if I think you need to be concerned."

"Really? You have been known to keep things from me before. Important things—because you wanted to handle it all by yourself."

"Believe me, I've learned my lesson when it comes to keeping things from you. We are a team."

Bree kissed him and turned back to the group. She watched as Noah took a sip of his water, wiping his mouth with the back of his hand afterward. Sam, sitting right beside him, mimicked the motion almost exactly a couple seconds later.

They spent the next two hours making steady progress through the wilderness. Tanner and Noah took multiple opportunities to indicate different plants and animals along the way. They showed some edible berries, but then were quick to point out the poisonous berries that looked very similar.

They identified poison oak and other plants to avoid, as well as specifying the multiple different trees and flowers that made up the beauty of this part of Colorado. Their respect for the wilderness around them was evident in every sentence. It was nearly impossible not to get caught up in their passion for the land.

The running theme was obvious: *respect nature*. Nature wasn't always gentle, but even in its harshness there was beauty.

They came across all sorts of animals. The racer snake they saw along one rocky ridge was Sam's personal favorite, even though it had everybody else squealing in fear.

Noah pointed out the tracks from deer and elk, and even the signs that a bear had passed through at some point. When Eva's eyes grew wide, Tanner took the time to explain the best way to defend yourself against a bear was actually to avoid it in the first place. Talking out loud and letting a bear know you were nearby was the best way to get it to move along in the opposite direction. Most bears weren't looking for a confrontation.

Sam wanted to press about what should be done if the bear didn't move along and charged instead, but that topic of conversation was obviously a little upsetting for Eva, who was soon near tears. A look and nod passed between Tanner and Noah, before Tanner grabbed Eva's hand to show her a caterpillar that was climbing up a tree. Noah placed a light hand on Sam's shoulder and led him a few steps over to the side.

Concern clouded Marilyn's face.

"Don't worry," Bree whispered to her. "Noah won't let the details get too out of hand. Although the way Sam got excited about that snake, I think he could probably handle details about a bear attack."

"Oh." Marilyn relaxed. "A bear attack. Right. Yeah, Sam can handle that."

Marilyn hadn't been worried about the topic, Bree realized.

"You know Noah would never hurt Sam, right?" she whispered.

Marilyn gave a shaky laugh. "I know that. Of course, I know that."

"Oh, my gosh, really? That's awesome!" Sam's excited voice called out from next to Noah, who was obviously imparting some vast wilderness secret to the boy. "It's so gross! Mom would never do it." Sam bellylaughed.

They watched as Noah leaned his head closer to tell Sam something else.

"I don't want him to live his life scared," Marilyn whispered. "I already hate myself enough for what I let them witness happen to me. I don't want to spend their whole childhood hovering over them and making them afraid to try new things and befriend new people."

Bree ran a hand along her friend's back, the gesture coming so much more naturally now than it would have a year ago, since she now had so many people in her life teaching her how to give and receive love.

"The world isn't always a safe place. Your kids learned that early, and, yeah, that's a tragedy of gargantuan proportions. But look at them, Marilyn." She gestured first at Eva, who was holding Tanner's hand and pressing her face close to a tree so she could see the critter, giggling every few seconds. Then over to Sam, who was staring at Noah with huge, wide eyes, obviously completely entranced with whatever the man was saying.

"Yeah?" Marilyn asked. "They don't seem to be doing anything particularly amazing."

Bree smiled. "Exactly. They're kids getting excited about caterpillars and probably some gross story about peeing on a tree to keep away a bear. And they're fine. Whatever you did, whatever you suffered through to protect them? It worked."

"I'm totally going to try that!" Sam yelled.

Noah chuckled. It was the first time Bree had heard him laugh. Even Tanner turned around at the sound.

"We'll check with your mom first. And you definitely have to make sure there is an adult around."

Noah looked over and winked at Marilyn, causing her to blush. Bree bit her tongue to keep from teasing her about it.

"Noah and I have been spending a little bit of time together," Marilyn said so softly Bree could hardly hear her.

"Spending time together as in dating?"

Marilyn flushed even more. "Not really. I mean he did have dinner with us once last week before the fire."

Bree nudged her hip against her friend. "That sounds a little bit like a date."

"Mostly he comes by after the kids go to bed at night."

Bree tried not to do a double take at that news. Certainly, they were both consenting adults, and although Marilyn may be technically still married to Jared on paper, it was safe to say the marriage had ended sometime around when he'd dislocated her shoulder, broken her nose, cracked her ribs, fractured her wrist and sent her into a coma.

If Marilyn could find a little bit of happiness with Noah—and vice versa—then damn all the people who would judge her for it. But Bree was still a little surprised.

"Good for you. I say get as much action as you can."

Marilyn's jaw dropped and her eyes got wide. "Oh, my God, it's not like that. Noah doesn't come over to have sex." Although the woman didn't look too distraught about that idea. "He's been teaching me self-defense moves."

Now, *that* sounded like Noah.

"Well, there's no one better you could learn them from," Bree said, meaning it.

"I know."

"And heck, that sort of is dating for Noah."

"I know," Marilyn whispered again.

Tanner and Noah got everyone moving forward again, focusing more on the smaller, gentler animals rather than predators. They answered any questions the kids or Barb or Francis had, while Bree and Marilyn brought up the rear.

They'd gone about another thirty minutes when Tanner stopped and pointed out a group of marmots lying out on a rock, far enough from the humans not to be threatened. Noah handed everyone his binoculars so they could take a closer look at the large ground squirrels.

"Marmots are pretty cool," Tanner said. "They eat grass and flowers and live in groups of between ten and twenty. During warm weather, they pretty much spend all day eating and lying out in the sun, getting fat."

"Sounds kind of boring," Sam said.

Tanner rubbed the kid's hair. "The amazing thing about marmots is that they hibernate over half their lives. At least six months out of every year, they're underground, living inside a hole, just trying to survive."

"They stay inside a hole for six months?" Eva asked. "They don't come out to eat or anything?"

Tanner tapped her on her nose. "Nope. They just hunker down, breathe in and out, and survive. That's it."

"Boring," Sam muttered again.

"I have no idea how Tanner knows all this stuff," Bree murmured to Marilyn. "I'm not sure if it's the nerdiest thing I've ever seen or the sexiest."

She glanced over at Marilyn, but she was just staring out blankly ahead of her.

"You okay?" Bree asked.

"I'm a marmot," Marilyn finally said. "Spending half my life living in a hole, just trying to survive. That's basically what I've done."

She said it so softly there was no way anyone else could've possibly heard her.

But when Noah spoke again, he was looking directly at her. "I don't think marmots are boring at all. I think they're pretty amazing. They don't really have any true defense mechanisms like other animals do, and it's just sheer strength of will that keeps them alive during the winter. They survive because they are determined to. That's something to be respected."

Marilyn finally looked away from Noah.

"All right," Tanner said. "Let's get going. We've got about another mile until we get to the rafts."

Everyone picked up their pace. The rafting was the highlight of the trip for Sam. He liked the tents and the wilderness and whatever crazy stuff Noah had told him about escaping bears, but rafting was truly exciting.

"We'll only be on the water a couple hours," Tanner said. "And there aren't any real rapids until much farther down the river."

Sam let out a disappointed groan. Tanner chuckled and ruffled his hair. "How about you get some rafting experience under your belt today and we'll start building up from there. Everybody has to learn in the safe water."

"I'll bet you and Noah didn't have to learn in baby water like this," Sam said when they reached the area where the rafts were stored.

"Not only did we learn in water just like this, we learned in this *exact* water," Noah said. "Lips wasn't much more than your age, and I was just a couple years older when our dad brought us here for the first time. So don't be talking junk about this water."

Sam's eyes grew big. "Really? You first went rafting *here*?"

"Yep," Tanner said. "And a year later I was already doing class III rapids. So let's get to work."

Sam was a lot more focused after finding out this was where his two idols got their start.

Like they'd done everything else, Tanner and Noah

carefully explained the logistics of rafting. Noah readily admitted that Tanner was the better raftsman, although Bree was sure he could do it just fine.

Tanner pulled the map out of his backpack and showed everyone exactly where they'd be going.

"At this second fork, we'll take the left. Farther downriver is where the rapids get a little more exciting than what we're looking for today." He winked at Sam. "But maybe soon. If it's okay, Bree Cheese and I and the two rug rats will go down with the majority of the supplies. Noah will have the honor of escorting the rest of the lovely ladies."

Bree was going to offer to trade with Marilyn so she could be with her kids. But when she heard the other woman mutter "no marmot," she held her tongue. Marilyn was trying to face her fears by allowing the kids to be away from her. Bree wanted to help.

And when Noah gave Marilyn a reassuring nod and a small smile, Bree was even more convinced this was the right thing.

Soon they were on their way. The first hour on the river Bree just sat back and enjoyed herself. The water was moving at a fast enough pace to keep everybody interested and it felt like nothing could go wrong out here. The kids kept demanding Noah and Tanner race, and they took turns paddling hard to get in front of each other. About thirty minutes later they came up on the second fork and Tanner let Noah pull ahead.

"Aw, man," Sam said. "They're beating us!"

Tanner just smiled. "Noah's got to get ahead so he can help us dock and get the supplies out. And come on, you and I both know we could take them."

"Yeah, we could!"

Tanner slowed them down further with his oar as

Noah took the fork. Bree could see why he wanted to have Noah already stopped and ready to help them. The speed of the water had definitely picked up.

She was just about to ask him about it when an odd screeching noise came from the front of the raft. She looked back at Tanner, who was steering them with the paddle. "Do you hear that?"

When the sound got louder a moment later, everyone could hear it.

Tanner's muttered curse was cut off when the raft jerked suddenly, the front end collapsing, throwing them all forward.

Both kids screamed as they were thrown forcefully into the water. Bree grabbed for Eva, but the rapids pulled her away, then pulled Bree under.

Chapter Eleven

Tanner didn't even waste time trying to figure out what the hell had caused a large enough puncture in the PVC material of the raft to cause it to collapse so suddenly. They weren't near any severely jagged rocks, and even if they were, the raft material should've been able to handle it.

Instead he pushed off the remainder of the raft that was still above water and dived forward into the water.

The cold of it stunned him for second. It might have been May, but the water flowing down from the Rockies was still damn cold. And Bree and the kids were in it with not nearly the muscle mass he had to fight the cold.

All of them were wearing life jackets, but someone could still drown in one if they fought it or got pulled under the wrong way.

Out of the corner of his eye the fork where they needed to have turned floated by. There was no way they could make it over in this current, and now there was no way Noah would be able to get here to help them out. It was all up to him now.

Bree's voice reached him over the roar of the water. "Tanner… I… Sam… Find Eva!"

Praying that meant Bree had Sam, Tanner propelled himself as high up in the water as he could in his sopping clothes and boots to try to see. Two bright life jackets were closer to the shore. The other one, smaller—it had to be Eva—was still flailing in the middle of the rushing water. Tanner began to swim toward her with every bit of strength he had. If Eva got washed too far down the river, she'd be in the serious rapids.

He pushed himself hard, shoving away the fear that even though Bree and Sam were closer to the shore, they could still be in danger. Bree had become quite the outdoors woman, but this could be more than she could handle.

Saying a silent prayer on his bride-to-be's behalf, he swam the last dozen yards between him and Eva.

"Eva, I'm coming sweetheart!"

"L-Lips? I'm cold."

Her scared voice tugged at his heart, but she was alive. That was the most important thing.

"I'm coming up behind you and then we're gonna swim together to the shore."

"I'm not a good swimmer."

"You're doing just fine. Doing perfect, considering none of us had planned to be swimming down this river today, did we?" He closed the last yard, his fingertips grabbing the back of her life vest. "Got you."

"I—I didn't know what to do. I'm cold."

He pulled her up against his chest, wrapping his arm under her armpits, and began swimming toward the shore. "You did perfect. Absolutely perfect."

"Where's Sam?"

"He's with Bree. They are probably already on the shore. Let's go find them." Tanner prayed that was true.

Eva really was a little trouper. She didn't panic, didn't cry, just used her little legs as best she could to help propel them toward the shore. He'd known grown-ass adults who hadn't kept as much composure as this five-year-old girl did in the face of danger.

They made it to shore a few exhausting minutes later. Tanner made sure Eva was all the way out and safe before standing to see if he needed to go back into the water for Bree and Sam. His heart began thumping harder in his chest when he didn't see any sign of either life vest on the shore or in the water.

"Bree!" His voice came out much weaker than he wanted it to.

He wasn't even sure what direction he should look. He hadn't seen either of them after catching them out of the corner of his eye when he first went after Eva. Maybe they hadn't made it to the shoreline. Maybe they had gotten sucked back into the water and were rushing downstream.

"Bree!" he called again. When he didn't get an answer, he ran toward a boulder that would give him a better vantage point of the riverbank and the water itself. He scrambled up the rock, cursing as he fell, movements uncoordinated from the cold, scraping his hands. He ignored it. There would be time for first aid later.

From this higher vantage point he spotted Bree and Sam immediately. A relieved breath shuddered out of his chest when he saw they were alive and conscious. They were both hovering over one of the side whirlpools the rapids made, reaching for something.

Tanner scrambled back down the rock to get Eva, and they made their way over to Bree and Sam, Tanner carrying Eva's shivering body most of the way.

"Oh, thank God," Bree said when she saw them. She then tried to stand, clutching the emergency bag that they'd obviously fished out of the whirlpool to her chest.

"This bag has rope," she said between chattering teeth.

"Smart," he said, pulling her to his chest and letting Eva slide to the ground. If Bree had needed to get him out of the water, that rope would've been the best way to do it. Possibly the only way to do it.

"That bag has emergency supplies—Mylar blankets and waterproof matches. If we could only save one backpack, that's the one we want." He turned to the kids. "We're going to build a fire and we're going to get warm. I know this sounds weird, but I need everybody to strip down to just your T-shirts and undies."

He knew they were cold when nobody gave him any complaints. Tanner and Sam began gathering firewood while Bree helped the shivering Eva off with her wet clothes.

"I can get this, buddy, if you want to go get your wet clothes off. I know you're cold."

"I'll—I'll help," Sam said through chattering teeth. "The sooner we get wood, the sooner we'll have a fire."

They began picking up twigs and branches. At least it hadn't rained, so nothing was wet.

Tanner nodded at the boy. "That's exactly what my father said to Noah and me when we fell into this river when we weren't much older than you."

"Really?"

"Yep. And I know your mom would be so proud of how brave and strong you're being. Noah too. Don't tell him I told you, but when he fell in the river, he cried like a little baby."

Arms full of wood, they headed back toward Bree and Eva.

"Noah really cried?" Sam asked.

"Yeah, of course, and I was crying too. It was damn cold." That got a small laugh from Sam.

Bree was holding a sleeping Eva on her lap wrapped in a blanket when they got to them.

Tanner began building a fire. Normally he would have taken this opportunity to teach Sam about it, but Sam probably wasn't up to learning much right now, and getting the fire going quickly was of the essence.

"She okay?" he asked Bree.

Bree rocked the girl back and forth in her arms. "Once I got her warm and fed her a protein bar, she was out like a light."

"Did you get something to eat too?"

"Yes. There isn't a lot in that bag, but I'm thankful for a little bit of food."

Tanner got the blaze going, then reached down and pulled off his wet jeans, glad he had boxers on. He held out the other thermal blanket to Sam, who took it, then removed his own wet clothing.

"I feel like I could sleep for a week. Getting tossed around like that takes it out of you."

"What happened?" Bree asked. "Did we run into a rock or something?"

Tanner looked over at Sam. The kid's eyes were already drifting shut. He grabbed a protein bar from the bag, unwrapped it and put a bite in the boy's mouth. He chewed without protest. Tanner took a bite himself, then put the rest of it in Sam's mouth.

"It shouldn't have mattered if we'd run into a rock. Rafts like that are meant to hit rocks regularly."

Feeling much better without his wet clothes on, Tanner grew the fire until it was a large blaze. Sam was already falling asleep on the ground next to him.

"The bag you saved wasn't the one with the emergency sat phone, was it?"

Bree shook her head. "No, it wasn't your backpack.

It was the emergency kit Barb was carrying. Blankets, some food, a water bladder and a flare gun."

"Flare gun. That's good."

"Do we need it?" she asked.

"Only to signal to the others that we made it and we're okay. I'm sure Marilyn is beside herself right now."

Bree pulled Eva more closely into her arms. "I would be too if I saw my kids go headfirst into a river and there was nothing I could do about it."

He got up and walked over to the wet backpack. Pulling out the flare gun, he also grabbed two of the four flares in the package.

"Two flares will let Noah know we don't need any assistance. Otherwise he'll be trying to sprint his way to us. Getting to the nearest bridge would take him hours, even at full speed. We don't want him doing that—the risk of injury is too high in the dark if we don't need help."

He kissed Bree on top of the head as he walked by to get far enough away not to wake the kids as he shot. He pulled out the flare gun, loaded and shot it, then repeated the process. He knew Noah would understand the message and just hoped he'd be able to keep Marilyn calm.

He added more firewood to the fire, then resumed his seat next to Sam.

"So what's the plan?" Bree asked, attempting to smother a huge yawn. "We've got, what, an hour or two before sunset?"

"Plan really doesn't change too much from the original camping plan, except to cut it short." Tanner looked up at the trees that were starting to sway more. "Honestly, we probably would've needed to cut the trip short anyway. The wind is picking up, which is going to blow in the storm that was coming this way a little faster."

She made a face. "Are we going to get rained on? I'm just getting dry."

"No, not tonight. Maybe late tomorrow night. But we'll be able to make it back to the vehicles by then. We'll meet Marilyn, Noah and the others at the first bridge where they can cross. Noah will know to rendezvous with us there. Besides that, we'll still have fun, learn as much about nature and the wilderness as possible and the kids will have a hell of a story to tell as they grow up about the time they almost drowned in the Colorado River."

She smiled. "I like that plan."

"We've got plenty of water and a way to carry it, some edible plants around and the basic supplies to fish tonight and tomorrow. We'll have to cut the trip short, but all in all, nothing too bad."

Bree shifted, scooting over so she could lean more of her weight back against a large rock behind her. She moved the sleeping Eva over so she was on the ground, but still next to her.

"Have you ever had anything like this happen before? I know you rafted in this area your whole life. What would've happened if something like that occurred once we'd hit the bigger rapids?"

He stretched his legs out in front of him, finally feeling, if not quite warm, at least not freezing. "No, I've never had anything like this happen to me, or even heard anything like it. And these rafts were inspected before they were brought here. A puncture would've been noticed."

"It definitely wasn't a slow leak. We jerked like we hit something."

"That shouldn't have made a difference either. These rafts are qualified for up to class V rapids. If they burst every time you hit a rock, there'd be people floating down the river all over the place."

And that was the problem, wasn't it? The raft had *burst*. Even if there had been some odd puncture, it should have been a slow leak, not that sort of explosion.

"I wish I could get my hands on the raft," he continued. "It had to have been some sort of manufacturer malfunction. It was dangerous enough as is, but like you said, on bigger rapids it could have been deadly."

"Could someone have tampered with the raft?"

Tanner thought about that for a minute. About the danger Noah had been sensing. But it just didn't make sense. "The short answer is yes."

Bree sighed, shifting her weight. "But the longer answer is that it wouldn't really make sense to tamper with the raft."

"Exactly. Too many unknown variables. We didn't decide who was going to be in each raft until just a couple minutes before we got in them. Plus, we were never in very dangerous waters. If we had been in the other raft, and Noah, Marilyn, Barb and Francis had been in ours, they would've just immediately swum to shore. Nothing but a big headache."

Bree wrapped her arms around her knees. "I guess I'm just jumpy after the fire and all the Jared stuff."

Yeah, Tanner didn't like that he now did not have any sort of communication with Risk Peak. Ronnie couldn't send him an update if something happened with Jared. And his Glock was now sitting at the bottom of the Colorado River. It was time to get home.

Tanner got up and moved over until he was sitting next to her, on the opposite side of the sleeping Eva, and wrapped an arm around her shoulders. "It's been a crazy couple of weeks, that's for sure. And in camping my dad always said you could count on some sort of calamity, but I'll be honest, I wasn't expecting this."

"Well, hopefully we've gotten our share of bad luck all used up. None left for the wedding."

He kissed her temple. "Nothing with us ever seems to go according to plan, does it?"

She snuggled into him. "Do you think that will be true our whole life?"

"Let's hope not. I hereby decree that we have officially gotten all our bad luck out of our system. From here on out, no more calamities."

"I'll second that."

They stared into the fire until they were both nice and warm. Tanner put his hiking pants and boots back on as the sun started to set. Sam woke up and the two of them headed to the river for fishing. Tanner explained about the flares so that the boy would know his mother wouldn't be worried.

They ate enough to at least not be hungry, then gathered firewood to have nearby to keep the blaze going all night.

They used what they could from the rescued emergency pack for pillows and covering. It was going to be a long night, but all things considered, it could've been much, much worse.

Chapter Twelve

Both kids were chattering nonstop the next morning as the four of them made their way toward the rendezvous point. They weren't in any hurry; coming from this side of the river meant they had a much shorter walk than Noah and the women did.

They'd eaten an odd breakfast of fish and protein bars, but it had given them the nourishment they needed.

Eva and Sam were bantering back and forth, talking at great length about all the details they were going to tell their friends—falling into the water, the snake, Sam's intel about how to avoid a bear.

Tanner met Bree's eyes, both of them struggling not to smile, as the kids decided that they would leave out any really scary parts so that their friends wouldn't be so frightened of rafting that they were afraid to try it.

"Wise." Bree nodded her head as she walked hand in hand with Eva. "You don't want to overwhelm your friends with too much action all at once."

They'd gone another mile before Sam lengthened his stride so he could be walking next to Tanner, leaving the females a little farther behind. The kid obviously had something to say.

"What's on your mind, buddy?"

"Do you think Noah is going to be mad at us?"

"Why would he be mad?"

Sam shrugged. "Because we had all the food and supplies in our boat. And he didn't really have anyone to help them out. Just Mom and Miss Barb and Miss Francis."

Tanner swallowed a laugh. "Although I'm sure he would have rather had you there to help him, Noah is capable of handling just about anything. Even three women who don't know much about the wilderness. Although your mom is pretty darn smart."

Sam nodded solemnly. "Oh, I know. But she's…"

Tanner knew the kids had been seeing a child psychologist. He wished he had a doctor's advice on what to say right now to the little boy. He would just go with his gut.

"She's what, buddy?"

"Broken," he whispered, then touched his chest. "On the inside. My dad…he hurt her."

"A man should never hurt a woman."

"I know." Sam's voice got smaller. "I tried to help, but Dad would lock us in our bedrooms."

"Hey." Tanner stopped and crouched down beside him so they could be eye to eye. The girls came up on them, but Bree just kept walking, giving them privacy.

"I know you and I don't know each other very well." He smiled and winked at the boy. "Although after our river adventure, I think we have a bond, right?"

Sam nodded solemnly. "Yes, sir."

"Then I want to say this man to man. Friend to friend. That stuff your dad did to your mom is on *him*, and nobody else. Not her, and especially not you or Eva. A real man should never raise a hand against a woman. Even if you could've gotten out of that room you were locked in, there's nothing you could've done."

Sam didn't look like he believed Tanner, but Tanner hadn't expected him to. It was going to take more than just a couple of sentences from someone the kid didn't really know very well to unpack all the emotional damage done in this situation. All any of them could do was to continuously reassure Sam, and Marilyn, that they weren't at fault for Jared Ellis's actions.

"Hey, you're not worried that Noah will hurt your mom, are you? Because I can assure you that will never happen."

"I know Noah wouldn't hurt her. I just didn't want him to get mad at her because she sometimes has bad days. Sometimes it's hard for her to get out of bed. Sometimes she cries."

God, Tanner's heart was breaking for this kid. When he and Noah had been this age, their biggest concern had been trying to talk their mom into letting them stay out past when the streetlights came on, and how to do enough car washes and lemonade stands to raise the money to buy the video game they currently wanted. There had been all sorts of laughter and chaos in their house. Never violence, and rarely tears.

"Don't you worry about Noah." Tanner stood and squeezed Sam's shoulder, and they began walking again. "You know Miss Cassandra is our sister, right? And she's kinda crazy. So Noah can definitely handle your mom, even if she's not having a good day."

"Oh, yeah." A smile broke through on Sam's solemn face. "Miss Cass is a little crazy. She's not quiet like Bree Cheese or my mom."

Tanner rolled his eyes. "You can say that again. Believe me, I had to live with her growing up."

He told a story of the time Cassandra made him so angry he'd accidentally thrown a baseball bat through a window as they caught up with the girls. It wouldn't take them much longer to reach the bridge. Probably an hour or two after lunch, the kids would be reunited with their mom and everyone would feel a whole lot better.

They were still a good six hours of hiking to where they'd left the cars, so there would probably be one more meal of eating fish and protein bars and whatever other edible plants he and Noah could find, but tonight everyone would be back together and in their own beds.

A flash of bright light reflecting from up on the ridge in front of them caught Tanner's attention, but by the time he could pinpoint where it had come from it was gone. A reflection of that type was almost always from something people had brought with them into the wilderness. Animals did their utmost to blend in. People were the ones who carried items that reflected and drew attention to themselves—binoculars, cameras, cell phones…

Rifle sights.

Seeing other people in this section of the wilderness wasn't completely unusual, although there were much more popular areas for both hiking and rafting. So Tanner wasn't concerned, but he was definitely aware.

When he saw the brief reflection again fifteen minutes later, on par with their location and pace, then he became concerned.

But not overly so. Yes, there were people ahead of them, moving at the same pace as them, and looking over their shoulder to make sure he and Bree and the kids were still moving. But whoever it was couldn't mean them harm, or at least didn't mean to shoot them outright, because they had more than enough opportunity to do it. Their watchers had the higher ground, they were hidden and Tanner was unarmed.

Until there was reason to change the plan, he wasn't going to. Nevertheless, he subtly picked up their pace.

He saw the reflective glimmer one more time before they curved around the ridge and came to the suspension bridge that would lead them over the river and back to safety.

Except the bridge had been destroyed. Pieces of rope and lumber hung in disarray, still attached to the cliff on the other side of the river, but completely removed from their side.

How the hell had that happened?

The bridge had been around as long as Tanner could remember. The river was relatively narrow at this juncture, so the catenary rope bridge had been built across it. The thing had scared him to death the first couple of times he'd crossed it, the way it would sway with each step. It was only as he got older and became more aware of physics and mechanics that he'd come to understand how safe and secure the bridge really was.

Of course, he hadn't been up here in at least two years, so it was possible there'd been some damage before now and Tanner just hadn't realized it.

"Houston, I think we have a problem," Bree muttered. "I hope this isn't the only way across the river."

"No, there are three more bridges farther downriver." And they would go to them—but first he wanted to check this one out. Handing out another protein bar to the kids for them to split, Tanner scooted down so he could get a better look at where the rope bridge had once been secured into the hard rock of the ravine.

When he saw it, he had to swallow his curse.

The bridge itself had definitely been cut by hand. More than cut. It had been completely destroyed. The rings attached to the wall of rock were still solidly embedded, but just beyond the metal the rope had been destroyed. It looked like someone had taken a blowtorch to it.

"Anything interesting?"

The kids were chattering as they continued munching on their bars.

"Definitely wasn't destroyed by mother nature."

Bree helped hoist him back up to ground level. "Why would someone want to destroy a bridge?"

That was the real question, wasn't it? And Tanner had a bad feeling about the answer.

There were three more bridges they could use, but getting to them was going to take them directly through an area that would leave them completely vulnerable, especially if the people who had been tracking them the last couple of hours intended them harm.

"What will Noah and Marilyn do when they get to their side of the bridge and see that it's unusable?"

"Noah knows about the other bridges. There is a secondary base camp five miles from here. If I were him, that's where I'd assume we would go."

Bree had already caught on to the tension in his voice. "Is it time to be concerned yet?"

Was it time to be concerned? At one point in their relationship Tanner would've tried to shelter her, to keep the truth from her. But he'd learned the hard way that wasn't a good idea. Bree could handle herself and was an asset in almost every situation.

He cupped her cheek. "There's no need to panic. And this could all still be coincidence. But yes, there is reason to think it might be time for concern."

Eva walked over to them and stood right next to Bree. "Are we not going to get to see Mommy?" she asked, her little lip quivering.

Bree smiled, but it was tight. "We are, pumpkin. We're just going to need to go to another bridge."

"Hey, Eva, you've been walking a long time. Can I give you a piggyback ride?" Tanner asked with a wink. "Then in a few minutes you can give me one."

The little girl giggled at his silliness and he took the opportunity to swing her up and around on his back. He gave Bree a nod, which she returned, and then looked over at Sam. "You ready to pick up the pace a little bit, champ? If we're going to beat your mom and Noah to the next bridge, we'll have to double-time it."

More like if they were going to make sure they beat the people who were tracking them, but no need to worry the kid with that info.

"Yeah, let's go!" Sam responded.

They walked at a pace faster than they'd been going before, but not fast enough to clue in the people watching them that Tanner was onto them. Bree did a great job keeping the kids talking—about computers, no less—and Tanner kept an eye on the ridge above them as the path they were on started to take them closer to the river's edge once again.

They'd gone about a mile when Tanner saw the light reflected up off the ridge again. When Bree stopped talking for a moment and caught his eye, he realized she'd seen it too. It wasn't until a couple of moments later when he saw a second reflection from the northeastern ridge that he realized they were actually in trouble.

It wasn't one person following them—it was two. At *least* two.

And if Tanner kept them on the path they were walking, they would be moving straight into an area where their followers held all the high ground, and all the advantages. It would make them sitting ducks.

He could be wrong. It could be two sets of hikers just out on their way not even thinking about the reflections their cameras or binoculars were making. It could be hunters up on the ridge, aware of his and the kids' presence but not intending any harm.

But it could also be someone who had already sabotaged their raft and forced their party to separate.

Tanner wasn't willing to take the chance.

There was only one way to know for sure, and that was to lead Bree and the kids deeper into the wilderness.

Catching Bree's eye, he tilted his head to the side and led them off the worn path.

She continued the ongoing conversation with the kids and Tanner didn't discourage it. Their followers were too far away to hear them at this point.

Away from the clearer path the ground was harder to navigate. Tanner would've liked to go much faster, but if somebody twisted an ankle it would definitely slow them down. He hated to add three or four extra miles to an already full day of walking for little legs, but doing this would give whoever was watching them the chance to move on.

Or let Tanner know for certain that they were in trouble.

The kids walked for a while, then Tanner gave Sam a piggyback. Bree, trouper that she was, held Eva for as long as she could, giving the little girl a break. After two miles Tanner swung them back toward the main path again. They walked parallel to it for a good half a mile, and even though he'd kept a close eye out, he didn't see any trace of anyone following them. Maybe he had been paranoid. A good cop was always a little paranoid, and maybe this time it was nothing.

"How are we doing?" Bree asked as the kids walked a few steps ahead of them.

"I haven't seen anything to make me suspicious for the last half a mile. I'm thinking maybe I was a bit overzealous."

She reached over and squeezed his hand. "I like it when you're overzealous. Although generally you're not in the middle of the wilderness when you decide to be."

He wrapped an arm around her shoulder and pulled her up against him, kissing her forehead. "Let's get back on the main path and deliver these kids to their mom."

They were almost to the clearing they would cut through to get back on the main path when Eva let out a disgusted sound.

"Ew. That's so gross."

When Tanner crouched down next to her to see what had gotten her attention, he expected some sort of bug or dead critter. But it wasn't. It was three cigarette butts.

"Mommy says smoking is gross," Eva informed him.

"Do people smoke even out in the woods?" Sam said.

"They do if they're addicted to cigarettes," Bree responded.

Tanner picked up one of the butts, much to the kids' dismay.

"You don't smoke, do you, Lips?" Sam asked.

Tanner brought the butt up to his nose and breathed in. The scent of tobacco was still very present. These butts weren't more than an hour old.

Someone had been sitting here, waiting. No hunter would smoke out in the open like that. It would scare all the prey away. Someone had been waiting for something much more specific.

"Everybody, back into the tree line," Tanner said, pushing them rapidly in that direction. He could tell by the kids' faces that he was making them nervous, but it couldn't be helped.

They were definitely being followed. And he was afraid not just followed...

Hunted.

Chapter Thirteen

Bree grabbed the kids' hands as Tanner led them deep into the thick shelter of the trees.

"I need to go check something out, okay? You guys stay here." He gave both kids a smile and a wink, which encouraged them a little bit, then turned to her. "I'm just going to see what I can find out. Info gathering only."

Obviously, his feeling that he was being paranoid had passed, and it had something to do with those cigarette butts. Someone had been there recently.

She nodded. "We'll be right here getting a little rest in case we need to do more walking."

The kids groaned at the thought of more walking.

"Whatever's left to eat in the backpack, go ahead and do it," Tanner said.

He didn't elaborate, but Bree could read between the lines: get calories into their system in case we need to run.

She nodded. "We'll be fine. You be careful."

With a nod he was gone.

"Bree Cheese, what's happening?" Eva asked.

"I'm not exactly sure, but I think we might be playing a big game of hide-and-seek."

The kids obviously didn't believe her, but they didn't

argue. They got out the last two protein bars and began splitting them, wrapping a chunk for Tanner.

With their bellies the slightest bit full, both kids' eyes began to droop. Bree couldn't blame them. They'd already walked at least five miles today. And given what they'd been through in the last twenty-four hours, they probably needed as much rest as they could get.

Bree didn't have that luxury. She kept her eyes open and her ears attuned for any sound of danger. Not that she knew what danger would sound like, or what she would do if an enemy—man or animal—attacked.

When she got back to Risk Peak, she was going to put some concerted effort into researching wilderness survival.

She grimaced. *After* she wrote her wedding vows. First, she had to put her researching abilities into that. Or…maybe whatever was happening right now would drag out to a month and they'd have to cancel the wedding. She and Tanner really could just go in front of the judge. It would solve all her problems.

All her problems except for whatever potential nicotine-riddled danger was out there. Plus, Sam and Eva would be miserable without their mom for that long. And she was sure Marilyn was already beside herself with worry. So she couldn't wish for that.

Tanner came back into their little hiding spot as silently as he'd left, nearly giving Bree a heart attack.

"Damn, you're spooky quiet," she said when she could get a word out. At least the kids were still asleep.

He didn't smile. "We're in trouble."

"For sure?"

He nodded and sat down, grabbing the water and the protein bar. "There are three people waiting for us up ahead. It's definitely a trap. They were waiting for us to pick up the main path again, and then we would've been sitting ducks for whatever they had planned."

"Who? Why?"

"I don't know. Someone from my past or yours? We've certainly found out over the last year that we're not without enemies." He pointed to the kids. "Or somebody attached to Ellis? Maybe he even found a way around his ankle monitor. Ronnie wouldn't have been able to get in touch with us if that happened. I couldn't get close enough to see their faces. All I know is that they were triangulated for a capture another mile and a half down, and we were about to walk right into them."

"So what's the plan?"

"We head deeper into the woods. I've been around this wilderness all my life, so that's an advantage. They're expecting us to show up on the main path in the next hour or two. It will take them a while to figure out we're not coming back that way, after all. That's the second advantage."

He sounded sure of himself. That reassured her. "Okay. Let's do it."

He touched her arm. "But we've also got disadvantages. Two kids who can be pushed physically only so far. No weapons. I could try to take them out myself, but that's risky, and would leave you relatively defenseless if I wasn't successful."

"Not to mention pretty damn lost."

He gave her a half smile that didn't hold much humor. "And as if that's not enough excitement, that storm is rolling in faster than we figured. It's going to hit in the next twenty-four hours."

She squeezed his hand. "Okay, that's a lot of variables to consider. So we try to backtrack our way around them?"

Tanner began packing the water bottle and trash into the backpack. "If we can. I have no idea how skilled they are at tracking. But we'll have to leave as small a trail for them to follow as possible." He shook his head. "It's going to be hard on the kids—scary and stressful. I don't think there's any way around that."

"I told them we were playing a game of hide-and-seek."

He smiled. "From here on out it will have to be as quiet a game of hide-and-seek as we can manage."

They both hated to traumatize these kids any further, but survival trumped everything else. Staying alive was the most important thing.

They woke the kids up and Tanner explained that they were going to do some serious wilderness training. Both kids looked a little skeptical, but Tanner got Sam on board by telling him it was similar to the training Noah had done in the army.

"I don't want to be in the army," Eva whispered to Bree. "I want to play soccer or work on the computer games you gave me. I'm not a soldier."

Bree buttoned up the little girl's jacket; now that it was late afternoon it was getting cooler. "I'm not a soldier either, sweetheart. So we'll just use our brains to help out as much as possible, okay? We'll just keep very quiet and use our eyes and ears to look out for what Tanner is talking about. I know you can do that. You're so good with computers, like your mom."

Eva nodded solemnly.

They moved out in a single-file line.

"Okay, here's the wilderness training game," Tanner said. "We're trying to make it so that nobody can follow us."

"Like hide-and-seek?" Eva asked.

"Yes. A little like hide-and-seek. But also wilderness hide-and-seek. That means we try not to break any branches or step in any soft soil."

"Because soft soil would leave a footprint?" Sam asked.

"For exactly that reason." Tanner beamed at him and the boy was obviously thrilled.

"We walk on rocks, if we can, and stay in a single-file line as much as possible."

Bree's heart swelled in her chest. This man was going to make such a wonderful father. To be so in tune with the danger around them, but calm and mindful of the children's needs also.

The kids were both smiling as they set off in a single-file line, Tanner leading the way and Bree bringing up the rear. Tanner held branches out of the way so that everyone could more easily proceed without them breaking. As he passed by plants that contained something edible, he pointed to it and he and Sam grabbed what they could and put it in the backpack.

The kids held tough for a long time. Longer than most kids their age would have, testament of what they'd survived earlier in their life. But when both of them began tripping, Sam falling and cutting his elbow, Bree knew they were in trouble. There was no way they were going to be able to double back as far as Tanner wanted. The kids weren't going to last that long.

The sun was beginning to set, making it even more difficult to see in the thick woods.

Tanner called them to a halt, and they began drinking from the canteen they'd refilled at the stream they'd crossed a mile or two back.

All the miles were beginning to blend together for

Bree; she couldn't imagine what it was like for the kids. And yet they didn't complain.

She looked up from sipping her water and found Tanner studying her.

"Circling back is not going to work tonight. It's too far."

She nodded. At this point she wasn't even sure *she* could make it, much less the kids.

"Do we have a plan B?"

He grimaced and nodded. "We get deeper in and find somewhere to hide until they pass."

The kids were listening intently, but there was no way to hide this from them, not anymore.

"Stranger danger?" Eva whispered.

"Yes," Tanner smiled at her. "Unfortunately, we've got some stranger danger. We need to hide and rest for a while. We'll let them pass, then go a different route home."

"What about Mom?" Sam asked.

"Noah will get her home. He'll be waiting for us with your mom. Both of them will be so happy to see us when we get there," Bree said.

"I'll carry both of them, if you get the backpack," Tanner said.

Bree shook her head. "There's no way you can carry both of them and continue to hide our tracks. I'll piggyback Miss Eva and you give Sam a ride."

"I can walk," Sam said. "I'm not a baby."

"I'm not a baby either," Eva said with a pout.

"Nobody's a baby," Tanner said, cutting them off. "We need to move as quickly as possible, with as few steps as possible. So if you happen to be the two shortest people here, then you get a piggyback ride. But listen, this is a wilderness piggyback. That means you need to hold on and help as much as possible with your legs and arms. Okay?"

They both nodded. Tanner walked over and cupped the back of Bree's neck. "You're going to have to dig deep, freckles. We need to move fast and find the best shelter we can get."

"I can take it."

He kissed her hard. "I know you can. Let's go."

Tanner hoisted Sam up onto his back, and Bree did the same with Eva.

Tanner hadn't been lying. He set a brutal pace, not slowing even as they headed uphill, over rocky terrain or through thick underbrush.

Bree forced herself to keep pace even when her lungs felt like they were on fire and she had stitches in both sides of her waist. Eva did what she could to help, keeping her legs hooked around Bree's hips and holding a lot of her own weight much of the time. But it was still agonizing.

Tanner periodically turned around to check on her but never offered to stop. That didn't make her angry. It meant he trusted her to do what had to get done.

But she hoped he was listening out for any trouble, because, honestly, someone could walk right up on her and she'd never hear them over the sound of her own labored breathing.

It was pitch-black by the time they stopped. Bree could barely see two feet in front of her.

"This," he said. She got a tiny bit of satisfaction to hear that Tanner was breathing hard too. "This is probably as best a place we're going to find. Everybody stay right here, and I'm going to make sure there's nothing living inside."

Inside what? Bree had no idea. Tanner took a sip

from the canteen, then handed it to Bree before disappearing into the darkness. She grabbed Eva's and Sam's hands just to make sure she didn't lose them in the darkness.

"What is Lips doing?" Sam asked.

"He's finding a safe place for us to rest. He'll be back in just a second." She prayed that was true, because she had no idea what she was going to do if she suddenly became the adult in charge.

But he was back just a few moments later. "Okay, no critters. At least, not now. We're safe to go in."

"In what?" Bree asked. "A cave?"

"It's really more of an overhang than an actual cave, but it's sheltered on three sides and can fit all four of us."

Tanner led them forward and down a small hill. The moon was finally coming out, so she could just barely make out the shape of the natural shelter he'd found. But he was right, it should keep them hidden for the most part.

"We can't make a fire," Tanner whispered. "So we're all going to need to huddle together with the blankets to keep warm. We'll have to eat whatever we collected on the way. But most important, we're going to have to be as still and quiet as possible, okay?"

The kids nodded. If they weren't too scared, they'd probably be out like a light as soon as they ate.

Tanner gave them all some more water and they got out the food they'd been collecting along the way today. The temperature was dropping now that it was dark, so Bree had the kids go ahead and wrap themselves in the blanket. Tanner ate a little, then whispered that he would be back in a few minutes.

"Where is he going?" Eva asked, worry evident in her little voice.

"Just to get something we need. He'll be right back." Bree didn't know exactly what Tanner was doing, but she knew her words were true.

Sure enough, he was back a few minutes later, two sticks in his hand. He laid them both by Bree.

"This is as close as I can get to weapons. Obviously, they're not going to be super useful against...more modern weaponry." She appreciated that he didn't say the word *gun* in front of the kids. No need to plant that in their minds right before they were stuck in the dark all night. "But it's something. Use it like a baseball bat. If someone who's not me comes in here, make your first shot count."

His giving her pointers on how to best use that large stick as a weapon was scaring her more than anything else he'd said today. Because he really thought she was going to have to use it.

But now wasn't the time to give in to panic. Tanner needed her to be strong. So she just reached over, found his hand in the dark and squeezed. "Okay."

As she'd predicted, it didn't take long for the kids to fall asleep. It was dark, they couldn't talk and there was nothing to see, not to mention their little bodies had been pushed hard today.

Once they were, Tanner brought his lips all the way to her ear and spoke quietly. "I'm going out. This place is good as a shelter, but if they find us here, we are basically sitting ducks. At least from out there if someone finds you, I can do something about it."

She nodded so he would know she understood.

"If I can take one or more out, I'm going to try to do that."

She stiffened. They undoubtedly had weapons. And he didn't know how many of them there were.

His hand came up and threaded into her hair on the other side of her head, the motion so Tanner-like and in control that it helped calm her.

"These guys have guns. They're dangerous, freckles—I can feel it in my gut. If I don't come back, at first light, you take the kids and run."

She shook her head frantically. There was no way she was leaving him.

"Yes." His fingers gripped her hair more firmly. "You go in the morning. You follow the direction the sun is rising until you run into the river, then turn right and follow the river south all the way until you hit the road. You get Noah, Whitaker, Ronnie...*everybody*. You send them all back up to help me."

"I don't want to leave you," she whispered.

"I'm going to be there for our wedding, don't you worry. But you have to promise me you'll go. I can keep myself alive, but I can't watch them hurt you or those kids."

"If you're not at the wedding, I'm going to make you wait another whole year to get married, with the no-touching rule still in effect," she lied. She'd never be able to live that long without touching him.

He kissed her forehead. "You can damn well bet I'm not going to miss our wedding night—you've got too many dirty debts to pay. I'll see you soon, freckles."

With a hard kiss on her lips, he disappeared silently into the darkness.

Chapter Fourteen

Tanner moved as silently as possible through the trees, stopping every so often to try to listen for anything out of place. Noah was so much better at this than he was. But to keep Bree and the kids safe, he would damn well learn how to do it fast.

He heard a soft bit of radio static crackle from a distance and knew it was the men signaling to one another. The good news was they were at a distance, nowhere near him or the hideout. The bad news was these guys were communicating via walkie-talkie.

And they were definitely around, and they were prepared.

Moving as silently as he could, Tanner made rounds farther and farther out from the hiding spot. He knew the men were out here, but he didn't want to stumble on one of them unaware.

What was the best plan? Try to lead them away? Would Bree run with the kids like he told her?

She would. If he didn't come back for one reason or another, he had to believe she would.

He shut his eyes again, focusing on the sounds around him. He heard the soft static again and moved silently in that direction. When he heard it again many minutes later he froze. That time it had been close. Way too close. He remained still. This might be his chance to take one of the men out.

He kept himself motionless to listen and figure out what direction he'd need to move, but this time it was voices that caught his attention.

"How many times are you going to let that damn thing give off noise?"

Tanner froze. That voice. He knew that voice. Where from?

"As many times as I have to until you all agree they might've moved on."

"They had two small children, no supplies, no food, no light. It made much more sense for them to stop once it got dark. So we keep searching around here, Paul."

Damn it, how did Tanner know that voice? He took a few steps to the side. If he was going to try to take both of them out, he would have to come from the best vantage point possible.

"Well, I've searched my quadrant twice, and there's nobody there," Paul hissed. "No sign of anyone. I think they moved on."

"If it wasn't for you and your damn cigarettes, we would've had them back near the trail."

Paul let out a curse. "I wanted to have a cigarette break. And how do you know they found them?"

"Well, they turned in a different direction and started covering up their tracks at that clearing where they obviously found your butts."

The voice clicked into place in Tanner's mind. It was Oscar Stobbart, Jared's lawyer.

"Shut the hell up, Oscar. You don't know for sure it was my cigarettes that tipped them off."

"And anyway," Paul continued. "That bitch isn't even

with them. We're not going to be able to bring her back to Jared if she isn't anywhere around."

"I'll admit, I didn't expect her to get in a different raft from her kids. She hasn't been five feet away from those brats for weeks," Oscar whispered. "If she hadn't separated from them, we could've taken them all at once. That tiny detonator was pretty effective."

Tanner took a couple steps closer so he could hear their low voices more clearly. He wasn't surprised at all to hear they'd sabotaged the raft.

"We work on the kids now and get them to Jared. It won't take much to get Marilyn to fall in line once they're gone."

"But what about the adults?" Paul said. "Jared doesn't want the kids hurt, but I've got the taste for a little hunting."

"The man is a cop," Oscar hissed. "It was one thing when we were just going to take out some woman. It's another thing to bring the entire police force of Colorado down on us."

"You worry too much. Always have. It's the wilderness. Accidents happen in the wilderness all the time. Even to cops."

"Right now, we stick to the plan. We can't get Marilyn, but we can get the kids."

"Fine," Paul said. "But if the cop or the woman poses a threat, I won't hesitate to do what needs to be done."

Tanner had to take them out now. Once they split up again the chances of him finding them both were slim. If he could eliminate these two, their odds of escaping the third were at least better.

Oscar and Paul both had weapons, but Tanner had the element of surprise. Even if he could take only one of them out, that would give Bree and the kids a better chance.

It was worth the risk.

He crouched, muscles flexing, about to spring, when he was tackled from the side and thrown into a tree.

"What was that?" Paul said.

Tanner couldn't say a word at all; fingers were pressed up against his windpipe, completely cutting off his ability to make any sound.

"Quiet, Hot Lips, it's me," Noah whispered into his ear.

Tanner stopped all struggle, and Noah immediately released his hold on Tanner's throat.

"We need to take them," Tanner whispered. "They're planning—"

Noah gave a sharp shake of his head. "Setup," he said in the lowest of voices.

Tanner kept completely still and silent. Noah knew something he obviously didn't. They waited there for what seemed like forever.

"It didn't work," said a third voice, one Tanner hadn't heard yet and had had no idea was around. "They must really not be anywhere around here. Otherwise the cop would've made a play. Trying to take you guys out would've been the smartest thing to do."

"It was worth a try. Let's split back up and make another round," Oscar said. "I still hold that they wouldn't have kept going with the kids. Too hard."

The other two men agreed and in a few moments there was silence once again as they faded back into the wilderness.

Tanner forced himself to count to five hundred before he even began to move, but once again Noah stopped him with a silent shake of the head and a hand on his shoulder.

Tanner was almost to a thousand this time before Noah finally moved.

"Being extra cautious?" Tanner whispered.

"There's a fourth, who was hanging behind just in case. I don't know where he was, but he was out there."

His brother was damn spooky sometimes.

"Are you sure there's nobody out there now?" Tanner whispered.

"Not near here. They're resuming their search."

"I'm pretty sure you just saved my life, so thanks."

Noah squeezed his shoulder. "Let's move. I've got to pick something up before we go to wherever you stashed Bree and the kids."

"Pick something up?" Tanner whispered. "Like a pizza?" Although, damn, pizza sounded good.

"Indefinitely more frustrating than pizza, trust me."

They made their way north, away from the hideout, but Tanner didn't question. Noah had a reason for whatever he was doing. Noah always had a reason.

"Did you track us?"

"Yeah. Damn near impossible to hide two kids and an inexperienced hiker, although you did a good job." His voice was so low Tanner could hardly hear him, and he was right next to him. "Tracking these guys was easier. I would've been here much sooner."

Tanner waited for him to finish the sentence but evidently it was complete in Noah's mind.

They walked for another five minutes, definitely not in a straight line. Then they came to an outcropping of rocks near a small drop off by a waterfall. Tanner had no idea what they were doing there, until a blur of white jumped out at them, stick in hand.

Tanner jumped out of the way, but Noah was obviously expecting it. He spun around, ducking from where the branch would've clobbered him in the head, and behind their attacker.

"Whoa there, tiger," he whispered, grabbing the attacker by the waist from behind and spinning her around.

"Noah?"

It was Marilyn. She lowered the stick, then looked between the two men.

"Tanner? Where are the kids?"

Tanner turned to his brother. "This is the *pizza*?"

"Like I said, more frustrating than a pizza. She followed me. We sent Francis and Barb home when we saw the bridge was out. Marilyn was supposed to go with them, but somebody is not great at following directions."

"I don't give a damn about your directions when my kids' lives are at stake," Marilyn spit out.

It was the most words, and definitely the most anger, Tanner had ever seen out of the quiet woman.

She turned to him. "Are they okay? We saw them fall out of the raft, but Noah assured me that the flares meant you guys were unharmed."

"We were. We are." He caught his brother's eyes in the dim light. "We survived the rafting accident with no problem. But we've got much bigger issues now."

The sound of the water covered most of their talking. "Your raft was sabotaged, wasn't it?" Noah asked.

"How did you know?"

"Found something similar on ours. Some sort of puncture mechanism on a timer. I don't know if it malfunctioned or if they only ever planned on taking down one raft."

Tanner muttered a curse.

"We would've gotten here a lot sooner," Noah continued, "but they took out not only the first bridge but the next two also."

"You must've been hauling ass the whole day to have gotten here by now."

Noah shrugged and turned to Marilyn. "It's Jared."

Even in the darkness Tanner could see the tension bolt through the woman. "He's here?"

"He's not here himself," Tanner said. "But I know for sure one of the men tracking us is Oscar Stobbart. The other guy's name was Paul. I'm assuming that's Paul Wyn."

Marilyn seemed to shrink inside herself. "I—I…"

Noah pulled her up against his chest. "Concentrate on what you know that might be able to help us right now. Leave the rest for another time. What do we need to know about these guys?"

She sucked in a couple of deep breaths. "They'll do anything for one another. I think Jared might've had something to do with Paul's wife's death, but I could never prove it."

Tanner barely refrained from rolling his eyes. "They're obviously used to working together."

"Where are the kids? Are they hurt? Scared? I just want to get to them."

"They're hidden with Bree. Sleeping. They're not hurt and have been absolute troupers today. They're hidden pretty well right now, but I don't want to leave them any longer than necessary. I was going to try to take out our hunters, but that was when I thought I was taking on two."

"We need a plan," Noah said.

Tanner nodded. "Let's get back to Bree. I know she's

worried sick. And then, yeah, a plan. Which probably involves us splitting up."

Noah gave him a nod. Neither of them liked the thought of splitting their defenses, but the most important thing right now was making sure to get those kids back safe. Out of Jared Ellis's clutches.

Chapter Fifteen

Every noise made by an animal, the break of a twig or even the leaves shifting in the wind sounded like desperate danger to Bree. She had long since placed herself in the mouth of their little overhang, determined to be a buffer between menace and these kids.

Whoever was hunting them might find them here, but they damn well weren't going to touch Eva and Sam without Bree getting a few good bashes in.

She refused to even think about Tanner not coming back, even when minute after minute marched closer to dawn and he still didn't return. Tanner was a hero; it was what he did by trade. But she didn't want him to be a hero tonight. She wanted him to come back and hide with her and find a way out of this by sneaking off in the dark, rather than facing the enemy head-on.

A silent tear ran down her cheek before she could stop it. Tanner's propensity for facing the enemy head-on was one of the reasons she'd fallen in love with him. But now she just wanted him back safe in her arms.

With every second she willed him closer until finally he was there right in front of her, crawling into the cave.

The branch shook in her hand and she swallowed a sob.

"I'm okay, freckles." His lips were on hers in a brief, hard kiss, then he scooted closer in next to her.

Two more people climbed in behind him. Bree couldn't believe it when she saw Marilyn and Noah.

Marilyn barely paid any attention to her, just crawled frantically past her to see the kids. The soft sobs coming from the woman were nothing less than heartbreaking. Quiet kissing noises filled the small space.

"Mommy?" Eva's sleepy voice said.

"Shh. I'm here. Go back to sleep."

"We played hide-and-seek. Soldier style."

"You can tell me all about it soon," Marilyn whispered.

In the darkness, Bree could barely make out Marilyn cuddling both kids to her.

"How did you find us?" Bree asked Noah.

"I had planned on tracking you, but Tanner did a pretty good job hiding those tracks. So I ended up tracking the guys hunting you. They weren't being nearly as careful."

"It's Jared Ellis's buddies," Tanner said. "I overheard them. They're after the kids."

"We need to get out of here, as soon as possible," Noah whispered. "Split up. They're not sure where you are right now, but they'll find you eventually."

"I'll lead them in the wrong direction. Give them just enough clues to have something to follow, then lose them when the storm hits," Tanner said. "You take Marilyn, Bree and the kids and get them to safety."

"You sure that's the best play?" Noah asked.

"I think it might be our only play. I can't justify leaving a trail of dead bodies when we don't know for sure what their purpose is and they haven't made any overt attempts on our life."

Tanner turned to Marilyn. "Their endgame is to bring you and the kids to Jared, right? Not to kill anyone?"

"He doesn't want to kill me. Even the last time when he put me in the hospital, I don't think he intended to kill me. And the kids have always been more of a means to an end to control me. Otherwise Jared mostly ignored them. But you guys… I don't know if they'll hurt you."

Noah turned to Tanner. "Why don't I lead the bad guys into the wilderness, and *you* take the merry gang back to town."

Tanner shook his head. "Because if they do come after you guys, I want you to use your skills and take them out. I'm handy with a gun, but I don't have the hand-to-hand combat skills you do. I'm not sure I'll be able to protect them the way you would. Better for me to be the decoy."

"I'm not letting you go alone," Bree interjected. "You're going to need more than one person if you're trying to fool them into thinking there're still four of us traveling through the wilderness."

"She's right, you know," Noah said. "They won't buy the ruse for long with you by yourself."

"I don't like it," Tanner finally said.

It was probably a good thing he couldn't see her roll her eyes in the dark. "You don't have to like it, you just have to do it."

Noah gave a low chuckle. "Consider it practice for marriage."

Silence from Tanner.

"I don't like it," he finally said again. "I don't know that I can protect you."

"I don't need you to protect me anymore. You've been

teaching me how to do that for myself since I've known you." She squeezed his hand. "We protect each other."

It was a testament to how far they'd come, how much Tanner now really looked at her as a partner in all areas of life—even the scary parts—that he finally muttered a soft agreement.

Noah slid toward the overhang entrance. "I'm going to go find a clear path for us. Try to get a bead on where they are searching now. I'll lead them farther out if I can. I'll be back in one hour. Be ready to move. That's when they're most likely to stop for a rest and we're going to use it to our advantage."

Without another word he was gone. Tanner looped his arm around Bree's shoulders and pulled her against him until his lips were at her temple. "You stubborn thing. I'm planning on all sorts of payback on our wedding night."

"It's a deal."

"Try to get a little rest before Noah comes back. We're going to have to move hard once he does."

She didn't think there was any way she would be able to sleep, but she scooted back toward Marilyn, who was hugging both her kids to her.

"Bree," Marilyn whispered. "I'm so sorry I brought this into your life."

"Don't even start with me. I'm thankful every day you are in my life. No one is to blame for Jared and his cronies except Jared and his cronies. So don't talk like that. Let's escape, get Jared thrown back in jail and get my wedding over with."

"You do know you just listed marrying the man you love as part of a series of traumatic events."

Bree wasn't facing Marilyn, and probably couldn't

have seen her face even if she was this far back in the shelter, but she could hear her friend's smile.

"Just the saying my vows part. Maybe running for my life will knock something loose and I'll be able to get them written."

She meant to say more, but the next thing Bree knew, Tanner was shaking her awake. Bree hadn't even realized she'd fallen asleep.

"It's time to go."

Noah was back. He was breathing heavy and drinking water from the canteen.

"I've got us a window open with them, led one of them in the opposite direction. We need to take advantage of it."

Marilyn woke up Sam and started talking softly to him. A moment later the little boy walked over to Noah.

Marilyn picked up the sleeping Eva in her arms. "We're ready. She'll wake up, but she'll keep quiet."

"That storm coming in is going to be worse than we thought," Noah told Tanner. "And it's going to hit soon."

"Good. We'll use it to our advantage."

"Go back toward the waterfall," Noah said. "It gives you multiple exit options. Once you're there, let out a scream or something to get them headed that way."

The two brothers hugged briefly, and Bree hugged Marilyn.

"Be careful," Tanner said. "They may not all come after us."

"We all better be back in time to be standing at that wedding, or Mom and Cassandra both are gonna kill us."

"Trust me, I know," Tanner muttered.

Less than a minute later they were all out of the shelter heading in different directions. Noah had Sam on his back and Marilyn was carrying Eva.

For them, stealth was more important than speed, at least right now.

Tanner grabbed Bree's hand, moving as quickly and silently as possible through the forest. He stopped every once in a while to listen, once completely changing directions, but it wasn't long before they made it to a small waterfall. They filled their canteen and caught their breath.

"This is it," Tanner said. "You ready to lead them in this direction? There's no turning back after this."

Was she ready? Was anybody ever actually *ready* to bring people with weapons hunting them in their direction?

She nodded. She knew the plan.

"Make it count. We want to make sure they hear."

Tanner kissed her, then stepped back.

Bree screamed.

Chapter Sixteen

Tanner never wanted to hear that sound from Bree again. She screamed his name like she was terrified out of her mind.

Which she may be, although she certainly hadn't shown any sign of breaking.

He kissed her again to stop the scream, then grabbed her hand. "Let's go."

They started pushing themselves almost unbearably hard. He could hear Bree's breaths behind him, sawing in and out, but she didn't complain, and he didn't stop. But after a couple of miles, they finally slowed.

These first few miles were critical. They had to get enough distance not to be caught, but not go so fast that the hunters figured out they were the decoys, not whom they really wanted.

But most important, they needed to provide Noah and Marilyn a chance to get back to safety.

They continued to move as the sun came up. They didn't speak, not knowing how far away the trackers might be. Tanner left very deliberate clues at first—ones they would have to be blind to miss.

They went deeper and deeper into the wilderness. If the men hunting them were as familiar with this area as he was, that would've been an instant clue that something was awry. It would be stupid to lead the children deeper into the wilderness with no supplies and a storm coming. At what point would that thought cross their minds? Would Noah have enough time to get Marilyn and the kids to safety?

Now that it was daylight, he and Bree had to move much more carefully, staying in the cover of the trees. If they went too much out in the open, they might be spotted with binoculars, or even worse, a rifle scope.

Like Marilyn had said, Jared wanted her and the kids alive, but anyone else might be considered expendable.

By midafternoon their energy was starting to fail. They ate some berries and drank water everywhere they could, but the calories they were getting into their bodies were nowhere near their output. That would begin to take a toll quickly.

Bree was amazing—not that he'd had much doubt she would be. She didn't complain, not even once. Not when he looked back and she was pale or sweating. She just kept pushing even when it got harder and harder.

The hunters were gaining on them. They had nourishment and equipment he and Bree didn't have.

Tanner wasn't exactly sure when they'd spotted him and Bree, but there was no doubt they had. The good news was they were still following, so that meant they must think the kids were still with them. The bad news was…everything else. No food or weapons, and moving farther from help with each step.

Noah would be back with the assistance they needed. Tanner just had to buy him more time.

A quiet cry fell from Bree's lips as she stumbled on the uneven ground and crashed hard onto her knees, barely catching herself before her face hit the ground. Tanner couldn't even move fast enough to stop her.

He let out a low curse. "We've got to stop. This is game over if one of us breaks a leg," he whispered.

"Where are they? They are still following us, right?"

"Yes, but it's harder for me to tell exactly where they are. The sun isn't shining so brightly, so I'm not catching any reflections off their scopes like I was yesterday. But then again, they're not exactly trying to hide, so I catch a glimpse of one of them every once in a while. Last time was over an hour ago."

He kept his voice low because over an hour ago was an eternity when you were talking about hunting someone in the forest. They could be much closer now.

"So we need to keep going." Exhaustion skirted across her face. She struggled to push herself back up into a standing position, but her movements were jerky and uncoordinated.

Damn it, she was more tired than she'd let on.

He sat down beside her and pulled her down next to him.

"I thought we needed to go? That they are gaining on us." But she didn't try to get back up.

He scooted down next to her and tucked them both up against the tree.

"No, rest for a while. At some point we need to turn back toward civilization."

She closed her eyes. "Have we given them enough time?"

The fact that she was asking that rather than demanding they continue to push forward told Tanner what he needed to know. Bree was getting awful darn close to her breaking point.

Mentally and emotionally she could keep pushing herself. She'd proved that over and over since he'd met her. But the body could go only as far as it could go.

"Quit looking at me like that," she said without opening her eyes.

"Looking at you like what? And how can you tell anything anyway if your eyes are closed?"

"I can tell just by the way you're breathing."

His eyebrow rose. "All right, smarty, exactly how am I looking at you, then?"

"Like you know I want to go on, but my body isn't going to make it."

Damned if that wasn't *exactly* what he was thinking.

"We can't keep going at this pace." He reached over and kissed her temple.

Now those green eyes opened. "But we can for another few hours. Give them the time they need to make sure they're out safely. My body will do whatever I tell it to. And if I tell it it's going hard for another few hours, that's what it's going to do."

Tanner sighed. "I'm sure that's true right up to the point where your body completely collapses. We don't want to let it get to that point."

But he knew they needed to get moving again.

And then it began to rain.

Storms in the Colorado wilderness weren't to be messed with at any time, and this one was a doozy. Rain was pelting them by the time he helped her to her feet a minute later.

"Hopefully this will work in our favor," he told her.

It would certainly make them less visible and might make the hunters stop altogether. They didn't know Tanner knew who they were. He may not have enough to arrest them—what he'd seen and heard had been minimal, and circumstantial—but he damn well wouldn't be taking his eyes off Jared Ellis or any of his posse for as long as needed. They would slip up, and Tanner would be there to take them down when they did.

But right now, they needed to survive this damn wilderness.

They began moving forward again at a slower pace this time, because no matter what Bree said, there was only so much her smaller body could handle.

They tried to keep out of the cold rain as much as possible, dashing from point to point under anything that would offer them shelter. But it still didn't take long before they were completely soaked.

The only good news was that the farther they went, the less Tanner saw any sign of the hunters.

As lightning lit up the late-afternoon sky, he prayed it was because they'd done the smart thing and chosen to wait out the storm. Of course, the storm was probably going to last another ten hours, but he doubted the men knew that. By the time they did, Noah would definitely have made it back to Risk Peak.

As the wind picked up and began whipping through the trees, Tanner knew they were going to have to find shelter themselves.

A quick look at Bree confirmed it. Her teeth were chattering, lips starting to turn a little blue, despite their exertion. He needed to get her someplace where they could stop, allow themselves time to dry off and raise their body temperatures. He knew just the place and would bet anything the hunters weren't aware of it.

They were almost back to the river. His original plan had been to cut back up the river, leading away from town. But not anymore. He and Bree had bought Noah and Marilyn and the kids plenty of time. If he knew his brother, he'd already gotten Marilyn and the kids to old man Henrikson's house. That old goat was the only person Tanner knew who disliked people more than Noah did. But he had a damn impressive collection of shotguns. And his place would be the first they'd come across on their way into town. Noah would be borrowing a couple of those shotguns his way back out here. The rest of the cavalry would be right behind him.

"Is the storm getting louder?" Bree asked as they stopped to catch their breath by a clump of trees. Right now, Tanner was playing a game of choose your enemy. Hanging out under the trees was a bad idea because of the storm, but they provided them cover from the hunters. Getting away from the trees would be better to avoid the lightning but might make them visible to the people with guns.

"No, that's the river. It's about twenty yards ahead of us, then about ten or fifteen feet straight down over the ledge."

"The same river you told me to run toward this morning with the kids if you didn't make it back?"

"Yep, although you would've hit it about three miles downstream and that's much closer to town."

Her mouth tightened at the thought of having extra miles to walk, he was sure, but she didn't say anything.

"Don't worry, we're not walking the whole way right now. It's time to get out of the storm."

Walking down by the riverbank would be easier but would put them in a weakened tactical position. If one of the hunters came up on the ridge, they'd have a clear shot at them even though the ridge wasn't very high here. They'd have to be doubly careful.

"Okay, let's—"

Tanner felt the burn in his upper arm at the same time the shot rang out. He and Bree were diving to the ground as a second shot exploded in the tree next to them. Those weren't rifle shots or Tanner would be dead right now. They were from a handgun. That explained why Tanner was still alive—rifles were a hell of a lot more accurate—but it also meant somebody was much closer than he'd expected.

And it also just changed all the rules of the game. Anything Tanner did now would be considered self-defense.

But that fact wouldn't help them if they were dead.

"Are you okay? Are you shot?" Bree began patting him all over his torso.

"Just a graze on my arm. I'm okay. But we've got to move right now."

"Okay."

He grabbed her hand with his, keeping his eye out for the shooter. "We're going to have to split up. Stay down and crawl toward the river. I think it's only one of them, or we'd already be in a lot more trouble."

Bree nodded and began crawling in the direction she needed to go.

Tanner doubled back toward where the gunfire had come from, ignoring the pain in his arm. He could move it, and it wasn't bleeding too much, so treating it would have to wait. Hopefully the rain had muffled the gunshot enough that it wouldn't bring the shooter's buddies into the area.

Tanner kept low and moved in a zigzagging motion, trying to make himself as hard a target to hit as possible.

But he was also moving blind, since he didn't know exactly where the shooter was.

Tanner let out a curse when another shot rang out. Near the water. Near Bree. The bastard had somehow circled back behind him.

He gave up all pretense of hiding or weaving and bolted toward where he'd sent Bree.

"Bree, stay down!" He yelled the words, hoping to redirect the danger back to himself. At least then it wouldn't be pointed at her.

He spotted the shooter at the very edge of the river-bank's cliff. The shooter was facing to the side, away from Tanner, gun pointed at something ahead of him on the ground. It didn't take a genius to figure out it was Bree in front of him, staying low the way Tanner had told her.

The guy was going to shoot her.

Tanner forced every ounce of energy into his legs and rushed as fast as he could toward the man with the gun, praying he'd reach the shooter in time.

Chapter Seventeen

A shot rang out over her head and Bree realized she was going to die.

It wasn't the first time she'd felt that way today. There'd been half a dozen times as they'd run like fiends through the wilderness that she was pretty sure she would either fall over and crack her spine, have a massive coronary from the exertion or step on some creature who decided it didn't like being stepped on and would make its displeasure known by poisoning her.

But this guy staring down the gun at her definitely left little doubt in her mind that she was, in fact, going to die.

"And here I thought I wasn't going to get to do anything interesting," the man said with a smirk.

At least that was what she thought he said, as it was nearly impossible to hear him over the storm and the river barreling below them. As he spoke, she got into a crouching position, trying to think of something to say, something she could barter with, but nothing came to her exhausted mind. She wiped the rain from her eyes and got a good look at the man for the first time.

"You. You're the paramedic from the night of the fire."

"Yep, and things could've gone much easier if you'd

just left those two brats with me. That's why we started the fire to begin with. To get them or Marilyn outside. But then that entire damn town showed up."

She leaped to the side while he was talking, knowing it wasn't going to be enough, that he'd still have an easy shot.

But the shot never came.

Instead, Bree watched, first relieved when Tanner crashed into the man, knocking them both to the side and the guy's gun out of his hand, then in horror as the momentum kept them moving forward and over the side of the ravine.

"Tanner!" Bree screamed, scrambling forward to get to him. But both men had already fallen into the water below by the time she got there. The ridge wasn't very high at this point, like Tanner had said—maybe fifteen feet. But how deep was the water? It was flowing pretty quickly, but she couldn't tell how deep it was. In the rain it was difficult to see either man.

When Tanner's head burst through the surface, Bree let out a sob of relief. He was alive. She looked along the ridge for a way to get down to him as he fought to make his way to the river's edge. Every stroke seemed like a struggle for him. Unlike when they'd capsized in the raft, Tanner didn't have on a life jacket. Waterlogged clothes and shoes were dragging him under.

She pushed herself to her feet. In the rain, she would've completely missed the guy's gun if she hadn't literally stepped on it. She knew only a little about handguns, based on what Tanner had taught her the last few months, but any weapon was better than nothing. She tried to keep an eye on him as she ran parallel to the river, looking for any way to get down.

Panic ate like acid through her gut when she finally

had to take her eyes off Tanner to find a way down from the ridge. How was she ever going to find him again? She finally found an overhang of rocks and slid and jumped down them as fast as she could, ignoring the burning cuts on her palms as her skin tore on the jagged edges.

"Hang on, baby. Hang on." She said the words over and over as she reached the riverbank and began sprinting back toward Tanner, cursing when she couldn't get enough speed out of her body.

Thunder crackled heavily overhead, lightning immediately flashing in the storm-darkened sky. Vaguely she wondered if the storm would kill them both, even if she could get to Tanner.

The longer she ran, the more panicked she became. Had she somehow missed him? Had he not been able to make it over to the edge? There wasn't any riverbank here, so she was forced to walk in the water. The air seemed to be sucked out of her lungs from the cold, and she was in only six inches of water. How could Tanner have survived completely immersed in the water?

She pressed forward, harder, drawing on energy from her innermost center. Tanner needed her. She had to get to him.

She rounded a small ledge and let out a sob of relief when she saw Tanner standing at the edge of the water. He was swaying almost drunkenly, his big body tilted at an odd angle, his shoulder held awkwardly.

He made some sort of jerky movement, shifting to the side clumsily, and Bree realized the paramedic guy was right behind him. They were fighting. Or...trying to fight. The awkward, stiff movements Tanner was making were definitely not the complex fighting maneuvers she knew he was capable of.

She winced as the paramedic got a solid hook into Tanner's jaw. Tanner stumbled to the side but didn't go down. His left arm still held awkwardly at an angle to his side, Tanner got his own punch in.

Bree kept moving toward them, not wanting to call out and distract Tanner. After another couple of minutes and a few more exhausted punches from both sides, it became evident Tanner was going to triumph.

She was almost to Tanner when his last brutal uppercut to the paramedic's chin sent the man flying back and into the water. He probably would've drowned, but Tanner grabbed him with his good hand and dragged him to the shore, leaving him.

The relief she felt at seeing him alive, and the other man unconscious, wiped the last strength she had, almost causing her to collapse in the water. She slowed to a walk, the fifteen yards she was from Tanner seeming like a mile. She yelled to him, but he couldn't hear her over the storm.

He was looking up at the ridge, and she realized he was looking for her. She called out to him, her voice sounding weak even to her own ears, and he turned. The relief she saw in his eyes, the way his posture relaxed to know that she was alive and unharmed filled her heart almost to bursting.

She stumbled toward him, her own movements jerky with cold and fatigue. She felt like she would never be warm again. She couldn't imagine what Tanner felt like with his body still submerged to midthigh.

Then the whole world seemed to turn black in front of her as the man behind Tanner got to his feet, a huge branch in his hand, held up like a club.

She opened her mouth to scream a warning to Tanner but knew he couldn't hear her. And it would come too late. She did the only thing she could—swung up the gun in her hand and pointed it in the man's direction.

But to Tanner it had to look like she was pointing it directly at him.

His face blanched, but then without her having to explain the plan, without her even knowing what the plan could be, he dropped like a rock into the water, giving her a clear shot of her target.

Tanner trusted her.

Bree didn't hesitate. She squeezed the trigger gently twice the way he'd taught her, aiming for the paramedic's chest—the largest mass.

Surprise lit his face as the force of the shots propelled him backward.

He took one more step forward before falling facedown into the water, the river carrying him away. Bree ignored him, moving as quickly as she could over to Tanner, who was struggling to regain his footing in the water.

She'd killed a man. She would have to deal with that later. Because unless she got them somewhere where they could dry off and warm up, there was going to be more than just one dead body.

She worked herself around to Tanner's less-injured side. Close up, she realized just how much worse his injuries were than she'd realized. His arm was definitely dislocated, but there was also a gash on his head and his face was chalk white.

She stuffed the gun into the waistband of her jeans as she wrapped her arm around Tanner's hips when he staggered. "We've got to get you somewhere you can get dry and warm."

He didn't argue. Couldn't even seem to find the strength to say anything, just nodded.

What was the best plan? Downstream toward the town? But what about the other hunters? They had to have heard all the gunfire and could show up any moment. How many bullets were left in the gun she had? She fought down her panic at not knowing what to do.

"Up—up bridge." His words were so jerky she almost couldn't understand them.

"You want us to go upriver? That's farther away from help."

"Shelter." He was already swaying on his feet. "Sh-shelter by bridge."

She moved directly in front of him, cupping his cheeks with her hands, looking deep into his eyes. It would've been romantic if they both weren't freezing, and he wasn't injured, and she hadn't killed somebody, and other people weren't still hunting them. Romantic.

"Tanner, I need to make sure you're lucid. If you send us upriver and there's nothing there…"

"Shelter. Trust."

She did trust him the same way he'd just trusted her rather than stop and ask why the heck she was pointing a gun at him. He would've been dead if he'd done that.

He knew these woods. He knew where they were. She would trust that the shelter was where he said it was.

They began walking up the riverbed, one slow step at a time. Within just a few minutes Tanner wasn't even trying to keep his weight off her. When he began wanting to rest, she knew they were in even bigger trouble. If Tanner sat down, there was no way she was going to be able to get him on his feet again. Tanner finally collapsed completely against her just about the time they rounded a corner and she saw the bridge.

"Tanner, there's the bridge. We're almost there."

"Leave me," he whispered.

Bree just rolled her eyes and kept walking forward. "Don't go all martyr on me now. If I was going to leave your heavy, muscled ass it would've been half a mile ago."

He didn't respond. And he stopped walking. That wasn't a good sign.

"Can't. You go."

Bree got in front of him again, grabbing him by his soaked shirt, careful not to hurt any of his many injuries. She was going to use his greatest weakness against him and didn't even care if that made her a bitch.

"You want me warm and safe inside that shelter, Hot Lips? Then you keep going. Because if you stop here, I stop here. That's it. End of story. Dig deep for me, baby."

His expression didn't change, but he started walking again.

She couldn't even see the crude door until they were right up on it. It was a small shelter that had been built into the highest section of the river's ravine walls. Unless you knew it was there, you'd never guess that was what it was.

She was carrying almost all of Tanner's weight the last dozen yards up the trail. He was almost unconscious on his feet.

And that damn storm never let up.

Leaning Tanner up against the side of the shelter, she pushed the heavy door open the only way she could, by throwing all her weight against it.

Nothing came flying, slithering or growling out. Anything else she didn't care. Grabbing Tanner on his good side before he fell face-first, she eased him inside the door. Then helped him as best she could down to the ground.

He was out cold.

"You made it, Lips." Not that she'd ever doubted he would. Not when it came to keeping her safe too.

She kept the door open to try to look around the shelter in the dark. There wasn't much. But what there was, was beautiful.

In one corner were five blankets wrapped and sealed in plastic. In the other corner, at least a dozen cans of food and a couple of can openers. She wouldn't be able to start a fire to cook whatever was in the cans, but she would gladly eat it cold at this point.

But first she had to get Tanner warm.

When she stumbled to the blankets and was assaulted by dizziness, she knew she was on the last of her own reserves. Tanner hadn't been the only one to draw on every remaining bit of strength.

She pulled the blankets over near him and began stripping off his clothes. He wasn't shivering—that was a bad sign. She dragged off every piece of clothing, then did the same for herself. Fingers nearly numb, she ripped open the packages containing the blankets. She immediately began wrapping them around Tanner, starting with his feet and head. She wasn't sure if what she was doing was technically right but figured anything had to be better than his cold, wet clothes. When she'd wrapped three blankets around him, she lay down beside him and wrapped the final two around them both.

And then she rubbed. She rubbed his chest and shoulders with her hands. She rubbed his legs with her feet. She rubbed her body all over his.

If he was awake, he would've teased her unmercifully about her gyrating, but at least it was creating warmth between them.

She rubbed until she wasn't able to find the energy to move anymore, then tucked his hands between their stomachs, and his feet between her calves.

She slept in fits and starts over the next few hours. At one point she got up and opened herself a can of what ended up being black beans, eating it with no hesitation whatsoever right out of the can using her fingers. But when she tried to wake Tanner up to get him to eat, he didn't even budge, not even when she wrapped his bullet graze with some gauze she found.

Shouldn't he be waking up? What if he had a concussion? Internal bleeding? She still had him wrapped in the blankets. It wasn't unbearably cold now that they were dry and out of the elements, but still his skin was cool to her touch. How many times this past winter had she called him her personal electric blanket, always rolling in toward him seeking out his warmth? But it wasn't there now.

Darkness had fallen, and there was nothing she could do right now anyway. If he still hadn't woken up by first light, she'd have no choice but to leave him and try to get help herself. She lay back down, pulling his body close to hers, resting her hand over his heart, assured somewhat by its strong, steady beat.

So many variables came into play, so many things that could still go wrong. Of course, she and Tanner had had all sorts of variables—good and bad—laid out in front of them before, and they'd always dealt with them one by one because...

Bree sat straight up, then lay back down.

She had her vows.

Just like that, they'd come to her. Right here, lying naked on the ground after eating a cold can of beans, she'd finally figured out her vows.

They'd been right in front of her all along.

She wrapped Tanner tighter in her arms.

Now she just needed to have the man with her in five days to say them to.

Chapter Eighteen

Tanner lay on the cold hard floor, consciousness coming back slowly. The first thing he became aware of was Bree pressed up against him, but that wasn't unusual. She was almost always the first thing he became aware of when he woke.

The second thing was that he wasn't cold. There'd been a time trudging up that riverbank where he was sure he would never be warm again.

He seemed to have all his fingers and his toes, so that was a good sign. Honestly, he was just surprised he was alive. He'd been sure he wouldn't make it. If it hadn't been for the fact that he knew Bree wasn't going to leave him, he'd be dead right now out in that water.

She sighed and moved against him, quickly proving the rest of his body was working just fine also, as her naked skin brushed against his.

She'd killed a man. In the midst of attempting to survive there had been no time to process that. He knew what it was like to take a life and wasn't going to allow her to feel any guilt over it. If she hadn't shot when she had, Tanner would be dead. She'd saved his life multiple times yesterday.

He pulled her closer until she was half lying on top of him, her favorite way to sleep. She let out a shuddery little breath and his heart clenched. He knew that sound. It was the sound she made when she had been crying. It didn't happen very often—for the longest time Bree had a difficult time accessing her feelings at all—and the sound gutted him now.

When he trailed his hand down her back, she shifted against him. "Tanner?"

"You went to an awful lot of trouble just to get me naked here with you, freckles."

She bolted upright. "You're awake!" She rubbed her face with the back of both hands. "I didn't mean to fall asleep. I'm not a very good watchman."

"You've got that gun right by your lap. I daresay if anyone came to that door you would've woken up. Your body needed rest."

He wanted to ask her why she'd been half crying in her sleep, but she was already starting to inspect his body for injuries.

"Your shoulder is definitely dislocated. If I had my computer, I could look up how to put it back into joint, but now it's so swollen you really need a medical professional."

He definitely already knew that from the fire shooting down his arm and chest every time he moved.

"I'll try to make some sort of sling out of your jacket. I don't know if that will really help, but it should at least take some of the weight off your shoulder," she continued. "I also think you have a concussion, but there's nothing I can do about that."

"Nothing is life-threatening—that's the most important thing, okay?" He trailed the fingers of his good hand up and down her arm. "Given the fact that I was shot at, fell over a ravine and was nearly clubbed to death, not to mention hypothermia... I feel pretty damn lucky."

She nodded. "You have to be hungry. There are some cans of food. Nothing particularly appetizing, especially since we've got no way to heat it up. But at least filling. I have no idea who keeps this place stocked, but the food isn't expired."

"Old man Henrikson. He lives just outside town, but comes through once a year and makes sure the three or four shelters in this area have some basic provisions."

"Henrikson? Who would've figured the most ornery man in town was a good Samaritan."

"When his grandson was a teenager, he got caught out in a freak June snowstorm. Broke his leg, couldn't get back home. He would've died if it hadn't been for a shelter that happened to be stocked by a hunter who'd been in a couple weeks before. Henrikson has come out every year for the past twenty years to make sure these shelters in the area are stocked."

She kissed his forehead. "Hopefully that lovely story will make your cold franks and beans taste better."

He ate the can she opened for him, careful to keep the Glock close to his side in case it was needed, while she laid their clothes out a little better to dry. Outside the rain continued to fall, although at least most of the thunder and lightning had stopped.

"How safe are we here?" she asked.

"This place is difficult enough to find in sunny weather. No one will stumble on it in this rain. It's possible they would know about it if they researched hiking and hunting up here, but otherwise I wouldn't count on anyone coming through that door."

Tanner remembered the maps he and Noah had seen Jared and his friends looking at the night they'd surveilled the town house. Could they have been looking at trails and shelters around here? It would've explained a lot: how they'd known where the rafts would be located, and the best place to puncture them. They could've studied the best places to try to ambush them.

He realized that Bree was sitting just out of reach, smoothing out the legs of his pants, then doing the same to hers. Her movements were jerky, almost frantic.

"Freckles, come here and sit by me."

"Why? Are you hurt? Why didn't old man Henrikson put some ibuprofen in the shelters, for goodness' sake?"

He smiled and held out his good hand. "Actually, I'm sure if you mention it to him, he will."

"Well, that's not exactly going to help you, is it?" Her voice was tight. Shaky.

"Bree." He patted the space beside him. "I'm okay. Come sit with me."

She did, although a little reluctantly. "We need to get back into town."

"We will. We've had rest, food. It will be much easier now. Let's just give the storm a few hours and see what happens."

If anything, that made her tenser.

He took her hand in his, twining their fingers together. "Why were you crying in your sleep, freckles? Not because of shooting that guy, right? His name is Paul Wyn. We have a file on him in the office and I recognized him when we were fighting. He's one of Jared Ellis's good friends."

Her eyes widened. "He was in Risk Peak the night of the fire. He'd been dressed as a paramedic and tried to get me to leave Sam and Eva with him while I got looked over in the ambulance."

Tanner let out a low curse. "Yeah, I think they knew

about this trip and have been planning a kidnapping the whole time. But you shouldn't feel guilty about shooting him. You know you had to do that, right? He would've killed me."

Tanner would give anything if he could take that weight off her. Carry it himself. Taking a life, even in self-defense, or defense of a loved one, was still weighty.

But evidently, not too much to Bree. "Oh, no, I know I had to shoot him. He definitely would've killed you with that club. Honestly, if I had had a clear shot while you were fighting, I might have taken it."

Tanner let out a short bark of laughter. God, he loved this woman. She was so damn practical.

"Well, as a law enforcement officer, I'm much happier that if you had to shoot Wyn, you did it when he was about to kill me, rather than when we were fighting. That's much more defensible in my report." He rubbed her hand. "If that wasn't it, then why the tears? You were crying in your sleep."

"It's nothing." She looked away.

"Freckles, you're the least prone person to hysterics that I know. So if you're crying in your sleep, it's a big deal. Is it everything we've been through in the last couple of days? That's understandable."

"No, I—I... Forget it. Don't worry about it. Let's just worry about you getting back home in one piece. I'm fine."

Now he was really worried. He hadn't even thought to ask her if she'd been injured in some way. Was she hurt and trying to play it off?

He swallowed a groan of pain as he shifted his weight so he could get a better look at her.

"Tanner, what are you do—"

"What aren't you telling me? Are you hurt?"

He didn't see any marks on her naked body, but a lot of her was covered in blankets. "Bree?" He caught her chin in his hand, forcing those green eyes to look at him. "We're a team, right? That means you tell me when you need help too. It goes both ways."

His heart sat heavy in his chest as big tears rolled down her cheeks.

"Fine," she finally murmured. "I was crying because I was relieved, okay?"

That definitely wasn't what he'd been expecting. "Relieved that we made it to shelter? That we are warm and dry?" That made sense, but why not just admit that?

"No, relieved that I finally came up with my wedding vows!"

She closed her eyes and bowed her head as if she'd just admitted to committing the most atrocious of crimes.

"You were crying over our wedding vows?"

"You do know we're getting married in four days, right? And we have to say vows." Her whole body seemed to deflate. "I've just been in a state of panic, thinking of standing up there in front of everyone… I'm already such a social spaz, and you're so important in Risk Peak. I wanted my vows to be perfect so I don't embarrass you in any way. It's just been stressful."

He trailed his fingers down her cheek. "More stressful than running through the wilderness with people trying to kill you?" Because she hadn't cried then.

She tilted her head, obviously seriously considering the stress levels of both. "Actually, about the same."

He wanted to yank her to him but couldn't force his left hand to work at all. Instead, he threaded the fingers of his right hand into the hair at the nape of her neck. He'd known the wedding planning had been stressful for her but had no idea she'd been feeling such pressure about the ceremony itself.

He leaned his forehead against hers. "If you got up there and couldn't say a single thing except 'I do,' I wouldn't care. All I care about is that you're willing to give me forever."

"I do. I do want forever. But everyone you've known your whole life is going to be there. All your people. I just don't want to mess it up."

He'd been selfish. He'd wanted a big wedding— talked her into it—and why?

Because he'd wanted to make his declaration of love for and commitment to her as public as possible. But he should've taken into consideration more what she really wanted. Bree could barely stand to be around a group of people at the best of times. And standing up in front of five hundred of them, many of them she barely knew… No wonder this had been so stressful for her.

He leaned forward and kissed her. "I never really thought about the wedding, the event itself, and how it would affect you emotionally. I've been joking all these months about taking you in front of the judge. Let's just do that. We don't need a big event. At the end of the day, our love, our marriage, is between you and me. Nobody else matters."

She smiled at him, the sight so beautiful and pure it nearly took his breath away. "Last week I might've taken you up on that. Hell, the night of the fire I almost got killed because I was in the office working on those stupid vows."

He smiled at her description. No one was ever going to accuse Bree of being overly sentimental. That was just fine with him.

"But they came to me while I was trying to sleep,"

she continued. "All this… And they just came to me. Honestly, that's why I was crying. I was just so relieved."

"Tell me them."

She reached up and kissed him softly. "I will. On Saturday. Four days."

He could wait. "Are you sure that's all that was upsetting you? You seemed flustered."

"I just want to get back so I can write all this down, so I don't forget them."

Tanner shook his head. "I've seen you memorize entire pages of coding after reading it just a couple of times. Your brain is like a computer."

"Exactly. I can remember coding, but words? Emotions? Not so easy."

He tucked her against his chest with his good arm, ignoring the pain as best he could in the other. "If you're worried you won't be able to remember the words, just write a program in your mind that includes them."

"What? I—" she paused. "Damn it, Dempsey, you're a genius."

She lay down next to him and he could almost hear her brain running like a machine. He had no idea what program she was writing, or what it would do, but knew whatever information she needed was now safely locked away in that brilliant mind of hers.

When she slept this time, there were no tears.

Chapter Nineteen

Two shots firing into the air woke Tanner immediately.
He and Bree had changed back into their clothes as soon
as they were dry in case they had to run again. They'd
slept side by side, but without her curled up next to him.
The slightest touch on his left arm sent spikes of agony
through his system. And he'd wanted to have his right
arm free in case he needed to get to the Glock quickly.

Five minutes later shots rang out again.

"Freckles, wake up."

"I don't want any more beans," she muttered, not
opening her eyes.

"We've got to get moving."

Now those green eyes popped open. "Did they find
us?"

"Not the hunters." He forced himself to stand, bent
over because of the low ceiling and, tucking the gun
inside the waistband of his pants, took a look outside.

No more rain.

Two more shots.

"Was that a gun?" She joined him at the door.

"Yes, a signal from Noah."

"Are you sure?"

"Yes. The double shot, just like how we used the
flare gun. He's signaling to let me know where he is."

"Won't that let the hunters know where he is too?"

Tanner nodded. "He wouldn't do it if he wasn't sure it was safe. I'm assuming he has backup. Normally I would use our gun to fire two shots in response, but I'd rather save those last two bullets in case we need them."

WHEN THEY FOUND Noah two hours later, he had more than enough backup. Sheriff Duggan, Whitaker and half the Grand County Police Department was with him. Not to mention two forest rangers and four citizens from Risk Peak who had exceptional experience in these woods, including old Mr. Henrikson.

And thankfully, a paramedic. Tanner's shoulder was the first line of business. There were things he still needed to do here before he could leave and go back into town.

Bree sat across from him, holding his good hand like they were about to arm wrestle, keeping his eyes pinned with hers as the paramedic rolled the swollen joint back into place.

Tanner's curse was low and ugly, but his eyes never left Bree's and she never flinched.

His shoulder immediately felt better, and he let go of her hand.

"I'm going to read up on how to do that," she said. "That's a good skill to have."

"And I hope one you'll never actually need to use."

Somebody offered him some ibuprofen and he took double the recommended dosage. His jacket would have to continue to second as a sling until he could see a regular doctor. But first there were things he needed to do here.

Noah looked almost as rough as Tanner felt when Tanner found him talking to Whitaker.

"Marilyn and the kids safe?"

"Yes. Ronnie Kitchens is keeping them in protective custody until we can prove who's behind this. I got her and the kids to Henrikson's house. Cass—I have to admit, I love our sister—had already sent somebody up there when Barb and Francis arrived and told her about the raft and the bridge being out."

"That was smart."

"At that point Cass still thought it was regular wilderness camping snafus but knew we'd head for Henrikson's house if we got in trouble. So she sent a phone with him, and once Marilyn was there, she sounded the alarm."

Tanner took a closer look at his brother. "You're looking a little bruised up. Run into a tree?"

Noah led Tanner off to the side where they could talk privately.

"I immediately came back out here to see if I could help you and Bree. Ran into a hunter who thought that his knife and my lack of one gave him an advantage. I'll be needing to take you to that body so you can do whatever cop paperwork is involved. I haven't mentioned it to anyone else because…"

Because Noah hadn't been sure how Tanner wanted to handle this. Because Noah still thought as a warrior; he'd never thought as a cop. And if Tanner just wanted these bodies to disappear, Noah would be willing to make that happen and never speak of it again.

"I'm going to have my own cop paperwork involved with the death of Paul Wyn, the guy Bree shot. Ends up he was in Risk Peak the night of the fire. So we'll report them both to Whitaker and process them officially."

"I didn't get a positive ID on my guy," Noah said.

"But I'm sure it was another one of Jared's posse. You know he's behind all this."

Tanner ran his good hand over his face. "Yeah, but proving it won't be as easy."

After convincing Bree to let someone take her back to town so she could reassure Marilyn and the kids that everything was all right, Noah and Sheriff Duggan headed toward one body and Tanner and Whitaker headed for Paul Wyn, finding him washed up downstream not far from where Bree had shot him.

Since he'd been involved with the situation, Tanner stayed to the side as Whitaker inspected the body, giving Whitaker the short version of everything that had happened.

"I sort of wish fewer of my murder cases involved you, Dempsey."

"At least you're not trying to arrest me for this one."

Whitaker looked up from where he was crouched over the body and gave him a smirk. "Not yet."

The man had been sure Tanner was involved in a series of murders a few months ago. But Tanner couldn't really blame him for that since someone had been going out of his way to frame Tanner.

Night was falling once again by the time both bodies were ready to be escorted back into town. Given the circumstances, and the number of witnesses involved, there wouldn't be any charges filed against Bree or Noah.

And given that the second body was George Pearson, also someone tied to Jared Ellis, Sheriff Duggan had ordered around-the-clock protection for Marilyn. Although Tanner suspected Noah would be providing that also.

Ronnie already had a report for Tanner and Sheriff Duggan when they stepped into the office. Jared's ankle monitor had not shown any unusual activity. Denver PD had already been to question Jared. Evidently he, Oscar Stobbart and Marius Nixon, the friend who had paid Jared's bail, had all been together for the past forty-eight hours, working on a business plan.

Willing to vouch for one another's whereabouts 100 percent.

The next day Tanner and Sheriff Duggan called in every favor they could and finally got a judge who was willing to have an emergency in-chambers session to hear the details that afternoon.

With one signature, Judge Osborne could require Jared to remain in jail until his trial, set for four months from now. Tanner was already sitting in the judge's chamber when Jared and Oscar Stobbart arrived.

And really wasn't surprised when he saw Oscar's hands had all sorts of cuts and abrasions on them, just like Tanner's.

Colorado wilderness can be a real bitch, can't it?

The judge entered and asked for Tanner to provide a summary of what had happened and what he was requesting. Tanner had already provided this to the judge in written form but forced himself to stay calm and focused as he reiterated the events.

What had happened in the wilderness. The two dead bodies lying in the morgue.

When Tanner was done, Judge Osborne asked Oscar for Jared's rebuttal.

Oscar's voice was solemn. "We are terribly sorry to hear about these awful events, Your Honor. But, respectfully, what does this have to do with my client?"

Ellis shot Tanner a smirk while the judge wasn't looking.

"Your Honor, both Paul Wyn and George Pearson are

known associates—*recent* known associates—of Mr. Ellis's. And, as I mentioned in my report, I overheard two men talking who mentioned Jared by name, and that he wanted possession of the children."

Tanner wanted to mention the fact that one of the men talking had been Oscar but knew that that would derail the situation in a heartbeat, since Tanner hadn't actually seen him and couldn't prove it. He had to pick his battles.

"Again, respectfully, Your Honor," Oscar said, "Captain Dempsey has been through quite an ordeal. Could it be possible that he misheard, or misunderstood the conversation? Nor, as I'm sure you realized, has Captain Dempsey identified the speakers. We're not even sure that the two men he overheard mentioning the children were George Pearson and Paul Wyn, since Captain Dempsey never actually saw them. Beyond that, my client can speak only to his own whereabouts and intents."

"The two dead men are not just passing acquaintances of Mr. Ellis." Tanner took out a folder that contained pictures of Jared with the two men he had taken last week with Noah. "Here they were together just last week. They've known one another for years—they were some of Jared Ellis's closest friends. These were the men hunting Marilyn Ellis and her children."

Oscar let out a disappointed scoff. "Surveillance, Your Honor? It seems as if Officer Dempsey has a personal vendetta against my client. This is borderline harassment and it's part of a pattern. I'm not sure if you're aware of this, but last week Officer Dempsey also brought in a civilian to study Mr. Ellis's ankle monitor."

"A civilian, but a renowned computer expert who has been utilized by law enforcement in the past," Tanner put in.

Oscar barely let him finish. "Officer Dempsey is determined to write Mr. Ellis's narrative the way he deems fit, not necessarily as the truth."

Tanner had been prepared for this.

"This is the only thing I'm interested in rewriting." Tanner slid another picture across the desk. "This is what Mrs. Ellis looked like during her last trip to the hospital. Jared Ellis gets his day in court for what he's been accused of. That's fine. But there was more than enough evidence to get a restraining order against him. The most important thing is keeping Marilyn Ellis and her children safe. And keeping Jared Ellis from doing something like this again."

"Allegedly, Judge." Oscar's voice was almost bored.

The judge turned to Tanner. "Did you see Jared in the woods? Do we have any reason to believe the ankle monitor is not working properly? You tell me that's the case and I'll sign the incarceration paperwork right now."

"Your Honor—" Oscar started until the judge held up his hand.

Tanner wanted to lie. More than any other time in his life he wanted to tell the judge there was reason to suspect Ellis could get out of the monitor. But he couldn't do it.

"Not specifically with Jared Ellis. But we can all admit that these monitors are not perfect."

"Actually, Your Honor, there has never been a reported case of this particular monitor being hacked or removed without intention. One hundred percent of the people who have attempted to remove this type of monitor had law enforcement at their location within minutes and were immediately apprehended."

The judge studied the reports on the technology

Oscar handed him. Tanner knew the information was impressive. Hell, even Bree hadn't been able to figure out a way to easily hack it.

"Based on this data, I'm not going to put Mr. Ellis back in jail to await trial."

"Thank you, Your Honor," Oscar and Jared both answered in unison. Jared had obviously been coached not to say anything during this meeting.

"But if there is so much as a hint of any of Mr. Ellis's other *known acquaintances* creeping around Mrs. Ellis or the children, then you can expect to be spending the rest of your time in holding. Got that, Mr. Ellis?"

Oscar immediately broke into protest. "Your Honor, I highly object to holding my client accountable for others' actions."

Judge Osborne very calmly turned the picture of Marilyn's battered body back around on his desk, pushing it to the edge.

"Save your objections for the court, Counselor. I have a feeling you're going to need it."

The judge turned to Tanner. "Captain Dempsey, I will request that the Denver marshals' office send officers over daily to make sure Mr. Ellis isn't having any difficulties with his monitor."

"Your Honor!" Oscar protested again.

"Your client is getting to stay out of jail. I'd be happy with that and concentrate on how you plan to convince a jury he deserves to stay that way."

Oscar grumbled under his breath, but it was Jared who spoke.

"That's fine, Your Honor. I just want to get this whole misunderstanding behind me. I look forward to my chance in court to show what really happened."

The judge nodded, lips pursed. "Yes, I'm sure you do."

Oscar and Ellis left, and Tanner thanked the judge for his time. On his way back out of town, Tanner stopped by the Denver marshals' office himself. These were the ones who would be first on the scene if anything so much as beeped concerning Jared.

They had already heard what had happened over the past two days and took his concerns seriously. Jared's whereabouts were a top priority for them.

They even took the time to double-check the monitoring system, bringing Tanner to the room where Bree had worked last week. While Tanner watched, they got the coordinates of Jared's location, then sent an officer out to make sure that was correct.

It was.

By the time Tanner left, he wasn't thrilled that Jared wasn't back behind bars, but at least he knew the people here cared what happened. It wouldn't be long before that bastard was behind bars for good.

Chapter Twenty

"It really is a beautiful dress, Bree. Tomorrow is going to be amazing."

Bree took a sip of her wine. She, Cassandra and Marilyn were sitting in her apartment, in three chairs across from the couch where her wedding dress was laid out carefully.

The rehearsal dinner had gone without a scratch. Yes, half the town had been there, but Bree had just been able to relax and enjoy it. After everything she and Tanner had been through, she didn't want her own wedding to stress her out. Like Cassandra had told her, if you did it right, you only got married once.

Looking over at Tanner tonight as he walked around the Sunrise Diner, where they'd decided to hold their rehearsal dinner, talking and joking with all their family and friends, Bree knew she was doing it right.

Tomorrow morning, she would become Mrs. Tanner Dempsey. Bree Dempsey.

When she'd first heard that unexpected knock on her door in her nearly empty apartment in Kansas City, she'd never dreamed it would lead her here. To this place. To this moment.

But how thankful she was that it had.

Everything; the danger, the pain, the fear… It was

all worth it because it had made them the Bree and Tanner they were now.

All those variables.

"What's that little smile?" Cassandra asked, taking another sip of wine.

It was after 10:00 p.m., the wedding was in the morning and her two best friends were here for a few more minutes. Tonight was her last night in this apartment. Bree doubted she would sleep very much, but that was okay.

"I'm ready," she said. "In every way that someone can be ready to marry someone else, I'm ready. It's time for Tanner and I to start our forever."

Cassandra let out a string of curses that would make a sailor blush, then burst into tears. "That's the most beautiful thing I've ever heard. And I love it even more that my brother feels the exact same way."

Marilyn smiled too. "It's going to be an amazing day." She turned back to the dress. "And that dress is just so…"

"Ornate?"

Marilyn chuckled. "It is ornate. It's beautiful, Bree. Of course, I got married in a denim skirt, so I'm probably a little bit partial to big, beautiful wedding dresses."

It still wasn't the dress Bree would've picked out if she'd gone with her heart. But there was no doubt the dress was beautiful, and it would be beautiful tomorrow when she wore it down the aisle.

She was about to say so when a distinct beeping noise began shrieking from her computer. It took her a moment to realize exactly what it was.

Jared Ellis's ankle monitor had just gone off.

She scrambled over to her laptop and began typing in information. Not ten seconds later everybody's phones began beeping—they were all receiving the alarm she'd set up as an app on their phones.

Bree's phone rang and she lifted it to her ear as she continued typing.

"Are you looking up the details on Jared?"

She loved that Tanner knew her well enough to cut straight to the chase, even the night before their wedding, not wasting time with greetings.

"Yes. It looks like he's still at his apartment. So if it went off, it was because he was trying to remove it from his body."

"I'm calling the Denver marshals. Noah is on his way to your place already. I'll make the call and be right behind him."

Bree disconnected the call and looked over at Marilyn. Every bit of color in the other woman's face had leached out.

Cassandra rushed over to her, grabbing her hands.

Bree brought the laptop over so Marilyn could see it. "Look, the monitor is still on, and still in his apartment. I won't say there's no cause to be alarmed, but let's get all the information before we panic."

Marilyn nodded. "I need to get to the kids. They're asleep at New Journeys."

Cassandra nodded. "I'm going to call Barb right now and have her put the building on lockdown, okay? There's absolutely no way Jared could get in that building. Hell, the kids will be safer than we are."

Marilyn nodded and Cassandra got on the phone.

When the alarm on her laptop screeched again, Bree opened the program to see what new data had come in.

Jared's monitor was now offline altogether.

Before Bree could even give anyone the bad news,

Noah walked through the door. He went straight over to Marilyn and pulled her against his chest.

"We've already got Ronnie standing guard over at New Journeys," he said. "The kids are safe."

"Jared's tracker just went offline," Bree told him.

"What does that mean, exactly?" Noah asked.

Bree looked at him and then at Marilyn. "Technically, it means we no longer know exactly where Jared is."

When Tanner walked in a few moments later, some of Bree's tension eased. He looked calm, not panicked the way she felt. He was on the phone with someone. Cassandra, always in wedding-planner mode, threw a blanket over Bree's wedding dress on the couch.

"I'll call Sowers myself if that's okay with you, Marshal, just to double check. I've got his number." Tanner nodded as he listened to whatever the marshal was saying. "Will do. Thanks for calling us first."

Tanner ended the call. "Adam Sowers, one of the marshals I met personally two days ago, is already on scene. Everything is okay. Sowers was nearby when Jared's alarm went off and he got the call. He immediately went to Jared's town house, arriving within two or three minutes of the alarm. Jared was still there."

"The monitor is offline now," Bree said.

"Yes, Sowers confirmed this. Evidently Jared developed some sort of rash under the monitor. He was trying to loosen it to keep it from chafing and knocked it offline."

"You met this guy Sowers, and he's on the up-and-up?" Noah said.

Bree was already sitting down at her computer. She wanted to know everything there was to know about this Adam Sowers. There wasn't time to go through legal channels, so she just wasn't going to mention what she was doing to her husband-to-be.

"Yeah," Tanner said. "He's young. Enthusiastic about the job and about making a difference. I'm going to call him myself right now."

Bree didn't pay attention to Tanner's call. Tanner was much better at telling if someone was lying than she would be. She was good at digging up facts.

By the time Tanner was off the phone with Sowers a few minutes later, Bree was feeling much better about him too. Sowers seemed to be exactly what Tanner had said. He'd been out of the police academy and part of the marshals' office for two and a half years. He was married with a six-month-old daughter. No indication of any sort of questionable finances, infidelity or bad habits.

"Sowers is a good cop. I believe him," Tanner said from across the room.

"I concur," Bree said, closing her laptop.

Tanner narrowed his eyes at her. "Don't even tell me what you were doing. Do not make me arrest you the night before we're getting married."

"Moi?" She gave him her most innocent shrug, and he just rolled his eyes. She was pretty sure he wouldn't arrest her, but not 100 percent.

But at least it broke the tension in the room.

"It's really safe?" Marilyn asked.

"Jared will either go into holding until the ankle monitor can be fixed or someone will keep him under surveillance." Tanner gave Marilyn a kind smile. "We'll be notified if anything changes."

She still looked pretty worried, and after what she'd been through, Bree couldn't blame her.

Bree came over and rubbed Marilyn's shoulder. "This actually reassures me that the monitor is working the way it's intended. I don't doubt that Jared was probably trying to test it out and see if the cops came running to his door if he tried to remove it. Now he knows it works and they will."

Tanner slipped an arm around Bree's waist. "And we might be able to use this with Judge Osborne to get Jared moved back into jail until the trial. The judge isn't going to put up with this nonsense."

"I know I was supposed to hang over here with you tonight," Marilyn said. "But I just need to go check on the kids."

Bree pulled Marilyn in for a hug. "I'm fine. Go be with your kids. I totally understand. I'll just see you bright and early in the morning."

A midmorning wedding had seemed like such a romantic idea at the time Bree had let Cassandra and Cheryl talk her into it. And Bree had to admit that watching the sun make its way past her beloved Rockies was definitely her favorite time of day.

"Okay, I'll see you tomorrow. Get some sleep." Marilyn pointed at Tanner. "And you get out of here. You're not allowed to stay with her, because we all know what's going to happen if you do."

Tanner smiled. "Yes, ma'am."

Cassandra grabbed her jacket. "I'm going to head home to my family too. Wrap that dress back up as soon as we leave and hang it on your bedroom door. No point in inviting disaster. I cannot even think of red wine coming anywhere near it."

"Fine. I'll keep it safe, I promise." Marilyn hugged her again and Noah escorted her out the door, Cassandra right behind them.

Tanner walked to the door himself, then turned back.

"I don't suppose I could talk you into letting me see that dress," he said with a smile.

"Nope. Cassandra and Marilyn would both kill me. They think it's the most beautiful thing since sliced bread."

Tanner laughed but then the smile fell from his face. "But you don't?"

This was going to be the problem with being married to such a good cop. She wasn't going to be able to hide stuff from him. "You know me, not big on dressing up in girlie stuff."

"How about you wear that dress for me tomorrow morning at our wedding and I'll make it worth your while tomorrow night."

He held open his arms, ignoring his stiff shoulder, and she walked into them. "It's a deal." One she definitely didn't mind making. "And the dress is beautiful. It's gorgeous, even."

"You are what will make it gorgeous. It wouldn't matter what you wear."

He kissed her. Soft, sweet, light. The same sort of kiss he'd started with her all those months ago.

"That's our last kiss when we're not husband and wife," she whispered when they finally broke apart.

He leaned his forehead against hers. "I promise, the kisses just get better from here. But now I better get going or not only will that not be our last kiss—I might really decide I want one more last something else before we get married."

She gave him a scandalized grin. "What would Marilyn say?"

He smiled too and cupped her cheeks. "I'll see you tomorrow."

"I'll be the one in white."

"I can't wait. Lock the door behind me." He kissed her on the forehead and walked out the door.

Bree locked it, then turned and walked over to the couch and pulled the blanket off her dress. It really was beautiful. Not *her* maybe, but beautiful. It would make Tanner proud of how she looked when he saw her in it. And that was close enough to perfect for her.

She walked into the small bedroom to get the plastic garment bag.

A knock on the door had her turning away. Maybe it was Marilyn having decided to come back. Good. She could help Bree get the dress into the garment bag. Or maybe it was Tanner wanting more kisses—that was even better.

But when she opened the door it was neither. Jared Ellis stood on her doorstep.

After a moment of shock, she tried to slam the door in his face, but he was too quick. His backhand caught her across the cheek, and she stumbled backward. He quickly took the opportunity to enter her apartment, closing the door behind him.

"You're going to help me get my wife back."

Bree spun around, running for her phone. Tanner couldn't be but half a block away. One message and he'd be back here in under a minute.

But then Jared pulled out a gun.

"If you grab that phone, I'm going to have to shoot you. That's going to be inconvenient for me and painful for you."

She was tempted to go for the phone anyway. Given what she knew about Jared, being shot may be more of a mercy than some of the other things he was capable of.

He grabbed her and threw her onto the couch—onto

her beautiful wedding dress—before she could make a decision.

"How did you fool the monitoring system?" she asked, keeping her eyes on the gun still trained at her.

Bree wasn't conceited, but she found it nearly impossible to think that this guy had found a way around the system that she had missed.

"It's all about weaknesses," Jared said. "Pressure points in the system. I'm very good at finding pressure points."

"The system didn't have any pressure points. I searched it myself."

He gave a shrug and cocky half grin. "The computer system wasn't the weakness. It only needed to be circumvented."

He pulled up the leg of his khaki pants to show the monitor was gone.

"So that alarm I got was correct. You had taken it off. You must have bribed Sowers. He lied about you still being in Denver."

Jared shrugged. "*Bribe* is not really the correct word. Like I said, I'm very good at finding pressure points. Sowers's is his wife and newborn daughter. Once I applied a little pressure to that point, he was willing to do whatever I wanted, including say he was still with me if anybody called."

His eyes were so cold. So dead. This man was a sociopath.

He pointed the gun a little closer at her. "I'm going to need you to call my Marilyn."

There was no way in hell.

"She won't answer. Thanks to your little stunt, when we got the alarm that there was something wrong with your ankle monitor, she went into hiding with the kids."

His eyes narrowed. "But surely she'll come if her dear friend needs her the night before the wedding. Maybe tell her you got cold feet, you need her to help you figure out what you should do."

"You don't think she's going to be a little suspicious of that? An hour ago I couldn't wait to get married, then all of a sudden I'm calling saying I'm about to skip town? Oh, and it just happens to be when there was indication that you were messing with your ankle monitor. Hmm, I wonder if she'll be suspicious about that at all. I wonder if maybe she'll go to the police. I wonder if maybe you've underestimated Marilyn for way too many years and she's never going to put herself in a position where you have control over her again."

Bree spit the words out and finally got some real emotion in his eyes. *Anger.*

"I'm not afraid of you," she lied with a steady voice.

But she was. He had a gun. And she might know some self-defense moves, but most of them weren't going to do much good against someone determined to shoot her.

Jared shook his head. "Marilyn used to be a lot more like you when I first met her. Feisty. Wanted to fight back. But eventually I taught her to heel. She's very well trained now. Which is why I am, in fact, going to need you to call her and get her to come over."

Bree stood. No matter what he threatened, Bree wasn't going to allow Marilyn to put herself back in this man's clutches. "Even if she would come, which I don't think she's stupid enough to do, I won't do it. I won't call her. You'll have to shoot me."

For a second she thought he was actually going to do it, but a knock on the door stopped him.

"Bree, it's me. I couldn't leave you on the night before your wedding."

Bree's eyes met Jared's cold ones.

It was Marilyn.

Chapter Twenty-One

Tanner walked into Micky's, one of the two bars in Risk Peak. He'd had his first legal drink here when he turned twenty-one. It was only right that he'd have his last drink as a single man here also.

Noah would be buying him both.

"Marilyn and the kids okay?" he asked Noah as his brother joined him at the booth. "Can't blame Marilyn for being nervous after everything that's happened in the last week."

"Yep. Kids were sound asleep."

Tanner took a sip of his beer. "The way Marilyn looked when that alarm went off about Jared's monitor… I wouldn't have been surprised if she'd taken the kids and fled the country."

"I'm trying to give her whatever she needs to work through this at her own pace." Noah spun his beer around between his fingers. "But believe me, it's only out of respect for you that this situation hasn't already been completely handled."

"Let the justice system work its process." But Tanner grimaced even as he said it.

"What was that look for?"

"In some ways I would totally approve of you handling it yourself. I got the case files. I know Marilyn told us some about what Ellis did to her, but it's bad, Noah."

Noah stared down into his beer. "She's told me a little. Sick stuff. The physical abuse was what got him arrested, but the other stuff he did to her…" He trailed off. "And I don't even think she's told me all of it."

"Then I'm sure most of it isn't in the police report either. But hell, what is in the report is bad enough. Jared should be looking at eight to ten years."

Noah shook his head. "Not long enough, if you ask me."

"It's too bad we can't pin the stuff in the wilderness on him. Whitaker is still looking into that. He's gotten warrants to go through Paul Wyn and George Pearson's phone records and texts. If he can tie it to Jared, you know he will."

"Good. Accessory to attempted murder is going to hold a much longer sentence, I'm assuming."

"Yeah, and that would be much better because I really don't like how Oscar Stobbart seems so confident about the case. That Jared won't see jail time."

"That's his job, right? Hell, someone who's as good at this sleazy lawyer stuff as he is knows that the appearance of confidence can get them a long way."

"I thought that too. But it's almost like they have a plan. They aren't worried at all. And that worries me. I know confidence is his business, but I have no idea how Oscar can look at this evidence and be so sure Jared's not going to jail."

"Maybe they plan on paying off jurors or something. I know most of Jared's accounts are frozen, but you know he has to have stuff stashed away somewhere."

"Yeah, I'm sure he'd be great at finding the weakest link in jurors." Tanner took a sip of beer, another thought coming to his head. "Or maybe they don't plan on going to trial at all."

"You mean making a run for it?" Noah's eyes lit up, and Tanner knew he relished the chance to go after Ellis if he ran.

Tanner shook his head. "He would have to go before the trial, but the ankle monitor is unhackable. Bree would've found it. You saw how quickly her program worked to let us know Jared had even messed with it tonight. There are no weak links in the computer system."

Damn it. Of course not. Jared knew that.

Jared wouldn't be looking in the computer system for weakness. He'd be looking for weakness in *people*.

At the end of the day, Jared Ellis was a *bully*. He wouldn't try to buy people off when attempting to get them to do what he wanted them to do. He would use what he knew worked best. *Force.*

Tanner pulled out his phone and hit Send on the last call he'd made.

Noah had already noticed Tanner's tension and was pushing his drink to the side. "Who are you calling?"

"A hunch. It may not lead anywhere."

Noah just nodded.

The call went straight to voice mail. Tanner tried it again, but the same thing happened. Sowers wasn't answering.

"Adam Sowers, the guy who was checking on Jared, isn't answering."

"You think that means a problem?"

"I just don't like it," Tanner said. He tried one more time for good measure, but still nothing.

His next call was to Marshal Brickman to see if Sowers had checked in.

"Dempsey. I don't have any new information for you.

I assure you, as soon as I have info, you'll be the first to know."

"Marshal, has Sowers checked in? I just tried to reach him on his phone and there was no answer multiple times. I was wondering if you'd heard from him."

"I personally haven't. Hold while I get in touch with the appropriate person."

Tanner pushed his beer to the side as he waited for the marshal to come back. He'd definitely lost his taste for it.

"Nobody has heard from him. I'm sending someone over to Ellis's house right now."

But if Jared was doing what Tanner was afraid he might be doing, sending more officers to the town house wasn't necessarily going to help.

"Instead of sending someone to Ellis's place, will you send someone over to check on Sowers's wife and baby?"

There was silence from Marshal Brickman for a long moment. "What exactly do you think is happening?"

"I'm just wondering if maybe Jared Ellis didn't find a weakness none of us were considering."

"Adam Sowers is a good man. A good cop."

"Everybody has their weakness. We all know that's true."

Marshal Brickman muttered a curse. "Fine. I'll keep you posted if we find anything of interest."

Noah was already paying for the beers by the time Tanner disconnected the call.

"This all may be nothing," he told his brother. "I could be grasping at things that aren't there."

"Until we know that for sure, I think we need to head back to New Journeys. No harm in checking on Marilyn and the kids and standing guard there until we have multiple eyewitness accounts that Ellis is, in fact, still in Denver."

"I don't want to get Marilyn nervous if there's no reason to."

Noah shook his head. "Believe me, I don't want to either."

They rode together in Tanner's SUV to New Journeys. Both of them were checking the darkness for anything unfamiliar, person or otherwise, as they walked to the door. Tanner rang the bell, keeping his face clearly in range of the security camera so whoever was checking it would know it was him. Within just a few seconds the door was opening.

"Hi, Tanner," Francis said. "Bree isn't here."

He smiled. "I know. Actually, we're looking for Marilyn and the kids."

"She's not here either."

Noah's head shot around. "What? I just brought her back over here myself not even an hour ago."

The woman shrank back a little at Noah's tone. Tanner provided his most reassuring smile. "How about the kids? Are they here?"

Had they misread Marilyn? Had she decided to make a run for it since it looked like Jared might have made progress in attempting to escape his monitor?

"Yes, they're both in bed asleep. Marilyn went back out to see Bree. Said something about how she wasn't a marmot and that a good bottle of wine was a terrible thing to waste."

"That's good." Tanner smiled again, and the woman relaxed just a little bit. "It's good for Bree to have someone hanging out with her the night before her wedding."

Francis nodded. "That's what Marilyn and I thought too. Is everything okay?"

Tanner nodded. Noah had already gone back to staring out at any possible shadows in the darkness. "Yes, everything's fine. Just do me a favor. Call it prewedding jitters or whatever, but just don't open the door to anyone you don't know personally, okay?"

Francis smiled. "Trust me, I never do. But I'll make sure."

"I'll see you at the wedding tomorrow."

The door closed and locked behind him as Tanner turned and walked back toward his SUV with Noah.

"Maybe I'm looking for trouble that's not there. Maybe—"

The phone rang in his hand. "That's probably Marshal Brickman now. Telling me that Sowers requests that I stop being such an overprotective jackass and let him do his job."

Tanner pressed the receive button. "Marshal. I'm sure I probably owe you an apol—"

Brickman cut him off. "Dempsey, you were right. Ellis had someone holding Sowers's wife and baby hostage. Ellis is gone."

Brickman kept talking, but Noah and Tanner were already sprinting for his car. Jared was out and no doubt wanted to get his hands on Marilyn. And Marilyn might have led him straight to Bree.

Chapter Twenty-Two

Bree opened her mouth to scream and warn Marilyn, but Jared was expecting that. She ducked as his fist flew at her face, missing most of the blow, but it still caught her and spun her around back onto the couch. A drop of blood dripped from her nose.

Right onto her wedding dress.

That bastard had just stained her wedding dress. Who cared if she didn't like it—it was still *her* damn wedding dress.

"You keep the hell quiet." Jared stormed over to the door and yanked it open. Before Marilyn could do so much as give a terrified little shriek, he yanked her inside and shut the door behind her.

Bree's heart broke at the abject terror that carved itself into Marilyn's features at the realization that she was once again in this madman's power.

"Well, I guess this solves the whole problem on how to get you over here," Jared sneered. "Hello, wife."

Marilyn darted for the door, but Jared just snagged an arm around her waist, then flung her against the wall like she was a rag doll. "So predictable. You're always so predictable and stupid, Marilyn. It's why you'll always belong to me. You should be happy I even want to keep you."

Marilyn seemed to almost collapse in on herself, wrapping her arms around the side of her head in a protective gesture. Bree didn't know if it was physical or emotional protection or maybe both.

Bree stood up. She wasn't going to sit and watch him batter her friend.

"You made me get a drop of blood on my wedding gown," she announced with a calm she didn't feel. "Do you know how hard it is to get blood out?"

She had no idea what she was saying. She was just trying to buy time. But buy time for what to happen? Tanner had no idea Jared was in Risk Peak, and Marilyn obviously wasn't going to be in any shape to provide assistance against her ex.

Jared tilted his head to the side and directed the gun straight at her. "I think a spot of blood on your precious gown is the least of your problems. You're not really needed anymore."

"Jared—" Marilyn pushed herself off the wall.

He turned and pointed a finger at her. "You shut up. It's your fault that we're in this situation to begin with. Deciding to air all our dirty laundry with the cops. Every couple has an argument here and there. You didn't need to bring the cops into it."

"Leave her alone and I'll go with you." Marilyn's voice was soft, but not shaky.

"Marilyn." There was no way Bree was letting her leave with him willingly. "No."

Marilyn just ignored her, keeping her eyes trained on Jared.

"You leave Bree alone and you don't try to have any contact with the kids. That's the deal." Marilyn took another step toward Jared. "You want me to go with you, that's what you have to do."

Jared's cold eyes narrowed as he stared at Marilyn. He obviously wasn't used to her putting up any sort of argument.

"What's to stop me from killing her right now and dragging you anywhere I want to go?"

"Because if you're going to start killing, I'm going to start screaming my head off. I may not be able to stop you from killing her, but I will damn well make sure you go down also."

Marilyn took another step. Now Bree studied her friend more closely. Marilyn wasn't acting like Marilyn at all, and the truth became clear to Bree.

Marilyn wasn't going to wait for someone to rescue her. *She was going to rescue herself.*

Jared gritted his teeth. "Look at you. You get away from me for a few months and all of a sudden you're full of sass. Don't worry, I have lots of ideas of how to modify that behavior."

Marilyn flinched but didn't back down.

Jared took a step toward Marilyn and quick as a flash swung his fist with the gun toward the tiny woman's face. God, he was so quick.

Marilyn was quicker.

Tanner had been teaching Bree some self-defense moves, but it was nothing compared to what Noah had obviously taught Marilyn. She ducked under the punch aimed for her jaw. Jared obviously never expected any sort of countermove and had put all his weight behind the hit. It would've broken Marilyn's jaw, without a doubt, if it had connected.

Marilyn brought her knee up to his groin at the same time she reached up with both hands and clawed at his eyes. Jared let out a roar before stumbling back, tripping over Bree's coffee table. She jumped out of the way as he fell back on top of her couch.

Bree couldn't care less about her wedding dress under the man. He'd just dropped his gun.

Marilyn reached down and grabbed it, pointing it directly at Jared.

"You bitch!" Jared was clutching at his bleeding face. "You stabbed me with those claws of yours."

"Congratulations, jerk," Bree said. "You just graduated from assault and battery charges to attempted murder. You're going away for a long, long time."

Bree glanced over at Marilyn. The woman was pale, but steady.

Jared's face turned purple with rage. He reached into his pocket and pulled out a switchblade, flicking it open with his wrist.

"I don't think you're really going to shoot me, Marilyn." He stood up. "I think if you had really wanted to get away from me, you could've done that. Couldn't you have? I mean, how hard would it have been to leave for good? You stayed in the same state I was in. That's how I knew you didn't really want to get away from me. That you remembered how I rescued you when you needed it."

Marilyn's hand with the gun began to shake.

"Don't listen to him," Bree said. "You made the best decisions you could in the situation you were in. It doesn't matter what happened then. It only matters what happens now."

Jared took a step toward Marilyn. Bree wanted to grab her phone and call Tanner but knew there was no way he could get here in time, and she might distract Marilyn.

"If you take one more step, I'll shoot you," Marilyn said. But her voice was shaky. So very shaky.

"Come on now, sweetheart." Jared took another step toward her. "We both know you used up all your bravery on that little self-defense move you pulled a minute ago. How about if our deal still stands? You leave with me now, and nobody gets hurt."

Marilyn widened her stance and shook her head, her arm with the gun becoming steadier. "How about if Bree calls the police and you are out of my life for good? You'll never have me again, Jared. That teenage girl you rescued from the trailer park? I'm not that same person. I know my value. And I'm way too valuable for someone like you."

With a yell, Jared launched himself across the table, arm raised with the knife.

Marilyn didn't hesitate. She fired a double shot to the chest.

Shock blanketed Jared's features before he stumbled back and collapsed onto the couch.

Not a half second later both her front and back doors burst open, Tanner coming through the front, Noah the rear.

Bree just stared at him, the echo from the gunfire so close it caught her off guard. Processing seemed impossible.

Almost from a daze she saw Tanner checking for a pulse from Jared on her couch.

"He's dead."

It was Noah who came up to Marilyn and helped take the gun from her shaking hand.

Marilyn was staring at Noah with huge eyes. "You told me to attack at the beginning. That when he first saw me was my best chance for escape, but I froze. I froze."

Noah pulled her against his chest. "You didn't get him at the start, but you got him at the end. And when it's all said and done, that's all that matters."

Bree was still staring at Jared's body. Oh, God. He was on her wedding gown. Bleeding all over her wedding gown. She couldn't even think about that now.

Tanner was on his phone and soon all sorts of people were filing into her apartment. Ronnie, a paramedic, other people she didn't know.

Bree just stood there, almost numb.

Finally, it was Tanner's face right in front of hers that zapped her back into reality. "Freckles? You okay? Two dead bodies in one week is a lot for anybody to handle."

"I'm not sad he's dead. After what he did to Marilyn? This is the only way we'd know for sure he'll never hurt her again. He found a way around the ankle monitor. Something I missed."

Tanner shook his head. "He had Oscar Stobbart and Marius Nixon holding Adam Sowers, his wife and his baby hostage. That's how he got out of the ankle monitor—not something you *missed*, something you never even considered, because you're not a psycho like Jared. So Oscar will be going to jail for a long time too."

"Good."

She felt his fingers trail down her cheek. "Maybe we should get you checked out. You're looking a little pale. And you haven't taken your eyes off Jared since I got here. He can't hurt anyone anymore."

"I know. It's just that…he just bled out all over my wedding gown."

Chapter Twenty-Three

"They're supposed to leave tomorrow late afternoon for their honeymoon. It would be nice for them to be married before that happened."

"Not to mention there's no way we're going to get the church again any Saturday soon. It was hard enough to get it this weekend when we booked it six months ago."

"Plus, Bree's cousin Melissa and those sweet babies will be here only for this weekend."

Bree sat in a booth at the Sunrise Diner listening to the women talk around her, not even sure who was saying what. It was after midnight, her wedding dress was currently part of a crime scene and even if it was released, there was no way she was getting married in that thing.

Marilyn was sitting across from her in the booth, sipping coffee. They'd both already given their statements to the police. The fact that Jared had been coming at her with a knife when she'd shot meant there'd be no criminal charges brought up against Marilyn. The woman had a lot she needed to process, but so far, she was holding up like a champ.

Marilyn had been sitting across from Bree for the past thirty minutes as more and more of the women from Risk Peak heard about what had happened and filled the diner around them.

"What's your plan?" Marilyn finally asked softly as the talking continued. "You know we can make the wedding work later if you want to wait. Don't worry about that."

But Bree didn't want to wait. She was ready. Ready for her always to start. Ready to say the vows that had become so clear to her.

Damn it. *Ready to have sex with Tanner.*

But she didn't want to do it without Marilyn up there with her. If she wanted to wait, Bree could wait too.

"What about you? I want you standing beside me when I do this. You've kept me sane over the past few months with all the wedding planning. If you're not up to it, then we'll reschedule."

Marilyn shook her head. "I refuse to give that man even one more hour of my life. Please get married tomorrow, Bree Cheese. Give us even more reason to celebrate *life.*"

Around them someone was talking about whether they needed to wake up the church secretary right now and see if there were any other possible weekends available.

"No." Bree stood. Enough. "The wedding is still on for tomorrow. As long as Tanner can be there, I'll still be walking down the aisle in the morning."

"Tanner will be there," Cassandra called out. "I already asked—since I'm the bossy little sister and allowed to ask questions like that. He says there's nothing about this situation that will keep him from the church if that's what you want."

But there would be no time to get another dress.

"I'll just wear a sundress or something," she said.

That was okay. The important thing was that she would get to marry Tanner tomorrow. She tried not to cringe at the thought of him in his tuxedo and her walking down the aisle in a sundress. But she didn't own anything fancier, and there was no way to get to a wedding dress shop before the ceremony in the morning.

"Oh, no you won't." Cheryl came and put her arm around Bree. How many times had she done that over the last year since Bree arrived in town? This woman had become a surrogate mother to her. Someone Bree treasured. "Leah and I have already been talking about that."

"You have?" Bree hadn't even realized Tanner's mother was here.

"We have a plan. We're going to make you a dress using sections of all of our own wedding dresses."

"But… I don't understand. Using pieces of your own dresses? Won't that ruin them?"

Cheryl pulled Bree in for a hug. "You're the only bride I know who's concerned about *our* wedding dresses, not about what *hers* might look like when it's all done."

Bree shrugged with one shoulder. "I can't envision it, to be honest. And is this even possible? How will you do it?"

"It won't be as ornate and detailed as your dress. There's no way we could make something like that probably *ever*, let alone in one night."

"Oh, well, that's okay. Nobody could actually make a dress like that one. I would never expect it."

"And would never want it either," Cheryl said with a smile. "Dan told me that as soon as he saw it. He admitted it was beautiful but said it wasn't a *Bree* kind of beautiful. I just wrote him off, convinced he was a man who didn't know anything about wedding dresses."

Bree couldn't stand that she might be hurting Cheryl's feelings after all the woman had done for her. "It is—*was*—a beautiful dress. Truly. I never would've picked out anything so beautiful without your help."

Cheryl smiled. "Oh, I know it was beautiful, but as painful as it is for me to say this, Dan was right. It's beautiful, but not a *Bree* kind of beautiful."

"I don't even know what Bree kind of beautiful is."

Cheryl reached in and kissed her on her cheek. "And that's exactly why it's such a unique beauty. Because you don't see it in yourself. Now, if you'll excuse me, I've got a wedding dress creation to supervise. We'll have you ready to walk down that aisle in the morning."

Bree squeezed her hand. "Okay. Thank you."

The older woman spun around and started announcing the plan. Everyone cheered, and within minutes they were running out into the darkness to grab their wedding dresses out of closets and mothballs and cedar trunks.

Others were running off to grab sewing machines.

Someone grabbed Bree and pulled her into the middle of the floor and began measuring her around her pajamas.

Dan, the lone male voice in the whole place, yelled, "I'll start the breakfast food. Y'all are going to need it."

"And coffee!" Cheryl yelled.

"Of course coffee!" Dan returned with a grin. He winked at Bree as she held up her arms so someone could measure her bust. "It's not my first day."

Bree just watched it all with a smile. What else could she do?

The women came back, carrying their wedding

dresses, laughing and joking and telling stories from their own wedding days. A few were telling interesting stories about the day they got divorced too.

None of them uttered a word of complaint as pieces of their dresses—usually parts of the train or underskirt that wouldn't ever be noticed, but sometimes more— were measured for the pattern they developed and cut.

It was the bodice of Gayle Little's dress that ended up fitting Bree perfectly. The woman had lost her husband of sixty years just a few months ago. Bree couldn't even believe somebody Mrs. Little's age would be here helping in the middle of the night. But she was, and she was more than happy to provide this part of her dress, even though it meant taking the dress apart.

"I never had daughters. And it just wasn't the right style for the women my boys married," Mrs. Little said. "My Stanley would've been thrilled at the thought of you wearing it to marry Tanner. He always loved that boy."

Bree held the older woman's hand as Cheryl and the other seamstresses gently removed the bodice of Mrs. Little's gown from the skirt portion.

"You're going to make a beautiful bride, dear," she said.

The commotion continued around her and all Bree could do was watch and smile. Eventually she started serving food and coffee to the women who were working so hard for her.

It was nearing dawn when she found Cassandra on one side of her and Marilyn on the other.

"You okay?" Cassandra asked.

"I'm getting married in a few hours and it's going to be perfect." Bree had no doubt about it.

Cassandra nodded and put an arm around her.

"You were wrong when you said the church would tip over with Tanner's family," Cass whispered, looking around at the beautiful chaos surrounding them.

"I know. Because they're my family too."

Bree sat down in the booth where she'd first sat that day with the twins.

She'd been exhausted, at her lowest, empty.

And oh, so alone.

They'd helped her that day too, the people of this town. Her family.

She laid her head down on the booth table, just like she'd done that day. Her eyes closed as the sounds of laughter, talking and fellowship surrounded her.

Her family was here.

She woke to a gentle hand on her shoulder.

"Bree," Marilyn whispered. "The dress is done. It's time to get ready."

Bree looked out the window. The sun was already shining brightly.

"What time is it? How long did I sleep?"

How unfair was it of her to fall asleep while everyone else was working hard.

"I don't know. I conked out too."

Bree looked around. It was much quieter now, much less frantic. Three different sewing machines were still set up in the middle of the diner, but most of the women were now sitting around, drinking coffee and chatting.

Bree looked over at Cheryl. "I'm so sorry I fell asleep. I should have stayed awake and helped."

"Do you know how to sew?" Cheryl asked.

"No, but—"

"Then there wasn't any point in you being awake."

"Plus, we all know my brother is not going to let you

get any sleep tonight!" Cassandra yelled from across the room. Even Mrs. Little chuckled.

"Come try on your dress," Cheryl said softly. "It's hanging in my office."

Cheryl kept her office purposely dim as she and Cassandra helped Bree put on the gown, the tiny buttons traveling all the way up her spine taking the longest time to fasten. With every second Bree got more and more nervous.

Finally, they were finished, and Cheryl ran a smoothing hand over Bree's shoulders.

"Okay, let's go see if this was more like what you'd envisioned when you'd never envisioned what your wedding dress would look like."

Bree took a deep breath and followed Cheryl and Cassandra out of the room. It didn't matter. No matter what the dress looked like, Bree was going to smile and act like it was the most beautiful thing she'd ever seen.

The women had the full-length mirror set up in the middle of the dining area. Sniffles and murmurs broke out as soon as Bree stepped foot inside. She looked at Marilyn, knowing how much the woman had loved the other gown, trying to see if there was any hint of disappointment at seeing this one.

Marilyn was crying. That probably wasn't a good sign.

I love it. It's absolutely perfect.

She rehearsed the words in her head. No matter what, she would smile and tell them she loved it.

She looked at her reflection in the mirror and promptly burst into tears.

She was immediately surrounded by a gaggle of women.

"No crying on your wedding day."

"We know it's not as gorgeous as that other gown, but Tanner will be thrilled to see you in this."

"I think you look lovely."

Everyone was talking so fast and all over one another that Bree couldn't even pick out who was saying what.

"Ladies, give Bree a little space," Cheryl finally said. It was her diner, after all.

They quieted and stepped back so Bree could once again see herself in the mirror. She trailed her fingers from her shoulders down over her chest to her waist and hips.

Her dress was a rainbow of white. No one piece matched exactly with the next.

Her eyes met Cheryl's in the mirror, then Cassandra's, then Mrs. Little's.

"It's absolutely perfect. It's what I never even knew I wanted."

"Now there's a beautiful bride, right there." Mrs. Little stood beside Bree, looking at her in the mirror, wrapping an arm around her waist.

"There's a lot of love sewn into the dress you're wearing," the older woman continued. "Love the brides had for their grooms when they were first worn, and love for you, and what an important part of our community you've become. Now let's finish getting you ready, because I'm pretty sure there's a deputy captain who will arrest us all if you're not on time coming down that aisle."

Chapter Twenty-Four

By the time Tanner got to the church he was feeling a little like a zombie. Murder was a messy business in every possible way. Not just the physical part of it, although that was bad enough in this case. Making sure all the evidence was gathered properly, then working with the coroner's office to have the body removed.

Even in a cut-and-dried case such as this one, it was still labor intensive. Particularly since it was a murder that also involved a hostage situation in a separate county. So lots of hours of extra communicating and paperwork.

Whitaker showed up right before dawn to take over everything. Tanner let out a sigh of relief. He really hadn't wanted to miss his own wedding and honeymoon.

"Thank you, Richard," Tanner said as he shook the man's hand. He hadn't been required to come, since this wasn't the normal section of the county he worked in. He'd done so without anyone asking him to.

"I figured it was better for me to miss the wedding than you. But seriously, the next dead body? Please do not let it have anything to do with you or your bride."

"Deal."

By that point, there hadn't been any point in trying

to get any sleep. Tanner tried to call Bree, to make sure she was okay.

He had no idea what he was supposed to say to a bride a few hours before her wedding when there was a dead body on top of her wedding dress. Even when he knew that bride probably better than anyone else in the world.

He just wanted to assure her that he was willing to do whatever she wanted to do. If she wanted to reschedule the whole thing, he would do that. If she wanted to get married in their jeans and T-shirts, he would do that. If she wanted not to have a big wedding at all, he would drag her in front of the judge in the next five minutes.

He just wanted her to know that he loved her.

But he didn't get to talk to Bree. Cassandra had answered the phone and explained to him what the women of the town were doing. She told him to hang out with Noah and to be at the church on time.

His breakfast with Noah had been pretty somber. A man was dead. And neither of them felt bad about it.

"Do you think Marilyn is going to be okay?" he asked in between bites of the breakfast food they had to get at the next town over because the Sunrise was currently a wedding dress factory.

"She'll have her ups and downs. Even knowing this was the only way she and the kids would truly be safe, it will still weigh on her. Make her wonder if there might've been a different way."

"Not in the eyes of the law. Ellis had every intent of hurting her and Bree, or worse."

Noah nodded. "That doesn't mean someone as tenderhearted as Marilyn won't still struggle with it. I would've taken that burden from her if I could."

Tanner wondered how long it would be before his brother realized he was in love with this woman. "I know you would, bro, but believe it or not, not all burdens are meant for you to carry."

"That woman has carried enough. She damn well doesn't need to carry any more."

Neither did Noah, not that he was going to be able to hear that. "Take a word of advice from your wise younger brother."

Noah snickered. "And what's that?"

"You two find a way of *sharing* the burden. I know that was one of the most fundamental lessons your time in the Special Forces taught you. A shared burden is easier to carry."

Noah nodded, then sat back and stared at him. "Dude, you're getting married in a couple hours. You nervous?"

"No." Tanner didn't hesitate. Didn't have any doubt. There was nowhere on earth he'd rather be than at that church watching Bree walked down the aisle.

And that was where he was two hours later when the wedding march played and Bree walked toward him slowly, escorted by Dan and Cheryl on either side of her.

Tanner knew he should look at her gown. Knew the women of the town had worked all night for Bree to have something to wear. But all he could see was her. It wouldn't have mattered what she'd been wearing— hell, it could've been a ten-thousand-dollar gown or a trash bag and he wouldn't have noticed.

She was stunning. She was perfect.

She was *his*.

And with every step she took toward him he was more in awe of that fact. When Dan flipped her veil over her head and she turned to him, trust and love shining out of those green eyes, Tanner felt it in every fiber of his being.

The minister said words, and Tanner repeated what he was supposed to and completed the tasks he was asked.

His eyes never drifted from Bree's face.

Only when it came time for the vows did he get snapped back into the ceremony. Bree had been nervous about this. With everything that had happened, they hadn't had much more time to talk about it.

He wanted to reassure her now that it didn't matter. That no matter what she said, he understood. That if she couldn't say anything at all, he would still know.

As Noah handed them both the rings, Tanner grabbed Bree's hands.

"We don't have to say anything if you don't want to," he whispered. He should've made this offer months ago and saved her so much stress. "We can just slip the rings on. You and I will both know what we're saying to each other without words."

Bree's smile was dazzling. "Don't worry. I've got this, Hot Lips," she whispered back.

The reverend indicated it was time for Tanner to say his vows.

It was easy for him. "You're every part of me I never knew was missing. Your intellect is astounding, but it's dwarfed by your beauty, your courage and your passion. I vow to cherish, honor and protect you all the days of the rest of our lives.

"You are my other half, my perfect fit, my forever partner. You are my greatest risk, my greatest reward, and I will thank God every day that you wandered into this town and not another."

A tear leaked out of Bree's eyes, but she was still beaming.

The reverend indicated it was her turn for the vows. She slid the ring onto his finger, but hesitated.

Tanner rubbed his thumb across the back of her small hand that was holding his. He would stay here as long as she needed him to. Or would help her out if she wanted. But mostly he would trust.

She said she had this, so he knew she did.

When the words came, there was no quaver, no problem being heard, no sign of nervousness. He would never have thought she could sound so confident in front of so many people.

He should've known better.

Her green eyes met his. "We both have known much loss in our lives, but we both found so much more. You are who I choose. You are who I choose to stand beside me when I need a partner, in front of me when I don't need a shield but you insist on being it anyway—" there were more than a few chuckles at that "—who I choose to stand behind me when I need support.

"I will fight back-to-back with you when our enemies surround us. I will fight shoulder to shoulder with you when injustice surrounds us. And I will fight face-to-face with you when you're being a jackass."

More laughs, and even he had to chuckle this time. Only his Bree could incorporate a mild swear word into her wedding vows so perfectly.

"You saved me in every possible way a person can be saved. You are my hero. And I know whatever risks the future brings, we will be fine."

She squeezed his hands, and her words slowed, took on depth. These were the words she'd found in the wilderness, he knew. "I don't care what all the different variables are, as long as the constant is us."

He kissed her. He was supposed to wait for the minister to say something, but he didn't care. She was his and he was hers.

The minister said something behind them and the entire church broke into applause. The organ started playing the song they were supposed to exit to.

But it was only when Cassandra snickered and said, "Get a room," did Tanner finally let go of Bree's lips and open his eyes, finding her grinning just as hugely as he was.

He grabbed her hand and turned, walking her down the aisle to their forever.

* * * * *

COLD CONSPIRACY

CINDI MYERS

To the ladies of GJWW.

Chapter One

"Come on, Donna. We need to head back to the house or I'll be late for work." Rayford County Sheriff's Deputy Jamie Douglas turned to look back at her nineteen-year-old sister, Donna, who was plodding up the forest trail in snowshoes. Short and plump, her brown curls like a halo peeking out from beneath her pink knit cap, cheeks rosy from the cold, Donna reminded Jamie of the Hummel figurines their grandmother had collected. On a Monday morning in mid-January, the two sisters had the forest to themselves, and Jamie had been happy to take advantage of a break in the weather to get outside and enjoy some exercise. But now that she needed to get home, Donna was in no rush, stopping to study a clump of snow on a tree branch alongside the trail, or laughing at the antics of Cheyenne, one of their three dogs. The twenty-pound terrier-Pomeranian mix was the smallest and easiest to handle of the canines, so Donna had charge of him. Jamie had a firm hold on the leashes for the other two—a Siberian husky named Targa, and a blond Lab mix, Cookie. "Donna!" Jamie called again, insistent.

Donna looked up, her knit cap slipping over one eye. "I'm coming!" she called, breaking into a clumsy jog.

"Don't run. You'll fall and hurt yourself." Jamie started

back toward her sister, but had taken only a few steps when Donna tripped and went sprawling.

"Oh!" It was Jamie's turn to run—not an easy feat in snowshoes, though she managed to reach Donna's side quickly. "Are you okay?"

Donna looked up, tears streaming down her plump cheeks. "I'm all wet," she sniffed.

"Come on, let's get you up." Jamie took her sister's arm. "It's not far to the car." Though Down syndrome had delayed her development, Donna was only a few inches shorter than Jamie and outweighed her by twenty pounds. Getting her to her feet while both women were wearing snowshoes made for a clumsy undertaking. Add in three romping dogs, and by the time Donna was upright, both sisters were tired and damp.

Once she was assured Donna would stay on her feet, Jamie took charge of Cheyenne, adjusting her grip on all three leashes. But just then, something crashed through the undergrowth to their left. Barking and lunging, Targa tore from her grasp, quickly followed by Cookie and Cheyenne. All three dogs took off across the snow, on the trail of the mule deer buck who was bounding through the forest.

"A deer!" Donna clapped her hands. "Did you see him run?"

"Targa! Cookie! Come here!" Jamie called after the dogs, even as the clamor of their barking receded into the woods. Silently cursing her bad luck, she slipped off her pack and dropped it at Donna's feet. "Stay here," she ordered. "I'm going after the dogs."

Running in snowshoes was probably like dancing in clown shoes, Jamie thought as she navigated through the thick undergrowth. She could still hear the dogs—that was good. "Targa, come!" she shouted. She needed to find the dogs soon. Otherwise, she'd be showing up late for the mandatory meeting Sheriff Travis Walker had called, and she hated to think what he would have to say. As the department's newest deputy, she couldn't count on him cutting her much slack.

The dogs' tracks were easy to follow through the snow, which was churned up by their running paws. Here and there she spotted the imprints of the deer, too. She replayed the sight of the big animal crashing out of the woods toward them. What had made the buck run that way—before the dogs had even seen it? Was a mountain lion stalking the animal?

Fighting back a shiver of fear, she scanned the forest surrounding her. She saw nothing, but she couldn't shake a feeling of uneasiness—as if she really was being watched.

She crashed through the underbrush and emerged in a small clearing. The dogs were on the other side, all wagging tails and happy grins as they gathered around a man on snowshoes, who scowled at the three of them. Jamie's heart sank when she recognized the uniform of a wildlife officer—what some people called a game warden. He looked up at her approach. "Are these your dogs?" he asked.

"Yes, Nate. They're my dogs." She crossed the clearing to him and gathered up the leashes. Worse even than having her dogs caught in the act of breaking the law by a wildlife officer was being caught by Nate Hall. The big blond outdoorsman managed to look like a conquering Viking, even in his khaki uniform, though Jamie could remember when he had been a gawky boy. The two of them had been pretty successfully avoiding each other since he had moved back to Eagle Mountain four months ago, after an absence of seven years. "My sister fell and I was helping her up when they got away from me," Jamie said.

"Jamie, you ought to know better," Nate said. "The deer

and elk are already stressed this winter, with the deep snow. Allowing dogs to chase them stresses them further and could even result in their death."

What made him think he had the right to lecture her? "I didn't *allow* the dogs to chase the deer," she said. "It was an accident." She glared down at the three dogs, who now sat at her feet, tongues lolling, the pictures of innocence.

"Hello!" They both turned to see Donna tromping toward them. She towed Jamie's pack behind her, dragging it through the snow by its strap.

"Donna, you were supposed to wait for me," Jamie said.

"I wanted to see what you were doing." Donna stopped, dropped the pack and turned to Nate. "Hello. I'm Donna. I'm Jamie's sister."

"Hello, Donna," Nate said. His gaze swept over Donna, assessing her. "Your sister said you fell. Are you okay?"

"Just wet." Donna looked down at the damp knees of her snow pants.

"We really need to be going." Jamie picked up her pack with one hand, while holding all three leashes in the other. "I have to get to work."

"Let me take the dogs." Not waiting for her reply, Nate stepped forward and took the leashes. She started to argue, then thought better of it. If the dogs got away from him, maybe he wouldn't be so quick to blame her.

"Nice day for snowshoeing," he said as he fell into step beside Jamie, Donna close behind.

She didn't really want to make small talk with him. The last real conversation they had had—seven years ago— had not been a pleasant one. Though she didn't remember much of anything either of them had said, she remembered the pain behind their words. The hurt had faded, leaving an unsettled feeling in its place.

The dogs trotted along like obedience school protégés.

When Targa tried to pull on the leash, Nate reined her in with a firm "No!" and she meekly obeyed—something she never did for Jamie. Apparently, muscles and a deep, velvety voice worked to impress female canines, too.

"It's a beautiful day," Donna said. "It's supposed to be Jamie's day off, but now she has to go to work."

"Something come up?" he asked. His gray eyes met hers, clearly telegraphing the question he didn't want to voice in front of Donna—*Any more murders?* Over the past three weeks, a serial killer had taken the lives of five local women. Dubbed the Ice Cold Killer, because of the calling cards he left behind with the words *Ice Cold* printed on them, the serial murderer had eluded all attempts by local law enforcement to track him down. Heavy snow and avalanches that closed the only road out of town for weeks at a time had further hampered the investigation.

"Nothing new," Jamie said. "The sheriff has called a meeting to go over everything we know so far."

Nate nodded and faced forward again. "When I moved back to town I was surprised to find out you were a sheriff's deputy," he said. "I never knew you were interested in law enforcement."

"There's a lot you never knew about me." She hadn't meant the words to come out so sharply and hurried to smooth them over. Otherwise, Nate might think she was still carrying a torch for him. "I stopped by the department one day to get an application to become a 911 dispatcher," she said. "I found out they were recruiting officers. They especially wanted women and would pay for my training, as long as I agreed to stay with the department three years. The starting salary was a lot more than I could make as a dispatcher, and I thought the work sounded interesting." She shrugged. "And it is."

"A little too interesting, sometimes, I imagine," Nate said.

"Well, yeah. Lately, at least." She had been one of the first on the scene when the killer's third victim, Fiona Winslow, had been found. Before then, she had never seen the body of someone who had died violently. Then she had responded to the call about a body in a car in the high school parking lot and found the killer's most recent victim, teacher Anita Allbritton. The deaths had shocked her, but they had also made her more determined than ever to do what she could to stop this killer.

"The sheriff is getting married soon," Donna said.

"Yes, he is." Nate looked back at her. "I'm going to be in the wedding."

"You are?" Donna sounded awed, as if Nate had announced that he was going to fly to the moon.

"I'm one of the groomsmen," Nate said.

"I didn't know you knew Travis that well," Jamie said.

"We ended up rooming together in college for a while," Nate said. "He's really the one who talked me into coming back to Eagle Mountain, when an opening came up in my department."

So Nate had returned to his hometown because of Travis—not because of anyone else he had left behind.

They reached the trailhead, where Jamie's SUV was parked. Nate helped her get the dogs into the vehicle. "Where is your car?" Donna asked, looking around the empty parking area.

"I hiked over from the base of Mount Wilson," Nate said. "I'm checking on the condition of the local deer and elk herds. The department is thinking of setting up some feeding stations, to help with survival rates this winter. All this snow is making it tough for even the elk to dig down and get enough food."

"I could help feed deer!" Donna's face lit up.

"I appreciate the offer," Nate said. "But they're too wild

to come to people. We put out pelleted food and hay in areas where the animals congregate, and monitor them with remote cameras."

Nate had intended to study wildlife biology in college, Jamie remembered. He was in his element out here in the snowy woods. That his job involved carrying a gun and arresting poachers would only make the work more interesting to him. He had always had a strong sense of wrong and right. Some people might even call him idealistic.

She didn't have much room for idealism in her life these days—she had to focus on being practical. "We have to go," she said, tossing her pack in after the dogs and shutting the hatch. "Buckle up, Donna."

She started around the side of the car to the driver's seat, but Nate blocked her way. "I'm glad I ran into you this afternoon," he said. "We didn't have much chance to visit at the scavenger hunt at the Walker Ranch."

She shook her head. Fiona Winslow had died that day—no one had been in a visiting mood. "I'm sure we'll run into each other from time to time," she said. Eagle Mountain was a small town in a remote area—she saw a lot of the same people over and over again, whether she wanted to or not. "But don't get any ideas about picking up where we left off." She shoved past him and opened the car door.

After she made sure Donna was buckled in, she backed the SUV out of the lot. Donna waved to Nate, who returned the wave, though the look on his face wasn't an especially friendly one.

Donna sat back in her seat. "He was cuuuute!" she said.

"Don't you remember Nate?" Jamie asked. "He used to come over to the house sometimes, when he and I were in middle school and high school."

"I remember boys," Donna said. "He's a man. You should go out with him."

"I'm not going out with anybody," Jamie said. She wasn't going to deny that Nate was good-looking. He had been handsome in high school, but time and working out, or maybe the demands of his job, had filled out and hardened his physique. Though the bulky parka and pack he had on today didn't reveal much, the jeans and sweater he had worn to the party at the ranch had showed off his broad shoulders and narrow waist in a way that had garnered second and third looks from most of the women present.

"Why don't you have a boyfriend?" Donna asked. It wasn't a new question. Donna seemed determined to pair up her sister with any number of men in town.

"I'm too busy to have a boyfriend," Jamie said. "I work and I take care of you, and I don't need anyone else."

"But I want you to have a boyfriend," Donna said.

"Sorry to disappoint you."

"I have a boyfriend!" Donna grinned and hugged herself.

"Oh?" This was the first Jamie had heard that Donna was interested in anyone in particular. "Who is your boyfriend?"

"Henry. He works in produce."

Donna worked part-time bagging groceries at Eagle Mountain Grocery. Jamie made a note to stop by the store and check out Henry. Was he another special-needs young adult like Donna, or the local teen heartthrob—or even an adult who might have unknowingly attracted her? It was an easy mistake for people to think of Donna as a perpetual child, but she was a young woman, and it was up to Jamie to see to it that no one took advantage of her.

She slowed to pass a blue Chevy parked half off the road. The car hadn't been there when they had come this way earlier. If she had more time, she would stop and check it out, but a glance at the clock on the dash showed she was cutting it close if she was going to drop Donna off at Mrs. Simmons's house and change into her sheriff's department uniform before the meeting.

"What is wrong with that car?" Donna looked back over her shoulder. "We should stop and see."

"I'll let the sheriff's office know about it," Jamie said. "They'll send someone out to check."

"I really think we should stop." Donna's expressive face was twisted with genuine concern. "Someone might be hurt."

"I didn't see anyone with the car," Jamie said.

"You didn't stop and look!" Donna leaned toward her, pleading. "We need to go back. Please? What if the car broke and someone is there, all cold and freezing?"

Her sister's compassion touched Jamie. The world would be a better place if there were more people like Donna in it. She slowed and pulled to the shoulder, preparing to make a U-turn. "All right. We'll go back." Maybe the sheriff would accept stopping to check on a disabled vehicle as an excuse for her tardiness.

She drove past the car, then turned back and pulled in behind it, angling her vehicle slightly, just as if she had been in a department cruiser instead of her personal vehicle. "Stay in the car," she said to Donna, who was reaching for the buckle on her seat belt.

Donna's hand stilled. "Okay," she said.

Cautiously, Jamie approached the vehicle. Though she didn't usually walk around armed, since the appearance of the Ice Cold Killer, she wore a gun in a holster on her belt at all times. Its presence eased some of her nervousness now. The late-model blue Chevrolet Malibu sat parked crookedly, nose toward the snowbank on the side of the road, the snow around it churned by footsteps, as if a bunch of people had hastily parked it and piled out.

She leaned forward, craning to see into the back seat, but nothing appeared out of order there. But something wasn't right. The hair rose up on the back of her neck and she put a hand on the gun, ready to draw it if necessary.

But she didn't need a gun to defend herself from the person in the car. The woman lay on her back across the front seat, eyes staring at nothing, the blood already dried from the wound on her throat.

Chapter Two

Nate reached his truck parked at the base of Mount Wilson just as his radio crackled. Though a recently installed repeater facilitated radio transmission in this remote area, the pop and crackle of heavy static often made the messages difficult to understand. He could make out something about needing an officer to assist the sheriff's department. He keyed the mic and replied. "This is Officer Hall. What was that location again?"

"Forest Service Road 1410. That's one-four-one-zero."

"Copy that. I'm on my way." The trailhead on 1410 was where he had left Jamie and her sister. Had they found something? Or had something happened to them?

He pressed down harder on the gas pedal, snow flying up around the truck as he raced down the narrow path left by the snowplow. The Ice Cold Killer's next to last victim, Lauren Grenado, had been found on a Forest Service road not that far from here. Maybe Nate shouldn't have left Jamie and her sister alone. He could have asked them to give him a ride back to his truck, as an excuse to stay with them. But Jamie had said she was running late for work, so she probably would have turned him down.

Who was he kidding? She definitely would have turned him down. She clearly didn't want anything to do with him, apparently still holding a grudge over their breakup all those years ago.

And yeah, maybe he hadn't handled that so well—but he'd been nineteen and headed off to college out of state. He had thought he was doing the right thing by ending their relationship when it was impossible for them to be together. He had told himself that eventually she would see the sense in splitting up. Maybe she would even thank him one day. But she wasn't thanking him for anything—the knowledge that he could have hurt her that deeply chafed at him like a stone in his boot.

He spotted her SUV up ahead, parked behind a blue sedan. Jamie, hands in the pockets of her parka, paced alongside the road. He didn't see Donna—she was probably in the car.

He pulled in behind Jamie's SUV and turned on his flashers. Jamie whirled to face him. "What are you doing here?" she demanded.

"I got a call to assist the sheriff's department." He joined her and nodded toward the car. "What have you got?"

"Another dead woman." Her voice was flat, as was her expression. But he caught the note of despair at the end of the sentence and recognized the pain shining out from her hazel eyes. He had a sharp impulse to pull her close and comfort her—but he knew right away that would be a very bad idea. She wasn't his friend and former lover Jamie right now. She was Deputy Douglas, a fellow officer who needed him to do his job.

"I've got emergency flashers in my car," he said. He glanced toward her SUV. Donna sat in the front seat, hunched over and rocking back and forth. "Is your sister okay?"

"She's upset. Crying. Better to leave her alone for a bit."

"Do you know who the woman is?"

She shook her head. "No. But I think it's the Ice Cold Killer. I didn't open the door or anything, but she looks like his other victims—throat cut, wrists and ankles wrapped with tape."

He walked back to his truck, retrieved the emergency beacons and set them ten yards behind his bumper and ten yards ahead of the car. As he passed, he glanced into the front seat and caught a glimpse of the dead woman, staring up at him. Suppressing a shudder, he returned to Jamie, as a Rayford County Sheriff's cruiser approached. The driver parked on the opposite side of the road, and tall and lanky Deputy Dwight Prentice got out. "Travis is on his way," he said, when they had exchanged greetings.

"I was headed back to town to get ready for our meeting when I saw the car," Jamie said. "It wasn't here when I drove by earlier, on my way to the Pickaxe snowshoe trail."

"The meeting has been pushed back to four o'clock." Dwight walked over to the car and peered inside. "Do you know who she is?"

"I don't recognize her, and I never opened the car door," Jamie said. "I figured I should wait for the crime scene team."

"Did you call in the license plate?" Dwight asked.

Jamie flushed. "No. I... I didn't think of it."

"I'll do it," Nate said.

Radio transmission was clearer here and after a few minutes he was back with Jamie and Dwight, with a name. "The car is registered to Michaela Underwood of Ames, Iowa."

The sound of an approaching vehicle distracted them. No one said anything as Sheriff Travis Walker pulled in behind Dwight's cruiser. Tall and trim, looking like a law enforcement recruiting poster, the young sheriff showed the strain of the hunt for this serial killer in the shadows beneath his eyes and the grim set of his mouth. He pulled on gloves as he crossed to them, and listened to Jamie's story. "What time did you drive by here on your way to the trail?" he asked.

"I left my house at five after nine, so it would have been about nine thirty," she said.

"Your call came in at eleven fifty-two," Travis said. "How long was that after you found her?"

"I had to drive until I found a signal, but it wasn't that long," Jamie said. "We stopped here at eleven forty-five. I know because I kept checking the time, worried I was going to be late for work."

Travis glanced toward her car. "Who is that with you?"

"My sister, Donna. She never got out of the car." One of the dogs—the big husky—stuck its head out of the partially opened driver's-side window. "I have my dogs with me, too," Jamie added.

"All right. Let's see what we've got."

The others stood back as Travis opened the driver's-side door. He leaned into the vehicle and emerged a few moments later with a small card, like a business card, and held it up for them to see. The bold black letters were easy to read at this short distance: ICE COLD. "Butch is on his way," Travis said. Butch Collins, a retired doctor, served as Rayford County's medical examiner. "Once he's done, Dwight and I will process the scene. I've got a wrecker on standby to take the car to our garage."

"It must be getting crowded in there," Nate said—which earned him a deeper frown from the sheriff.

"Nate, can you stay and handle traffic, in case we get any lookie-loos?" Travis asked.

"Sure."

"What do you want me to do?" Jamie asked.

"Take your sister home. I'll see you at the station this afternoon. You can file your statement then."

"All right."

Nate couldn't tell if she was relieved to be dismissed—or upset about being excluded. He followed her back to her SUV and walked around to the passenger side. The dogs began barking but quieted at a reprimand from Jamie. Donna eased the door open a crack at Nate's approach. "Hello," Nate said. He had a vague memory of Donna as a sweet, awkward little girl. She wasn't so little anymore.

"Hello." She glanced toward the blue sedan, where Dwight and Travis still stood. "Did you see the woman?"

"She's not anyone we know," Nate said. "A tourist, probably." More than a few visitors had been stranded in Eagle Mountain when Dixon Pass, the only route into town, closed due to repeated avalanches triggered by the heavy snowfall.

"Why did she have to die?" Donna asked.

Because there are bad people in the world, he thought. But that didn't seem the right answer to give this girl, who wanted reassurance. "I don't know," he said. "But your sister and I, and Sheriff Walker and all his deputies, are going to do everything we can to find the person who hurt her."

Donna's eyes met his—sweet, sad eyes. "I like you," she said.

"I like you, too," he answered, touched.

"All right, Donna. Quit flirting with Nate so he can get back to work." Jamie turned the key in the ignition and started the SUV.

"You okay, Jamie?" he asked.

The look she gave him could have lit a campfire. "Why wouldn't I be okay?" she asked. "I'm a deputy. I know how to handle myself."

"I wasn't implying you didn't." He took a step back.

"But this kind of thing shakes up everybody. If you asked the sheriff, he'd probably tell you he's upset." At least, Nate had known Travis long enough to recognize the signs that this case was tearing him up inside.

"I'm fine," Jamie said, not looking at him. "And I need to go."

Look me in the eye and let me see that you're really okay, he thought. But he only took another step back and watched as she drove away. Then he walked into the road, to flag down the ambulance he could see in the distance.

JAMIE SHIFTED IN the driver's seat of the SUV, as uncomfortable as if her clothes were too tight. Nate had looked at her as if he expected her to dissolve into tears at any minute. He ought to know she wasn't like that. She was tough—and a lot tougher now than she was when they had been a couple. She had had to develop a thick skin to deal with everything life had thrown at her.

She was a sheriff's deputy, and she had seen dead people before. She wasn't going to fall apart at the sight of a body. Though she had forgotten to call in the license plate of the car, which she should have done, even if she wasn't on duty. And she should have stayed and helped process the crime scene.

If she had been a man, would the sheriff have asked her to stay? No, she decided, her gender didn't have anything to do with this. Travis Walker was as fair a man as she had ever known. But she had had Donna with her. She had to look after her sister, and the sheriff knew that. They had discussed her situation before he hired her. With their parents dead and no other relatives living nearby, Jamie was responsible for Donna, and might be for the rest of her life. While Donna might one day want to live on her own, with some assistance, most programs that would allow that were only available in larger cities—not small towns like Eagle Mountain. As long as Donna wanted to stay in their childhood home, Jamie would do whatever she could to make that happen.

She was happy to take care of her sister, but it meant making certain adjustments. She wasn't free to go out whenever she liked. She couldn't be spontaneous, because she had to make sure Donna was safe and looked after. She didn't think many men her age would be open to that kind of life.

Which was fine. She didn't need a man to make her complete.

She didn't need Nate Hall. When his plans changed and he decided to go away for college, he had shed her as easily as if he had been getting rid of last year's winter coat or a pair of shoes he'd outgrown.

He had told her he loved her, but when you loved someone, you didn't treat them like you were doing them a favor when you said goodbye.

"I'm hungry. We missed lunch."

Jamie guessed Donna wasn't too traumatized, if she was thinking about food. "I'll make you a sandwich before I drop you off at Mrs. Simmons's," she said. "I think there's still some tuna in the refrigerator. Would you like that?"

"I don't want to go to Mrs. Simmons's house," Donna said. "I want to stay home."

"I have to work this afternoon," Jamie said. "And I may be late. You can't stay in the house by yourself."

"Why not?" Donna asked. "I know how to dial 911 if something bad happens."

Jamie tightened her hands on the steering wheel until her knuckles ached. "It's not safe for you to stay by yourself," she said. Even if Donna's mental capacity had matched her physical age, Jamie wouldn't have wanted to leave her alone. Not with a killer preying on women in Eagle Mountain.

"I'm old enough to stay home by myself," Donna said.

"Mrs. Simmons's feelings will be hurt if you don't stay with her," Jamie said. For sure, their older neighbor would miss the money Jamie paid her to watch over Donna while Jamie worked.

"You could explain it to her." But Donna sounded doubtful. She was very sensitive to other people's feelings—perhaps because her own had been wounded so often by unthinking remarks.

"If you don't go see her, you'll miss your shows," Jamie said. Every afternoon, Mrs. Simmons and Donna watched old sitcoms and dramas on a classic TV station. Since Jamie didn't subscribe to the expensive cable package required for such programming, Mrs. Simmons was Donna's only source for her beloved shows.

Donna sighed—a long, dramatic sigh that would have done any teen girl proud. "I guess I had better go, then."

"Thank you." Jamie leaned over and squeezed her sister's arm. "I really appreciate you being so nice about it."

"What time will you be home?" Donna asked.

"I don't know. I have this meeting, but if the sheriff wants me to work after that, I will." She sat up straighter, her next words as much a pep talk for herself as for her sister. "The work I do is important. I'm helping to keep people safe." Though she and her fellow deputies hadn't been able to keep Michaela Underwood and the Ice Cold Killer's other victims safe. The knowledge hurt, and it goaded her to do more. To do better.

"Will you see Nate at the meeting?" Donna asked.

Jamie frowned. "Nate is a wildlife officer—he doesn't work for the sheriff's department."

"He's nice," Donna said. "And cute."

"You think every man you see is cute," Jamie teased.

"I don't think Mr. McAdams is cute." Donna made a face. Mr. McAdams was the meat market manager at Eagle Mountain Grocery. Jamie had to admit he bore a startling resemblance to the photo of last year's Grand Champion steer that graced the door to the meat freezer at the grocery.

"Is Henry cute?" Jamie asked.

Donna grinned. "Oh, yeah. Henry is cuuuute!" She dissolved into giggles, and Jamie couldn't help giggling, too. She could never feel gloomy for long when she was with Donna. Her sister had a real gift for bringing joy into the lives of everyone she knew.

They reached home and the dogs piled out of the SUV and raced into the house, then out into the backyard, through the dog door Jamie's father had installed years before. Three laps around the yard, noses to the ground, then they were back inside, lined up in formation in front of the treat cabinet. "Treat!" Donna proclaimed and took out the bag that held the beloved bacon snacks. She carefully doled out one to each dog, pronouncing "Good dog!" as each treat was devoured.

The next hour passed in a blur of lunch, changing clothes and hustling Donna two houses down to Mrs. Simmons, who met them at the door, a worried expression on her face. "There's some cookies for you on the table," Mrs. Simmons said to Donna. "You go get them while I talk to Jamie."

When Donna had left them, Mrs. Simmons said, keeping her voice low. "I heard they found another woman's body."

"Yes." There was no sense denying it. Half the town listened to the emergency scanner, the way some people listened to music on the radio. "I don't know anything to tell you," she added quickly, before Mrs. Simmons could press her for more information.

"I never thought I'd see the day when I didn't feel safe around here," Mrs. Simmons said.

Jamie wanted to reassure the woman that she would be fine—that there was nothing to worry about. But with six women dead and the department no closer to finding the killer, the words would be empty and meaningless. "I have to go," she said. "I'm not sure how late I'll be. If it will be later than nine, I'll call you."

"Don't worry about us," Mrs. Simmons said. "Donna is welcome to spend the night if she needs to. She's good company."

Ten minutes later, Jamie parked her SUV in the lot behind the sheriff's department. She stowed her purse in her locker and made her way down the hall to the conference room. Dwight and Travis's brother, Deputy Gage Walker, were already there, along with Ryder Stewart from Colorado State Patrol, and US Marshal Cody Rankin, his arm in a sling.

"How's the arm?" Jamie asked as she took a seat at the table across from Cody.

"The arm's fine. The shoulder hurts where they took the bullet out, but I'll live." He had been shot by an ex-con who had been pursuing him and the woman who was catering Travis's upcoming wedding. "I'm not officially on duty," Cody added. "But Travis asked me to sit in and contribute what I could."

The sheriff entered and everyone moved to seats around the table. Though newspaper reports almost always included at least one reference to the sheriff's "boyish good looks," today he looked much older, like a combat veteran who has seen too many battles. He walked to the bulletin board in the center of the wall facing the conference

table and pinned up an eight-by-ten glossy photo of a smiling, dark-haired woman. The image joined five others of
similarly smiling, pretty females. The victims of the Ice
Cold Killer.

"Her name is Michaela Underwood," Travis said.
"Twenty-two years old, she moved to Eagle Mountain to
live near her parents. She recently started a new job at the
bank." He turned to face them. "These killings have got
to stop," he said. "And they have to stop now."

Chapter Three

The meeting at the sheriff's department had already begun when Nate arrived. He slipped into the empty seat next to Jamie. She glanced at him, her expression unreadable, then turned her attention back to the sheriff, who was speaking.

"We're putting every resource we've got behind this case," Travis said. "We're going to look at every bit of evidence again. We're going to reinterview everyone even remotely connected with the women who died, everyone in the areas where they were killed—anyone who might have possibly seen or heard anything."

"What about suspects?" Nate asked. He indicated a board on the far left side of the room, where photos of several men were pinned.

"Where we can, we'll talk to them again." Travis said. "We've ruled them out as the murderers, but they may know something." He rested his pointer on photos of a pair of young men at the top of the chart. "Alex Woodruff and Tim Dawson drew our attention because they were at the Walking W Ranch the day the third victim, Fiona Winslow, was killed. They didn't have an alibi for the previous two murders, of Kelly Farrow and Christy O'Brien. Once the road reopened, they disappeared. I'm still trying to confirm that they returned to Fort Collins, where they're supposedly attending Colorado State University."

He shifted the pointer to a photo of a handsome, dark-haired man. "Ken Rutledge came to our attention because he lived next door to Kelly Farrow and had dated her business partner, Darcy Marsh. When he attacked Darcy several times and eventually kidnapped her, we thought we had found our killer. But since his arrest, there have been three more murders."

Quickly, Travis summarized the case against the remaining suspects—three high school students who had been seen the night Christy O'Brien was murdered, and a veterinarian who resented Kelly Farrow and Darcy Marsh setting up a competing veterinary practice. "They all have solid alibis for most of the murders, so we had to rule them out," he concluded.

He moved back to the head of the conference table. "We're putting together profiles of all the victims, to see if we can find any common ground, and we're constructing a detailed timeline. If you're not out on a call, then I want you studying the evidence, looking for clues and trying to anticipate this killer's next move."

They all murmured agreement.

"Some of this we've already done," Travis said. "But we're going to do it again. The person who did this left clues that tell us who he is. It's up to us to find them. Colorado Bureau of Investigation has agreed to send an investigator to work with us when the road opens again, but we don't know when that will be. Until then, we're on our own. I want to start by considering some questions."

He picked up a marker and wrote on a whiteboard to the left of the women's pictures, speaking as he wrote. "Why is this killer—or killers—here?"

"Because he lives here," Gage said.

"Because he was visiting here and got caught by the snow," Dwight added.

"Because he came here to kill someone specific and found out he liked it," Jamie said. She flushed as the others turned to look at her. "It would be one way to confuse authorities about one specific murder," she said. "By committing a bunch of unrelated ones."

Travis nodded and added this to their list of reasons.

"Are we talking about one man working alone, or two men working together?" Ryder asked.

"That was my next question." Travis wrote it on the whiteboard.

"I think it has to be two," Gage said. "The timing of some of the killings—Christy O'Brien, Fiona Winslow and Anita Allbritton, in particular—required everything to be carried out very quickly. The woman had to be subdued, bound, killed and put into her vehicle. One man would have a hard time doing that."

"Maybe he's a really big guy," Cody said. "Really powerful—powerful enough to overwhelm and subdue the women."

"I agree with Gage that I think we're probably looking at two men," Travis said. "But that should make it easier to catch them. And if we find one, that will probably lead us to the second one." He turned to write on the board again. "What do we know for certain about these murders?"

"The victims are all women," Dwight said. "Young women—all of them under forty, most under thirty."

"They're all killed out of doors," Nate said. "Away from other people."

"Except for Fiona," Jamie said. "There were a lot of people around when she was killed."

"They were all left in vehicles, except Fiona," Ryder said. "And they were alone in their vehicles."

"The killer uses the weather to his advantage," Gage

said. "The snow makes travel difficult and covers up his tracks."

"I think he likes to taunt law enforcement," Ryder said. "He leaves those cards, knowing we'll find them."

"He wants us to know he's committing the murders, but is that really taunting?" Dwight asked.

"He killed Fiona at the Walker Ranch," Gage said. "When the place was crawling with cops." He shifted to look at Jamie and Nate. "I wouldn't be surprised if he knew the two of you were nearby when he killed Michaela this morning."

Jamie gasped. "That deer!"

Nate touched her arm. "What deer?"

"When my sister and I were on the trail this morning, a buck burst out of the underbrush suddenly, as if something had startled it," she said. "That's what my dogs were chasing. I wondered at the time if a mountain lion was after it. And when I was trying to catch the dogs I felt...unsettled." Her eyes met his, tinged with fear. "As if someone was watching me."

"That could be a good thing, if he thinks he's taunting us," Travis said. "We might be able to draw him out into the open."

"So far he's been very good at evading us," Gage said.

"He has, but from now on, we're going to be better." Travis pointed to Nate. "Did you see anyone else when you were in the area near the murder this morning?"

"I talked to an ice fisherman—checked his fishing license. A local guy." He searched his memory. "Abel Crutchfield."

"Gage, find him and interview him," Travis said.

Gage nodded.

"Anyone else?" Travis asked.

Nate shook his head. "Nobody else—except Jamie—Deputy Douglas—and her sister."

"Jamie, did you see anyone while you and your sister were out there?"

"No one," she admitted. "We didn't even pass any cars once we turned off the main highway."

"You start with the women," Travis told her. "See if you can find any commonalities—or any one woman who had a reason someone might want to kill her. Enough that he would kill others to cover up the crime."

"Yes, sir."

Travis gave the others their assignments—Nate was going to work with Gage on re-canvassing people who might have been in the vicinity of the two murders that occurred on forest service land.

The meeting ended and they filed out of the conference room, unsmiling and mostly silent. Nate stayed close to Jamie. "Is Donna upset about all this?" he asked.

"A little." She shook her head. "Not too much. She does a good job of living in the moment, and I try to keep things low-key—not bring the job home or act upset around her."

"These killings have everyone on edge," he said.

"It's frustrating, having him do this right under our noses. I realize it might be more than one person, but it's awkward to keep saying 'killer or killers.'"

"I get that," Nate said. "We all say 'he,' even though we suspect more than one person is involved."

"This is a small community," Jamie said. "We ought to be able to spot someone like this."

"He knows how to blend in," Nate said. "Or to hide."

She rolled her shoulders, as if shrugging off some burden. "I was surprised to see you here this afternoon," she said.

"The sheriff asked me to sit in. I've been one of the

first on the scene for three of the murders. I spend a lot of time in the backcountry, where several of the women were found. He's trying to pull in every resource that might help. And I want to help. There's not a law enforcement officer in the county who doesn't want to catch this guy."

"Of course. Well, I'd better get to work. I'm going to start reviewing all the information we have about the victims." She started to turn away, but Nate touched her arm, stopping her.

"Now that I'm back in Eagle Mountain, I'd really like us to be friends again," he said.

The look she leveled at him held a decided chill. "I don't have a lot of time for hanging out and reminiscing about the old days," she said.

She shrugged out of his grasp and started down the hall but was stopped by Adelaide Kinkaid. The seventy-something office manager alternately nagged and nurtured the sheriff and his deputies, and kept her finger on the pulse of the town. She peered over the tops of her purple bifocals at Jamie. "Where's the sheriff?" she asked. "There's someone here to see him."

"I think he's still in the conference room, talking to Gage," Jamie said.

"I'll get him." Adelaide started to move past Jamie, then said, "You go on up front and stay with the couple who are waiting. I'm thinking this might benefit from a woman's touch."

Nate followed Jamie into the small front lobby of the sheriff's department. A man and a woman in their early thirties huddled together near the door, arms around each other, the man's head bent close to the woman's. They both looked up when Jamie and Nate arrived, the woman's face a mask of sorrow, her eyes puffy and red from crying.

"I'm Deputy Douglas." Jamie introduced herself. "The sheriff will be here shortly. Can I help you in the meantime?"

"We're Drew and Sarah Michener." The man offered his hand. "We came to find out everything we could about… about Michaela Underwood's death." He looked down at his wife, who had bowed her head and was dabbing at her eyes with a crumpled tissue. "We just heard the news, from her parents."

"Michaela is…was…my sister," the woman—Sarah—said. "We heard she was killed in the woods near here this morning. I want to know if that man—Al—killed her."

"Who is Al?" Jamie asked.

"The man she was supposed to meet this morning, to go snowshoeing," Sarah said. "If you found her by herself, and he wasn't there, he must have been the one to kill her."

"I'm Sheriff Walker." Travis joined them in the lobby. "I understand you wanted to talk to me."

"This is Drew and Sarah Michener." Jamie made the introductions. "Michaela Underwood's sister and brother-in-law."

Travis shook hands with the Micheners. "We'd better talk about this in my office," he said. Jamie started to turn away, but Travis stopped her. "Deputy Douglas, you come, too."

Nate moved aside to let them pass, Travis leading the way to his office, Jamie bringing up the rear.

Gage joined him in the lobby. "What's up?" he asked, watching the couple disappear into Travis's office.

"Michaela's sister and her husband think they know who killed her," Nate said. "Or at least, she was supposed to meet a man—someone named Al—to go snowshoeing this morning."

"And you didn't see any sign of him out there with her, did you?" Gage asked.

"No." He continued to study the closed door, wishing he could hear what was going on in there. "Even if he didn't kill Michaela, the sheriff is going to want to find him and talk to him."

Gage put his hand on Nate's shoulder. "Right now, the sheriff wants me to talk to this ice fisherman, Abel Crutchfield. You up for coming with me?"

"Sure." He'd planned to finish his report on the condition of elk and deer herds in the area, but that could wait. A murder investigation took precedence over everything.

JAMIE FOLLOWED THE Micheners into Travis's office, closing the door after her. She stood by the door, while the Micheners occupied the two chairs in front of Travis's desk. Even if Jamie could have found more seating, there wasn't room for it in the small room.

Travis settled behind the desk, a neat, uncluttered space with only a laptop and a stack of files visible. "I'm very sorry for your loss," he said. "Losing a loved one is always hard, but losing them to murder is especially tough. We're doing everything we can to find who did this, but if you have anything you think can help us, we certainly want to know."

Sarah looked at her husband, who cleared his throat. "Can you tell us more about what you already know?" he asked. "We got the call this morning from Sarah's father—Michaela lived with them, so I assume that's how you knew to contact them. But they're understandably upset and didn't have a lot of details."

"We found Michaela's body in her vehicle on the side of Forest Service Road 1410," Travis said. "The medical examiner thinks she was killed earlier this morning. Do you know why she would have been in that area?"

"She had a date to go snowshoeing with a man," Sarah

said. "Someone named Al. I don't know his last name." She leaned forward, clenched hands pressed to her chest. "I told her not to go out with someone she didn't know—especially not to someplace where there weren't a lot of other people around. Especially not with this…this mad-man going around killing women. But she wouldn't lis-ten to me." Her face crumpled. "If only she had listened."

Drew rubbed his wife's back as she struggled to pull herself together. "Michaela was young," he said. "Only twenty-two. And she trusted people. She still thought she was invincible."

"How did she meet this man?" Travis asked.

Sarah sniffed, straightening her shoulders. "She met him at the bank. She just started the job on the first of the month. She's a teller. I guess they flirted, and the next day he came back and asked her out. She said…she said he was really nice and cute, and that she thought the idea of going snowshoeing was fun, and would be a good way to get to know each other without a lot of pressure."

"When was this—when they met?" Travis asked.

"I think it was Thursday when he first came into the bank." Sarah nodded. "Yes, Thursday. Because Friday she and I met for lunch and she told me about him—then she called me later that day to tell me he'd come back in and they'd made a date for Monday. She had the day off, and I guess he did, too."

"Did she say where he worked?" Travis asked. "Or what kind of work he did?"

"No." Sarah sighed. "I asked her that, too. She said she didn't know and it didn't matter, because that was the kind of thing they could get to know about each other on Monday. She told me I was too uptight and I worried too much. But I was right to worry! He must have been the one who killed her."

"What time were they supposed to meet?" Travis asked. "Or did he arrange to pick her up at your parents' house?"

"She said they were meeting at eight thirty at the trail-head for the snowshoe trails," Sarah said. "She told me she was being smart, driving herself, because if the date didn't go well, it would be easy for her to leave."

Travis looked to Jamie. "You said you got to the trail-head about nine thirty?"

"Yes," Jamie said. "There wasn't anyone else there. And no other cars in the parking area. We didn't pass any cars on the way in, either."

"Her parents said she left their house at eight," Drew volunteered.

"She didn't tell them she was meeting a man," Sarah said. "Just that she was going snowshoeing with friends."

Travis nodded. "Tell me everything your sister said to you about this man—even if you don't think it's important. Did she describe what he looked like? Did she say where he lived, or if he gave her his phone number?"

"She just said he was cute. And funny. I guess he made some joke about how nobody could rob the bank with the road closed, because they wouldn't be able to go very far and she thought that was funny."

"What was he doing at the bank that day?" Travis asked. "Was he making a deposit or cashing a check?"

"I don't know. Sorry. I don't know if she had his number, though I think she said she gave him hers." She shook her head. "I've been thinking and thinking about this ever since we got the call from my dad, and there really isn't anything else. She got kind of defensive when I started quizzing her about the guy, and I didn't want to make her mad, so I changed the subject. I made her promise to call me when she got back to the house and let me know how things went, but I wasn't worried when I didn't hear from her by lunch. I just figured they were having a good time and decided to go eat together. But all that time, she was already dead." She covered her hand with her mouth and took a long, hiccupping breath.

Travis took a box of tissues from a drawer of his desk and slid it over to her. "Thank you for coming to talk to us," he said. "We'll follow up with the bank, see if anyone there remembers this man. If we're lucky, he'll be on the security footage. And we may want to talk to you and to your parents again."

"Of course," Drew said. He stood and helped his wife to her feet, also. "Please keep us posted on how things are going."

"We will." Travis came around the desk to escort the Micheners to the lobby. Jamie stepped aside, then followed them into the hall. She was still standing there, reviewing everything the Micheners had said, when Travis returned.

"I've got Dwight checking Michaela's phone records for a call or text that might be from Al," he said. "Meanwhile, I want you to come to the bank with me. I'll call Tom Babcock and ask him to meet us there. We need to get those security tapes and see what this guy looks like. Maybe we'll recognize him."

"Do you really think he's the Ice Cold Killer?" Jamie quickened her steps to keep up with the sheriff's long strides.

"He's the best lead we've had so far," Travis said. "I'm not going to let him get away."

Chapter Four

Abel Crutchfield lived in a mobile home on the west side of town that backed up to the river. His truck sat beneath a steel carport next to the trailer home, which was painted a cheerful turquoise and white. A trio of garden gnomes poked out of the snow around the bottom of the front steps, and a Christmas wreath with a drooping red ribbon still adorned the door.

Abel answered Gage's knock and his eyes widened at the sight of the two officers on his doorstep. "Is something wrong?" he asked.

"We'd like to ask you a few questions." Gage handed him a business card.

Abel read it, then looked past Gage to Nate. "You're the game warden I talked to this morning, aren't you?"

"Yes." Nate gave him a reassuring smile. "This isn't about that. We're hoping you can help us with something else."

"You'd better come in." Abel pushed open the screened door. "No sense standing out in the cold."

The front room of the trailer was neat but packed with furniture—a sofa and two recliners, a large entertainment unit with a television and a stereo system, and two tall bookshelves filled with paperback books and ceramic figurines of dogs, bears, more gnomes, angels and others

Nate couldn't make out. Abel threaded his way through the clutter and sat in one of the recliners and motioned to the sofa. "It's my wife's afternoon for her knitting club," he said. "So I'm here by myself. What can I help you with?"

"Did you see anyone else while you were fishing this morning?" Gage asked.

"Nope. I had the lake to myself."

"What about on the way to and from the lake?" Nate asked. "Did you see anyone on the road, or in the parking area?"

"What's this about?" Abel asked. "Not that it makes any difference in my answers, but I'd like to know."

"Another young woman was killed in that area this morning," Gage said.

Abel sat back, clearly shocked. "You don't think I killed her, do you?" he asked. "I was just out there fishing. I go fishing every Monday. Usually I bring home something for supper."

"We're not accusing you," Gage said. "But we're hoping you might have seen or heard something that could help us find the killer. Where were you between eight and ten this morning?"

"I was at the lake. I always try to get there by eight, and I leave about eleven to come home for lunch." He turned to Nate. "You saw me there. It must have been about nine or so when we talked."

Nate nodded. "That's about right. And you didn't see anyone else while you were at the lake?"

"Not a soul. I passed a couple of cars on the highway on my way out there, but once I turned onto the Forest Service Road, I didn't see any other cars, and none in the parking lot. I saw a woman out walking, but that was all."

Gage tensed. "A woman out walking? Where? What did she look like?"

"She was on the forest road, about a mile before the turnoff to the lake. She was tall and thin, with long blond hair—a lot of it."

"What was she doing?" Gage asked.

"Just walking along, talking on the phone. She didn't even look up when I passed."

"What else can you tell me about her?" Gage asked. "Did you recognize her?"

"She was wearing jeans and hiking boots and a black parka. I didn't get that good a look at her. She had her head bent, with that phone pressed to her ear and her hair falling all in her face."

"Had you ever seen her out there before?" Nate asked.

"No. I usually don't see anybody—not in the winter, anyway," Abel said. "I don't think there are any houses out that way."

"Didn't you think it was odd she was walking out there by herself?" Gage asked.

Abel shrugged. "People like to walk. It's none of my business. She didn't look like she was in trouble or anything. Just walking along, talking on the phone."

"What time was this that you saw her?" Gage asked.

"Well, it was before eight. Maybe seven fifty."

"Which direction was she walking?" Nate asked.

"North. Same direction I was headed."

They talked to him a few more minutes, but he couldn't tell them anything further. They said goodbye and returned to Gage's cruiser. Neither man spoke until they were headed back to the sheriff's department.

"The woman he saw wasn't Michaela," Gage said. "She has short, dark hair. And what was a woman doing out there by herself at that time of morning, anyway?"

"Something else really strange about that whole story," Nate said.

"I know what you're thinking," Gage said. "What was she doing on the phone?"

"Right. Jamie had to drive a ways to call in when she found Michaela. There's no phone signal out that way. None at all."

BANK PRESIDENT TOM BABCOCK met Travis and Jamie at the Mountain States Bank, a worried expression on his face. "I hope we can help you," he said as he led them past the teller windows to the back of the building. "It's unnerving to think a murderer is one of our customers."

"If he is a customer, it will make it easier for us to find him," Travis said.

"You said on the phone you wanted to see footage from our security cameras," Babcock said. "I've asked our IT specialist, Susan Whitmore, to meet with us. She knows her way around the system much better than I do." He opened the door to a small office filled with computer equipment. "While we wait for her, can you tell me a little more about this? You said our teller, Michaela Underwood, was murdered? And this man she met at the bank might be her killer?"

"We don't know that he killed her," Travis said. "But he was supposed to meet her this morning. It may be he knows something about what happened. Were you here on Thursday?"

"Yes. Michaela worked eight to five that day. She took lunch from eleven thirty to twelve thirty, and was the only teller on duty from twelve thirty to three."

"Do you remember her talking to a young man?" Travis asked. "Flirting with him?"

"I can't say that I noticed anything like that." He frowned. "Michaela was always very friendly. Customers liked her.

We're going to really miss her. I can't imagine anyone wanting to hurt her..."

His voice trailed away as a chime sounded. "That will be Susan now." He leaned out of the open door. "We're back here, Susan," he called.

Susan Whitmore was a trim woman with very short platinum hair and piercing blue eyes. "Tom filled me in on the phone," she said after introductions were made. "Just tell me what you need, Sheriff, and I'll do my best to help."

"Michaela Underwood made a date to go snowshoeing this morning with a man she told her sister she met here at the bank Thursday," Travis explained. "He returned Friday and asked her out. We need to find this guy and talk to him. All we have is a first name—Al. If we can spot him talking to her on your security footage, we're hoping that will help us locate him."

"If you find him, we can look at the time stamp on the image and I can link him to a particular transaction," Tom said. "That should give you a name if he was cashing a check or making a deposit, or a payment on an account with us."

"Do you have a particular time you want to look at?" Susan asked. "Or the whole day?"

"Let's start with twelve thirty to three," Travis said. "When Michaela was the only teller working."

"All right." Susan inputted information into a computer and pulled up a black-and-white image showing four screens—ATM, front door, back door and a wider shot that took in most of the lobby. She clicked on the lobby view and enlarged it. "We'll start here, since this gives us a good view of Michaela. I'll scroll forward and stop on any male customers."

Jamie and Travis leaned in as Susan began to forward the film. Michaela waited on an older couple, a young woman with a child and two middle-aged women. Then a single man approached the counter. "Stop," Travis ordered.

Susan stilled the film. Jamie studied the image of a slender man, maybe six feet tall or just under. He wore a dark knit hat pulled down on his head, the collar of his dark coat turned up.

"Can you zoom in?" Travis asked.

Susan enlarged the image until it began to blur. Travis furrowed his brow. "Is there another camera, focused on the teller, which would give us a view of his face?" he asked.

"No," Susan said.

Travis sighed and stepped back. "The way he's standing, we can't tell anything about his face. We can't even tell whether his hair is light or dark."

"Do you think that's deliberate?" Jamie asked.

"Maybe," Travis said. "If he is the killer, he wouldn't want to be seen on video. The hat and coat do a good job of obscuring his face. He's wearing jeans and hiking boots."

"Maybe the brand of the boots will tell us something," Jamie said.

"We'll try," Travis said. He nodded to Susan. "Advance the tape again. Let's see what he does."

They had a clear view of Michaela, smiling and at one point even laughing, as the man stood in front of her. Then he left. But instead of turning to face the camera, he took a few steps back, still talking to Michaela. When he was almost out of reach of the camera, he whirled, head down, and hurried out of the frame.

"I'm willing to bet he knew about the security camera and didn't want to be seen," Travis said. "Let's see the footage for Friday."

But the footage from Friday yielded no sign of the man. They spent almost an hour running through everything and saw no images of him. "Maybe she met him outside the bank," Jamie said. "On her lunch break or something."

"Maybe," Travis said. "It would be easy enough for him to wait for her in the parking lot or on the sidewalk and stop her before she went into the bank." He turned to Tom. "Did anything about him look familiar to you—like someone who had come into the bank before?"

Tom shook his head. "I'm sorry, no."

"What about the name Al? Does that make you think of anyone in particular?"

"I know an Allen and an Alvin, but both of them are in their fifties or sixties. And that wasn't them we saw on the video just now."

"I'm going to need all your security footage from the past week, including what we looked at today. It's possible this guy came in earlier, checking things out."

"Of course. Susan will get it for you."

"Can you tell us what kind of transaction he was making here Thursday?" Travis asked. "The time stamp on the security footage showed he walked up to the teller window at two sixteen."

Tom walked to a computer farther down the counter and began typing. A few moments later, he groaned. "Looks like it was a cash transaction."

"Such as?" Jamie asked.

"Breaking a large bill or cashing in rolled coins," Tom said.

"Here are the security discs for the time period you wanted." Susan handed Travis an envelope. Travis wrote out a receipt for her, then he and Jamie left.

"I got chills when Tom said it was a cash transaction," Jamie said when they were in Travis's cruiser. "Al had to know we couldn't trace that."

"Or maybe he was using the transaction as an excuse

to hit on the cute teller," Travis said. He rubbed his hands along the steering wheel. "Not that I really believe that. I think we're on to something."

"This might be the killer." A shiver ran through Jamie as she said the words.

"Maybe." He shifted the cruiser into gear and began backing out of the parking spot. "In any case, this feels like the closest we've gotten."

NATE AND GAGE returned to the sheriff's department and waylaid Travis and Jamie as soon as they returned. "We got something from Abel Crutchfield that might be useful," Gage said as they followed Travis into his office. Jamie hung back, then followed, too, squeezing in to stand next to Nate. The soft, herbal scent of her hair made his heart race with a sudden memory of the two of them making out in the old Ford pickup he had driven at the time. Hastily, he shoved the memory away and focused on the conversation between the sheriff and his brother.

"Abel says he saw a woman—tall, thin, blonde—walking along Forest Service Road 1410 this morning," Gage said. "She was alone, no car around. He said he didn't get a real good look at her, because she had her head bent, talking on her phone."

"Except there isn't a phone signal out there," Nate said. "For any carrier."

"That does seem suspicious," Travis said.

Beside Nate, Jamie shifted. "Maybe it isn't really suspicious," she said.

She flushed when all three men turned to look at her but continued, her voice even. "Maybe she was nervous, being out there alone. She heard the guy's truck and pulled out her phone and pretended to be talking to someone so whoever was driving past would get the idea she could summon help if she needed to."

"Do women really do things like that?" Nate asked and wished he could take the words back as soon as he said them.

"Yeah, they do," she said, the expression in her eyes making him feel about three feet tall. "Because you know—men."

None of them had a good response to this. The silence stretched. Finally, Travis said, "Let's see if we can find anyone else who saw this woman. I also have a list of bank employees. Let's talk to them and see if any of them remember 'Al.' Jamie, I want you to help with that. Most of the employees are young women—they might be more willing to open up to you." He clicked a few keys on his laptop. "I just forwarded the list to you."

"I'll get right on it," she said, then slipped out the door.

"I'll see if I can find any campers or snowshoers or skiers or fishermen who might have seen a woman who fits the description Abel gave us," Nate said.

"Let's not drop the ball on his," Travis said.

"Right," Nate said. He wasn't going to drop the ball on Jamie, either. He'd do whatever it took to make her see he wasn't the boy who had hurt her seven years ago. She might never feel close to him again, but at least they could be friends.

Chapter Five

Jamie left the sheriff's department at nine o'clock, after working her way through half the bank employees on the list Travis had forwarded to her. So far, none of the people she'd spoken to remembered Michaela talking to anyone special, and they had no recollection of a single man who stood out for them.

She picked up a sleepy Donna from Mrs. Simmons's house. Donna had already taken a bath and changed into a pair of flannel pajamas with large, colorful dogs all over them. Jamie had a pair just like them. Over the past couple of years, Donna had gotten into the habit of keeping a number of clothes at the caregiver's house, which made things easier for everyone. As Jamie put an arm around Donna and escorted her into their house, she caught the smell of the coconut shampoo her sister used. The scent and the feel of the soft flannel beneath her hand transported her back to the days when Donna was little and Jamie, seven years older, often helped her get ready for bed. Once Donna was bathed and dressed in pajamas, the sisters would snuggle together in Donna's bed, and Jamie would read to her until she fell asleep.

Tonight, she led her upstairs to the room across the hall from Jamie's own and tucked her in. Donna turned on her side and studied the big whiteboard on her bedroom wall, where Jamie drew in a calendar every month and noted both sisters' schedules. Donna liked knowing what was supposed to happen each day. "Work tomorrow," she said. "I'll see Henry."

Right, Jamie thought as she kissed her sister, then switched out the light. Sometime tomorrow she'd have to find time to stop by the grocery store and check out Henry. He was probably harmless, but it didn't hurt to be careful.

She walked across the hall to her room and exchanged her uniform for yoga pants and an oversize sweatshirt. Taking off the heavy utility belt and body armor was the definite signal that she was off duty. Time to relax. Except she was too restless to settle. She went downstairs and wandered through the familiar rooms—the kitchen, with its white-painted cabinets and blue Formica countertops; the formal dining room she had turned into a home office; and the wood-paneled living room with its comfortable tweed-covered sofa and chairs and heavy wood tables. The house was out of style but comfortable and familiar.

She and Donna had grown up in this house and had lived here together until Jamie had gone off to college. She hadn't gone far—only across the mountains to Boulder, and the University of Colorado. She had studied business, thinking she would look for a job in Junction, so that she could be close to Donna and her parents. Then, her parents had been killed in a car accident, plowed into by a tourist who was texting while driving. The tourist had walked away with only a few bruises, while her parents had both been pronounced dead at the scene.

So much for a business career in Junction. Jamie needed to be in Eagle Mountain, with Donna. She might have sold the family home and moved with her sister to Junction or Denver or somewhere else, but the thought made her heart ache. Eagle Mountain was home. And Donna didn't do well with change. She needed familiar things—her home, the neighbors she knew, her job at the grocery store—to keep her firmly grounded.

Jamie had moved back to Eagle Mountain for good four years ago. After a series of low-paying clerical jobs, the opportunity at the sheriff's department had been a welcome relief—a way for Jamie to stay in Eagle Mountain and earn a living that would support her and her sister. But it had also been a lifesaver because it gave Jamie a focus and purpose. She had discovered, somewhat to her surprise, that she loved the work. She liked looking out for her hometown and the people in it, and she liked being part of a team that was trying to protect everyone here.

Oh, it wasn't all good feelings and easy times. She had been sworn at by people she stopped for traffic violations, kicked and punched by a shoplifter she had chased down on Main Street, with half a dozen locals and tourists standing around watching the battle and no one lifting a finger to help her. And she had looked on the bodies of those murdered women and felt a mixture of sickness and anger—and a fierce desire to stop the man before he hurt anyone else.

The loud trill of an old-fashioned phone startled her. She raced to grab her cell phone off the hall table, and frowned at the screen, which showed Unknown Number. A sales call? A scammer? Or maybe one of the bank employees, calling her back because he or she had remembered something. She answered, cautious. "Hello?"

"It's Nate. I called to see how you're doing."

The deep voice vibrated through her, making her heart flutter, but she steeled herself against the sensation. The question—coming from him—annoyed her. "I'm fine. Why wouldn't I be?"

"Finding a dead woman shakes up most people. It shook me up."

She settled onto the sofa, a pillow hugged to her stomach. "I'm fine," she said. "It's part of the job. I knew that going in."

"From what I saw today, you're good at your job."

Was he flattering her, trying to persuade her to forgive him? She sighed. "Nate, I don't want to do this."

"Do what?"

"I don't want to pretend we're friends. We're not. We can't be."

"Why not?"

"You know why not."

A long pause. She began to wonder if he had hung up on her. Then he said. "So, because we were once lovers—each other's first lovers—we can't be friends now? Jamie, that was seven years ago. We were kids."

"And now we're adults, and we don't have to pretend we're two old pals."

"I don't know why not," he said. "There was a time I knew you better than anyone—and you knew me better."

"Like you said, that was seven years ago." A lot had happened since then. She wasn't the same woman anymore.

"We're going to be working together on this case," he said. "We shouldn't be enemies."

"You're not my enemy." Did he really think that? "But we can't be…close…anymore."

"Why not?"

Because if she let him too close, she knew she would fall for him again. And she couldn't trust him to not leave her again—at the next promotion, or if someone better came along. He had proved before that he looked out for his own interests and he wasn't one to stick with a relationship if things got tough. "It would be too complicated," she said. "I know you don't like that." He had said that when he broke up with her before. *There's no sense us staying together. It would be too complicated.*

Was that sound him grinding his teeth together? "You've got a lot of wrong ideas about me," he said.

"You're the one who gave them to me."

"Fine. Have it your way. We won't be 'close'—whatever that means to you. But we can be civil. Don't make this more difficult than it has to be."

"I wouldn't dream of it. Now I'd better go. We'll have another long day tomorrow. Good night."

She didn't wait for him to answer but hung up. She'd handled that well, she thought. No sense starting something that was bound to end badly. She'd been very mature and matter-of-fact. She ought to be proud of herself.

She knew a lot about grief now. The pain never went away, but with time, it always got better.

NATE SCANNED THE sheltered meadow at the base of Mount Wilson with his binoculars, counting the number of elk in the small herd gathered there. Most of them still looked to be in good shape, but this would be a good place to put one of the feeding stations the Department of Wildlife had decided to set up starting this weekend. Local ranchers and hunters had volunteered to help distribute the hay and pellets to the three main feeding sites in the area. The supplies were being delivered by helicopter, which meant the project wouldn't be hampered by the still-closed highway.

He entered the information about the herd into a database on his phone, then snowshoed back to the trailhead where he had left his truck. Once inside the cab, with the heater turned up high, he headed down the road, his speed at a crawl, alert for signs of anything unusual. As he passed the turnout toward a closed campground, he caught a flash of color through the trees and stopped. The binoculars came out and he zeroed in on a dark gray SUV parked up against an icy expanse of exposed rock. He scanned the area and focused in on two climbers halfway up the ice.

He followed the SUV's tracks in the snow and parked behind the vehicle. By the time he got out of his truck, the two climbers were headed down. He walked over and met them when their feet hit the snow. No helmets, he noted, and no ropes or harnesses or other safety gear. Maybe they thought they didn't need it, that their spiked shoes and ice axes were enough.

The first man, about six feet tall, with a slight build and sandy hair cut short, eyed Nate suspiciously. "You need something?" he asked.

"You and your friend climb here often?" Nate asked as the other young man, who was a couple of inches taller than his companion and had a head of brown curls, joined them. Something about these two was familiar, but he couldn't place them. Maybe he had seen them around town somewhere.

"Sometimes," the first man said. "There's no law against it." He ran his thumb along the edge of the ice ax he hefted. It wasn't a threatening gesture, but it made Nate aware of the ax as a weapon.

"No, there's not." He addressed the second young man, who also had an ice ax, which he held down by his side. "Were the two of you around here yesterday?"

"Not yesterday," the dark-haired man said. "Why do you want to know?"

"I'm looking for anyone who might have seen a blonde woman in this area, alone, yesterday morning," Nate said. "What are your names?"

"I'm Lex." The blond offered his hand, and gave a firm shake. "This is Ty."

"Did the two of you see a woman around here yesterday morning—blond hair, walking alongside the road?"

The barest flicker of a glance passed between the two climbers. "We weren't here yesterday," Lex said.

"Right," Nate said. "What about the other times you've been out here? Have you ever seen a woman like that in this area?"

A longer exchange of glances, then Ty shook his head. "No. We've run into women climbing at the park in town but not out here."

"I wouldn't think any woman would risk walking along the road by herself around here," Lex said. "Not with that serial killer going around offing women." His expression became more animated. "Somebody at the restaurant last night said something about another woman being killed yesterday. Was this blonde the Ice Cold Killer's latest victim?"

"No," Nate said. "The sheriff would just like to talk to her."

"This guy's sure making the sheriff look like an idiot," Lex said. "Killing all these women practically under his nose."

"I heard one of the victims was even done in on the sheriff's family ranch," Ty said. "That's got to have him furious."

"The sheriff definitely isn't an idiot," Nate said. "Have you seen anyone else in the area—fishermen, hikers, other climbers? It's possible one of them was here yesterday and saw this woman."

"We see people all the time," Ty said. "But most of them we never know their names."

"You're kind of grasping at straws, aren't you?" Lex

asked. "Questioning random people in the woods isn't going to help you find this killer."

Three years on the job had given Nate plenty of experience dealing with the public. He'd gotten into the habit of identifying them as particular types. He'd learned to deal with each type a different way. Nate cataloged these two as civilian know-it-alls, always happy to tell him how to do his job. "Do either of you know a guy named Al?" he asked.

Lex laughed. "There was a guy named Al in my organic chemistry class last semester. Do you think he's your killer?"

"Have you met anyone named Al in Eagle Mountain?" Nate asked.

"Nope," Ty said. "But then, we don't know many people here."

"So you're students?"

"Graduated," Lex said.

"What do you do now?" Nate asked.

"Right now, we're going to try another route up this ice." He turned back toward the rock face. "Good luck with your search."

Not waiting for Nate to say anything else, Lex stepped up onto a small protrusion in the ice, swung his ax over his head and buried the tip with a heavy thud. Ty moved ten feet farther down the face and began to climb also. Nate might not even have been there, for all they were concerned.

Their disdain grated, but Nate knew he was better off ignoring them the same way they ignored him. They didn't have anything to tell him. But he made note of the license tag on their SUV as he walked back to his truck. When he had a better cell signal, he'd call it in.

From there, he drove past the spot where they had found

Michaela in her car. Crime scene tape still festooned the area, and someone had left a bouquet of flowers in the snow on the shoulder of the road, the blossoms of what might have been daisies and carnations wilting and turning brown in the cold.

He passed the parking area for the snowshoe trail and thought of Jamie, and the anger with which she had confronted him yesterday. He was aware she had been cool to him since his return to Eagle Mountain, but her coldness had surprised him. Her initial agitation over her runaway dogs had morphed into real ire—almost as if she was continuing the last conversation they had had, like it was the next day instead of seven years later. At one time, her reaction might have caused him to respond in anger, also. Now, with time and maturity, the fact that she still had such strong feelings intrigued him.

Jamie had been his best friend at one time, the one person in the world he knew he could always count on. Things had ended badly between them—and he was willing to take his share of responsibility for that. But life was too short to throw away a friendship like that.

He was close enough now to a group of private summer cabins that he decided to go a little out of his way and check them out. Though not strictly part of his duties, he liked to do a regular drive-by of the properties, to check for any vandalism, break-ins or maintenance issues. The cabins, a cluster of seven log structures of one or two rooms each, were privately owned, but on Forest Service land. Most of the cabins had been built eighty or a hundred years ago and the owners were allowed to continue to use them after the land was turned over to the Forest Service. They weren't allowed to enlarge the cabins or use them for any other purpose. Most of them weren't suitable for year-round living, anyway, being uninsulated and off-grid, and Nate had yet to encounter anyone out here after the first snow.

He turned onto the road leading up to the cabins and parked in front of the heavy chain that blocked the way. Half a dozen heavy locks hung from the chain. Cabin owners or friends would have combinations or keys that allowed them to open the chain and pass through. Nate studied the obviously fresh tire tracks on either side of the chain. Someone had entered and exited this way in the last day or so—maybe even this morning. Possibly one of the cabin owners had stopped by to check on his property.

Leaving his truck parked, Nate stepped over the chain and followed a winding track to the first cabin. Old wooden shutters covered the windows of the structure—protection against weather and both four-legged and two-legged animals. A hand-painted sign hung over the door, *Lazy Daze* burned into the wood.

Nate followed the tire tracks past four more cabins, all the way back to the most remote in the grouping, set a short distance from the others. No one was at the cabin now, but tracks in the snow showed where a vehicle had parked, and where at least two people had walked around. Like the first cabin, wooden shutters covered the windows and the door was padlocked. Nate studied the door, unable to shake the uneasiness that had his nerves on hyperalert. Something wasn't right here. He sniffed the air and caught the sharp tang of wood smoke, and shifted his gaze to the chimney of the cabin. No smoke emanated from it now, but someone might have had a fire in there recently.

He walked around the side of the cabin, hoping to find an uncovered window that would allow him to peek in. He spotted a door that provided access to a covered back porch and headed for it, intending to check if it was locked. But he hadn't gone far when something clamped onto his ankle, pain lancing through him, stealing his breath. Vision fogged with shock, he stared down at the jagged steel trap clamped around his foot.

Chapter Six

"We've had a garbled radio transmission from one of our officers." The woman from Colorado Parks and Wildlife who contacted dispatch spoke with a distinct Texas drawl. "All of the personnel in this area are involved in the supply delivery near County Road Two. I didn't get a reply when I tried to make contact again, but reception is very bad in that area. Could one of your officers check it out for us?"

"I can take that," Jamie said. "I'm headed out now." She had stopped by the dispatch center to say hello to her friend, Anong, who was on duty that afternoon.

Anong keyed her microphone. "I have a deputy here who can check out that call for you," she said. "What is the location?"

"We think it came from somewhere around Sundance cabins—the summer cabins off Forest Service Road 1410? Wildlife officer Nate Hall."

Jamie bit back a groan of annoyance. Was this some twisted way for Nate to make sure he saw her again? But she immediately dismissed that notion, and a tickle of fear replaced her irritation. Was Nate in some kind of trouble? "I'm on my way," she said.

"I'll let the sheriff's department know what's up," Anong said, her wide face soft with concern. "Is Officer Hall a friend of yours?"

"Not exactly."

Nate wasn't a friend, but he wasn't her enemy. She had meant that. And even if she had hated his guts, he was a fellow officer who might be in trouble. She was in her cruiser headed out of town when the sheriff called her. "I'm sending Gage out as backup," he said.

"Nate's going to be really embarrassed if this is the radio equivalent of a butt dial," she said.

"Better embarrassed than in real trouble," Travis said.

"Yes, sir."

She punched the accelerator, going as fast as she dared on the icy roads. She resisted the urge to switch on her lights and sirens. That was a sure way to draw a crowd. She wouldn't mind embarrassing Nate a little but no need to go overboard. And if he was in a dangerous situation, no sense putting other people at risk.

She spotted his truck parked at the entrance to the enclave of summer cabins. The chain over the road was in place, and nothing looked out of order. She got out of her cruiser and spotted tire tracks leading toward the cabins. Had Nate seen someone and followed them—or was he merely checking the cabins for signs of vandalism or break-ins? It was something they had had trouble with in the past—usually bored teens breaking into a cabin to have a party or mess things up.

She cupped her hands around her mouth. "Nate!"

Her voice echoed back to her, followed by ringing silence. A chill wind buffeted her, and she rubbed her shoulders against the cold. Better to get back in the cruiser and wait for Gage to arrive. She turned back toward her vehicle, then froze as a cry reached her—an animal sound that sent an icy jolt through her. Heart hammering, she raced toward the sound. "Nate!" she shouted again.

The reply was stronger now, a strangled cry for help.

She ran faster, slipping and falling on the ice, but picking herself up and charging on. She found him alongside a cabin, hunched over on the ground, his face as pale as the snow around him. "Jamie!"

"Nate, what happened?" She fell to her knees beside him, then recoiled in horror at the sight of the trap around his foot. The steel teeth had sliced through his thick pack boots and blood stained the snow around him. She swallowed hard. "Who would have something like that out here?"

"I think it was a booby trap," he said. "It was covered up pretty well, and it's attached to the cabin, so that anyone caught in it couldn't get away." He indicated the thick chain that ran between the trap and the cabin wall, where it was fastened to an iron ring sunk into one of the logs.

She forced herself to ignore the blood and her thoughts of what the trap must have done to Nate's leg, and bent to study the contraption itself. Then she grasped the sides of the trap and pulled hard, but barely managed to move them. "You can't open it that way," Nate said. "You have to stand on it. See these pieces?" He indicated ear-shaped metal pieces on either side of the trap's jaw. "Stand on them and your weight will force the trap open."

"All right." She stood and he scooted back, giving her room to position herself. She straddled the trap, facing him. "I don't want to hurt you," she said.

"It already hurts like the devil," he said. "You can't make it worse. Just do it and get it over with."

Right. She took a deep breath, then stepped down on first one ear, then the other. The jaws eased open. With a groan, Nate pulled his foot from the trap. Jamie shoved the trap aside and knelt beside him once more. "I should go call an ambulance," she said. "Will you be okay if I leave you?"

"I kept waiting for whoever did this to come back." He lifted a pistol from the ground beside him. "But they didn't show." He frowned. "How did you know I was here?"

"Someone from your office called and said they had had a garbled transmission from you and asked us to check it out."

"And you were the lucky one." His eyes met hers. She wanted to look away but couldn't, mesmerized by the tenderness behind the pain. She remembered other times when he had looked in her eyes that way, moments when they had trusted each other with secrets, turned to each other for comfort or united in lovemaking. She leaned toward him, drawn by the pull of memories and a longing she hadn't even realized was in her, to feel that close again.

"Jamie! Nate! What's going on?"

Gage's shouts yanked her back to the present and she pulled away, then stood and went to meet him. "Someone set a leghold trap beside this cabin and Nate stepped in it," she said.

Gage followed her to where Nate sat. He had dragged himself over to lean against the wall of the cabin, a thin trail of blood marking his path. "How are you doing?" Gage asked.

"The bleeding has almost stopped. My boot is ruined, but it probably kept the trap from destroying my leg." He grimaced at his mangled boot. "The ankle might be fractured, but it's not a bad break. It doesn't hurt as much, now that the pressure of the trap is off."

Gage squatted down to get a better look at the trap. "I hope you're up on your tetanus shots," he said. "This thing is pretty rusty."

"It's an old trap," Nate said. "An antique. New ones have smooth jaws, not toothed ones. I seem to remember one of these cabins had some old traps hanging up on the wall. Not this one, but another in this group. Take a look for me, will you?"

"I will, after we get an ambulance for you," Gage said.

"I don't need an ambulance," Nate said. "The two of you can get me to one of your vehicles. That will be a lot faster than waiting for an ambulance to come all the way out here—especially since you'll have to drive halfway back to town to get a cell signal."

Gage studied him a moment, then nodded. "All right. I guess we could do that." He looked around them. "What about whoever did this?"

"I'd like to get a look inside this cabin," Nate said. "The tracks in the snow indicate someone has been here recently. Maybe someone is squatting here and they set the trap to discourage anyone investigating too closely."

"Then they're not very bright," Gage said. "They had to know someone getting hurt in a trap like that would bring the law down on this place."

"Maybe they thought they could get to whoever was caught before anyone else found out," Nate said.

"We'll get someone out here to take a look," Gage said. "First, let's get you to the clinic in town." He offered his hand and Nate grasped it and heaved to his feet.

Jamie rushed in to steady him, and Gage moved in on the other side. "We could make a chair and carry you," Gage said.

"I've still got one good leg," Nate said. "I might as well use it."

Slowly, awkwardly, they made their way around the cabin and onto the road. Nate gritted his teeth and breathed hard but made no protest. After what seemed like an hour—but was probably only fifteen minutes—they reached Jamie's cruiser. Gage opened the door and helped Nate into the passenger seat. "You take him to the clinic," Gage said. "I'll stay here and make sure no one disturbs the crime scene. You phone for help when you get into cell range."

"All right."

Nate said nothing on the drive into town. Eyes closed, he rested his head against the window. Jamie wondered if he was asleep. When they reached the turnoff onto the county road, Jamie called Adelaide and told her what had happened. She promised to call ahead to the clinic and to send Dwight and another deputy to assist Gage.

Jamie ended the call and looked at Nate. His eyes were open and he was watching her. "You okay?" she asked, focusing on the road again.

"I'm okay."

At the clinic, Jamie insisted on fetching a wheelchair from inside to transport Nate inside. He didn't object. When questioned by the staff about how he ended up with his leg caught in a trap, he said, "I'm a wildlife officer," as if that explained everything.

X-rays revealed his ankle was badly bruised, the skin mangled and requiring stitches, but it wasn't broken. "Those pack boots have a lot of padding," the doctor said as Nate completed the final paperwork for his visit. "That probably saved you."

He left with his ankle in an air splint, hobbling on crutches. "I'll drive you home," Jamie said.

He directed her to a cabin on a ranch on the edge of town. "The original owner built it as an artist's studio," Nate said as he unlocked the door. "Come in and take a look."

She moved past him, into a room with blond wood floors and large windows that flooded the space with natural light. A galley kitchen filled the corner of the room, and doors opened onto a single bedroom and bath.

"How did you ever find this place?" she asked, not hiding her admiration.

Nate sank onto the leather sofa and leaned the crutches against the wall behind him. "The officer who had my job before me lived here," he said. "When he moved to Cortez, he worked out a deal with the landlord for me to take over his lease."

It felt awkward standing while he was sitting, so she sat on the other end of the sofa. "I guess your parents don't still have a place in town, do they?" she asked.

"No, they sold out and moved to Texas three years ago. My dad said he got tired of shoveling snow, and my brother and his kids are in Dallas and my mom wanted to be closer to the grandkids."

"I guess I lost track of them," she said. "I had a lot going on just then."

"Your parents' deaths," he said. "I remember. My mom told me." He leaned over and fiddled with the fastening on his Aircast. "I kept meaning to get in touch with you, to tell you how sorry I was." He glanced at her. "I guess I messed that up, too."

She shook her head. "It's all right." She had been so devastated at the time she couldn't even remember who had or hadn't expressed their sympathy.

"That must have been rough," he said. "Losing both of them at once. Mom said you were living in Boulder at the time."

"Yeah. I came home to take care of Donna. She was so upset. It took her a long time before she could accept that they weren't coming back."

"You could have taken her with you, gone back to the city."

"I didn't want to do that to her. She had already lost her parents—I couldn't have her lose her home and her friends, all the things that were familiar to her. Routine is really important to her."

"What about all you lost?" he said. "You must have had a job, friends, a home?"

She shifted to angle her body toward him. "Eagle Mountain is my home. And I had just graduated. It's not as if I had a career or anything. Besides, if I hadn't come back here, I never would have gotten into law enforcement. I'd have probably ended up in a cubicle somewhere, bored out of my mind, instead of doing something active that I'm good at. Besides, who are you to give me a hard time about coming back here to live? You did it."

"Yeah, I did. It was a good opportunity for me." He shrugged. "And I missed it. I missed a lot of things." His gaze zeroed in on her.

She stood. "I'd better go. Somebody will return your truck tomorrow, I imagine."

Before he could protest, his phone rang. She headed for the door. He answered the call and said, "Wait up a minute. It's Gage."

Hand on the doorknob, she paused. Nate listened a moment, then said, "Jamie is here. I'm going to put you on speaker. Tell her what you told me."

"We found evidence that someone was squatting in that cabin," Gage said. "Maybe more than one person. We've got a reserve deputy sitting on the place waiting for them to come back. We'll want to question them about that trap. How's the leg?"

"Bad bruise, no break, some stitches," Nate said. "I have to stay off it a few days."

"You got lucky," Gage said.

"I guess you could look at it that way."

"We found two more of those traps—one on the other side of the cabin, and one near the front steps," Gage said.

"Looks like you missed that second one by inches, judging by your prints in the snow. And you were right—the traps were taken off the wall of a nearby cabin."

"Is there anything in the cabin to tell you the identity of the squatter?"

"Not much—some blankets, dishes, canned food. We talked to the owner—he lives in Nebraska—and it sounds like everything we found was stuff that he keeps there."

"How did the squatter get in? I didn't see any sign of a break-in."

"The owner keeps the key under a flowerpot on the back porch. It's not there now."

Nate rolled his eyes. "Well, it'll be interesting to see if anyone shows up and who they are."

"I'm wondering if it might be our killer," Gage said.

"What makes you think that?" Nate asked.

"Just a hunch. I mean, if you wanted to stay off the radar, this would be a good place to hide, wouldn't it?"

Chapter Seven

"Henry and I have a date!" Donna announced at breakfast the next morning. Sunlight streamed from the window behind her, promising another beautiful day.

"Oh?" Jamie tried not to show too much curiosity. She still hadn't gotten by the store to meet Henry, though she needed to do so soon.

"He's going to take me to dinner and the movies." Donna spoke around a mouthful of half-chewed cereal.

"Don't talk with your mouth full," Jamie chided. "And we don't have a movie theatre in Eagle Mountain."

Donna chewed and swallowed. "I know that," she said. "We're going to watch a movie at his house."

"When are you planning to do this?"

"Soon."

Which could mean next month or this afternoon. "You can't go out with Henry until I meet him," Jamie said.

"Why do you have to meet him? He's *my* boyfriend."

"I still need to check him out and make sure he's a good person for you to date." That he wasn't someone who was trying to take advantage of Donna's vulnerability.

"I don't have to approve of your boyfriends."

"I don't have any boyfriends." She had had only a few casual dates since breaking up with Nate. Thinking about that now made her feel pathetic. But she was far too busy to have time for a relationship.

"But if you did, you wouldn't wait for my permission to date them," Donna said. "I shouldn't have to, either."

"I'm your big sister. It's my job to look after you."

"I'm nineteen. I don't need you to look after me."

But you do, Jamie thought. Donna knew it, too, even if she wouldn't admit it. Jamie could understand that her sister was frustrated that she wasn't able to do the things other people her age could do. She was high-functioning, but she had led a sheltered life. She didn't understand that there were people in the world who would take advantage of her. "I'm not saying you can't go out with Henry," she said. "I just want to meet him first." She leaned across the table and put her hand over Donna's. "I would say that even if we switched places and you were just like me." The words weren't a lie. If Michaela's family had insisted on meeting "Al" before Michaela went out with him, maybe the bank teller would be alive today.

But Donna was in a stubborn mood this morning. "What if I don't want you to meet him?"

"Donna, please. If he's your friend, of course I want to meet him."

"He's *my* friend. Can't I have anything that's just mine?" She shoved back her chair and stomped off.

Jamie sighed and resisted the urge to get up and follow Donna. It wouldn't hurt to let her sulk a little. And her bad moods rarely lasted long.

Ten minutes later, after Jamie had finished breakfast and cleared away the dishes, she found Donna waiting by the front door, her backpack in hand. "Time to go to work," she said.

"It is," Jamie said. "When you get off at three, you know to come straight to Mrs. Simmons's?"

"I know." She headed out the door to Jamie's cruiser.

The two sisters didn't speak on the short drive to the grocery store. Donna could walk the few blocks from their house to the store, but Jamie liked to drive her when she could. "Is Henry working today?" she asked as she pulled into the parking lot.

"He is." Donna opened the door. "'Bye." She hurried into the store, not looking back.

Jamie made a note to swing by later and find out exactly when Henry would be working, as well as his last name and more about him.

She parked behind the sheriff's department and entered through the back door. Adelaide waylaid her as she emerged from the locked room. "We're holding a masquerade ball at the community center Friday night, all proceeds to benefit folks in town for whom the road closures have caused a financial hardship. I hope you plan to be there."

"Oh." Jamie blinked. "A masquerade party?"

"Wear a costume and a mask." Adelaide looked her up and down. "I'm sure you're creative enough to come up with something. If you can't, the volunteers at the Humane Society thrift store have combed through donations and assembled a number of suitable disguises at very reasonable prices. And you're not on schedule to work that evening—I already checked."

"I don't know." Jamie searched for some excuse, but it was tough to think straight with Adelaide's steel gaze boring into her. Seventy-plus years, much of it spent bossing people around, had made the sheriff's department office manager a formidable force.

"It's for a good cause," Adelaide said. "People who work on the other side of the pass haven't been able to get to work, and store owners have suffered losses with fewer tourists visiting and the inability to replenish their stocks. People are really hurting and we want to help them."

"Of course," Jamie said. "I'll be there." Maybe she'd take Donna. Her sister liked dressing up, and she would enjoy seeing everyone's costumes.

Satisfied, Adelaide let her pass. Jamie made her way to the conference room, helped herself to a cup of coffee but bypassed the box of doughnuts. She settled at the table next to Dwight. A few moments later Nate clumped in on crutches and sank into the chair across from her. He looked better than he had yesterday. "How's the ankle?" she asked.

"It's there."

The sheriff entered the room and they all settled in to listen to the usual bulletins and updates, including a summary of the previous day's events at the summer cabins, for anyone who might not have gotten the full story yet. "No one showed up at the cabin while our officer was there," Travis said. "We can't afford to post someone there full-time, but if any of you are in the area, make it a point to swing by." He glanced down at his open laptop. "Did we get anything from Michaela Underwood's phone records?"

"There was one call at eight oh two the morning she was killed," Dwight said. "That could have been from Al. It came from a payphone at the Shell station. It's probably the only payphone in town. The phone box is around the side of the building, out of view of the road, and no one remembers seeing anyone using it that morning."

"Where are we on the search for the blonde woman Abel Crutchfield saw walking along Forest Service Road 1410?" Travis asked.

"Nowhere," Gage said. "We haven't found anyone else who saw her, or any blonde woman who lives out that way. In fact, no one lives out that way."

"What about the bank employees?" Travis asked.

"I interviewed all the employees," Jamie said. She checked her notes. "One woman, Janis Endicott, remembers Michaela talking about Al, but none of them remember seeing him or could give any new details."

"Anything else on this case?" Travis asked. "Any thoughts or insights any of you might have had about it?"

"I thought of one thing," Jamie said. When every head swiveled to look at her, she fought down a blush and forced herself to keep her voice steady. "While the other women who were killed seemed like crimes of opportunity, he apparently targeted Michaela."

"We could be dealing with a copycat," Dwight said.

"Maybe," Travis said. "Though nothing we've learned about Michaela points to her having an enemy who would want to kill her. And we can't be sure our killer didn't target and stalk any of the other women." He turned to Jamie. "That's good thinking, Deputy."

She swallowed, steeling herself for her next words. "I also thought maybe we should give the killer a target and see if he takes the bait."

"What are you talking about?" Nate hadn't said anything so far in the meeting, but he spoke up now.

Jamie shifted in her chair. She had lain awake a long time last night, thinking about this. "I could drive around, out of uniform and in my personal vehicle, in some of the areas we know he's killed other women and see if anyone behaves suspiciously."

"No." Nate spoke loudly and leaned across the table toward her.

She shrank back. "I'd be smart," she said. "And we could have other officers watching me."

"It might not be a bad idea," Travis said. "You wouldn't have to be alone. We could have another officer hidden in the car with you."

Nate leaned back in his chair, silent, though he continued to glare at Jamie. She ignored him. "I think it's worth a try," she said.

Travis nodded. "I think so, too. We'll set something up for this evening. Dwight, you can go with her."

"Yes, sir."

Jamie struggled to remain composed, even as an adrenaline rush at the thought of possibly facing down a killer—or helping to capture him—made it difficult to sit still.

The rest of the meeting was a blur of routine announcements about training, schedules and upcoming events—including the masquerade party on Friday. When the sheriff dismissed them, she rose and left the room, intending to head out on patrol. Nate followed on her heels. "Jamie, wait up."

She stopped and looked back at him as he limped down the hallway toward her. "If you're going to lecture me about how I shouldn't put myself out there as bait for a killer, don't waste your breath," she said. "I'll be perfectly safe."

"More like it will all be a waste of time," he said. "I think this guy is too smart to fall for a trap like that."

"It's worth a try," she said.

He nodded. "I wish I could go with you."

She looked down at the cast on his foot. "I suppose you could bash the killer over the head with your crutches."

He laughed. "Yeah, well, just be careful."

"I'm always careful," she said.

"Yeah, you are, aren't you?"

How was she supposed to interpret the look he gave her? Equal parts frustration and—was that pity? She shook her head. She was imagining things. Nate might still have a few feelings for the girl she had been, but he didn't know enough about her now to really care.

"OFFICER HALL, AREN'T you supposed to be home, resting?"

Nate did his best to stand up straight—despite his cast and crutches—as he swiveled to face Adelaide. The septuagenarian eyed him over the top of purple-framed bifocals, her gaze taking in his khaki uniform. "Surely you aren't on duty?"

"I came in to give the sheriff my formal statement about what happened yesterday," Nate said. "And I'm in uniform because I'm here in an official capacity, as an officer of Parks and Wildlife." That was what he had told himself, anyway. It didn't feel right to show up at the sheriff's department in civilian clothing. Whether it was the uniform or the sheriff feeling sorry for him, Travis had asked Nate to sit in on the morning meeting.

"How long are you going to be laid up with your injuries?" Adelaide asked.

"Six weeks. Maybe less." He was determined to get back to work as swiftly as possible. The idea of sitting around the house with his foot up for the next month and a half was beyond depressing.

"If you're determined to be up and about so soon, you should come to the masquerade ball this Friday night." Adelaide handed him a postcard. The front of the card showed an attractive woman with a black, feathered mask hiding her features. "Proceeds benefit the folks here in Eagle Mountain who have been hit hardest by the heavy snow and road closures. There will be food, music and dancing, and prizes for the best costumes."

"I don't think I'll be doing any dancing just yet," Nate said. He tried to hand the card back to Adelaide, but she refused to take it.

"You can sit, have a drink and something to eat, and enjoy seeing everyone's costumes."

"What are you coming as?" he asked Adelaide.

The devilish look that came into her fading blue eyes made him take a step back. "You'll just have to wait and see. One more reason for you to show up."

"I'll, uh, think about it." He retreated to the door, moving faster than he would have thought possible in his condition.

His next stop was the grocery store. If he was going to be sitting home for the next few weeks, he needed to stock up on snacks and easy meals. He made his way to the produce section and was sizing up the potatoes when a familiar voice hailed him. "Hello, Officer Nate."

Smiling, he turned to greet Donna Douglas. Jamie's sister wore one of the grocery's blue aprons over a green sweater and jeans, her curly brown hair pulled back in a ponytail. He had never paid much attention to her when he and Jamie were dating. He'd thought of her as just a kid, seeming younger than her years because of her mental disability. "Hello, Donna," he said.

"You're Jamie's friend." Donna grinned. "Her boyfriend."

How was he supposed to answer that? "Jamie and I are friends."

"What happened to your foot?" She stared at the blue Aircast encasing his left foot.

"I hurt it at work."

"What kind of work do you do?"

"I work for Parks and Wildlife."

"I remember now. We met you when we were snowshoeing. Did a big animal step on your foot?"

"Not exactly."

"Hey, Donna."

They turned to see a stocky, moon-faced young man wheeling a produce cart toward them. His blue eyes shone from behind his black-framed glasses as he grinned at

Donna. Donna grinned back. It made Nate think of cartoons he had seen as a child, where a pair of lovers looked at each other and hearts exploded in the air around them. He couldn't see any hearts around these two, but he had no doubt they were there.

"This is Henry." Donna took the young man's hand when he stopped beside them. "He's my boyfriend."

Henry nodded. "Donna's my girlfriend."

"You look like you make a good couple," Nate said.

"Thanks." Donna released Henry's hand. "I have to get back to work," she said. "We don't want to get in trouble." She waved to Nate and hurried back toward the register area.

"Me, too," Henry said. He began unloading apples from a box on a cart, arranging them in a neat pyramid. "You should buy an apple." He handed Nate a large red fruit. "They're very good, and good for you."

"I think I will." Nate pulled a plastic bag from the roll at one end of the bin and selected three more apples to go with the one Henry had given him.

"Are you a police officer?" Henry was staring at Nate's khaki uniform and gun.

"A kind of police officer, yes." He didn't mention Parks and Wildlife. When he named his employer, people invariably thought he was a park ranger, not a cop. Never mind that he had the same training as any other law enforcement officer. He wrote tickets, investigated crimes and made arrests all the time as part of his job. And most of the lawbreakers he faced met up with him when he was alone in the wilderness—and almost all of them carried guns.

"Do you know anything about all those women who died?"

Henry's question startled him, but he told himself it shouldn't have surprised him. The Ice Cold Killer was the number one topic of conversation in Eagle Mountain these days. Henry had probably heard his customers and his family talking about the case.

"I'm trying to help find the man who killed those women," Nate said.

"Michaela was my friend." Henry's mouth turned down, and his lip quivered. He sniffed. "She worked at the bank and she helped me with my account."

"I'm very sorry you lost your friend," Nate said.

"I saw her the day before she died. She came in here to the store. She did that sometimes. She would buy a salad or fruit for her lunch and say hello to me."

"That's good that you got to see her."

Henry was frowning—or maybe concentrating very hard. Nate couldn't tell. "She was with a man," Henry said. "They were laughing and she was smiling at him—different from the way she smiled at me."

The hair on the back of Nate's neck stood up. "Who was the man, do you know?"

Henry shook his head. "I didn't know him. But I think maybe he was her boyfriend."

Nate set the bag of apples in his cart and moved closer to Henry, the way he might approach a skittish deer. "Henry, do you think you would recognize that man if you saw him again?"

He nodded. "I think so. I'm pretty good at remembering people."

"Could you come to the sheriff's department with me and tell them what you told me, and maybe describe the man to them?"

Henry's frown deepened. "I can't come now. I have to work." His voice rose. A couple of shoppers turned to stare.

"What time do you get off work?" Nate asked.

Henry tilted his head to one side, thinking. "I get off today at three o'clock," he said.

"If I come back here at three, will you go to the sheriff's office with me?" Nate asked. "Just for a little bit?"

Henry shrugged. "I guess so. Is it important?"

"Yes. It's important."

"Okay." He turned back to arranging the apples. "See you at three."

Nate finished his shopping, his mind racing. If Henry was telling the truth—and he would have no reason to lie—then he might have seen Michaela with her killer. This might be the break they had been waiting for.

Chapter Eight

Jamie didn't make it back to the grocery store until three fifteen. Donna got off at three, so Jamie reasoned this would be a good opportunity for her to meet Henry without upsetting her sister if things didn't go well. "I'm looking for someone named Henry, who works in your produce department," she told the young woman at the office, whose name tag identified her as Veronique.

"Henry?" Veronique's eyebrows rose. "He's not in any kind of trouble, is he?"

"No, no. I just wanted to meet him. He's, uh, he's friends with my sister, Donna."

"Oh, Donna! Of course." Veronique brightened. "She and Henry left at three. He said something about walking her home." She giggled. "They're so cute together."

So much for Jamie's plan to meet Henry alone. "What is Henry like?" she asked.

"Oh, he's a good kid. Like Donna. He came to us from the same program."

"You mean, he's developmentally disabled, too."

"Yeah. Down syndrome, I think. But a good worker. Friendly. Customers like him. They like Donna, too."

"How old is he?"

"Early twenties. He lives with his mother, I think. Why do you want to know?"

"Donna says he's her boyfriend."

Veronique giggled again. "Yeah, those two are really sweet on each other. It's cute."

"Thanks." Jamie left the store and returned to her cruiser. Henry didn't sound like a serial killer who was going to lure her sister to a remote location and kill her. But she still wanted to meet him. She checked her watch. They might already be at Mrs. Simmons's, but since they were on foot, and Donna was never one to hurry, Jamie ought to be able to catch up with them en route and introduce herself.

She cruised slowly through the streets of Eagle Mountain, waving to people she passed and keeping an eye out for her sister and the mysterious Henry. She pulled into Mrs. Simmons's driveway, wondering if her sister had arrived ahead of her. She hoped Henry hadn't already left. Knowing Mrs. Simmons, she would have invited him in.

The sitter met Jamie on the front porch. "I was getting ready to call you," she said, before Jamie could speak. "Donna isn't here. It's not like her to be so late.'

Jamie tried to push back the fear that climbed in her throat and the painful drumming of her heart. "She left the store at three," she said. "And I didn't see her on the drive over. Maybe I misunderstood where she was going." She squeezed Mrs. Simmons's clasped hands. "I'll go back to the store and talk to them again. Call me right away if she shows up."

Mrs. Simmons nodded, her face creased with worry.

Before heading to the store, Jamie stopped at her house. Donna was always going on about wanting to stay by herself. Maybe when she said she was going home, she meant exactly that, and she had brought Henry here to the house.

But the house was locked up tight, and only the dogs responded to Jamie's calls.

Back at the store, Jamie had to hunt up Veronique in the bakery, where she was accepting an order from a vendor. "Are you sure Donna and Henry said they were headed home?" she asked.

"Yes." Veronique looked up from her clipboard. "I spoke to him myself when he was punching out."

"Maybe he meant his home. Can you give me his parents' number?"

Veronique's brow furrowed. "We're not supposed to give out personal information about our employees."

"I'm a sheriff's deputy. And I'm trying to make sure my sister is safe." Jamie couldn't rein in her impatience.

"Oh, uh, okay."

Jamie followed the woman to the front office, and a few moments later was dialing the number for Mrs. O'Keefe. While she listened to the phone ring, she thought about the approach she should take with these people. She didn't want to send them into a panic. "Hello?" a woman answered.

"Hello, Mrs. O'Keefe?"

"Yes."

"This is Jamie Douglas. I'm Donna Douglas's sister. She works with your son, Henry, at the grocery store."

"Oh, yes," the woman's voice softened. "We've met Donna before." She chuckled. "Henry is quite taken with her.'

"Have you seen Henry, or talked to him, since he got off work at three?"

"No. He mentioned this morning that he was going to walk Donna to the house where she stays every afternoon while you work. It's only a few blocks, and we do like to encourage Henry to be as independent as possible. He's really very responsible."

Jamie took a deep breath. She hated worrying this

woman, who sounded very nice. But in Mrs. O'Keefe's position, she would want to know. "Donna and Henry never showed up at the sitter's," she said. "I'm trying to find them now."

"Oh, no! That doesn't sound like Henry at all." Her voice broke. "You don't think this horrible killer has decided to go after them, do you?"

"I'm sure that's not it," Jamie said, as much to reassure herself as to allay Mrs. O'Keefe's fears. "They probably decided to stop off at a restaurant or something. Donna mentioned this morning that she and Henry wanted to go on a date."

"Yes. Yes, that sounds reasonable." Mrs. O'Keefe was clearly trying to keep it together.

"I'm a sheriff's deputy," Jamie said. "We'll start looking for them right away. I'll call you as soon as I know anything."

"Please do. This is so unlike Henry. He's such a good boy. Well, he's a man now, of course, but he'll always be my boy."

"I understand." Jamie sometimes had to remind herself that, while Donna would always be her little sister, she was a grown woman.

"Is everything all right?" Veronique asked when Jamie ended the call.

"I'm sure they're fine," Jamie said. "I'm going to look for them."

She checked the most likely spots first—the Cakewalk Café, Peggy's Pizza and Kate's—but no one had seen Donna or Henry, together or alone. As Jamie cruised down Eagle Mountain's main drag, she scanned the sidewalks and shops for any sign of the two young people.

Tense with worry, she headed for the sheriff's department. She hated to involve the department in her family's business, but she needed her fellow officers' help in tracking down Donna and Henry before they got into trouble. Anyone could take advantage of two such trusting souls.

She parked on the street and entered through the front door. If Travis wasn't in his office, Adelaide would know where to find him.

But when Jamie approached Adelaide's desk, she discovered the office manager wasn't alone. "Hey, Jamie!" Donna stood and hurried around Adelaide's desk to hug her sister.

Jamie hugged her back and had to wait a few seconds before she felt safe speaking. "What are you doing here?" she asked Donna.

"I'm waiting for Henry," Donna said, as if this explained everything.

"Donna's friend is giving a statement to the sheriff," Adelaide said.

"A statement about what?"

"I don't know," Adelaide said. "Nate brought him in."

"Nate Hall?" How was Nate involved in any of this?

"He gave us a ride in his truck," Donna said. "He has a set of deer antlers and a shotgun in it."

"I don't understand," Jamie said. "Did something happen?" She addressed her sister. "Did someone try to hurt you and Henry while you were walking home?"

Donna looked puzzled. "No. We came here with Nate, in his truck."

"I'm sure he'll be finished in a few minutes," Adelaide said. "Then you can ask the sheriff what this is about."

Not knowing what else to do, Jamie sat, only half paying attention to the conversation Donna and Adelaide were having about the masquerade ball on Friday. After about five minutes, the door to the sheriff's office opened and Nate emerged with a stocky young man who wore black framed glasses. The young man—Henry—grinned as Donna rushed to meet him. "I still need to walk you home," he said.

"Hello, Henry. I'm Donna's sister, Jamie." Jamie offered her hand and Henry solemnly shook it.

"Nice to meet you," he said.

Jamie looked past him to address Nate, who supported himself with crutches. "What are Henry and my sister doing here at the sheriff's department?"

"Henry was friends with Michaela Underwood," Nate said. "He saw her in the store the day before she died, with a man he thought was her boyfriend."

"Al," Jamie said. The man who might have been her killer.

"He gave us a very good description of the man," Nate said. "He's been a big help to us."

"I need to walk Donna home now," Henry said.

"I'll drive Donna home," Jamie said. "And I need to call your mother, Henry. When you didn't come home, she was worried. The way Mrs. Simmons and I were worried about Donna when she didn't show up on time." She glared at Nate as she said the last words. He had the grace to look chagrined.

"I'll give you a ride to your place, Henry," Nate said. "After we call your mom."

Jamie already had her phone out and was dialing the O'Keefes' number. Mrs. O'Keefe answered after the first ring. "Henry is fine," Jamie said. "He and Donna are here at the sheriff's department. Everything is all right. They're not in trouble. Henry was able to give some evidence in a case we're working on. An officer is going to bring him home… Of course, if you would rather. I understand." She chatted with Mrs. O'Keefe for another minute and then ended the call. "Your mother is coming to get you," she told Henry.

"I'll wait with him, if you want to go," Nate said.

"No, I do not want to go." Jamie took Nate's arm and tugged him toward the hallway. Reluctantly, he hobbled after her.

She led the way into the empty conference room and shut the door behind him. He held up his hand to stop her speaking. "Before you lay into me, I realize I screwed up," he said. "I should have let you know what was going on and that your sister was safe. I didn't mean to worry you."

"You didn't mean to worry me? There is a killer out there who preys on women. My sister would be an easy target. I wasn't worried—I was petrified."

"I get that, and I'm sorry." He took her hand, his thumb tracing the contours of her knuckles, the touch reassuring—and unsettling. "I'm really sorry. I promise not to do that to you again."

She wanted to continue to rage at him but feared that if she opened her mouth again, she'd start crying. She forced back the tears and pulled her hand away from his. "How did you find out Henry knew Michaela?" she asked.

"I was buying groceries and we got to talking. He saw my uniform and asked if I knew about the murders—then he told me he had seen Michaela the day before she died, with a man he hadn't seen her with before."

"Then how did my sister get involved?"

"When I showed up at three to pick up Henry and bring him here to make his statement, Donna was with him. He said she needed to come with him and I didn't see any harm in it." He grimaced. "I should have realized you'd be worried."

"I know. And really, Donna should have called me herself. She knows she's supposed to."

"Am I forgiven?" he asked.

His contrite tone almost made her laugh. The tension of the afternoon had her emotions ricocheting all over the place. "I'll think about it," she said, moving past him.

Henry and Donna waited where Nate and Jamie had left them, seated in chairs by the door, holding hands. "I want to take Donna to the party Friday night," Henry said, standing as Nate and Jamie approached.

"We're supposed to wear costumes," Donna said, bouncing on her toes with excitement.

Jamie opened her mouth to say no. Donna needed to stay home, where she would be safe. But she couldn't keep her sister a prisoner. And Jamie had planned to attend the masquerade party anyway. "All right," she said.

Donna looked to Henry, who nodded. "Good," he said.

Jamie took her sister's hand. "Come on. I'll take you to Mrs. Simmons's," she said.

"See you tomorrow," Henry said. He stopped and blew Donna a kiss. She returned the gesture, blushing and giggling. Jamie couldn't help smiling. Veronique was right—Donna and Henry made a cute couple. She was happy Donna had found a friend, but her heart ached at the knowledge that no matter how hard she tried, she could never protect her sister from all the ways the world could hurt her.

NATE HAD JUST settled onto the sofa, feet up, a cup of cocoa in one hand, a suspense novel in the other, when someone rapped on his door. "Who is it?" he called. He could count on the fingers of one hand the number of people who had stopped by for a visit since he had moved in four months ago.

"It's Travis."

Intrigued, Nate levered himself to his feet and clomped

to the door with the aid of one crutch. He unlocked it and opened it to admit the sheriff. "I wanted to see how you're doing and check if you needed anything," Travis said.

"Thanks, but I'm okay." Nate dropped back onto the sofa. He doubted the sheriff had really come over to check on him. Travis had something on his mind. Even back in college, when they had roomed together, Travis had a tendency to brood. "Have a seat," Nate said.

Travis sat, elbows on his knees, hands clasped in front of his mouth, saying nothing.

"How are the wedding preparations going?" Nate asked. "It won't be long now."

"They're going okay. Lacy is a little anxious about the weather. Some of the guests won't be able to attend if the road doesn't open."

"You won't be able to get away for your honeymoon, either," Nate said.

"I'm not going anywhere until this killer is caught. Lacy knows that."

"You never were one to leave a job unfinished. What's the latest?"

"We can't get a police artist to come here, because of the road closures, but I've arranged for one to Skype with Henry O'Keefe. I'm hoping we can get an image we can publish in the paper and distribute around town. Someone knows this guy."

"He may not be the killer."

"Maybe not. But he might have seen something that morning that could help us find the killer." He sat up straight. "He's going to strike again, I'm sure."

"What about the plan to have Jamie drive around, trying to attract the killer's attention?" Nate didn't like the idea, but it wasn't his decision to make.

"We're going to do that tonight," Travis said. "I put it

off one night after we got the description from Henry. I
wanted to see if that led to anyone obvious. It didn't, but
maybe we'll have better luck with the drawing. Meanwhile,
Dwight is going out with Jamie tonight. Gage and I will
be on duty nearby, ready to close in."

"Jamie is pretty new to the force, isn't she?"

"She's been with us almost a year. She's been a good
addition to the department."

"I knew her growing up," Nate said. "I never would
have dreamed she'd go into law enforcement. It's not anything she ever talked about." Whereas he had decided to
aim for a job with Parks and Wildlife when he was still
in his teens. The idea of being able to study wildlife and
actively protect it, while also helping to educate the public, had appealed to him, as had the freedom to spend lots
of time outdoors.

"She's hardworking and good with people," Travis said.
"She's smart. And we're working to diversify the force to
better reflect the population we serve. We're hoping to re-
cruit more women like her."

"She seems to really like the work. But are you sure
she's up for this decoy exercise tonight? This killer—or
killers—has made a habit of killing women very quickly."
His stomach clenched as he spoke.

Travis's gaze met Nate's, unwavering. "I wouldn't ask
Jamie to do this if I didn't believe she could handle it," he
said. "So, what's going on between you two?"

Nate looked away. "Nothing is going on between us."

"I thought I sensed some…tension."

Nate laughed. "Oh, there's tension all right. She can't
stand me."

"And why is that?"

He blew out a breath. Travis wasn't the type to press
if Nate told him to mind his own business, but maybe

getting his levelheaded friend's perspective would help. "Jamie and I dated during high school," he said. "We were really close. I guess you could say we were each other's first love. But then it was time to go to college and I was going away. I didn't think it was fair to ask her to wait for me, so I broke things off with her. I thought we could still be friends, but she didn't see it that way." His shoulders sagged. "I guess you could say things ended badly. Apparently, she's never forgiven me. Maybe because I wasn't around to support her after her parents died."

"It takes a lot of energy to hold on to anger that long," Travis said. "It makes me think there's more than animosity behind it."

"Think that if you like, but she's made it clear she doesn't want to have anything to do with me."

Travis's phone rang and he answered. He listened for a moment, frowning, then stood. "I'm on my way." He pocketed his phone again. "That was Adelaide," he said. "The Ice Cold Killer has struck again—only this time, the woman got away."

Chapter Nine

"You're going to be all right, Tammy. You're safe now." Jamie handed the distraught young woman a cup of water, then sat next to her, pulling the chair close. Tammy Patterson, reporter for the *Eagle Mountain Examiner*, had stumbled into the sheriff's department ten minutes before, her clothes torn, her face bloodied, tears running down her cheeks. She had sobbed incoherently, something about the Ice Cold Killer coming after her. "You're safe now," Jamie murmured again and pressed a cold compress to the swelling on the side of Tammy's face.

"The sheriff is on his way," Dwight Prentice said from the doorway of the conference room. "The paramedics are coming, too."

Jamie nodded. It wouldn't hurt to have Tammy's bruises checked. "Drink some water," she urged. "When the sheriff gets here, we'll need you to tell us what happened, but remember, you're safe and you're with friends."

Tammy nodded and drank. Her hands didn't shake as badly now, and the flow of tears had subsided.

Dwight glanced over this shoulder. "Sheriff's here." A moment later, Travis entered.

"Hello, Tammy," he said. "I understand you've had a frightening time of it."

She drew in a deep, shuddering breath. "I was terrified. But I'm alive and safe now—that's what counts."

Travis pulled up a chair across from Tammy. "You may be able to help us catch this guy and stop him from hurting other women. So I need you to tell me everything you can remember about what happened—even if the detail seems too small to be important. Can you do that?"

She nodded, licked her lips and began speaking, hesitantly at first, then with more assurance. "I was out on County Road Two. Colorado Parks and Wildlife is going to start putting out food for the deer and elk who have been stressed by all this snow, and they have a staging area out there for the supplies and volunteers. I went out there to get photos for the paper."

She took a sip of water, then continued. "I was on my way back to town, maybe three miles from the staging area. It had started snowing, and visibility wasn't that good. Then all of a sudden, I saw a woman standing on the side of the road. She was waving her arms. I had to stop. I pulled over to the shoulder and she ran up to the passenger side of the car. I rolled down the window and she told me she had had a fight with her boyfriend, who was drunk. She needed to get to town—or at least to borrow a phone so she could call a friend to come get her. Of course I said I'd help her. She was so distressed—clearly, she had been crying, and her hair was all down in her eyes, and she sounded almost hysterical. I unlocked the car and leaned over to clear stuff off the passenger seat so she could get in."

She closed her eyes and a shudder went through her. "All of a sudden, the driver's-side door opened and someone grabbed me and started hauling me out of the car. I screamed and started trying to fight him off. I thought at first it was the woman's boyfriend, angry because I was getting involved. But then the woman came around to the side of the road. While he held my arms, she grabbed at my legs and started trying to wrap them with duct tape."

"The woman was helping him?" Jamie asked.

Tammy's eyes met hers. "Looking back now, I don't think it really was a woman," she said. "This person was really strong."

"Do you think it was a man, dressed up like a woman?" Travis asked.

"Maybe," Tammy said. "She was tall for a woman, and she had lots of blond hair, all falling in front of her face. She never really looked directly at me. I think the hair might have been a wig. And like I said, she was so strong."

Travis nodded. "All right. Tell us about the other man. The one who grabbed you."

Tammy shook her head. "There's not much to tell. He was behind me most of the time. I only saw him for a few seconds, from the side. He was dressed all in black, with a ski mask pulled down over his head."

"How tall do you think he was?" Travis asked. "How much taller than you?"

"He was taller than me—most men are. But he wasn't really tall, so I'd say, maybe five-ten. But the ground was really uneven there, and he was behind me, so he might have been six feet tall, just standing on lower ground."

"What about build?" Travis asked. "Was he stocky, or really muscular?"

She shook her head. "No, he was just, you know, average. I wish now I had paid more attention, but I was so scared. I was sure he was going to kill me."

"You got away," Jamie reminded her. "You're safe."

"What did you do?" Travis asked. "How did you get away?"

"I fought so hard. When he grabbed me, I had picked up

my notebook off the passenger seat so the woman could get in. It had a pen clipped to it. I grabbed the pen and stabbed at him—at his hands, his face. And I kicked at the woman. She dropped the duct tape and it rolled into the dirt." Tammy's eyes widened. "I remember now—she swore, and her voice was different—deeper. A man's voice."

"Did he say a name, or address the other man in any way?" Travis asked.

Tammy closed her eyes. Jamie imagined her putting herself back in that place. "No. They didn't say anything to each other. The man in the ski mask was angry that I fought, and he hit me—hard." She put a hand to her bruised face. "But I was so terrified. I knew if I didn't get away from them, I would die. So I did everything I could think of. I kept stabbing with the pen, and I spat at him and tried to bite him. When he dragged me from the car, I hooked one foot onto the bottom of the seat. It threw him off balance. The side of the road is really rough over there, and there's a lot of snow. He slid down into the ditch, away from me. I got up and crawled back into the car and slammed the door. The engine was still running, so I just floored it. I almost ran over the woman.

"I don't even remember getting here. I just drove, as fast as I could. I kept looking in the mirror, to see if they followed me, but they didn't."

"Where were you, exactly, when this happened?" Travis asked.

"On County Road Two. There's that little neighborhood of houses in there, then a stretch of woods, then a big curve. This was right after the big curve."

"You want me to go out and take a look?" Dwight spoke from the doorway.

"Take Gage with you. Find the scene and cordon it off. Do a search, then hit the houses around there. Talk to everyone you can. Find out if they know anything. Or saw or heard anything"

"That's only a few miles from where Michaela's body was found," Jamie said. "The killers might live in one of those houses."

"I want to go out there tonight, see if we can draw them out." Travis said. He turned to Jamie. "If you're still up for it, Deputy."

"I am."

"I'll call Gage," Dwight said, and left them as two paramedics entered. Travis and Jamie moved away to let them check out Tammy.

"You don't have to do this decoy op if you're uncomfortable with it," Travis told Jamie. "There's no doubt these two are dangerous."

"I want to, sir," she said. "This may be our best chance to catch them. They'll be frustrated that Tammy got away."

"I agree." He clapped her on the shoulder. "Go home now and change."

"Yes, sir." She glanced at Tammy. "What about her?"

"She lives with her parents here in town. I'll call them in a minute and they can come pick her up. She should be safe there, but I'll put a reserve deputy on the house tonight, just in case. Be back here at seven o'clock."

"Yes, sir." She hurried from the room, buzzing with excitement. She might be able to catch these killers—tonight.

"YOU'RE BEING AN IDIOT," Nate mumbled to himself as he grabbed his crutches and swung out of the cab of his truck. He had just pulled into Jamie's driveway. It was six thirty at night. Her car was in the driveway, and most of the windows of the house were lit up, so he was pretty sure she was home. She'd probably be furious to see him. He should leave her alone. But, knowing she was going out there tonight, possibly to face a serial killer—or more than one serial killer—he couldn't stay away.

He positioned the crutches under his arms and paused a moment to look up at the house. The place didn't look that much different than it had when he was in high school, at least in the dark. The same stone lions sat on either side of the steps leading up to the wide front porch, and the same wooden swing hung from the porch rafters. He and Jamie had spent many hours on that swing, sometimes making out, but mostly talking, about everything. He hadn't been able to talk to anyone like that since. Maybe it was only as a teenager that a man could be comfortable baring his soul that way. Or maybe he could only do it with Jamie.

He clumped his way up the walk, navigated the steps, crossed the porch and rang the doorbell. It echoed loudly through the house. "I'll get it!" a voice shouted, followed by the thunder of running feet on a hardwood floor.

The door opened and Donna peeked out. "Hello," she said, then held the door open wider. "Come in."

Jamie appeared behind her sister. She caught the door and held it. "What are you doing here?" she asked.

"I just wanted to talk, okay? Please?"

Reluctantly, she let him in. "I don't have much time," she said as he moved past her. "I have to be at the sheriff's department at seven."

"I know what you're going to do tonight," he said.

"I'm going to do my job."

"You're sure dressed up for work," Donna said.

Nate let his gaze slide over the short blue dress, with its low-cut neckline and full, swirly skirt. It was made of some soft fabric that hugged her curves, and the skirt stopped several inches above the tops of the tall black boots she wore. A sudden pull of attraction caught him off guard.

"Donna, I left my purse upstairs," Jamie said. "Could you get it for me, please?"

When Donna had left them, Jamie turned back to Nate. "Why are you staring at me that way?"

"Is that what you're wearing tonight?" he asked.

"Yes.'

"You'll have on a coat, right?"

"My car has a heater. I don't want these two to have any doubt that I'm a young woman."

Yeah, there was no doubt of that. "You should wear a vest," he said.

Her eyebrows rose. "You mean a tactical vest?"

"Yes."

"These two use a knife," she said. "They don't shoot people. And they slit throats. A tactical vest wouldn't be any help at all."

"You don't know they don't have a gun."

"They didn't use it on Tammy today. If they had one, you'd think they would have."

"Tammy? Is that the woman who got away from the killer? Travis got the call while he was at my house."

"Killers. There are two of them."

"What happened this afternoon?" he asked. "You can tell me—I'm part of the team and I'm going to hear about it in the briefing tomorrow morning anyway."

She crossed her arms over her chest. She probably didn't realize how much it enhanced her cleavage. Nate shifted, hoping she didn't notice the effect she was having on him. "Aren't you on medical leave?" she asked.

"From my Parks and Wildlife job—not from the team that's hunting this killer. I can sort data and do research with one foot in a cast. So what happened to Tammy? And Tammy who?"

Jamie glanced up the stairs, then lowered her voice.

"Tammy Patterson—the reporter for the paper? She stopped to help a woman who flagged her down. Only it wasn't a woman—it was a man in a wig. A second man came out of the woods and grabbed Tammy and he and the one dressed like a woman tried to wrap her up in duct tape. Tammy fought like a wildcat and managed to get away."

"She was lucky."

"Yes. And she may be our lucky break. I'm really hoping we catch these two tonight." She took a step back. "You still haven't told me why you're here."

"I just—" He shoved his hands in his pockets. He'd feel better if he could pace, but that was impossible on crutches. "I just wanted to tell you to be careful." He couldn't believe how lame he sounded, but he hadn't thought this out very well—he had just gotten in his truck and started to drive, and ended up here.

"I'm not an idiot," she said.

"I know that. But neither are these killers."

"Why do you care, anyway?" she asked.

"Because I do." Their eyes met and the heat in her gaze rocked him back. Jamie might *say* she couldn't stand him, but that was not what it felt like right now. He leaned toward her. Another half second and he would have to kiss her. She looked like she wanted to kiss him back. He just needed to be a little closer...

"Here's your purse. It wasn't upstairs, it was on the kitchen table." Donna came into the room, the purse dangling from her wrist. Jamie looked away and Nate suppressed a groan of disappointment. "Are you going to stay with me while Jamie goes out?" Donna asked.

"Nate isn't going to stay with you," Jamie said. "You're going to Mrs. Simmons's."

"I could stay with her," Nate said. "I don't mind." And

he'd be here when Jamie got home, to make sure she was all right.

"Yay!" Donna clapped her hands. "Do you like to play cards? We can play cards."

"Donna, I don't think—" Jamie began.

"Really, I don't mind," Nate said. "Let me stay."

"Pleeeease!" Donna put her hands together as if praying. "I don't want to go to Mrs. Simmons's all the time. I want to stay here."

Jamie blew out a breath. "Okay." She frowned at Nate. "I guess I will feel better, knowing she's with you."

"She'll be safe with me," Nate said. If he couldn't look after Jamie, at least he could look after her sister.

"This feels really weird," Jamie said, as she drove slowly along County Road Two, constantly scanning the side of the road for any sign of life. The afternoon's snow had stopped, and the plows had left fresh drifts on the roadside that reflected back the glow from her headlights.

"Imagine how I feel." Dwight Prentice spoke from his position on the floorboard of the back seat.

Jamie grimaced, remembering the awkward contortions required for the six-foot-three deputy to hide in her car. "We're passing that neighborhood Tammy mentioned," she said.

"The place where she pulled over is around the next big curve," Dwight said. "By the time we got there, the new snow had almost covered the area. By now the plows will have wiped out everything—not that there was anything to find. We didn't see so much as a hair or a button."

Jamie cruised slowly past the spot, where yellow crime scene tape fluttered from roadside brush. "We haven't even passed another car in ten minutes," she said.

"When you can find a place to turn around, go ahead

Cindi Myers 99

and do so," Dwight said. "We'll make one more pass past that neighborhood. Pretend you're looking for an address. If you don't attract any attention after that, we'll call it a night."

"Maybe Tammy getting away scared them off," Jamie said, as she pulled over onto the shoulder and prepared to turn around.

"They can't have gone far," Dwight said. "The highway out of town is still closed."

She swung the car around, then gasped and slammed on the brakes as her headlights lit up the figure of a man on the side of the road. He put up one hand to shield his eyes, then hunched over and turned back toward the woods. Jamie shoved open the door and bailed out of the car, her Glock already drawn. "Stop, police!"

Jamie heard Dwight move in behind her. The man, who wore a fur cap with earflaps and sported a full beard, dropped two items and raised his hands over his head. "Don't shoot," he pleaded.

"Get on your knees," Dwight ordered. "Hands behind your head."

The man did as asked and Dwight moved in closer, Jamie behind him. She nudged at the rifle the man had dropped and what she now recognized as a hand-held spotlight. The first rush of adrenaline was fading, leaving behind a sinking feeling. "Who are you, and what are you doing out here in the middle of the night?" he asked.

"It's only nine o'clock," he said.

"What's your name?" she asked.

The man—who up close looked to be at least seventy—looked away and didn't answer.

Dwight rummaged in the man's pocket and pulled out a wallet. He flipped it open and read. "Mitch Oliphant."

He looked at the man. "What were you doing out here, Mr. Oliphant?"

Again, no answer.

Jamie nudged the spotlight with her toe. "It looks to me like you were spotlighting deer," she said. "Which is against the law."

"You ain't no game warden," Oliphant said.

No. The local game warden was currently at Jamie's house, babysitting her sister.

"In fact, how do I know you're even a cop?" Oliphant continued. "You sure ain't dressed like one." He leered and she suppressed the urge to tug on her short skirt.

"We can still enforce the law," she said. "How long have you been out here tonight?"

"There's no law against being out at night. I was taking a walk."

"With your rifle and a spotlight?" Dwight asked.

"I couldn't find my flashlight. And a man's got a right to defend himself, with that crazy killer running around."

"What do you know about the killer?" Jamie asked.

Oliphant glared at her. "Nothing."

"Have you seen anyone else while you were taking your walk?" Jamie asked. "Anyone at all?"

"No. Can I get up now? Being down on the ground like this hurts my knees."

Jamie and Dwight exchanged glances. "You can get up," Jamie said. "Slowly."

"At my age, that's the only speed I got." Grunting, Oliphant rose to his feet. "Are you gonna keep me standing out here in the cold all night?" he asked.

"Where do you live?" Dwight asked.

"The address is on my license." Oliphant stared at Dwight, who didn't back down. Jamie focused on the two, trying to ignore her freezing feet and wishing she had thought to get her coat from the car. "I live out on Fish Camp Road," Oliphant finally said.

Jamie gaped. That had to be at least eight miles from where they were standing. "Did you walk all the way from there?"

"No. My truck is parked up the road about a quarter mile." He jerked his head toward town.

"We'll let you go if you promise to go home and stay there," Dwight said. "Don't be out here at night where you don't have any business."

Oliphant muttered something to the effect that it was a free country and turned away, but Jamie called after him. "Mr. Oliphant?"

He glanced back at her. "What?"

"Do you come out here often? Walking?"

"What's it to you?"

"You might be able to help us. We're looking for a woman—a tall blonde. A couple of people have seen her out here, walking along the road. She told one woman who stopped to help her that she had a boyfriend who beats her. We want to make sure she's all right." It was close enough to the truth.

The lines between Oliphant's brows deepened. "I think I saw her, once. But when she saw me, she took off—right into the woods, like a scared rabbit."

"Did you get a good look at her?" Dwight asked. "Do you think you'd recognize her again?"

The old man shook his head. "I only saw her for a few seconds. She was tall and thin, with a lot of blond hair, all hanging down in her face."

"Where were you when you saw her?" Jamie asked.

He looked around them. "I don't know. Somewhere around here. I can't remember."

"When did you see her?" Dwight asked.

"A week ago? Maybe more." He shrugged. "It was just a few seconds. I didn't mark it on my calendar or anything."

Jamie glanced at Dwight. He shook his head slightly, indicating he didn't have anything to add. "All right, Mr. Oliphant, you can go," Jamie said. "If we have any more questions, we'll be in touch."

He picked up his rifle and the spotlight, then shuffled away, down the shoulder of the road. Jamie got back into the car and turned the heat up to high. Dwight slid into the passenger seat. "What do you make of his story about the blonde?" he asked, as she turned onto the highway and headed for town.

"It sounds like these two troll for women pretty regularly," she said. "The guy dressed up in the wig is the bait to get the women to stop, then his friend comes out of the woods. Together, they subdue and kill the women." She shuddered. "Creepy."

"Travis is going to get a police artist with Tammy and see if we can get a portrait we can circulate," Dwight said.

"He probably only wears the disguise when they're out hunting," Jamie said.

"Maybe the artist can give us an idea of what the guy looks like without a wig."

"Maybe." She yawned. "I hate that we didn't lure them out tonight."

"You didn't hesitate when we saw Oliphant," Dwight said. "That was good."

"I knew you had my back."

She drove to the sheriff's department, where she and Dwight made their report to the sheriff, then she headed for home. It was all she could do to stay awake for the drive. The tension of the day had drained her. As she pulled into the driveway, she saw that someone had left the porch light on for her. The door opened while she was still standing on the porch, fumbling for her keys, and she walked in— right into Nate's arms.

Chapter Ten

The strength of Nate's embrace felt so familiar—so right. Jamie closed her eyes and rested her head on his shoulder, breathing in the clean, masculine scent of him, feeling as if she could let go completely, and he would continue to hold her up. "Tough night?" he asked after a moment, his voice low, his warm breath stirring her hair.

She lifted her head and looked up at him. "We didn't see the killers," she said. "We stopped and questioned an old man. I think he was spotlighting deer, but we couldn't prove it, so we had to let him go."

"Who was it?" Nate asked.

"Mitch Oliphant."

He nodded. "I know Mitch. And yeah, he was probably spotlighting deer." He frowned. "Did he do something to upset you?"

"No. I'm just tired. Seeing Tammy this afternoon and then going out there tonight—it's a lot to take in."

"You've had to be strong for a long time." He smoothed his hand down her arm. "You've carried a lot of weight on your shoulders for the past few years. I'm sorry I wasn't there for you then. But I'm here for you now."

His words—and the meaning behind them—were more seductive than any sexy love-words. She prided herself on standing on her own two feet, but sometimes—times like tonight—it was so hard. To be able to lean on someone else, just for a little while, was a luxury she craved the way some people wanted sex or money. She stared into his eyes, trying to figure out the catch to his words—to figure out what he expected from her in exchange for his help. But she saw nothing but tenderness, and allowed herself to let down her guard just a little.

Just long enough for one kiss. She closed her eyes as his lips met hers, letting her body soften and mold to his. They kissed as if they had been apart only a few hours instead of seven years. She tilted her head to deepen the kiss and he tasted both familiar and new. She had missed this—this closeness, this communicating without words, this swell of desire and need and the promise of fulfillment. She had been here before with him, and yet she wasn't kissing a boy this time but a man, with a man's power and knowledge and patience. The thought thrilled her and had her wondering if they could sneak upstairs to her bedroom without Donna hearing them.

She eased back slightly and opened her eyes. He was smiling—a look filled with triumph. That gleam of victory set her back on her heels. She shoved away from him and raked a hand through her hair, trying to think. "Hey." He reached for her. "It's okay."

"No, it is not okay," she said. Her heart hammered and her buzzing nerves left her feeling shaky and off-balance. "This is a mistake. A big mistake."

"YOU'VE GOT TO give me something to do." The next morning, Nate leaned on one crutch in front of the sheriff's desk and pleaded with Travis. "I'm going nuts sitting at the house staring at the walls." With nothing else to occupy his mind, he kept replaying that kiss with Jamie. He'd finally broken through the wall she had erected between

them, and she'd let him know she still cared for him—
and the next thing he knew, she'd been shoving him out
the door, muttering that she "couldn't do this," deaf to his
pleas for an explanation.

Travis shifted his gaze to the dark blue Aircast that
encased Nate's left ankle. "How long are you off duty?"
he asked.

"Until the doctor clears me to return. He says that could
be as long as six weeks, but I'm going to be back before
then."

Sure you are. Travis had the grace not to say the words
out loud, but Nate could read his friend well enough.
"Look," he said. "My ankle is busted, not my brain.
Haven't you got data that needs crunching, or investigation notes that need reviewing? You need help, don't you?"

"Yes." Travis shoved back his chair and stood. He motioned for Nate to follow him and led the way to a room
that was apparently dedicated to the investigation. Photographs of the victims and their crime scenes filled the
walls, two long tables contained tagged evidence, and another table held a computer terminal and stacks of paperwork.

Jamie looked up from her seat at this table. Her face
paled, then reddened as she stared at Nate. With her cheeks
flushed and several tendrils of hair escaping from the knot
at the base of her neck, she struck Nate as incredibly de-
sirable—a thought he immediately shoved to the back of
his mind. "Nate's going to help you with that witness database," Travis said, then left them.

The sound of the door closing behind Travis echoed in
the still room. The plastic chair Nate grabbed from a row
against the wall protested loudly as he dragged it to the
table. He sat opposite Jamie, who focused on the computer screen. He waited, deciding he'd let her speak first.

"I'm compiling a database of every witness we've in-terviewed so far," she said after a long, uncomfortable moment. "We need to review their statements, look for similarities, or anything that stands out, and decide if we want to interview them again. You can start reading over their statements while I input the data." She nodded to the stack of file folders at her elbow.

"All right." He took a couple of inches of folders off the top of the pile and placed them in front of him but didn't open one, his eyes steady on her.

After another long moment, she looked over at him. "What?" she asked.

"We need to clear the air between us," he said.

She looked back at the computer, though her hands re-mained motionless on the keyboard. "I don't know what you're talking about."

"Yes, you do. Ever since I came back to town, you've been giving me the cold shoulder."

She started to shake her head, but he continued. He hadn't really planned to say all this, but now that he was talking, it felt good to get his feelings out in the open. "I get that you were hurt when I broke things off when I went to college," he said. "I'm sorry about that. I really am. But that was seven years ago. We're both adults now. I can't believe you're still holding a stupid thing I did back then over my head."

"I'm not!" She put both hands to her head, as if she wanted to yank out her hair, then lowered them to the table, fists clenched. Her eyes met his and he saw again the pain there, and felt the corresponding ache in his own chest. "You think because we were…involved before, we can be again," she said. "And that's not going to happen."

"You say that—but when you kissed me last night, I wasn't getting that message at all."

Now she looked as if she wanted to throw something at him. He prepared to duck. She glanced toward the door, as if to reassure herself they were still alone. She shifted her gaze back to him. "That kiss last night wasn't about any emotional attachment," she said. "You want me to admit I'm attracted to you—all right, I will. I'm sure that makes you very happy. But you were right when you said we're both adults now. I'm mature enough to know that a relationship between the two of us would be a bad idea."

"Why do you say that?" He leaned across the table toward her, his hands inches from hers, though not touching. "I was serious when I said I care about you," he said. "There was a time when you were the best friend I had. You probably know me better than most people. Why would it be so horrible if we got together?"

"It might be wonderful, for a while." She sounded wistful. "But it wouldn't last. There's no point putting myself through all that."

How do you know it won't last? he started to ask, but couldn't get the words out. Because really, she was right. He had dated at least a dozen women since he had moved away. None seriously. And he wasn't looking for serious with her. At least he didn't think so. She really did know him better than anyone else, didn't she?

He slid his hands away and sat back. "Then we don't have to be lovers," he said. "If I agree to respect that boundary, can we at least be friends? Can we work as a team on this case without this—this coldness between us?"

She hesitated, then looked him in the eye. "Yes. We can do that."

He was a little embarrassed at how much he wanted to whoop and celebrate over such a simple thing. He settled for nodding and opened the file folder on the top of his pile. "All right," he said. "Glad we got that settled. Let's get to work."

JAMIE WAS SURPRISED to find she missed Nate after he left at two for a doctor's appointment. After their awkward—but she could admit now, probably necessary—conversation, they had settled into an efficient and, yes, friendly, work pattern. She was reminded of how smart he was—organized and quick to winnow out nonessential information and grasp patterns, traits that probably helped him with wildlife research. She couldn't help but be reminded of all those afternoons they had spent studying together—he coaching her through chemistry and advanced algebra, she helping him with English and history. They each brought different strengths to the table, and it was the same this afternoon. With his help, she was able to get every witness into the database, and had almost completed summarizing what each one had to say by the time she clocked out at six. Tomorrow she'd finish up and begin indexing by keyword, and focus on people they needed to interview again.

Donna also worked until six today, so Jamie swung by the grocery store and picked her up. She was waiting out front with Henry, the two holding hands. Jamie smiled in spite of herself. They really were a cute couple, and they looked so happy. There was something to be said for the naivety of first love—before you knew how much it hurt when things turned sour.

Nate hadn't even tried to deny that he wasn't interested in a long-term romance. At least he'd been honest, and he had confirmed her instinct to avoid falling for him again. They would keep things friendly but platonic.

If Jamie had thought Donna would distract her from thoughts of the handsome wildlife officer, her hope was in vain. "Did you see Nate today?" Donna asked as Jamie drove toward home.

Jamie tightened her hands on the steering wheel. "Why would I see Nate?" she asked.

"You work together, don't you?"

Not exactly. Of course, they had worked together today. "I saw Nate at work today," she said.

"He's cuuuute," Donna said, using one of her favorite descriptions. "I like him. Is he going to come over again soon?"

"I don't think so," Jamie said.

"Why not? You like him, don't you?"

"I like Nate as a friend."

Donna giggled. "I think you like him more than that."

"No. I do not."

"Then why did you kiss him last night? You don't kiss friends like that."

"Donna!" She glanced at her sister. "What were you doing watching us?"

"I heard you come in last night. I wanted to say goodnight. Then I saw you two kissing." She put a hand to her mouth, giggling again. "Is he a good kisser?"

Jamie groaned. She couldn't begin to explain her complicated feelings for Nate—and how much she regretted that kiss—to her sister. "You shouldn't spy on people," she said. "It isn't nice."

"Henry kissed me."

Jamie blinked and almost missed the turn into their driveway. At the last minute, she braked and steered the car up to the garage. She had talked to Donna about sex more than once over the years, and was confident her sister understood what was and wasn't appropriate behavior. But how much of a defense was that understanding when it came to overheated hormones? Jamie had all but thrown herself at Nate last night in a moment of weakness. She needed to know more about how Donna felt about this new relationship with Henry.

Jamie switched off the car, took a deep breath and

turned to her sister. "When did Henry kiss you?" she asked, sounding much calmer than she felt.

"In the break room last Friday. We had our break together, then he leaned over and kissed me on the cheek." She put a hand to her cheek, a dreamy look in her eyes. "He had really soft lips."

Jamie melted a little, from both relief and a rush of tenderness. "That's very sweet," she said. "Henry sounds like a real gentleman."

"He is," Donna said. "He said his mother told him he has to respect me."

Thank you, Mrs. O'Keefe, Jamie silently breathed. She opened her door. "Come on," she said. "Let's make dinner. How does ravioli sound?"

"Ravioli sounds great!" Donna jumped out of the car and raced up the walk, all thoughts of Nate and kissing gone.

Together, the sisters made dinner. Donna's job was to set the table and put ice in glasses, a job she did with minimal mess. When she dropped an ice cube, one of the dogs was happy to snatch it up and carry it off to chew. Over supper, Donna told Jamie about helping Mrs. Simmons fold laundry that morning, and a boy she had seen at the store who wore a knit cap made to look like a dinosaur. "I want a hat like that for Christmas," Donna declared.

They were doing dishes when the doorbell rang, sending the dogs into a barking frenzy, toenails scrabbling on the wood floors as they raced to hurl themselves at the intruder. Jamie shouted for them to quiet as she hurried to the front door, then peered out the sidelight at their visitor.

When she opened the door, Tammy Patterson gave her a faint smile. "Hi," she said. "Do you think I could talk to you for a minute?"

"Sure." Jamie's gaze shifted to the street, where a compact car idled, a man at the wheel.

"That's my brother," Tammy said. "He drove me over." She waved at him and he lifted his hand, then put the car in gear and drove away. "He'll pick me up when I call him."

"Come on in." Jamie held open the door. The dogs surged forward to inspect the new arrival, but Jamie shooed them away. Donna watched from the bottom of the stairs. "This is my sister, Donna," Jamie said. "Donna, this is my friend, Tammy."

"Hi, Donna," Tammy said.

"Hi." Donna nibbled her thumb. "Can I watch my show?" she asked.

"Sure. Tammy and I will talk in the kitchen."

Donna hurried off to the living room to insert the cartoon DVD she loved, while Jamie led the way to the kitchen. "Do you want some tea?" she asked, as she filled the kettle.

"Sure." Tammy sat at the table. "I hope you don't mind my coming by," she said. "I had some questions."

"Sure." Jamie put the kettle on, then took the chair opposite Tammy. The bruise on the reporter's cheek had turned a sickly yellow and purple, and there were gray shadows under her eyes. "What can I help you with?" Jamie asked.

"Do you know when I'll get my car back?" Tammy asked.

"I'm not sure. But I can check. You need your car for work, don't you?"

"My mom said I could borrow hers. I just wondered." She ran her thumb back and forth along the edge of the table. "Maybe it's better if I drive my mom's car for a while. The killers wouldn't recognize it."

"You're worried those two are going to come after you, aren't you?" Jamie asked.

Tammy raised her head, her expression bleak. "Shouldn't I be? I'm the only person who's seen them. Well, one of them. If they go ahead and finish the job they started, I won't be able to identify them."

Tammy had a legitimate concern. Under other circumstances, Jamie might have advised the reporter to take a vacation somewhere else until the killers were caught, but that wasn't possible with the roads closed. "I think the best thing you can do right now is to not go anywhere alone," Jamie said. "You were smart to have your brother drive you tonight."

"Yeah, well, that might make it tough to do my job. Of course, I haven't gone back to work yet, though I'll need to soon."

The teakettle whistled and Jamie got up and made the tea. As she poured the water, the smell of apples and cinnamon wafted up on the steam. She hoped the homey smell would help comfort Tammy.

"Do you have any leads in the case?" Tammy asked when Jamie joined her again. "I'm not asking as a reporter."

"You've given us our best lead so far," Jamie said. "But we haven't identified a suspect yet."

"The sheriff has set up a teleconference with a police artist tomorrow," Tammy said. She smoothed her hands down the thighs of her jeans. "I'm really nervous about getting it wrong. I mean, everything happened so fast."

"Police artists are used to working with nervous people," Jamie said. "He—or she—will help you provide the details they need. You probably remember more than you think."

"That's something else that worries me. I know you'll probably think I'm being stupid. I mean, of course I want to find out who is doing this and stop them from killing anyone else. But all along, I've told myself it had to be someone from outside—a stranger to Eagle Mountain who got trapped here by the weather and for whatever reason decided to go on a killing spree."

Jamie nodded. "I think that's a perfectly natural reaction. This seems like such a safe place."

"Right." She bit her lip and looked down at her lap.

"What is it?" Jamie leaned toward the other woman. "Do you know something—have you remembered something—about the killers that might help us catch them?"

Tammy shrugged. "It's nothing, really. Not anything helpful. It's just, well, ever since it happened, I can't shake the feeling that the man in that wig was someone I know. There was something familiar about him. I've tried and tried to think who it could be, but I can't even imagine. But I can't shake the idea that the killer really isn't a stranger. He's someone who lives here. Someone I might even be friends with."

Jamie nodded, an icy knot in the pit of her stomach. "It's always been a possibility—a probability, even. And it would be horrible to find out these two are people we all like, even admire. It's the kind of thing that makes you question your judgment about everyone."

Tammy sighed. "So you don't think I'm crazy?"

"Of course not."

"I promise, I'd tell you if I remembered anything definite," Tammy said.

"You may remember more when you talk to the artist," Jamie said. She pushed the tea toward Tammy. "Drink up."

Tammy took a long sip of tea, then set the cup down. "I already feel better, talking to you," she said. "Though I don't see how you do the job you do. I mean, I see enough nasty stuff as a reporter, but I only have to take pictures and report. I don't have to wade right into the awful, dangerous stuff or deal with truly horrible people."

"Most of the time the job isn't like that," Jamie said. "The work is interesting, and I believe it's important."

"Good for you." Tammy picked up her cup and smiled at Jamie over its rim. "When this is over, maybe I'll interview you for the paper."

"Why would you want to do that?"

"Eagle Mountain's first female deputy—that's newsworthy, don't you think?"

"Only if we were in the 1950s. I really don't want to call attention to myself."

"I'll keep asking, until you change your mind."

"Right. So what else can we talk about?"

Tammy laughed. "Fair enough. Are you going to the charity masquerade tomorrow night?"

Jamie had already forgotten about the party. "I promised I would. I have to figure out some kind of costume. Will you be there?"

"You bet. I'm even looking forward to it. I mean, if no one else can recognize me in my costume, that means the killers can't, either. I'm hoping I can relax and have a good time."

The two chatted about possible costumes and the weather forecast while they finished their tea, then Tammy phoned her brother. When he arrived, Jamie walked her to the door, but the gist of their conversation kept replaying in her mind. Jamie hadn't thought about the killers being at the party. But if they were locals, why wouldn't they attend and mingle?

And maybe even pick out their next victim.

Chapter Eleven

"Now you remember what I told you?" Jamie adjusted the cat ears atop Donna's head, then looked her sister in the eye. "Tell me."

"I'm to stay with Henry and his mom and not talk to strangers." Donna smoothed the end of the long tail attached to the back of her leggings. "But if everyone is in costume, how will I know if they're a stranger or not?"

Donna had a point. Jamie figured most people would recognize her and Donna, despite Donna's painted-on whiskers and pink nose, and the feathered mask Jamie had added to her own jester's getup. But if someone went all out with a full mask or a furry suit or something, identification might be difficult. "If you're not sure you know someone, ask their name," she said. "If they won't tell you, or you don't recognize the name, walk away. But the best thing is to stay with Henry and Mrs. O'Keefe." Henry's mom had volunteered to chaperone the couple, for which Jamie was deeply grateful. Though she and Donna were attending the charity ball to support those in need, Jamie planned on working, too, trying to spot a killer or killers among the partygoers.

To that end, she'd chosen a costume that allowed her to move, and run if necessary, and that made it easy to conceal her weapon. The multicolored satin tunic, black tights and flat shoes fit the bill perfectly, though she was sure she was in for a night of teasing from her fellow officers. She picked up the jester's hat from the table by the door and handed Donna her coat. "Come on. We don't want to be late."

Volunteers had transformed the Eagle Mountain Community Center into a ballroom that was one part Mardi Gras excess and one part high school prom sentiment. Swaths of black and purple fabric draped the walls and white twinkle lights glowed everywhere. A mirrored disco ball straight out of the 1980s cast spangled light across the dance floor, where a Tyrannosaurus Rex gyrated with a veiled belly dancer and a firefighter in full bunker gear swayed with a woman in a hot pink, retro ski suit.

"Wow!" Donna gasped as she and Jamie waited in line to surrender their tickets.

"Hello, ladies." Adelaide greeted Jamie and Donna when they reached the front of the line. "You both look very nice." Adelaide had teased and sprayed her hair into a 1960s-style beehive and wore oversize hoop earrings and a pink-and-orange paisley minidress.

"What are you supposed to be?" Donna asked.

"I'm a go-go dancer." She stood and lifted one leg to show off orange tights and white, knee-high boots. "Before your time, of course, but I remember those days fondly."

Jamie returned the older woman's grin. She could picture a younger Adelaide grooving to the beat in her psychedelic finery.

They moved farther into the room and surveyed the packed house. Most of the town must have turned out for the fund-raiser. "How are we ever going to find Henry?" Donna asked.

"We'll look for him," Jamie said. "If he's here, we'll find him."

She scanned the milling crowd and spotted Travis right away. No costume and mask could disguise the sheriff's erect form and focused expression. In any case, he was dressed as an Old West lawman, complete with a silver star pinned to a brocaded vest. Next to him his fiancée, Lacy Milligan, looked stunning in a short red-and-black flounced dress that pegged her as an old-time saloon girl.

Gage Walker continued the Old West theme with a mountain man getup, including a fringed buckskin shirt, coonskin cap and what might have been a coyote pelt thrown over one shoulder. The woman in the calico dress, her hair in a prim bun that effectively hid the blue dip-dyed ends, must be his wife, Maya. She was carrying an old-fashioned slate and chalk. Of course. Maya was a school-marm—fitting, since she taught at the local high school.

"There's Henry!" Donna jumped up and down and waved enthusiastically at a brown-clad figure hurrying toward them. As he drew nearer, Jamie realized Henry was dressed as a dog, with floppy ears, whiskers and a shiny black nose.

Mrs. O'Keefe followed him across the floor. A white wig and a cap covered her brown hair, and a dress so wide it must have been held out by a hoopskirt forced her to turn sideways as she maneuvered through the crowd. She held a large plush bone in one hand. "I'm Old Mother Hubbard," she said after they had exchanged greetings. She tapped Henry on the shoulder with the stuffed bone. "This is my poor dog."

Henry paused only a moment to grin at his mother before turning back to Donna. "We want to go get some food," he said.

"All right," Mrs. O'Keefe said. "I'll come with you." She picked up her skirts. "Do you want to come, too?" she asked Jamie.

"Thanks, but I need to check in with the sheriff."

Jamie worked her way through the crowd, past two superheroes, a soldier, three princesses, a witch and many other costumes she couldn't recognize. While she could guess the identity of almost everyone she passed, a knight in full armor and a six-foot rabbit confounded her.

Gage and Maya had moved on by the time Jamie reached Travis and Lacy, and the DJ had turned up the music, so that they had to lean close to hear each other. "Any instructions?" she asked.

"Mingle," Travis said. "Keep an eye on other single women to see if any strangers approach them."

"Stranger is a relative term," Lacy said, scanning the crowd. "There are some wild costumes. Did you see the guy dressed as an octopus?"

"Just keep your eyes open," Travis said. "And have fun."

Lacy linked her arm in his. "Speaking of fun, I want to check out the silent auction table."

The normally stern sheriff's face transformed as he smiled at Lacy—a smile so full of love and tenderness that it made Jamie's breath catch. What would it be like to have a man look at her that way?

"Hello, Deputy. That's a very amusing costume you have."

She whirled around to find herself face-to-face with a melodrama villain, complete with an outrageously curled black mustache, black suit with a black string tie and a dapper cane. Nate shook one pointed end of her collar, making the attached bell jingle. "Do you know how to juggle?" he asked.

"I do it every day," she deadpanned.

He nodded slowly. "Yes, I guess you do." Leaning on a polished black cane, he looked out at the crowded dance floor. "I'd ask you to dance, but this cast is seriously cramping my style."

She had a sudden memory of dancing with him in a crowded high school gym. They hadn't worried about style back then, content to hold each other close and sway in time to the music. She looked away, afraid the unexpected swell of longing for that time showed on her face. "Don't take this wrong," she said. "But I'm trying to look like I'm at this party alone. Nothing personal."

"Single and vulnerable," he said. "Still trying to lure the killer?"

She shrugged. "It's worth a try."

"What will you do if he takes the bait?"

"I won't let him reel me in, if that's what you're worried about. The idea is to string him along, and find out as much about him as I can."

"Of course, you might just end up with a perfectly innocent man who has a thing for women wearing bells."

She was pretty sure her mask diluted the effect of the scowl she aimed at him, but he got the message. "All right." He held up his hands and took a step back. "I'll see if I can find any tall, sort of masculine women with long blond hair."

He hobbled away into the crowd and Jamie moved toward the buffet table. She caught a glimpse of Donna and Henry on the edge of the dance floor, moving to an upbeat rock song. They made up for their awkwardness with enthusiasm and joy. Donna stood with her hands in the air, swiveling her hips, her tail switching from side to side, while Henry pumped his arms and bent his knees, his puppy-dog ears flopping as he nodded in time to the music. Jamie put a hand to her chest as if she could contain the sudden, fierce swell of love for her sister.

Jamie had been seven when Donna was born. Her parents had explained that Donna was different and would need Jamie's help growing up. But all Jamie had seen was her sister's perfection—her round, dimpled face and trusting brown eyes. As soon as she was able, Donna watched Jamie's every move and tried hard to imitate her big sister. Jamie cheered her on, helped with the exercises and therapy doctors prescribed, played games with her and read to her. Other little girls played with dolls, but Jamie had a real live doll in Donna.

In high school things had changed some, as Jamie grew more independent, working a job, dating, going out with friends and doing so many things that didn't include Donna. And Donna had her own friends, too. She participated in Special Olympics and worked part-time after school. But her sister was always important to her. One of the toughest things about leaving to go to college had been moving away from Donna. Jamie had told herself it would be good for her sister to not be as dependent on her, but she had never hesitated to come home after her parents had died. Donna needed her—and Jamie needed Donna, too. Caring for her sister had helped heal her grief. Donna had given her a purpose and a focus at a time when her life seemed so out of control.

She moved around the room, greeting people she knew, talking briefly, but always moving on. She wanted anyone watching to know that she was here alone, the kind of woman who might be easy prey. After an hour or so she moved on to the buffet table and began filling her plate with food contributed by restaurants in town. She leaned over to snag a mini kebab and jostled a man dressed as a pirate. "Sorry," she said, stepping back.

"Oh, no, ma *cher*. It is *moi* who should apologize." The French accent was cheesy and obviously fake, but it went with his over-the-top costume—satin-clad pirate, complete with dreadlocks, a fake beard and eye patch. A chill raced up Jamie's spine as she studied him. She was sure she didn't know this guy. She was also sure the costume—and the accent—were designed to hide his identity.

She shifted her plate to her left hand and stuck out her right. "I'm Jamie," she said.

"So charmed, I am sure," he oozed, then bent and kissed her hand. She had to restrain herself from snatching it back, and suppressed a silent *ew*.

Instead, she forced herself to smile and to look at him with what she hoped was a flirtatious expression. "Are you new in town?" she asked. "I don't think I recognize you."

"That is the idea, is it not?" He grinned, revealing a gold tooth—fake, she was sure. It was the kind of thing that might distract a person from looking too closely. But she wasn't distracted. She studied him, searching for any identifying marks. But the wig, beard and eye patch did a good job of hiding most of his features. The one eye that looked back at her was brown, but since that was the most common eye color, the detail might not be significant.

He noticed her studying him and looked away. "I have seen you around town, I think," he said. "Do you live here?"

"Yes. And you?"

"I am a pirate. I live a life of adventure on the high seas." He turned away and selected a cheese puff from a tray. "Have you tasted these?" he asked. "Delicious."

"Yeah. They look great." She added one to her plate and pretended to survey the rest of the offerings in front of him, while observing him out of the corner of her eye.

"You are here alone?" he asked after a moment.

"Yeah. Uh, my boyfriend and I just split and I've been

kind of bummed. But I figure it's time I got back out there and circulated, you know?" Maybe if he thought she was on the rebound, he'd mistake her for an easy mark.

"Ahhh." Hard to interpret that remark. And the fake beard was so full she couldn't tell much about his expression. Had the sheriff or one of her fellow deputies noticed her talking to this guy yet? It wouldn't hurt to have another person she could compare notes with later about his appearance. "Are you here alone?" she asked.

"Yes. Like you, I am all by myself." He set aside his half-eaten food. "Would you like to dance?"

"Sure."

They moved toward the dance floor. When he took her hand, she pretended to look eager, though she couldn't hide her shock when he pulled her so forcefully against him. Still smiling, she pushed back, putting a few inches between them, primarily because she didn't want him to discover that she was armed.

"You do not like me to take liberties," he said, in that same cheesy accent.

"Well, I hardly know you." She forced herself to smile into his eyes. "Though I wouldn't mind getting to know you better."

"That can be arranged." They swayed together until the song ended, then he led her from the dance floor. "Why don't we go outside, where it's quiet, so we can talk," he said, taking her hand and pulling her toward the door.

The last thing she intended to do was go out into the parking lot with him. She resisted. "I'm having fun," she said. "Let's have another dance." Maybe she could get some of his DNA under her fingernails—scratch him or something. She'd have to make it look like an accident…

"I want to talk, not dance." He pulled her toward the

door once more. He was really strong. He wouldn't have had much trouble overpowering the women who were killed, especially with another man helping him.

"Jamie! Jamie! Where are you going?"

Jamie stopped and spun around as Donna jogged up to her. "Where are you going?" Donna asked.

"Nowhere." She pulled free of the pirate's grasp and smoothed Donna's hair. "Are you having a good time?" she asked.

"Yes." Donna looked at the pirate. "Who is this?"

"A friend," the pirate said. He moved as if to take Donna's hand, but Jamie blocked him. The thought of this creep touching her sister made her skin crawl.

"Do you need something?" Jamie asked Donna, pulling her sister's attention away from the pirate.

"I want to go with Henry and his mom back to his place. She said we could watch a movie and make popcorn. All this noise makes my head hurt."

Jamie glanced over Donna's shoulder and saw Mrs. O'Keefe and Henry approaching. "If it's all right with you, I thought Donna could spend the night," Mrs. O'Keefe said. "We can swing by your house and get her things. She can sleep in the guest room, right across the hall from me. I'll take good care of her."

"Please, Jamie! Please let me go." Donna put her hands together, begging.

"All right," Jamie said. "That sounds like a good idea." A great one, really. Donna would be away from the pirate and his friend and safe, and Jamie would be free to focus on her work.

"Thanks!" Donna kissed Jamie's cheek, then hurried away.

Jamie turned back toward the pirate, but he was gone.

She scanned the crowd, searching for him, but he had vanished. Had he left the party—or only gone in search of his next victim?

AFTER MAKING A TOUR of the room and greeting a few people he knew, Nate made a few bids on silent auction items, then filled a plate with food from the buffet and found a chair against one wall. He would have preferred to spend the evening with Jamie. He had looked forward to catching up on all that had been happening in their lives the past four years. He wanted to prove to her that he could be her friend, without demanding more from her than she wanted to give.

Which meant he had to respect this crazy idea she had about putting herself out there as bait for the Ice Cold Killers. No doubt she was capable of looking out for herself, but it wouldn't hurt for him to act as backup, so he made sure to choose a chair that gave him a view of most of the room. He munched chicken wings and cheese balls as she made her way around the room, then stiffened and set aside his plate as a man in a pirate costume started hitting on her. Nate wasn't close enough to hear what the man was saying, but he could read the guy's body language well enough.

When the pirate grabbed Jamie's hand and kissed it, Nate gripped the curved handle of the cane until his knuckles ached. It was made of stout wood and could serve as an effective weapon if need be. He imagined breaking it over the head of this guy, who was standing much too close to Jamie. Who was this joker, to think he could get away with leering at her that way?

Was that the kind of man she wanted—one who leered and kissed her hand, and came on too strong? Was she falling for charm that was as fake as his dreadlocks?

"Do you know him?"

Nate turned to find Travis had taken the chair next to him. The sheriff nodded toward the man with Jamie. "Can you tell who he is under the wig and beard?"

"No." Nate went back to studying the man. The fake beard, mustache, dreadlocks and eye patch covered three-fourths of the man's face. "I don't think I've seen him before."

"Me, either," Travis said. "And Jamie doesn't act as if she recognizes him."

"What makes you think that?" Jamie was smiling at the man now.

"She's leaning away from him," Travis said. "And there's a lot of tension in her shoulders."

Nate saw what Travis meant and felt his own shoulders relax a little. Jamie was flirting with the man, but she wasn't truly attracted to him. She was interested in him as a suspect. "Do you think he's one of the guys you're looking for?" Nate asked, keeping his voice low.

"Maybe," Travis said.

Nate shifted his weight to one hip and slid his phone from his pocket. "Face me and pretend to be posing for a picture," he said. "I'll zoom in for a shot of the pirate."

"Good idea." Travis angled toward Nate, his back to Jamie and the buccaneer. Nate snapped a few photos, zooming in as far as the camera would go. He tucked the phone into his pocket and both men sat back in their chairs again. "I'll send you the files and maybe your tech people can do something with them."

"Thanks," Travis said.

The pirate led Jamie onto the dance floor, where he plastered himself to her. Nate had to grip the edge of his seat to keep from storming out there and prying the two apart. But Jamie put some distance between them and managed the rest of the dance with a pained expression on her face. The song ended and a tug-of-war between the two followed. "I think he's trying to get her to leave," Nate said. He shoved to his feet. "Maybe I need to go interrupt."

Travis put out a restraining hand. "Give it a minute."

Nate stilled but didn't sit back down. Jamie and the pirate continued to argue, and then Donna, Henry and Henry's mother hurried toward her. The pirate stepped back, then began to melt into the crowd.

"I'm going to follow him," Travis said and left.

Donna and the others exited the room and Jamie looked around. Nate hurried toward her, moving as fast as he could with the cane. "I watched the whole thing," he said by way of greeting. "Are you okay?"

"I'm fine." She searched the crowd. "I think he might have been one of the men we're looking for," she said, her voice tight with excitement.

"Travis is following him," Nate said. He touched her shoulder, forcing her to look at him. "What did he say to you?"

"He flirted in this horrible French accent," she said. "In fact, it was so bad, I think that was the point."

"He wanted to disguise his voice," Nate said.

"Yes, I think so."

"After you danced—was he trying to convince you to leave with him?" Nate asked.

"Yes," she said. "But when Donna and the O'Keefes interrupted, he slipped away."

"He didn't want anyone else to see him with you," Nate said.

"I tried to memorize everything I could about him," she said. "But his costume covered up everything. And he didn't have any really outstanding features—no visible moles or a crooked nose or anything."

"I took a few pictures of him with my phone," Nate

said. "Travis will have them analyzed. Maybe he can get something from that."

"That was a good idea," Jamie said.

Travis joined them once more, a little breathless. "I lost him," he said. "I saw him slip out the back door to the parking lot, but by the time I made it out there, he was gone."

"Did you get a look at his car?" Nate asked.

Travis shook his head, then turned to Jamie. "What information did he give you?" he asked.

"Not much," she said. "He avoided any of my questions about who he was or where he was from. The costume hid most of his face, and he spoke with a terrible French accent." She sighed. "About all I can tell you is that he has brown eyes, good teeth and is about six feet tall, average build. And he's strong. I think he probably works out. He could have easily overpowered those women."

"I think he's fairly young," Nate said. "He moved like a younger man."

Jamie nodded. "Yes. In his twenties, I think. Maybe early thirties."

"That doesn't give us much to go on," Nate said.

"Send me those photographs you took," Travis said. "We'll print them up and try to find out if anyone else talked to him tonight." He looked around the room. "We'll talk to as many women here as we can tonight. Let's find out if he approached any of them. Maybe they saw or heard something we didn't."

"Adelaide is taking tickets at the door," Jamie said. "She probably saw him when he came in, and she talks to everyone."

"I'll question her," Travis said. "We'll also compare the photograph to the sketches the police artist did from Henry and Tammy's descriptions."

"Were the sketches of the same man?" Nate asked.

"Two different men," Travis said. "If we're right, the man Henry saw with Michaela—the one who called himself Al—is the masked man who came up behind Tammy. The man she described to us is the decoy and accomplice."

They separated to question the other party guests. Though a couple of people Nate talked to had seen the pirate from a distance, none of them had spoken with him. By midnight, the party began breaking up. Nate met up with Travis and Jamie once more. "Adelaide remembers the guy," Travis said. "But she couldn't tell us anything we didn't already know."

"I found one woman he approached," Jamie said. "He asked her to dance, but then her boyfriend returned with a drink and he left in a hurry."

"He doesn't want any witnesses," Travis said. "I'm becoming more and more certain that this is one of the killers." He watched guests file toward the exit. "I don't think there's anything more we can do here tonight. Let's go home, and in the morning we can take a look at the photos Nate took."

He left them. "I'd better get my coat," Jamie said, heading for the cloakroom.

Nate limped alongside her. "Where's Donna?" he asked.

"She's going to spend the night at Henry's house."

"So you're going home alone?"

"I guess I am." A smile ghosted across her lips. "That's something I haven't done in a very long time."

"I'll follow you home," he said.

"You don't have to do that." She accepted her coat—the same down parka she had worn the day he met her and Donna snowshoeing—from the man behind the counter in the cloakroom.

"I know." Nate took the coat and held it for her. "But

there's a killer out there who may have been targeting you. I think it's safer if I follow you."

She slipped her arms into the coat, then glanced up at him. "Okay. Thanks."

They fed into the stream of vehicles leaving the community center parking lot, and he followed her to the bungalow on Oak Street. At one time he could have driven to this place blindfolded. He had spent as much time here back in high school as he had in his own house. He parked behind Jamie and followed her to the front door.

"I'll be all right now," she said, as she unlocked the door.

"Humor me and let me make sure," he said.

As soon as she opened the door, the three dogs galloped toward them, barking furiously when they saw Nate. "Quiet!" Jamie shouted. "It's only Nate."

He had removed the fake mustache in the truck on the way here, along with the hat, so that he hoped he looked more like himself. He bent and offered the back of his hand to the biggest dog—the husky—to sniff. The other dogs followed suit and soon he was patting all three while they jostled for attention.

"They're obviously fine," Jamie said. "They wouldn't act like this if someone had managed to break in."

Nate said nothing, but stumped through all the downstairs rooms, looking for signs of any disturbance. Though, since he didn't live here, how would he know if something was out of place or not, unless the intruder had done something obvious like leave a window open?

"Do you want to look under the bed, too?" she asked, when he returned to her in the foyer, at the bottom of the stairs leading to the second floor.

No, but he wouldn't mind looking *in* her bed. He didn't say the words out loud, but they must have shown on his face. She blushed. She looked so impossibly sweet and sexy. He reached out and removed the jester's hat, and smoothed back her hair.

"What?" she asked.

"Are you sure you'll be okay here tonight, by yourself?" he asked. "If you're nervous, I could stay. I'd sleep on the couch, I promise."

"I'll be fine." She took his arm and led him to the door. "Go home and I'll see you tomorrow at the sheriff's department."

"All right." Maybe he wouldn't go right home. Maybe he'd park his truck down the block and watch her place for a while, just to be sure. She didn't have to know.

He opened the door and started to step onto the porch, but the sight of a dark-colored SUV cruising slowly as it approached made him freeze. "Who's that?" he asked, nodding toward the vehicle.

Jamie peered past him, one hand on his shoulder. "I don't know."

He reached behind her and switched off the porch light, plunging them into shadow. He was aware of her labored breathing as the vehicle drove slowly past. Though the driver was hard to make out in the darkness, Nate was sure he turned his head to look at them.

"The license plate on the car is obscured," Jamie whispered.

Nate pulled her back into the house, and shut and locked the door. "Do you think that was him?" Jamie asked. "The man at the dance?"

"I don't know. It could have been." Nate pulled her close, his heart pounding. He needed to reassure himself that she was safe. She didn't fight him, but relaxed in his embrace, her head nestled in the hollow of his shoulder. "I'm not leaving you here alone," he said.

"No." She lifted her head, her eyes searching his. Then she rose up on tiptoe and pressed her lips to his, her eyes still open, still locked to his.

Chapter Twelve

Nate closed his eyes and gave himself up to the kiss, caressing her with lips and hands, welcoming the tangle of her tongue with his, the soft sweetness of her mouth, the dizzying *want* her touch sent blazing through him.

He didn't know how long it was before she pulled away. He was breathing hard, half wondering if he was dreaming, telling himself he had to keep it together. She had to set the pace here. He had promised himself he wouldn't take more than she would give, and it was a promise he was determined to keep.

"I don't think you should sleep on the couch," she said.

He released his hold on her and took a step back. He couldn't think clearly when she was so close. "Are you sure about this?" he asked, his voice hoarse, not sounding like his own.

She nodded. "I know if I turn my back on these feelings—if I don't give us this chance—then I'm going to regret it."

"Yeah." He raked one hand through his hair. "Yeah, I'll regret it, too." It felt big and important, a move that would change him—would change them. But it felt right, too.

She leaned past him and double-checked the door lock, then took his hand and led him up the stairs.

JAMIE CLIMBED THE STAIRS, Nate's grip firm and reassuring in hers, helping to calm the butterflies going wild in her chest. She led him down the hall, but not to the room that had been hers growing up. Nate had sneaked up to that room one night, climbing the drainpipe and shimmying across the porch roof to climb into her window. They hadn't really done anything—too fearful of the consequences if they had been caught. But there had been something so thrilling about cuddling together on her bed—she in flannel pajamas decorated with pink hearts, he in jeans and a sweatshirt. They had kissed and whispered to each other until, hearing her father get up to go to the bathroom and sure his next stop would be her bedroom, he had slipped out the window and to the ground once more.

But she didn't take him to that room. About a year after her parents' death, she had moved into the master bedroom. She had given away their king-size bed and replaced it with an iron four-poster she had purchased from a local antique shop, making payments each pay period for three months until the bed was hers. She had stored the family photos that had adorned the walls and replaced them with black-and-white photos of Eagle Mountain landscapes, also purchased from a local shop.

Nate stopped in the doorway and surveyed the room. "What?" she asked. "Are you weirded out because this used to be my parents' room?"

"No. I'd forgotten this was theirs. I was just admiring it. Admiring you."

"You were looking at the walls—you weren't looking at me."

"I was admiring what the walls tell me about you."

She faced him, hands on his shoulders. "What do they tell you?"

His eyes met hers. "That you love beautiful things. Not

frilly or over the top, but beautiful." He tossed the cane aside and fit his hands to her waist. "That you love this place—you love Eagle Mountain."

"I do," she said. That was one of the things that made her so uneasy about him. Nate had come back to Eagle Mountain, but she didn't sense that it was home for him— not the way it was home for her.

But she didn't want to think about that now. And she didn't want to talk anymore. When he opened his mouth as if to speak, she put two fingers to his lips to silence him, then she began loosening the knot of his string tie.

Tie loosened, she began working her way down the buttons on his starched white shirt. He slid his hand around to lower the zipper on her tunic, the sudden rush of cool air on her back mitigated by his warm hand smoothing down her spine. Impatient to be closer still, she pushed his jacket off his shoulders, then his shirt, her heart thudding harder as she admired the defined muscles of his chest and shoulders. Stripped of camouflaging clothing, he resembled a Viking warrior.

"Your turn," he murmured and pushed the tunic over her shoulders and down to the floor, followed quickly by the tights, until she was standing before him in her bra and panties, goose bumps prickling her arms and shoulders. He stripped out of his trousers and stood before her in boxers—which did little to hide his desire. She was contemplating this, dry mouthed and breathless, when he forced her attention to more practical concerns. "What about protection?" he asked.

"In the drawer by the bed."

He moved the short distance to the bed, opened the drawer of the nightstand and took out a package of condoms, and gave her a questioning look.

"Don't flatter yourself," she said, her face burning.

"I didn't say anything."

"You didn't have to—I could see it in your eyes." She joined him by the bed. "You thought I bought these, planning to bring you up here."

"It's none of my business why you bought them," he said. "I'm just glad you have them." He sat on the side of the bed and began to open the package.

But she couldn't not tell him now. "There was this guy I went out with a few times. I thought maybe…" She shook her head. "Nothing came of it." She pressed her lips together. She had said enough. She didn't want him to know there hadn't been anyone else since him. She hadn't dated much, what with Donna and her job. And when she did go out with someone, she found it difficult to let down her guard with men.

He set aside the condom box and reached for her. "It's okay. Come here."

She crawled onto the bed next to him, nerves warring with excitement. She wanted this—needed this. But she was afraid of making a mistake.

Then he was kissing her, hands gently exploring, warm fingers coaxing delicious sensations from her. She began to relax and to make her own discoveries about his body. Everything about him—about being here with him—was both familiar and new. He was Nate—the first man and the only man she had ever made love with. The man she had trusted with all her secrets. He was the same—yet very different. He was bigger than she remembered. Broader and more muscular. A man, where he had been a boy.

"You've grown into a beautiful woman," he said, shaping his hand to one breast.

"I guess we've both changed," she said, breathless again as he dragged his thumb across her sensitive nipple.

"For the better." He kissed her fiercely, his hand moving

down to stroke her sex, until desire all but overwhelmed her. She felt impatient, desperate and a little out of control.

"I really don't want to wait anymore," she said, digging her fingers into the taut skin of his shoulders.

In answer, he held her close and plunged two fingers into her, then began to stroke more deftly. She came fast and hard, thrusting against him, crying out in relief. He held her a little while longer and then, smiling, he reached for the box of condoms.

When they came together again, she felt more in control, though no less eager for him. As he filled her she let out a long sigh that grew to a low moan as he began to move. Nervousness long vanquished, she matched his rhythm, every sense focused on the moment. Desire began to build once more, lifting her up, climbing with him to that wonderful height. When at last she could wait no longer and leaped, he followed, the two of them clinging tightly together for the glide back down to earth.

Neither of them said anything for long minutes. She rested her head on his chest and reveled in the strong, steady thud of his heartbeat, and the rise and fall of his body beneath hers with each breath. She felt so connected to him it took all her strength to shove off the bed and head to the bathroom.

When she returned a few moments later, she thought from the steady, deep rhythm of his breathing that he was asleep. She slid in next to him and he reached for her. "I was afraid for you tonight," he said.

It took her a moment to comprehend that he was talking about earlier in the evening, when the pirate had approached her. "I was never in any danger," she said.

"I know. But if that was one of the killers—he's murdered six women, seemingly at random. Someone with a mind like that—it's terrifying."

"Yes, it is." She propped herself on one elbow, wanting to see his face. "Thank you for following me home and for offering to stay."

"You would have sent me away, if we hadn't seen that car driving past."

"I would have regretted it. I might even have called you back before you got to your truck."

He laughed and pulled her close in a bear hug. "I was going to park my truck at the end of the block and watch your house all night, to make sure you were safe."

The words brought a lump to her throat. To think that he cared so much. Fearing losing control, she rolled onto her back and searched for a less emotional topic of conversation. "How is your ankle?" she asked.

"Sex is a terrific pain reliever." He lay back beside her. "I figure in another week or so I'll be able to ditch the cane."

"I'm glad it's not bothering you too much."

"The worst part is the boredom. I haven't been off work this long since I graduated college. I used to think I was lazy, but I've discovered I really hate being idle."

"Me, too." She laughed. "Though sometimes I think it might be nice to try out a life of leisure—for a few days, anyway."

He reached down and laced his fingers in her hand. "You've got a lot on your plate. Tell me about Donna."

The question surprised her. It wasn't as if Nate hadn't known Donna almost as long as he had known Jamie. "What about her?"

"She seems to have things together and is pretty smart. Will she ever be able to live on her own?"

Jamie tensed and took her hand from his. Why was he asking that question? Why now? "Maybe. But she'll always need help. The man I end up with has to take Donna as part of the bargain." Might as well be up-front about that now. She held her breath, waiting for his answer.

"Of course," he said. "I like Donna. I always have. It's good to see her so happy."

She relaxed again. He wasn't lying. His acceptance and even affection for Donna was one of the reasons she had fallen in love with him. "I hope she does okay tonight. She's never spent a night away from home before. She's never wanted to."

"And it feels strange to you," he said.

"Yes. But everything about this night is a little strange."

"You didn't think I'd be here with you."

"No. But I'm glad you are." She took his hand again.

He rolled over to face her and pulled her close once more. "I'm always here for you," he said. "I'm going to keep saying that until you believe it."

She believed he meant his words, but she didn't trust him not to break his own promise. She owed it to herself not to let him break her heart, too.

NATE LEFT JAMIE'S place after breakfast the next morning. She didn't come right out and say so, but he sensed she wanted him gone before her sister returned home. He could understand explaining his presence might be awkward, and he was willing to let her ease into the idea of the two of them being together again.

He headed toward the sheriff's department, and along the way found himself searching driveways and side streets for the dark SUV that had driven past Jamie's house the night before. Had the driver really been the man in the pirate costume—the murderer? Or had he and Jamie let paranoia and fear get the better of them? In broad daylight, it was easy to think the latter, but he decided to reserve judgment until after he talked to the sheriff.

Travis was at his desk and hard at work. Upcoming wedding or not, the sheriff was going to spend every spare hour on this case.

"Any luck getting an ID from the photo I sent, or the police artist sketches?" Nate asked, after Adelaide had escorted him to Travis's office.

"No." Travis passed a sheet of paper to Nate. "Take a look."

The paper featured side-by-side comparisons of the photograph Nate had taken of the pirate and two sketches of men. "Are these the police artist sketches from the information Henry and Tammy provided?" Nate asked.

"Yes. Do either of them look familiar to you?"

Nate studied the images, comparing each to the photograph of the pirate, and to his mental images of people he knew. "I don't recognize them," he said. "And neither of them looks like the pirate to me."

"The police artist thinks the guy in the pirate costume may have made his nose look larger with makeup, and the gold tooth is probably a fake," Travis said. "He suggested we look for someone with a theatrical background, so I asked the local theatre group to give me a list of any men who have been involved in their productions." He passed Nate a second sheet of paper. "I've highlighted the names of men who fall into the right age group. There are only half a dozen."

Nate's eyebrows rose. "Gage's name is on here."

"Yeah. He was in a comedy revue they did a couple of years ago. I left it on there to give him a hard time, but he was with me when several of the murders occurred, so we can safely rule him out."

Nate tossed the papers back onto the desk and lowered himself into the visitor's chair. "Last night, I followed Jamie home from the community center," he said.

"I was worried about her being alone. I know she's a cop, but these two killers seem to have a knack for eluding us."

"Never a bad idea to be safe," Travis said.

"Yeah, well, I was saying goodnight to her when a dark-colored SUV passed. It could have been dark gray or black, and I think it was a Toyota. It passed the house very slowly, and it seemed the driver was looking at the house—though it was dark, so I can't be sure." He gripped the arms of the chair and leaned toward Travis. "The license plate was obscured—the license plate light was out and it looked as if mud or something else had been smeared over most of the plate."

"Whoever was driving the car didn't want the plate read," Travis said. "What did you do?"

"We decided I should spend the night at her place, in case the guy came back." He kept his expression blank, letting Travis use his imagination to fill in any details on sleeping arrangements. No way was Nate going to elaborate. Travis was his friend, but he was also Jamie's boss, and there were some things he didn't need to know.

"I'll add your description of the vehicle to the other information we've collected," Travis said.

Nate sat back again, frustration churning his stomach. "What's your gut tell you on this?" he asked. Travis would have made it his business to know everything there was to know about this case, and he was good at spotting patterns and making connections.

Travis drew in a deep breath and waited a long beat before he spoke. "We're looking for two men—young and strong, from five-nine to, say, six-two," he said. "They're working together. One of them can pass as a woman while wearing a wig, and probably acted as a decoy to induce the victim to stop, so that the other man could overpower her. That decoy technique may be a new twist or something they've done all along."

"You know most of the people around here," Nate said. "Do you have any suspects in mind?"

"There were two men who were on my radar from the very first," he said. "College students who were here over winter break. My sister invited them to the scavenger hunt at the ranch where Fiona Winslow was killed."

"I think I remember them," Nate said. "Cocky young guys. They got in an argument with Fiona and Ken Rutledge."

"Right. They may have been the last to see Fiona before she left Ken and went looking for a couple of the other women."

"You said they were on your radar? But no longer?"

"They supposedly left town when the road reopened briefly earlier in the month. At least, I haven't seen them around, and they moved out of the cabin where they were staying."

"But they could still be here," Nate said. "Hiding."

"They could."

"I assume you contacted the school they attend?"

"I did. Neither of them reported for classes. But they could have decided to quit school."

"What about parents? Friends?"

"I don't have that information," Travis said. "The aunt who owns the cabin here where they were staying hasn't heard from them. If the roads were open, I'd send someone to Fort Collins to talk to people. I contacted a local investigator and asked him to do some checking, but we don't have much of a budget for that kind of thing, and so far he hasn't come up with anything significant. No one can say for sure these two are in Fort Collins—but no one is sure they aren't, either."

"I've got lots of time on my hands," Nate said. "I could drive around the county, do some checking. Tell me who I'm looking for. I sort of remember them from before, but not clearly."

"I'll print out their ID photos for you. Their names are Alex Woodruff and Tim Dawson."

"Alex. That could be the Al who was with Michaela," Nate said.

"Maybe. Tammy and Henry are coming in this morning to look at some photographs, including the one you took last night. We'll see if they can pick out Alex and Tim."

"I have a few ideas of places they might be staying," Nate said.

"Tell me, and I'll send a couple of deputies out to check," Travis said.

Nate shook his head. "I want to look around first before you waste any of your resources. I'll let you know if I see anything suspicious."

"If you find these two, call for backup," Travis said. "After what they did to these women, they won't think twice about killing you."

"I'm no hero," Nate said. "If we find them, we'll send in our own army to take them. They won't know what hit them."

"The women they killed probably didn't, either," Travis said. "I want to make it tougher for them to take anyone by surprise, so I'm holding a press conference at eleven. I'm going to let everyone know about the possible use of a decoy, as well as release the photograph of the pirate and the two police sketches. Maybe we'll get lucky and someone knows where these two are hiding."

"What about releasing the photos of Tim and Alex?" Nate asked. "That's probably your best bet of finding out if anyone around here has seen them lately."

"I may do that, too." The printer that sat on the credenza behind Travis whirred and he leaned back and plucked a sheet of paper from the tray. "These are Alex Woodruff and Tim Dawson's driver's license photos," he said as he handed the printout to Nate.

Nate studied the photos of the two young men—one with straight, sandy hair cut short, the other with a mop of brown curls. His eyes widened and his heart beat faster. "I know these guys." He looked up and met the sheriff's gaze. "They're definitely still in the area. I talked to them only four days ago."

Chapter Thirteen

Donna returned from her stay with the O'Keefes full of descriptions of what she saw, what they ate and everything she had done. Jamie listened to this nonstop narrative as she cleaned up the kitchen, delighted the evening had gone so well—and only a little guilty that she had scarcely missed her sister, focused as she was on Nate. Donna, so caught up in her own happy memories, never asked how Jamie had spent her evening.

At nine forty-five, she and Donna loaded all three dogs into the car for their annual checkups. Darcy Marsh was the newest veterinarian in town, a pleasant young woman who had a real rapport with animals. She greeted Donna, Jamie and the three dogs enthusiastically. "I saw you at the masquerade last night but never made my way around to you," she said, as she washed her hands before examining the dogs.

"I'm sorry I missed you," Jamie said.

"What was your costume?" Donna asked. "I was a cat."

"You were a very cute cat," Darcy said. "Ryder and I went as Roy Rogers and Dale Evans—complete with stick horses." She laughed. "At least they raised a lot of money to help people who have been hurt by the road closures. And we had a lot of fun."

"How is Ryder?" Jamie asked. Darcy's fiancé, Ryder Stewart, was a Colorado State Highway Patrol trooper.

"He's great." Darcy put her stethoscope to Targa's chest and for a few moments, the only sound in the room was the dogs panting loudly. "She sounds good," Darcy pronounced at last. "Now let's hear the rest of them."

Some fifteen minutes later, after Darcy had examined ears, teeth and every other accessible part of the three dogs, she pronounced all the canines in good health. While Jamie paid the bill, Donna and a vet tech took the dogs out to Jamie's SUV. "At the party last night, did either of you notice a guy dressed as a pirate?" Jamie asked Darcy and her receptionist, Stacy. "He had long dreadlocks, a beard and mustache and an eye patch, and he spoke with a cheesy French accent."

"I didn't see anybody like that," Stacy said as she accepted Jamie's credit card.

"Me, either." Darcy leaned toward Jamie. "Why do you ask?"

Jamie shook her head. "I was just wondering."

But Darcy wasn't going to be put off so easily. "Are you working on this Ice Cold Killer case?" she asked.

"I think it's safe to say every law enforcement officer in the county is working on this case," Jamie hedged.

"Yeah. But the sheriff's department would know more than anyone." Darcy rubbed her arms, as if she was chilled. "I just wondered if you're any closer to finding out who is killing all these women. I'm still trying to wrap my head around Kelly being gone."

Kelly Farrow had been Darcy's partner in the veterinary business—and the Ice Cold Killer's first victim. Had that really been less than a month ago?

"We have some leads," Jamie said. "I can't say anything more, but it feels like we're making progress."

"Thanks," Darcy said. "That helps a little, I guess."

It didn't really help, Jamie knew. Nothing would until the killings stopped. Even she, with all her law enforcement training, didn't feel safe alone anymore. She signed the credit card slip, said goodbye, then headed across the parking lot to where Donna and the dogs waited in the SUV. Jamie stopped short, her hand on the door handle, as a dark SUV pulled out of the lot. The hairs on the back of her neck stood up as she tried to read the vehicle's license plate and realized it was obscured.

Heart racing, she yanked open her car door and slid into the driver's seat. She started the engine with one hand and fastened her seat belt with the other, then took off out of the parking lot, tires squealing.

"Why are you driving so fast?" Donna asked, steadying herself with one hand on the dashboard.

"I thought I saw someone I know and I want to catch up with him," Jamie said. She scanned the road ahead and the driveways they passed, but there was no sign of the SUV.

"Who are you trying to find?" Donna asked.

"A man I met at the party last night."

"The pirate? Henry and I saw you talking to him." Donna shook her head. "He didn't look very nice to me."

For all her innocence and tendency to be too trusting, Donna sometimes had very good instincts about people. "I don't think he is very nice," Jamie said. "If you see him again, don't say anything to him, just come find me. If you're at work, you can call me."

"Is he a bad man?" Donna sank down in her seat, her face creased with worry.

"I don't know," Jamie said. "But you remember we talked about this before. It's good to be careful around people you don't know."

"I know."

Jamie pulled into the parking lot of the history museum and turned the SUV around. "Let's go home," she said. "We both need to get ready for work." She would tell the sheriff about the dark SUV with the obscured plate. They'd have a better chance of finding it if everyone in the department was looking. The killer had been able to hide from them so far, but as long as the roads stayed closed, he wouldn't be able to run far.

"I MET THESE two while I was on patrol Tuesday." Nate tapped the photos Travis had given him. "They were ice climbing that exposed rock face by Snowberry campground. I'm sure it was the same two, though they introduced themselves as Lex and Ty. I even thought they looked familiar, but I didn't connect them to the scavenger hunt at your ranch."

"Did they say anything to indicate where they were staying?" Travis grabbed a notepad and prepared to take notes.

"No. But they did tell me they were college graduates. They shut down my attempts to get any more information." Nate grimaced. "I stopped to ask them if they'd seen a woman with long blond hair in the area. They said no, but they mentioned the Ice Cold Killer. They seemed eager to talk about it, in fact."

"Oh? What did they say?"

"Mainly, they talked about how good the killer was at eluding you. Their exact words were that the killer was making you look like an idiot."

Travis nodded. "That fits with the suggestion we've had that the killer likes taunting law enforcement. He wants to prove he's smarter than the people who are pursuing him." He pushed his chair back. "I'm going to put out an APB on these guys, and I'll mention them at my press conference this morning. If they're in the area, someone will see them and we'll find them."

"Let me know if I can do anything to help," Nate said.

He left the sheriff's department, but instead of going home, he headed to the national forest, to the campground where he had encountered Alex and Tim. He parked at the entrance to the closed campground and walked over to the rock wall where the two had been climbing. A cold wind buffeted him as he got out of the truck. A low, gray sky promised more snow soon. The drifts at the foot of the wall lay undisturbed. Leaning heavily on his crutch, Nate scanned the area for any trace the two might have left behind. They had been meticulous about cleaning up their crime scenes, but they might not have been so careful here.

But any evidence they might have left had been buried by four inches of fresh snow. Nate returned to his truck and sat, thinking. The two young men had abandoned their aunt's cabin, perhaps because they sensed the sheriff was closing in on them. Though they had had a chance to leave town when the road opened briefly, they had elected to stick around and continue the killings. Three women had been murdered since the road had closed again. Alex and Tim had to be living somewhere. Somewhere without neighbors who might get suspicious and report them to the sheriff's department. Somewhere near here—the area where the murder of Michaela Underwood and the attack on Tammy Patterson had occurred.

Of course! He slapped the steering wheel, then started the truck. Why hadn't he seen it before? The squatters in the summer cabin—the ones who had set those animal traps around the hideout—they had to be Alex and Tim.

He drove to the cabin and parked past the cabins, at a trailhead that was little used this time of year, then hiked back to the cabins. At the chain across the road, he unholstered his weapon and took a firmer grip on his cane. He didn't intend to confront anyone who might be here, but he wanted to be prepared in case they spotted him first.

The snow on the road leading to the cabins had been packed down by the sheriff's department vehicles, making walking less arduous than the last time Nate was here. He paused halfway up to take in the scattering of cabins, each a short distance from its neighbor, with its own picnic table and outbuildings. In summer, these cabins would form a thriving community. The same families had owned these little getaways for generations, and each summer would be a reunion of old friends. Grandparents and grandchildren, parents who had come here as children themselves and new people who had married into the families would gather for barbecue and picnics, volleyball games and horseshoe competitions. With no cell phone or television service, and little space inside the small dwellings, they looked to each other and the outdoors for entertainment. Cherished memories and soul-deep relationships kept families returning year after year, and made them guard jealously what was, for many, a little piece of heaven.

In the cold of winter the cabins didn't look so inviting. They stood with shuttered windows and padlocked doors in the ringing silence of the forest, like a forgotten ghost town. Nate moved silently through the deep snow, a wraith himself, slipping between the trees.

Alert for any sign of more traps, he approached the cabins slowly, moving as stealthily as possible, hampered as he was by the crutch and the awkward air boot. He reached the cabin the traps had been taken from first. He could see them piled on the front porch, and the pale outlines where they had hung on the side of the building.

He passed the other six cabins, pausing to scan the snow around each one for any sign of activity before moving on to the cabin where he had been snared. There were more signs of activity here—depressions covered over by fresh snow that marked the path of law enforcement vehicles in and out, churned earth where he had sat waiting for rescue, and new, stout padlocks on the front and back doors.

Nate stood on the back porch of the cabin, searching through the trees. Though this cabin was the furthest back in the grouping, the forest road looped around behind it, so that anyone sitting on this porch, or looking out the back picture window, could hear approaching traffic, and even catch a glimpse of the vehicle through a gap in the trees.

Nate studied that gap, then started walking, making his way through the trees until he reached an opening that widened out to provide access to the road. Someone could park a vehicle here, access it via the path through the woods, and be gone before anyone driving on the road reached the cabin.

At the sound of an approaching vehicle, he shrank back into the trees, and watched as a Rayford County sheriff's department vehicle sped by. Grinning, Nate made his way back to the cabin.

He was waiting on the front porch when Travis and Gage pulled in. "Where's your truck?" Travis asked as he mounted the steps.

"I parked at a trailhead down the road," Nate said.

"That's a long way to walk with a busted ankle," Gage said.

"I didn't want anyone to see me."

"Whereas, we didn't care." Gage looked around them. "I guess you had the same idea we did."

"Alex and Tim must have been the squatters in this cabin," Nate said.

"It's a good place to hide," Gage said. "But they risked being trapped in here. There's only one entrance or exit."

"Not exactly." Nate stood. "Let me show you what I found." He led them back through the woods to the clearing next to the road. "If they kept a lookout, they could be out of the cabin and gone before law enforcement reached them," he said.

"They could even set up an alarm to warn them when someone was coming," Gage said as the three of them walked back to the cabin. "One of those cables you drive over and it rings a bell or something. Or a camera focused on the drive."

"We didn't find anything like that when we searched the place," Travis said.

"It's like the crime scenes," Gage said. "They know how to clean up after themselves."

"We're going to look again." Travis paused at the door and pulled on a pair of gloves. "You can help if you want, Nate."

"Sure." He accepted a pair of gloves. "It's not as if I have anything better to do."

An hour later they had combed every inch of the small cabin and come up with nothing to link Alex and Tim to either the cabin or the murders.

"They've cleared out of here," Travis said. "We'll check the other cabins, but I don't think we'll find anything."

"I walked around all of them when I arrived today," Nate said. "I didn't find any sign of activity at any of them."

"There are more of these summer cabins, aren't there?" Gage asked.

"There's one more grouping like this, with six cabins, on the other side of the county," Nate said.

"Then that's where we look next," Travis said.

"Let me go with you," Nate said.

Travis looked at the cast boot on his leg.

"I'll stay out of the action," Nate said. "I won't get in your way. But you need me there."

"Why is that?" Gage asked.

"Because I have a key to the gate," Nate said. "I can get you in there without anyone else knowing."

Chapter Fourteen

When Jamie arrived for her shift Saturday afternoon, Nate met her in the hallway. He had shed the cast boot and traded the crutch for a cane, which recalled the costume he had worn last night—and everything else about last night. But Jamie was pretty sure he could have greeted her dressed as a clown and she would have still thought about last night. "Hello," he said, the warmth in his smile making her heart beat a little faster.

"Hi." She nodded and started to move past him, determined to remain professional while she was on the job.

He turned and walked alongside her. "Busy morning?" he asked.

"Uh, yeah. We took the dogs to the vet." Should she mention the dark SUV she had seen pulling out of the lot?

"Did you catch the sheriff's press conference this morning?" Nate asked.

"No. I didn't know there was one." Was she supposed to have been there? No one had notified her. "What was it about?"

"He'll fill you in. There's a meeting in five minutes."

"I saw the notice in the locker room." Maybe she would bring up the SUV in the meeting.

Jamie and Nate were the last to enter the situation room, where Travis stood at the end of the conference table, be-

side a large poster on an easel. The poster featured the enlarged photos of two young men, two sketches of men and
a photograph of the man dressed in the pirate costume.

"For those of you who might not have heard the press
conference this morning, these are two men we want to
question regarding the Ice Cold Killer murders." Travis
indicated the left photo, of a slender young man with light
brown hair. "This is Alex Woodruff, also known as Al,
also known as Lex. He may be using other names." Travis consulted his notes. "He's twenty-two years old, until
recently an undergraduate at Colorado State University,
where he was studying psychology. He was also involved
in the university's theatrical company, where he met Tim
Dawson."

Travis indicated the second photograph, of a young man
with dark, curly hair. "Tim, also known as Ty, is twenty-
one, also a psych major, also active in the theatre company. As far as I have been able to determine, the two did
not return to classes when they started up again last week.
Previously they were staying in a cabin belonging to Tim's
aunt, on County Road Five. They left there some time before last week and may have broken into and been living
at Sundance cabins, though they are no longer there."

Jamie and several others at the table looked at Nate.
"Yeah, that's the cabin where I was hurt," he said.

"Alex and Tim may have set those traps to slow down
anyone who came after them," Travis said. "Nate talked
to them that morning near Snowberry campground. They
were climbing, and introduced themselves as Lex and Ty."

"They're not very creative with their aliases," Gage
observed.

"They were driving a dark gray Toyota Highlander,"
Nate said. "I made note of the license plate and the vehicle
is registered to Timothy Dawson."

"Alex Woodruff and Tim Dawson were suspects for the first three murders," Travis said. "We ruled them out after they supposedly left town. Now that we know they're back in town, we need to bring them in and question them."

He tapped the drawings in the middle of the poster. "These are drawings the police artist from Denver made after Skype sessions with Henry O'Keefe and Tammy Patterson. As you can see, they bear some resemblance to Alex and Tim, though nothing definitive. We brought Henry and Tammy back in this morning, and Henry picked out Alex's photo from a selection of photos we gave him, and identified him as the man he saw with Michaela Underwood the day before she was murdered. Tomorrow we'll take the photo to the bank and see if any of Michaela's co-workers recognize him. Tammy wasn't able to identify the man who was posing as a woman who lured her to stop, probably because of his disguise."

Travis moved on to the photograph at the bottom of the poster. "This man was at the masquerade party at the community center last night," he said. "He approached Deputy Douglas and tried to persuade her to come into the parking lot with him. When they were interrupted, he fled. He could be Alex or Tim in disguise, but we can't be sure."

He laid aside the pointer and faced them. "I've released these images to the media, and I've issued a BOLO for Alex, Tim and their vehicle. We're hoping someone will spot them and report the sighting."

"In the meantime, we're going to keep hunting for them. Dwight, I want you and Jamie to come with me and Gage this afternoon. We're going to check another set of summer cabins. These two have to be living somewhere, and since they broke into one cabin, they might try another."

He looked around the table. "Does anyone else have any questions, or anything to add?"

Jamie raised her hand.

"Yes, Deputy?"

"This morning, as I was leaving Darcy Marsh's veterinarian office, I saw a dark gray SUV, with the license plate obscured, exiting the parking lot."

"Do you think this was the same vehicle that drove by your house last night?" Travis asked.

Jamie stared. How had Travis known about that vehicle?

He must have read the question on her face. "Nate mentioned a vehicle fitting that description drove slowly past your house late last night," he said.

Nate! What else had he told his buddy, Travis, about last night? She tried hard to fight back a blush but wasn't sure she succeeded. "Yes, I think it was the same vehicle," she said. "A dark gray SUV—it could have been a Highlander—with the license plate obscured."

"We'll add that information to what we already know," Travis said.

She sat back, avoiding looking at Nate—or at anyone else. If the sheriff knew about her and Nate, how long would it be before everyone knew? Not that she was ashamed of having him spend the night, but she liked to keep her private life private. She didn't want to be the subject of gossip.

As soon as the meeting was over, she stood and made for the door. But Nate waylaid her in the hallway. "Jamie, wait up!" he called. "I'll ride with you to the cabins."

She pretended she hadn't heard, but that only made Nate raise his voice. "Jamie!"

She whirled to face him. "What?"

The word came out louder than she had intended. Now everyone was staring. She wished a hole would open in the floor and she could drop down into it.

Nate clomped up to her. "What's wrong?" he asked. "You look upset."

Aware of the others around them, she made for an empty office. Nate followed and shut the door behind him. If any of the others had seen them come in here—and they probably had, because cops didn't miss much—they'd talk. But at least what they said would only be speculation. "Did you tell Travis you were at my house last night?" she asked.

"Yes," Nate said. "He needed to know about the SUV we saw. It could be important to the case."

"Did you tell him you spent the night?"

"Yes."

She wanted to shake him but settled for clenching her hands. "Nate, how could you? He's my boss."

"I told him I stayed in case the guy in the pirate costume decided to pay you a visit. For all he knows, I slept on the couch." He put his hands on her shoulders. "I respect your privacy," he said. "And I'm not the kind of guy who shares private details like that with anyone else."

"Travis is your friend."

"Yes, but like you said, he's your boss. I'm not going to talk about you with him. It wouldn't be right."

She had never known Nate to lie to her before. Some of the tension in her shoulders eased. "Thank you. I'm sorry I overreacted. I just…" She shook her head.

"You want to take things slow," he said. "I understand. But remember—we're both single. We don't work for the same department. There's nothing wrong with us having a relationship."

"I know." She reached up and caressed his forearm. "But this is all so new…"

He kissed her forehead. "I know. You want to be sure this is going to work for you before you say anything. I get that. And I can be patient."

"Thanks for understanding." She wanted to melt into his arms and enjoy more than that gentle peck on the forehead. But she was on the clock, and they both had work to do. "Come on," she said. "We'd better get going."

The Juniper Creek cabins were tucked alongside a frozen creek in a section of national forest up against the base of Dakota Ridge. Since Nate was riding with her, Jamie ended up leading the convoy of sheriff's office vehicles. She stopped at the pipe gate that blocked the entrance to the cabins and Nate got out and post-holed through the snow to unlock one of half a dozen padlocks affixed to the chain around the gatepost.

"Why do you have a key?" she asked, when he returned to the cruiser.

"A buddy of mine owns one of the cabins. He lives in Denver now, so he gave me a key so I could check on the place for him."

As Travis had instructed, Jamie parked in the road at the bottom of a hill that led up to the cabins. The other deputies and the sheriff arranged their vehicles around hers to form a barricade across the road. Then they got out and gathered around the sheriff.

"We'll pair up and search every cabin for any signs of recent occupation," Travis said. "Nate will wait here and radio if anyone approaches. If you see anyone, or anything that raises concern, radio for backup. And be very cautious. They set a booby trap at the other cabin, so it's likely, if they've moved here, they've done the same."

Jamie and Deputy Dwight Prentice were tasked with searching the first three cabins. Six little residences formed a semicircle at the top of a rise, identical square cottages with front and back porches, metal roofs and board-and-batten siding painted forest service green. Heavy wooden shutters covered the windows, and stovepipes protruded from most of the roofs.

They approached up the road. As Jamie followed Dwight, trying to walk in the tracks he left in the deep snow, she was uncomfortably aware that anyone at the top of that hill would be able to see them coming. Though they all wore ballistic vests, a shooter could still do a lot of damage, and even kill them.

But no one fired on them, and the only sounds were the movements of the other members of the sheriff's department. "It doesn't look like anyone has come this way in a while," Dwight said when they reached the first cabin. A set of elk antlers hung over the front door, and a breeze stirred wind chimes that hung from one corner of the eaves.

Dwight tried the door, then knocked. "Sheriff's department!" he called loudly. "Open up!"

No one answered. She and Dwight hadn't expected them to. A stout padlock secured the front door. But they had to follow procedure.

Jamie peered through a gap in the shutters over the big front window, but could make out nothing in the darkness. "Let's check the perimeter," Dwight said.

They each circled around one side of the structure and met at the steps leading up to the rear porch, which had been screened in. The screen door was open, revealing a patio table and a stack of lawn chairs. The back door into the house was locked.

"Let's check the other cabins," Jamie said.

She led the way this time to the second cabin in the circle. The front door of this one featured a hand-carved wooden sign identifying it as McBride's Place. Snow had drifted around the foundation and buried the back steps.

As with the first cabin, Dwight and Jamie found no sign that anyone had been here in weeks.

They had the same results at the third cabin. To Jamie, the whole enclave felt deserted, preserved under a blanket of snow, waiting for spring. If Alex and Tim had ever been here, they had moved on before the last big snow.

They met Gage and Travis in front of the sixth cabin, and walked together back along the road toward the vehicles. "We didn't see any sign that anyone has been here," Dwight reported.

"Some here," Gage said. He scanned the thick woods around them. "It's a good hiding place, but maybe too remote for our killers. The other cabins were closer to town and other people."

"None of the murders have occurred near here," Travis said. "But they have to have shelter. We chased them out of the other cabin, so where did they go?"

"Maybe they have a friend who's putting them up," Jamie said.

"Or they broke into a summer home," Dwight said. "There are plenty of those in the area."

Travis nodded, but said nothing.

Nate met them at the gate. "Did you find anything?" he asked.

"Nothing," Travis said. "You should have waited in the cruiser. It would have been warmer."

"I've been doing some investigating of my own," Nate said. "I can't let you have all the fun."

"What did you find?" Travis asked.

"It might be nothing. Then again, it might be something." He led them back through the gate, up the Forest Service road about fifty feet to a trailhead. "I started thinking," Nate said. "This trail runs along behind the cabins, on the other side of the creek. It might be a back way in.

And someone's used it recently." He indicated tracks from snowshoes. "Two people, as close as I can figure."

"But we didn't find any tracks by the cabins," Gage said. "Unless someone is flying in through a window, we'd have seen signs of their passage in the snow."

"It could just be recreational snowshoers," Dwight said.

"It could," Nate agreed. "I still think it's worth following them, at least until you're past the cabins."

"Dwight and I can check them out," Jamie said.

"All right," Travis said. "We'll wait at the vehicles."

Jamie and Dwight headed up the trail. The snow was soft, which made the going slow. Deeper in the woods, the snowshoe tracks were more clearly visible, oval outlines in the snow. "I'd guess two men, from the size of the tracks," Dwight said.

"Yeah," Jamie said. "And it probably is just a couple of guys out for the day. We know no one went near the cabins."

"The killers have done a pretty good job of staying one step ahead of us," Dwight said. "If they were the ones at the Sundance cabins, they might have figured we'd look here next—it's a similar setup."

"Maybe," Jamie said. "But it doesn't hurt to check." When they had traveled about a quarter of a mile up the trail, she glimpsed one of the cabins through the trees. "If someone was going to cut over to the cabins, they'd do it somewhere in here," she said.

"Right here." Dwight stopped and indicated where the tracks turned off.

Picking up their pace, Dwight and Jamie followed the tracks to the edge of the icy creek, where they lost them in the deep snow along the creek bank. A bitter wind rattled the branches of the scrub oak that crowded the creek bank. Jamie hugged her arms across her chest against the cold.

"Did they wade across the creek?" she asked. "I don't see any tracks on the other side." Across the creek, the snow covered the open expanse between the creek and the cabins in a smooth white blanket.

"Me, either," Dwight said. "Let's see if we can pick up the tracks somewhere on this side of the creek." He headed one direction, while Jamie started off in the opposite direction. Carefully picking her way around the scrub oak and deadfall, she searched for some sign of the snowshoe tracks they had been following.

After about two minutes, she came upon a place where snow had been cleared away to reveal a stone campfire ring, logs drawn up on three sides for seating. Smoke curled up from the blackened contents of the ring, the scent of wet ash leaving a bitter taste in her mouth. "Dwight!" she called. "I've found something." She leaned over for a closer look and her heart hammered in her throat as she spotted what looked like blond hair.

Crashing sounds heralded Dwight's approach. He jogged up to her. "What is it?" he asked.

She pointed to the fire ring. "The ashes are still hot."

He found a tree branch and used it to poke at the smoldering fire. "There's some cloth in here," he said.

"And what looks like hair," she said. She put a hand to her mouth, fighting a wave of nausea. "You don't think it's a body, do you?"

"It's not real hair, I don't think." He fished a mane of yellow hair, half-melted and streaked black with ash, and held it up. "It's a wig," he said. "A woman's blond wig."

Chapter Fifteen

Nate stood in the situation room at the sheriff's department, trying to ignore the throbbing in his ankle. His doctor probably wouldn't approve of him having ditched the cast boot so soon, but he was sick of hobbling around on it. And he had plenty to distract him from the pain. The evidence collected from the fire pit had been arranged on the table in front of him. In addition to the half-burned blond wig, Jamie and Dwight had retrieved the remains of a wig of black dreadlocks, a fake beard and mustache, and black fabric garments that may have been the pirate costume. Before removing the items, they had photographed and measured the scene, and these photographs were also part of the evidence now.

"Do you think you can get DNA from the wigs?" Nate asked Travis.

"Maybe," the sheriff said. "If they aren't too badly burned. But that doesn't do us any good right now, since we can't get the wigs to the lab to test for DNA."

"I'll get to work adding all of this to our database," Jamie said, moving to the computer in the corner of the room.

"Lacy and I are supposed to have dinner with our officiate," Travis said. "But if you need me for anything…"

"You'll be the first to hear if there's a new development," Jamie said.

Travis left and she looked at Nate. "You might as well go home, too."

"I was thinking I could go and get us some dinner," he said.

"I packed a sandwich," she said. "It's in my locker."

"Doesn't something hot from Moe's Pub sound better? My treat." It wasn't the most romantic date he could think of, but it would give them a little time alone to talk.

"All right," she relented. "I guess I could go for a burger."

"No cheese, no onions, right?"

She smiled. "You remember."

"Some things you don't forget." And some people. Even in the years they had been apart, he hadn't forgotten about her. For a long time, she had been his fondest memory from his past. Returning to Eagle Mountain had made him wonder if they could make new memories together in the future.

Go slow, he reminded himself as he headed for his truck. Jamie had made it clear she wouldn't be rushed.

When he returned with their food half an hour later, she was bent over the computer. She looked up when he deposited the brown paper bag containing their burgers on the desk beside her. "Good timing," she said. "I was just finishing up."

He pulled a chair up across from her and handed her the diet soda he knew she preferred, then began distributing the food. "Thanks," she said, unwrapping her burger. "I really am starved."

"Tromping around in the woods in the cold burns a lot of calories," he said.

She nodded as she chewed, then swallowed. "How is your ankle?"

"It's there." He sipped his iced tea. "I guess Donna got home okay this morning?"

"Yes. She had a great time. Mrs. O'Keefe is so nice to take her."

"Are things serious between her and Henry?" he asked. "I mean, are they in love?"

Jamie frowned. "I don't know. They really like each other, but it's hard to say. I mean, Donna loves a lot of things. She loves her favorite TV shows and her stuffed cat and our three dogs. And she loves me. If I asked her, she would probably say she loves Henry, but I'm not sure if she knows what romantic love means."

"We all talk about loving lots of different things," he said. "Donna might not have the vocabulary to describe how her feelings for those things are different, but I'll bet down inside she knows the difference. I think that's part of being human." She stared at him a long moment, until he began to feel uncomfortable. "Did I say something wrong?" he asked.

"No. I think you said something very wise. I have to remind myself sometimes that my sister is her own person. I'm so used to looking after her and making decisions for her that I forget that sometimes. Her feelings and thoughts are real and valid even if I don't understand them. She's growing and changing all the time, though I don't always remember that."

"What does she do while you're working late like this?" he asked.

"She stays with our neighbor, Mrs. Simmons. She's a retired nurse and she and Donna really get along great. I was lucky to find her."

"I don't imagine that's cheap."

"No. But Donna gets some disability income that helps pay for it, and it's not like I spend my money on much else."

She said this as a kind of a joke, but he knew it was true. Jamie had never been one for fancy clothes or expensive hobbies and as far as he could tell, that hadn't changed. He had dated women who spent more on clothes and shoes and hair care, or cars and theatre tickets and furniture, than Jamie probably made in a year. It wasn't that she didn't care about her appearance or her surroundings, but she considered other things more important. She had dealt with more challenges than most women her age and had had to grow up much faster.

She finished her burger and stuffed the wrapper in the bag, then glanced up at the wall clock. "I should call Donna and tell her goodnight," she said. "I try to do that whenever I'm working late."

While she made the call, he stood and wandered over to the evidence table. The items they had pulled from the fire ring still reeked of smoke, along with the burnt-plastic smell of the singed artificial hair from the wigs. He picked up the evidence bag that contained the blond wig and examined it more closely.

Jamie joined him at the table. "Where in Eagle Mountain would someone get a wig like this?" he asked.

"The volunteers at the Humane Society thrift store put together a bunch of costumes for the masquerade ball," Jamie said. "When they open Monday morning I thought I'd go over there and ask if they had a blond wig, and if they remember who they sold it to. And the pirate costume. There couldn't have been too many like that, so I'm hoping they'll remember selling it."

Nate laid the wig back on the table. "I don't think it was an accident that they left this stuff near those cabins," he said.

"I don't, either," she said. "They guessed we would look for them there, because they had used that other cabin."

"They're taunting us," Nate said.

"Yes. They've done it before. They killed Fiona Winslow at the scavenger hunt, when there were off-duty officers all around them. They got a charge out of getting away with murder right under our noses."

"That's why the pirate focused on you at the party last night," Nate said. "It's why he drove by your house, and why he was hanging out at the vet's office this afternoon. Your spotting him wasn't an accident. He wanted you to see him and to know he's keeping tabs on you."

She shrugged. "It's creepy, but he's not going to do anything to me. I'm not going to let him trick me into coming with him somewhere. And I'm not going to mistake either Alex or Tim for innocent college students who need a lift somewhere, or a woman who needs help. I know better."

"You need to be careful," he said. "And you shouldn't go out alone."

"I'm alone in my patrol cruiser every time I work a shift," she said. "I know how to handle myself."

"There are two of them and only one of you," Nate said. "Maybe you should partner with another officer until this is over. Talk to Travis."

"No!" Her eyes flashed with anger. "You wouldn't suggest something like that to a male deputy."

"These two aren't killing men," he said.

"And they aren't going to kill me." She sat in front of the computer once more. "I appreciate your concern, but I can look after myself. I've been doing it a long time."

"I know." He shoved his hands in his pockets and stared at the floor, trying to rein in his emotions. "But that doesn't stop me from worrying."

"Nate." Her voice held a note of warning.

"What?"

"If we're going to bc a...a couple, then you can't do this."

"I can't worry about you? I don't know how to stop it. Or is it that you don't want me to talk about being worried?"

"You can worry—just don't try to stop me from doing my job."

If the shoe was on the other foot—if she objected to him going to work every day because it was dangerous—he would hate it. And they would probably fight about it. He wasn't going to let that happen. "I don't want you to give up your job," he said. "And I was out of line, suggesting you partner up with another deputy. I shouldn't have said that."

"Apology accepted." She hesitated, then added. "And it's nice to know someone is concerned about me. It means a lot."

He nodded. What he really wanted was to pull her to him and kiss her, but now wasn't the time or place. "I'd better go," he said. "You've got work to do and I should probably put this ankle up and slap an ice pack on it or something."

"You do that," she said. "I'll see you tomorrow."

He left, leaning more heavily on his cane as he crossed the parking lot to his truck. A thin sliver of moon shone overhead, amidst about a million diamond-bright stars. With few streetlights and most of the businesses shut down for the evening, there was little to compete with the nightly show in the heavens.

Nate drove slowly down Main, past silent storefronts and empty curbs. Moe's Pub, with its single lit sign, was the only business open, and only half a dozen cars and trucks remained in the gravel lot next to the tavern. A man emerged from Moe's front door and waved as Nate drove past, and Nate lifted one finger in salute. When Nate was a teenager, he had hated how quiet things were here after six or seven o'clock. The nearest movie theatre was an hour away and there had been nothing to do and nowhere to hang out with friends, away from the scrutiny of parents and teachers.

Now that he was older, he appreciated the peace and quiet. After a couple of years of partying in college he had had his fill, and these days he would rather watch a movie from the comfort of his couch, or visit with friends in their homes. He chuckled. Was this a sign of maturity—that he had no desire to hang out all night?

He approached the turnoff toward his house but instead of taking it, he drove half a mile farther and made the turn onto Jamie's street. He would just cruise by and make sure everything was all right. Just to help him sleep easier.

He slowed as he neared her house, and tightened his hands on the steering wheel as he took in the dark shape of an SUV in her driveway. Jamie's SUV was parked at the sheriff's department. So who was this? He flicked on his brights, trying to make out the figure in the driver's seat.

Just then, the vehicle in Jamie's driveway roared to life. The SUV reversed out of the driveway and barreled straight at Nate, who only had time to brace himself for the crash.

Chapter Sixteen

"Officer, please respond to MVA, Oak Street."

Jamie keyed her mike and responded. "Unit five responding."

"Copy that, unit five. EMS and fire are also on the way."

Jamie switched on her lights and siren and punched the accelerator. Oak was her street, with little traffic during daylight. Had one of her neighbors come home after too much to drink and clipped another car? Or had the deer who liked to wander into town and eat people's landscaping leaped out in front of a motorist?

As she turned onto the street, her headlights illuminated a pickup truck in front of the house. With a start, she realized it was Nate's truck. He stood beside it, head in his hands. She braked to a stop and, leaving the cruiser running, jumped out of the car and raced to his side. "Nate, what happened?" she asked. "Are you all right?"

"I'm fine. But my truck…" He pointed to the front of the truck. Jamie took a few steps forward and stared at the pile of bricks that had once been her mailbox surround, and at the crushed front end of Nate's pickup, steam hissing from the radiator.

"What happened?" she asked again, but before he could answer, an ambulance approached and parked across the street, followed by a fire truck. Merrily Rayford and Emmett Baxter climbed out of the ambulance and headed for Nate and Jamie, while a trio of firefighters in yellow bunker gear surrounded the truck.

"Is this our victim?" Merrily, a wiry blonde, set down a plastic tote and swept the beam of a flashlight over Nate's face. "That's quite a knot you have there. Did you hit your head on the dash?"

Nate put up a hand to shield his eyes as the EMT spotlighted a golf-ball-sized knot near his right temple. "It was a pretty hard impact. The air bags exploded and I couldn't really see anything for a few seconds." He brushed at the front of his jacket, which was coated in fine white dust. "What a mess."

"Lower your hand so I can see your eyes, please." He did as instructed and Merrily finished her examination. "Are you experiencing any pain?" she asked. "Neck, back, ribs, chest?"

"Just my head."

Merrily flicked a glance at Jamie. "How much did you have to drink tonight?" she asked.

"Nothing," Nate said.

"He hasn't been drinking," Jamie affirmed. "He and I were working at the sheriff's department until twenty minutes ago."

"Then how did you end up taking out this mailbox?" Emmett asked.

"Another vehicle ran me off the road," he said.

Merrily nodded and pressed a gauze square to the knot on Nate's head, which was seeping a little blood. "I don't see any sign of a concussion," she said. "But you ought to have someone with you tonight. And you could have whiplash or other injuries. Sometimes the shock of the accident masks pain. If you start experiencing any other symptoms, you should see a doctor right away."

"All right," he said. "Thanks."

While Merrily and Emmett packed up their gear and returned to the ambulance, Jamie pulled Nate aside. "Who forced you off the road?" she asked.

"That dark gray SUV that's been following you around was parked in your driveway," he said. "I slowed down to get a better look and hit my brights. The vehicle came barreling out the drive and headed right toward me. I had to wrench the wheel over to avoid being hit head-on." He frowned at the pile of crumbled brick in front of his bumper. "Sorry about your mailbox."

"Who was it?" she asked. "Did you get a good look at the driver?"

"No. Whoever it was had a knit cap pulled down low over his forehead, and a scarf wrapped around the lower half of his face."

She stared, trying to take in all he had said. "Are you sure it was the same SUV?" she asked.

"Yes. A Toyota Highlander. He was parked in your driveway, lights out." She could feel his eyes on her, and she could feel the anger and concern radiating from him, though it was too dark for her to read his expression. "He was waiting for you."

She gripped his arm, as much to steady herself as to command his attention. "What were you doing here?"

He hesitated, then said, "I was headed home and decided to drive by, just to check on the place. I'm not sure why—maybe I had an idea he would try something like this. I don't think it was a coincidence that he drove by here last night, and that he was waiting when you came out of the vet's office this afternoon."

Jamie didn't want to believe that this killer had targeted her. But she had been trained to draw conclusions based on evidence, and the evidence—as well as intuition—told her Nate was right.

"Jamie!"

She turned at the sound of her name. Donna, her puffy purple coat pulled on over pink flannel pajamas, jogged across the lawn toward her. Mrs. Simmons, swathed in a drab car coat, followed at a more sedate pace. "Jamie, what is going on?" Donna asked, throwing her arms around her sister.

"It's okay," Jamie said, hugging Donna to her. Feeling her sister's bulk calmed her. Donna was safe. Nate was going to be all right. That was all that mattered right now. "Just a little accident."

Donna turned to look at Nate. "Nate, are you hurt?" she asked.

His smile was more of a grimace, but Jamie was touched by the effort. "Just a bump on the head," he said. "I'll be fine."

"Your poor truck!" Donna pointed at the crumpled vehicle. "And the mailbox. How will we get the mail?"

"We can get a new mailbox," Jamie said.

"Such a commotion." Huffing a little, Mrs. Simmons joined them. "We heard the sirens and saw the lights and Donna insisted on coming out to see," she said. Her eyes shone and she kept darting glances at Nate and the wrecked truck, and the firefighters, who had retreated to the fire engine. Jamie suspected the caregiver had been as eager as Donna to be a part of the excitement.

"Did you see what happened?" Jamie asked.

Mrs. Simmons shook her head. "We were watching TV in the back of the house."

"We were watching Bollywood," Donna said. "And I had it turned up loud. I love the music and the dancing."

"But then we heard sirens and I looked out and saw the

flashing lights," Mrs. Simmons said. She leaned in closer and lowered her voice to a whisper. "Was it drunk driving, do you think?"

"No," Jamie said. "What about earlier? Did you see anyone over here at my house—another car in the driveway?"

"No." Mrs. Simmons's eyes widened and she put a hand to her mouth. "Someone was at your house? Who?"

"I don't know." Jamie didn't want to frighten the older woman. "It was probably someone with the wrong address. They weren't looking where they were going when they backed out of the driveway and hit Nate who had to swerve to avoid them."

She jumped as the fire truck's siren bleated. The firefighters waved as they pulled away from the curb. Merrily and Emmett jogged toward the ambulance. "Another call just came in," Emmett said.

The street seemed eerily silent after the emergency vehicles had left them. Jamie's feet and fingers ached with cold. "You need to get inside before you freeze," she told Donna.

"When will you be home?" Donna asked.

"When my shift is over." Jamie patted Donna's shoulder. "You go on back with Mrs. Simmons and I'll see you after eleven." She hoped it wouldn't be much later than that.

"Are you sure everything is all right?" Mrs. Simmons asked.

"It will be fine." She smiled in a way that she hoped was reassuring.

Donna and Mrs. Simmons returned to the caregiver's house and Jamie took out her phone. "I'm going to take some photographs and then I'll call a wrecker for your car."

"I'll get the wrecker driver to take me home," Nate said. "I guess there's nothing else I can do tonight."

"You heard Merrily," Jamie said. "You shouldn't be alone tonight."

"It's just a bump on the head," he said. "I'll be fine."

She dug her house keys from her pocket and pressed them into his hands. "You can stay with me tonight. I'll make up the couch." She wasn't ready to deal with awkward questions from Donna just yet.

He looked at the keys. "Are you sure?"

"I'm sure. Make yourself at home. I'll see to your truck, file my report, then I'll pick up Donna and be home before midnight."

She started to turn away, but he touched her arm. "You know what this means, him parked in your driveway?" he asked. "He's decided to go after you."

Her stomach knotted, but she refused to acknowledge the truth of his words. "He may be going after me," she said. "But you're the one who keeps getting hurt."

"I'm tough," he said. "I can take it."

"You don't think I can?"

"You're the strongest woman I know," he said. "But I don't want to have to find out what it would be like to not have you around."

He turned and strode toward the house, with only a trace of a limp. Jamie's chest hurt as she watched him mount the steps to the porch and let himself inside her house, but she didn't know whether the fear that threatened to strangle her was because someone might be trying to kill her—or because Nate cared so much.

NATE WOKE TO a throbbing head, in a room where the light didn't feel quite right. As sleep fled and his vision cleared, he looked up at the woman leaning over him. Donna, a pink knit hat pulled down over her brown hair, a fuzzy pink robe over pink pajamas, looked at him with an expression of great concern. "Hello," she said. "Why are you sleeping on our couch?"

After confirming that he was still dressed, Nate threw off the quilt he'd been sleeping under and shoved into a sitting position. "Jamie thought it would be better if I stayed here instead of going home alone after I was hurt last night," he said.

Donna nodded. "Good idea. Do you want some breakfast? We have cereal, or toaster waffles."

"What kind of cereal?" Nate asked.

Donna scrunched up her nose. "The healthy kind."

He suppressed a laugh. "Then maybe waffles?"

"Good choice!" She whirled and skipped away.

Nate made his way to the bathroom, where he rinsed his mouth and washed his face, and grimaced at the haggard, bruised visage that stared back at him. He ran a hand over his chin, the sandpaper rasp of a day's growth of beard making him wince. Nothing he could do about that now.

The smell of coffee drew him to the kitchen, where Jamie stood before the toaster, an empty plate in one hand, a coffee mug in the other. "Nate's here," Donna announced, unnecessarily, as Jamie had already turned to greet him.

"How are you feeling?" she asked, as he took a mug from the cabinet and filled it from the coffee maker beside the sink.

"I've got a headache, but nothing two aspirin and a little caffeine won't cure." He sipped the coffee and closed his eyes, savoring the sensation of its warmth spreading through him.

"Waffles will make you feel better," Donna said.

"Sit down and I'll fix you some waffles," Jamie said.

"I can look after myself," he said.

"It's not like I'm slaving over a hot stove." She set aside her coffee and pushed him toward the table. The toaster dinged and she plucked two waffles from the slots, dropped them on the plate, then set the plate in front of him. Donna pushed the syrup toward him.

He started to protest that he hadn't meant to take her waffles, but she had already inserted two more frozen discs into the toaster and pulled another plate from the cabinet. Three minutes later, she sat across from him. "I have to take Donna to work at eight, so I can give you a ride to your place," she said.

"Drop me off at the station," he said. "I want to talk to Travis about what happened last night."

"All right." She turned to Donna. "When you get off work this afternoon, wait for Mrs. Simmons to pick you up," she said. "I don't want you walking by yourself today."

"I can walk." Donna mopped up syrup with a forkful of waffle. "I like to walk."

"I know you do, but it's safer right now for you to wait for Mrs. Simmons."

Nate waited for Donna to protest, or to ask why, but she only mumbled "All right," and remained focused on finishing her breakfast. Was she as aware as they were of the danger the Ice Cold Killers posed to a young woman walking by herself? Or had experience taught her she wouldn't win an argument with her sister?

"Remember to wait for Mrs. Simmons," Jamie said. "Don't leave the store on your own."

"I'd rather go home with Henry." Donna looked up from her plate. "His mom said I could come over any time."

"We don't want to take advantage of Mrs. O'Keefe's hospitality," Jamie said. "Besides, if you go over to Henry's house all the time, he might get tired of you."

"He won't get tired of me," she said. "He loves me."

The expression in Jamie's eyes softened, though her mouth was still tight with worry. Nate wondered if he would ever tire of watching her this way—he was beginning to think not.

"Henry asked me to a birthday party tomorrow night," she said. "His cousin's birthday. She lives in a big house and has a hot tub and a snowmobile. She's going to have music and cake, and at midnight, they're going to shoot off fireworks."

"How long have you known about this?" Jamie asked.

Donna stuck out her lower lip. "I forgot to tell you. But Henry's mom is supposed to call you."

"I really don't want you out so late," Jamie said. "Especially with people I don't know. Maybe some other time."

"But I want to go!" Donna stood, her chair skidding backward. "You can't tell me what to do all the time. I'm old enough to decide for myself." Tears streamed down her face as she stared at Jamie. "I want to decide for myself," she sobbed, then whirled and ran from the room.

Jamie stared after her, then laid down her fork and pushed back her chair. She started to rise, then sank back down and turned to Nate. "Do you think I'm wrong?" she asked. "I'm only trying to protect her."

Nate clamped his mouth shut. Getting involved in a dispute between two sisters sounded like a bad idea any time. "You know your sister better than I do," he said.

"She wants to be independent," Jamie said. "She wants to be like other young women her age and it hurts her that she isn't. She doesn't show it, but I know it hurts. It's so unfair—she never did anything to deserve this."

"Neither did you," he said.

The look she gave him was so full of anguish he ached for her. "I want her to be happy," she said. "But most of all, I want her to be safe. Especially now. Especially with this killer preying on local women." She leaned across the table and took his hand. "What do you think I should do? Please tell me."

He took a sip of coffee, buying time. "Why not wait and talk to Mrs. O'Keefe?" he said. "Find out more about this party—where it is and who else will be there. Then you'll have a better idea of the risk involved."

She nodded. "All right. That makes sense." She sat back and let out a breath. "Thanks."

She stood and began gathering dishes. He rose and helped. They worked silently. She filled the dishwasher, while he put away the waffles and syrup—as he had done after other meals he had eaten here when they were in high school.

She had just closed the dishwasher when the doorbell rang. The dogs erupted into barking, a mad scrabble of toenails on the wood floor as they raced for the door. "Company!" Donna called, stomping down the stairs.

By the time Nate and Jamie reached the foyer, Donna was peering out the side window. "It's the sheriff," she announced.

Jamie shushed the dogs and ordered them back, then opened the door for Travis. He had his back to them, surveying the ruined mailbox. When he turned around, he didn't seem surprised to see Nate standing with Jamie. "I heard about what happened here last night," he said. "Jamie's report said something about a dark gray Highlander?"

"Come in." Jamie stepped back and held the door open wider. "Donna, you'd better go upstairs and get dressed or you'll be late."

Nate braced himself for another protest, but Donna merely turned and headed upstairs again. "Would you like some coffee?" Jamie asked. "I can make a fresh pot."

"No, thanks." He turned to Nate. "Tell me what happened."

Nate repeated his story about seeing the SUV in Jamie's driveway and gave his description of the driver.

"To anyone passing, he'd look like someone bundled up against the cold," Travis said. "But he made sure you wouldn't be able to give a description of him."

"I'm sure it's Alex or Tim," Nate said. "Everything points to it. I'd recognize the vehicle again. If we can find it, maybe we can find them."

"That's another reason I stopped by this morning," Travis said. "We found the Highlander. The VIN matches the one owned by Tim Dawson."

"That's great," Jamie said. "If they've been using it all this time, there's bound to be evidence—hairs, fibers, DNA."

Travis didn't seem nearly as excited as Jamie about the find. Then again, the sheriff was not the most emotional person around. "Where did you find it?" Nate asked.

"Out on Forest Service Road 1410, near the Sundance cabins," Travis said. "A call came in about eleven last night that someone had seen a fire in that area. By the time the first pumper truck got there, it was burned down to the frame."

"Accident or arson?" Nate asked.

"Oh, it was deliberate," Travis said. "The fire crew said they could smell the diesel fuel before they even got out of their truck."

"They were destroying evidence," Jamie said.

"Yes," Travis said. "And destroying our best link to them."

Chapter Seventeen

"Some folks nicknamed it the green monster." Bud O'Brien slapped his gloved hand on the hood of a mostly-green vintage pickup truck with oversize tires. "It looks like crap, but it will get you where you want to go."

"I guess I don't have much choice," Nate said, accepting the keys from the garage owner. His own truck was awaiting an assessment by an insurance appraiser—something that wouldn't happen until the highway reopened. Estimates on when that would be varied from tomorrow to next week, or next month. It all depended on how fast a road crew could clear away the many avalanches that had covered the pavement and how long fresh snows held off.

Today was sunny, the glittering white of the landscape blinding, the sky the blue of lake ice, the air bitterly cold and sharp enough that a deep breath was painful. The green monster's tires crunched over the snow-packed road as Nate headed out of town. Though he had discarded the air boot on his ankle and managed to walk without limping at least half the time, he hadn't been cleared to return to work, and Travis had nothing new for him to do. He'd decided to check out the site where Alex and Tim had burned their truck, more out of curiosity than from any hope of finding a real clue.

Bud O'Brien had hauled away what was left of the vehicle that morning, but a blackened patch of earth and soot-stained snow marked the spot, at the entrance to the summer cabins. Nate parked his truck well past the site and walked back along the road, then circled the patch of melted snow and ash that formed a muddy slurry. The smell of burned rubber and diesel fuel lingered in the air, and bits of broken glass and melted rubber littered the area. The deep tracks of Bud's wrecker led from the site to the road.

Nate's examination offered no new insight, so he walked back up toward the cabins, retracing the path he'd taken the day he was injured, wondering if any evidence lay buried under the thick snow, and trying to piece together the events of the last twelve hours. Alex and Tim must have driven out here last night immediately after one of them tried to run him down. The other would have followed in whatever vehicle they were using now—a stolen car? Travis would have zeroed in on any recently stolen vehicles, but he hadn't mentioned anything in the briefing at the sheriff's department that morning.

He had almost reached the cabin where he had been injured when movement in the underbrush caught his attention. At first he thought he had startled a deer, but a flash of red and blue made him reject that notion. Someone—no, two people—were running away from the cabin.

He started after then, but the deep snow and his still-tender ankle brought him to a quick halt. He'd never catch those two this way. He held his breath and listened as his quarry moved away, thrashing and cursing marking their progress. They were headed toward the road that ran behind the cabins, but thick brush and snow impeded their progress. If Nate hurried, he might be able to head them off.

Ignoring the pain in his ankle, he took off running

again, this time along the road, the snow there still packed down from sheriff's department vehicles, making movement easier. When he reached his truck, he gunned the engine. For all its dilapidated appearance, the vehicle had plenty of power. He raced around the hairpin curve where the road wound behind the cabins. He spotted the truck, and two figures emerging from the woods and climbing the snow-covered embankment toward a dirty brown Jeep Wrangler.

Nate braked hard and angled the truck in front of the Jeep. They wouldn't be able to move forward without hitting him, and backing up would send them perilously close to the embankment. As the two suspects reached the Jeep, Nate emerged from his truck, his Glock drawn. "Stop, and put your hands up where I can see them," he ordered.

The two young men—teenagers, he guessed—inched their hands into the air. This wasn't Alex and Tim. So why had they run from him? "Don't shoot," the slighter of the two said, staring out from beneath a red knit beanie and a fringe of blond bangs with frightened blue eyes.

"Who are you?" His companion, a handsome, broad-shouldered kid dressed all in black, demanded.

"Officer Nate Hall," he said. "Who are you?"

The teens looked at each other. "We haven't done anything wrong," the blond said.

"You were trespassing on private property," Nate said. Technically, the land on which the cabins sat belonged to the Forest Service, but the cabins themselves were private. "What were you doing at the cabins?"

"We were just looking for a friend," the blond said. His voice wavered and his hands shook.

"Who were you looking for?"

"We don't know their names," the boy dressed darker said. His expression wasn't exactly a sneer, but he showed none of his friend's nervousness. "They're just a couple of climbers we met. We followed them here and figured they were staying at the cabins."

"When did you meet them?" Nate asked.

The darker boy shrugged. "I don't know. A week ago?"

"It was last Monday," his friend said.

"Turn around and place your hands against the vehicle." Nate motioned with the Glock.

"You don't have any right—" the dark-haired boy said.

"He's got a gun," the other boy said. "Just do what he says."

Nate frisked each of them. They weren't armed, but he extracted their wallets and flipped them open. "Giuseppe Calendri and Greg Eicklebaum," he said, examining the driver's license photos, which gave local addresses. He holstered the Glock and returned the wallets, then took out the flyer with the pictures of Alex and Tim and held it out to them. "Are these the two climbers you met?" he asked.

The darker boy—Giuseppe—stuck out his lower lip. "I don't know."

"They had on stocking caps and sunglasses," the blond, Greg, said. "These look like driver's license photos. Nobody really looks like their driver's license photo, do they?"

Nate folded the flyer and stuck it back in his pocket. "Why did you run from me just now?" he asked.

"We didn't know you were a cop," Greg said. "You could have been anybody. I mean, there's a guy running around killing people. For all we knew, that was you."

"The Ice Cold Killer only kills women," Nate said.

"So far," Greg said. "But what if he changes his mind?"

"And it's not like you're in uniform, or even in a cop car." Giuseppe frowned. "You didn't show us a badge, either."

Nate pulled out his ID and flipped it open.

The boys leaned over to study it. "Aww, man," Greg said. "You're not even a real cop."

"I'm a real cop." Nate returned his credentials to his pocket.

"Well, we aren't fishing without a license or hunting out of season," Giuseppe said, his cockiness back. "And we didn't do anything to those cabins. Maybe we just got lost while we were out hiking and decided to cut through there to our car."

Nate didn't waste time arguing with him. "You can go," he said. "For now."

He waited until the boys were in their vehicle before he got into his own and pulled up far enough to let them out. Then he fell in behind them and followed them all the way to town. They turned off toward the gated neighborhood where they both lived, and Nate headed to the sheriff's department, to find out more about Giuseppe Calendri and Greg Eicklebaum.

JAMIE AND TRAVIS were going over the evidence database she had compiled when Nate walked into the office. How long was it going to be before this goofy, lightheaded feeling stopped sweeping over her every time she saw him? She had to fight to keep a sappy smile from her face, though there was no way she couldn't look at him. If nothing else, she wanted to see if she could detect whatever Donna had seen that convinced her sister that Nate was in love with her.

Okay, so maybe there was a little extra warmth in his eyes. And he really looked at her, his gaze lingering, instead of just sweeping over her. But that didn't really mean he was in love—did it?

"What can you tell me about Giuseppe Calendri and

Greg Eicklebaum?" Nate asked, sinking into the chair Travis offered him.

"Where did you run into those two?" Travis asked.

"At Sundance cabins," Nate said. "I wanted to see where Alex and Tim burned the Highlander, then I walked up to the cabins. Those two took off through the woods like a couple of startled deer."

"Giuseppe goes by Pi," Travis said. "He and Greg and a third boy, Gus Elcott, got in a little trouble a couple of weeks ago. They had some kind of competition going, racking up points for whoever could do the most outrageous dare. I had them do community service, shoveling snow, as punishment."

"I think they know something about Alex and Tim," Nate said. "When I asked them what they were doing at the cabins, they said they met a couple of climbers last Monday. They thought they were staying at the cabins and were looking for them. I showed them the pictures of Alex and Tim and they said they didn't recognize them, but I think they're lying."

"Do you know Pi and Greg?" Travis asked Jamie.

She shook her head. "I remember seeing their names as possible witnesses for Christy O'Brien's murder."

"They were spotted near the site of the murder that night," Travis said. "But they swore they didn't see a thing." He stood. "I think you and I should have a talk with Pi. He's the ringleader of that group."

"He struck me as a smug brat," Nate said.

"He's smart," Travis said. "He'll make a good witness if we can get him to tell us what he knows."

"Why did you want to take me to question this boy, instead of Nate?" Jamie asked when she and Travis were in the sheriff's cruiser, headed toward the exclusive neighborhood where the Calendris lived.

"I could say I want to give you more experience questioning suspects," Travis said. "That's true, and it would be the politically correct answer. But also, Nate already struck out questioning the boys. He cornered them and they dug in their heels. Pi strikes me as the type who likes to be the star of the show. You're closer to his age, and a woman, so I think he'll want to impress you."

Jamie smiled. She could always count on the sheriff to be honest. "I'll do my best to appear to hang on his every word," she said.

Chapter Eighteen

The Calendris lived in an impressive stone-and-cedar home with views of the snow-capped mountains. The young man who answered Travis's knock was handsome as any teen heartthrob, with thick dark hair flopping over his brow and deep-set, intense brown eyes. "Hello, Sheriff," he said, showing no surprise at the lawman's appearance. He nodded to Jamie as she walked past. "Hello, Deputy."

He closed the door and led them into an expansive great room, with soaring fir-plank ceilings and a massive stone fireplace in which a fire crackled. "I suppose you're here to ask me more about the two climbers we told Officer Hall about," he said, taking a seat on an oversize leather ottoman. "I'm sorry, I really don't know anything else to tell you."

"Where did you meet them?" Travis asked.

"Those ice falls by the national forest campground," Pi said. "It's not an official climbing area, but with all the snow and cold we've had this winter, there are some impressive features there. We wanted to give it a try and they were just finishing up a climb, but they gave us some good route-finding tips."

"Who is we?" Travis asked.

"Gus Elcott and Greg Eicklebaum were with me." Pi flashed a smile at Jamie. "They were busy unloading our climbing gear, so I did most of the talking with the two climbers."

"Did they tell you their names?" Jamie asked.

Pi shook his head. "No."

"Did they say where they were from? Where they were staying?" Travis asked.

"No."

"You told Officer Hall that you had followed them to the cabins," Travis said. "When was that?"

Pi waved a hand. "Oh, after we finished climbing I thought I spotted the guys' truck on the side of the road. I slowed down, thinking I'd stop and thank them for their help, and ask if they knew other good climbing areas around there. But as I slowed down, they pulled out in front of me. So I followed them until they pulled into the cabins. When they saw me, though, they pulled out and left."

"If they left, what made you think they were staying there?" Jamie asked.

Pi shrugged. "Just a hunch I had. I believe in following hunches."

"Have you seen either of these two since that day?" Travis asked.

"No." He leaned forward, elbows on his knees. "Why are you so interested in them? Have they done something wrong?"

"We'd like to question them in connection with a case," Travis said.

Pi sat back and nodded. "You think they have something to do with those women who were murdered," Pi said. "Maybe they're the Ice Cold Killer. I'm right, aren't I?"

"Describe these two," Travis said, ignoring Pi's suspicions. "How old do you think they were? What did they look like?"

"They were in their twenties, I think," Pi said. "One

was about my height—six feet—and the other was an inch or two taller."

"What color hair?" Travis prompted.

Pi shook his head. "They were wearing knit caps and those face things—balaclavas? It was really cold out, and when you're climbing ice, it gets even colder."

"What color eyes?"

"They had on sunglasses."

"Anything else?" Travis asked. "Did they have accents? Say where they were from?"

"No. We just talked about climbing."

Travis frowned, but closed his notebook and stood. Jamie and Pi rose also. "What are you and Greg and Gus up to these days, besides climbing?" Travis asked.

"We're staying out of trouble," Pi said.

"No more dares?"

Pi laughed. "No more dares. Thought it was fun while it lasted. Gus ended up with the most points, though we never declared an official winner."

"Points?" Jamie asked.

Pi flashed his movie-star smile again—a smile that had probably left more than one teenage girl weak at the knees, Jamie thought. "We had a little competition going where we accumulated points for different accomplishments. Some of them were a little risky, but we didn't mean any harm." He glanced at Travis. "Though I guess things were getting a little out of hand there at the end. It was probably just as well that we stopped."

"Don't start up again," Travis said. "Someone might get hurt."

"We won't," Pi said as he walked them to the door. "Although I think about it sometimes, things I might have done to earn more points. Just as a mental exercise, of course." He opened the door and Travis and Jamie exited.

Pi followed them onto the steps. "I hope you catch your killers," he said. "That's something that would have been worth a lot of points when we were playing our game. Someone who caught a serial killer would have been the ultimate winner."

"This isn't a game," Travis said. "If you know something that would help us, you need to tell us."

"I don't know anything," Pi said, his expression remaining pleasant. "Just another mental exercise." He returned to the house and closed the door behind him.

"There's something he's not telling us," Jamie said as she buckled her seat belt. "We need to talk to Greg and see what he says."

"We'll talk to Greg." Travis started the cruiser. "And maybe Pi is hiding something. Or maybe he just wants us to think he's smarter than he is."

"He probably isn't smarter than the killers," Jamie said.

"They're making mistakes," Travis said. "Leaving behind more evidence. We're going to find them."

"That would be a nice wedding present, wouldn't it?" Jamie said. "Closing this case before you leave on your honeymoon."

"Yeah," Travis agreed. "I know Lacy would appreciate it if we could start our marriage without this hanging over us."

"They haven't killed anyone in six days," Jamie said. "Maybe because we're closing in on them, forcing them to spend more time running."

"I wish I could think that's a good thing," he said. "But everything I've read says serial killers feel compelled to chase the high they get from killing. It's like a drug and the longer they go without it, the more the craving builds."

She bit the inside of her cheek, trying to create some

saliva for her suddenly dry mouth. "Nate thinks the killers have targeted me," she said.

"I don't think he's wrong," Travis said. He glanced at her, then refocused his attention on the road. "That's another reason I wanted you with me this afternoon. I don't want you patrolling alone until this is settled. And before you say anything, I would do the same if a killer appeared to be stalking a male deputy."

"Yes, sir." As much as she wanted to protest that her training enabled her to look after herself, the truth was, these two killers frightened her. She never wanted to be in the position where she had to face them down alone.

MONDAY AFTERNOON, JAMIE devoted herself to helping Donna get ready for the party. Henry's mom had answered all her questions and reassured her that the birthday party would be well supervised and safe. Donna could enjoy the party and Jamie didn't have to feel like a terrible person for keeping her home. Donna had been ecstatic at the news and had spent hours going through her clothes, deciding what to wear

Though her sister had attended homecoming dances and senior prom with groups of friends, and she had met Henry and his mother at the masquerade ball, this was her first real date, and she threw herself into it with all the fanfare of a Hollywood actress preparing for her first red carpet premiere. A long bubble bath was followed by a session with blow dryer and curling iron. She sat in a kitchen chair before her dresser mirror and fidgeted while Jamie shaped her hair into dozens of short ringlets all over her head.

"Close your eyes," Jamie ordered before she sprayed a liberal application of hair spray. A sparkly pink bow carefully clipped over one ear formed the finishing touch. Though Jamie had feared the final effect would be more

French poodle than *femme fatale*, Donna ended up looking perfectly lovely.

"I need perfume," Donna said, jumping up from her chair. "Something that smells really good."

Jamie didn't normally wear perfume, but she unearthed a bottle of her mother's favorite scent in the back of a closet. She dabbed some on Donna's wrist and her sister sniffed appreciatively. "It smells pretty," she said. "Like Mom, when she dressed up to go out."

Jamie had a sudden memory of watching her mother put on her makeup before going out to dinner with their father. When she was done, she would call both girls to her and give them a little spritz of her perfume "to have a little bit of me with you while I'm away." Now it felt like she was here again with them. "Mama would be so proud of you now," Jamie said, then turned away before she started crying and Donna, always so sympathetic to others' emotions, joined in. "Let's finish getting you ready."

Half an hour before Henry and his mother were due to arrive, Donna stood before Jamie. The orange ribbed tights she had chosen to go with her pink party dress—because orange was Henry's favorite color—made her look like a sherbet dessert—but a charming one. Henry would no doubt be delighted. Jamie's gaze shifted to the silver high heels Donna had borrowed from Jamie's closet. "Are you sure you don't want your pink flats?" she asked. "They'll be more comfortable for dancing."

"I don't want to be comfortable," Donna said. "I want to be pretty."

"Your flats are very pretty," Jamie said, resisting the impulse to rant about a culture that made women believe beauty was something they had to suffer for. Donna didn't care about any of that—she just wanted to be like the other young women she saw, with their high heels and fancy dresses.

"Is my face okay?' Donna turned and peered anxiously into the mirror. With Jamie's help, she wore not only powder and lip gloss, but eye shadow and mascara, which made her look older and, yes, more sophisticated.

"You look beautiful," Jamie said, hugging her gently, so as not to muss her hair.

The doorbell rang and the dogs began to bark. The sisters raced downstairs to answer it, but instead of Henry and his mother, Nate stood on the doorstep, his arms full of flowers. "Hello," he said. He offered a bouquet to Donna. "These are for you."

"Flowers!" Donna buried her nose in the blossoms—a handful of pink and white carnations and a single over-blown rose.

"And these are for you." Nate extended a second bouquet—more carnations and alstroemeria—to Jamie.

"Where did you find flowers?" she asked. "I'm sure the florist hasn't had a delivery in weeks."

"They had a few blooms left," he said. He turned back to Donna. "You look beautiful."

She blushed and giggled, and teetered on her heels, so that Jamie reached out to steady her. She should find a way to pull Mrs. O'Keefe aside and give her the pink flats, in case Donna wanted to change later.

"What should I do with my flowers?" Donna asked.

"I'll put them in a vase," Jamie said. She took her sister's bouquet along with her own to the kitchen, glad for a few moments alone to organize her thoughts. Nate's arrival was a surprise, but it didn't feel wrong to have him here for this milestone. She wondered if he understood how important this was for her and for Donna, too, and wanted to celebrate with them. Maybe he did, since he had brought the flowers.

Voices drew her back to the foyer, where Henry stood, dressed in black jeans and boots, a Western-cut white shirt, black leather jacket and a string tie. "Henry, you look so handsome," Donna cooed.

"And you look beautiful," he said, eyes shining.

Donna turned to Jamie. "And look—he brought me a corsage."

Jamie duly admired the corsage—made of pink silk roses and silk ferns—and slid it onto Donna's wrist. "Before you go, I have to get a picture," Jamie said, rushing to retrieve her phone.

The resulting photos showed the couple arm in arm, grinning at the camera, then at each other. Donna had never looked happier, Jamie thought.

"We have to go," Henry said.

Nate helped Donna with her coat. He and Jamie followed the couple onto the front porch and waved to Mrs. O'Keefe, who waited in the car.

Back inside, Jamie stood for a moment with her head down, one knuckle pressed hard above her upper lip, determined to hold back tears. Nate put his arm around her. "I can't believe I'm being so silly," she said. "You'd think I was sending my only kid to war or something. It's just a dance."

"I'm wondering if it's because she's doing something you thought she might never do," Nate said. "She's going on a real date with a young man she loves. She's doing something other girls her age do all the time, but that not every girl with her disability gets to do or is able to do."

Jamie looked up at him, blinking hard and somehow managing to keep the tears from overflowing. "I never thought of that," she said. "I… I think you might be right."

He took her hand in his. "I figured you might appreciate a little distraction tonight, so I thought I'd take you out."

"A real date?" she asked.

"A real date." He surveyed the yoga pants and sweatshirt she wore. "I can wait while you change."

She laughed and punched his chest. Unlike her casual clothes, he wore pressed jeans, a dark blue dress shirt and sports coat. "What makes you think I need to change?"

He grinned and waggled his eyebrows. "I can help you, if you like."

"Then we might never leave the house."

"I'm liking this idea better and better." He lunged toward her and she danced out of his reach and raced up the stairs.

"I'll be down in ten minutes," she called over her shoulder.

A pleasant thrill of excitement hummed through her as she rifled through her closet, trying to choose the right outfit. She settled on a pale blue cashmere sweater, black tights, a short black skirt and tall leather boots. Warm, easy to move in, but still sexy.

She was leaning over the bathroom sink, finishing her makeup, when Nate entered, a glass of wine in each hand. "I thought you might like this." He handed her a glass.

She sipped, her eyes locked to his. Despite the fading black eye and bruised temple, he had never looked more handsome to her. Maturity sat well on him, and though she still recognized the boy he had been, she appreciated more the man he had become.

She set aside the wine glass and wrapped her arms around him. "This was a good idea," she said.

"The wine? Or the date."

"The date."

He set his own glass beside hers, then drew her close for

a kiss—not the eager kiss of an impatient lover or the per-
functory embrace of a man doing what was expected, but a
deep, tender caress that invited lingering and exploration.

She arched her body to his and angled her mouth to
draw even closer, sinking into the sensation of his body
wrapped around her and the response of her own. Her pulse
thrummed in her ears and all thought of anything or anyone fled, and with it every bit of tension that had lately
strained her nerves and disturbed her sleep.

She moaned in protest when Nate pulled away, and
opened her eyes to stare at him accusingly. "Your phone,"
he said, gesturing toward the bedroom.

Then she realized a tinny reproduction of an old-fashioned phone ring was echoing from the bedroom. She
pushed past him and retrieved the phone from the dresser.
When she saw Mrs. O'Keefe's name her relaxed happiness
vanished. "Hello? Mrs. O'Keefe, is everything all right?"

"Oh, Jamie!" Mrs. O'Keefe's voice broke in what
sounded like a sob. "I'm so sorry. I don't know what to do."

"What is it? What happened?" Nate moved in behind
her and she glanced back at him, sure her eyes reflected
her sense of panic, then held the phone a little away from
her ear so that he could hear, too.

"I stopped to get gas and went inside to pay," Mrs.
O'Keefe said, the words pouring out in a rush. "I was sure
Henry and Donna would be fine while I was away, but
when I came out, she was gone."

"Gone? Donna is gone?" Jamie's voice rose, on the edge
of hysteria. Nate's arm encircled her, holding her up as her
knees threatened to buckle. "Where is she?"

"I don't know!" Mrs. O'Keefe wailed. "Henry said two
men in masks grabbed her and dragged her from the car.
One of them hit him—he's bleeding, and when I got there

he was hysterical. A sheriff's deputy is here, but I knew I needed to call you."

"We're on our way." Jamie ended the call and grabbed her keys from the dresser. "We have to go," she said, already running for the stairs. "Someone's taken Donna."

Chapter Nineteen

Nate drove as fast as he dared from Jamie's house to the corner where Eagle Mountain's two gas stations stood opposite each other. It had started to snow again, and the streets were mostly empty. Mrs. O'Keefe's Honda sat beside the end gas pump, a sheriff's department cruiser behind it. Jamie was out of the truck before Nate had come to a complete stop, hurrying to where Gage stood with Mrs. O'Keefe beside her vehicle. When Mrs. O'Keefe saw Jamie approaching, she burst into sobs.

Gage moved to one side while Jamie embraced the older woman. Nate approached him. "What have you got?" Nate asked.

"Two men in a white soft-top Jeep pulled up. One got out, jerked open the back door of the O'Keefe car and slashed the seat belt. He clamped one hand over Donna's mouth and dragged her out of the vehicle. When Henry tried to go after them, he punched him—hard. I think the poor kid's nose is probably broken."

"Did anyone see what happened?"

Gage shook his head. "Mrs. O'Keefe was the only customer and the clerk was busy with her."

Nate nodded toward a camera mounted above the gas pumps. "Maybe we'll get something from that."

"Maybe," Gage said. "But the camera is focused next to

the pumps, to catch people who drive off without paying for their gas. The kidnappers pulled up on the far side of the O'Keefe car. Henry says they wore masks."

"We don't need to see them to know who did this," Nate said.

The ambulance pulled in on the other side of the gas pumps, followed by the sheriff's cruiser.

EMT Emmett Baxter climbed out and approached the car. Mrs. O'Keefe and Travis met him. Jamie walked over to stand with Gage and Nate, her arms hugged tightly across her chest. The lighting under the gas pump canopy cast a sickly yellow glow, and snow blew around them in dizzying swirls.

Nate went to his truck and retrieved his coat and put it around her shoulders. "It's freezing out here," he said.

"I don't even feel it," she said. "I don't feel anything." Her eyes met his, red-rimmed and bleak. "What if they kill her?"

"You can't think that," he said.

She glanced over toward the car, where Henry sat in the back seat. "Go see about Henry," she said. "He had to see it happen, and he tried to protect her." She covered her mouth with her hand. He started to reach for her, but she pulled away. "Go make sure Henry is okay."

Henry sat between Emmett and his mother in the back seat of the Honda. Nate opened the passenger door and leaned in. "How's it going?" he asked.

"His nose is broken," Emmett said. "We'll have to splint it." He turned back to Mrs. O'Keefe. "We can give him something for the pain first, if you think that's all right."

"Of course." Mrs. O'Keefe squeezed her son's hand. "It's going to be all right," she said.

"It won't be all right without Donna," he moaned.

"Give me your other hand," Mrs. O'Keefe said. "And look at me."

Henry opened his hand and stared at the crumpled rectangle of white pasteboard in it.

"What have you got there?" Mrs. O'Keefe asked.

Nate leaned in past her. "Let me see," he said.

Henry held out his hand and Nate stared at the crumpled business card. "Ice cold," he read.

"He shoved this into my hand before he took Donna away," Henry said.

Nate took the card carefully, holding it by the edges, and walked over to where Travis stood with Jamie. When she saw what he held, her face blanched white, but she said nothing.

Travis frowned at the card. "This doesn't fit the pattern for the other women," he said.

"No, it doesn't," Nate said. "The others were all alone, taken when no one else was around."

Travis turned to Jamie. "Did you see any strange cars around your house when the O'Keefes and Donna left there this evening?"

"No." She bit her lip. "But I wasn't really looking."

"I didn't see anyone, either," Nate said. He had been focused on Jamie. Still, if Alex and Tim had been there, wouldn't he have known?

"I think they were watching your house and followed Mrs. O'Keefe to the gas station," Travis said. "They saw their chance to grab Donna and took it."

"But why Donna?" Jamie asked. "She never hurt anyone!"

It was the question everyone left behind when a loved one senselessly died asked—the question the families of Kelly Farrow and Christy O'Brien and Michaela Underwood and all the other murder victims had asked. Usually, there was no explanation for a crime like this.

"I don't think they were really after Donna," Travis said.

"Then why?" Jamie looked dazed.

"I think they were after you," Travis said. "This was a way to get to you. To get to a cop. It's what they've wanted all along."

"They can have me," she said. "As long as they don't hurt Donna."

"They're not going to have either of you," Travis said.

"We have to figure out where they've taken her," Nate said. "They have to be holed up somewhere."

Gage emerged from the gas station office. "The security camera at the pump picked up a partial plate number for the vehicle the kidnappers were in," he said. He handed Travis a slip of paper.

"It's the last two numbers of a Colorado plate," Travis said. "That will help—the first three letters are the same for half the cars registered in the county, but the last three are different." He returned the paper to Gage. "Call this in to Dwight. Tell him to do a search for every white Jeep Wrangler in the county and see if he can match this."

"I'm on it," Gage said.

"Let me help," Jamie said. "I'm good on the computer and focusing on the search will help keep me from going crazy."

Travis looked at her a long moment, as if trying to decide if she was going to crack up. "All right," he said. "Go help Dwight."

"I'll take you," Nate said.

They drove to the station in silence. There was no sense trying to comfort Jamie with words. The only thing that counted was action. He parked in front of the sheriff's department and came around to open the door for her. She slipped off his jacket and pressed it on him. "Are you coming in?" she asked.

He shook his head. "No. I'm going to talk to Pi and Greg again. Neither were very forthcoming when we interviewed them earlier, but Travis thinks they know something they aren't telling us, and I'm going to find out what that is."

But when Mrs. Calendri answered the door and Nate showed her his ID, she told him her son wasn't at home. "He's with Greg and Gus," she said.

"Could you call him for me?" Nate shoved his hands in the pocket of his jacket, which still carried a faint whiff of the lotion Jamie used. "It's important."

She retreated into the house and returned with a phone in her hand. She held it to her ear for a moment, then shook her head. "He isn't answering." Another pause, then she said, "Pi, please call your mother as soon as you can. It's important." She ended the call.

"Do you know Greg and Gus's numbers?" Nate asked.

"No. I don't. What is this about? Is Pi in some kind of trouble?"

"I hope not, Mrs. Calendri. We're trying to find someone who may be involved in a crime, and we think your son might be able to help us."

The lines around her eyes tightened. "I don't have Greg and Gus's numbers, but I can tell you where they live."

Greg Eicklebaum lived only two blocks away. Nate drove there and found him and Gus playing video games in a den off the garage. "We don't know where Pi is," Greg said after Nate explained his mission. "He was supposed to come over this afternoon, then said he had something else to do."

Nate sat and faced the boys, so close to them their knees almost touched. "You've got to tell me everything you know about those two climbers you saw out near the camp-ground that day," he said. "We think they kidnapped a young disabled woman this evening. Her life may depend on us finding them." His throat tightened as he said the words, but he pushed the image of Donna, helpless and afraid, away. He had a job to do, and that meant staying focused on facts, not emotions.

The two boys exchanged glances, then Gus said, "We saw one of them this morning."

"Where?"

"We were walking over to the park to shoot hoops." He gestured to the north. "This white Jeep pulled up to the stop sign and we looked over and it was one of the guys—the taller one, with the lighter hair. I remembered his sunglasses—really sharp Oakleys. We waved, but I don't think he saw us."

"You don't know where he was driving from—or where he went?" Nate asked.

"No," Gus said. "But Pi figured he must live near here, because nobody else really drives around here. I mean, there aren't any through streets or anything."

"Can you think of anything else that could help us find this guy?" Nate asked.

They both shook their heads. "I wish we could," Greg said. "Really."

"If you think of anything, call the sheriff's office," Nate said.

He returned to the sheriff's department and found Gage and the sheriff huddled with Dwight and Jamie in the situation room. "We think we've got something," Gage said when Nate joined them.

"There are a lot of white Jeeps registered in the county," Dwight said, tapping the keys of a laptop open on the desk before him. "But only two with the two numbers the security camera caught. One is registered to Amber Perry of 161 Maple Court, the other to Jonathan Dirkson of 17 Trapper Lane."

"Trapper Lane," Nate said.

The others stared at him. "Trapper Lane is in the same neighborhood as Pi Calendri and Greg Eicklebaum," he said. "I just talked to Greg and Gus Elcott, and Greg said they saw one of the climbers they had run into earlier, driving a white Jeep in their neighborhood this morning."

"What's the contact information for Dirkson?" Travis said.

"I'm on it," Jamie said, furiously typing at a second laptop. "Jonathan Dirkson's contact information is in Phoenix," she said.

"That's it!" Nate said. "The house on Trapper Lane is probably a vacation home. Alex and Tim broke into an unoccupied home and made use of the vehicle that was probably in the garage."

"A lot of houses in that neighborhood are second homes," Gage said. "And a lot of people rent them out short-term. Alex and Tim could tell anyone who asked they were vacationing here and the chances of anyone checking with the house's owner are slim to none."

"Let's go," Travis said.

Jamie shoved back her chair. "I'm coming with you," she said. "And don't tell me to stay here. If I'm really the one they want, then maybe I can help to trap them."

"All right." Travis turned to Nate. "I suppose you're going to come, too."

"You could use another trained officer."

"Go with Jamie, in her cruiser," Travis said. "And try not to get hurt. I don't want to have to explain to your boss how you were injured yet again when you aren't even officially on duty."

FOUR SHERIFF'S DEPARTMENT CRUISERS—and most of the sheriff's department, plus Nate—blockaded both ends of Trapper Lane. They surrounded the house, and the sheriff used a bullhorn to demand that Tim and Alex release Donna and come out with their hands up. But the only reaction they received was silence, and furtive looks through the curtains from the neighbors.

Dwight approached the house from the side, then returned to the others. "The Jeep isn't in the garage," he said. "Maybe they aren't here."

"Then we search the house," Travis said.

While the others hung back to provide cover, he and Gage approached the front door. Travis knocked, then tried the knob, and the door swung open. They disappeared into the house and emerged a long five minutes later. "It's clear," Travis called.

The others entered the empty, though orderly, house. Dust covers draped the furniture in every room but the kitchen and a small den where Tim and Alex had apparently established themselves. A couple of sleeping bags were rolled up on the floor of the den, and a few empty cans in the kitchen garbage can were the only evidence of occupation.

"Search every room," Travis said. "I want anything that might be tied to them, or that might tell us where they are now."

Dwight found Donna's corsage on the floor of the mudroom, the flowers crushed. Jamie stared at the forlorn flowers, then turned away, breathing hard.

"I noticed a shed out back," Dwight said. "Someone should check that."

"I will," Jamie said. She needed to get out of this house where her sister had been held.

The shed was a prefab wooden structure, about five feet

by seven feet, with a single door. The door wasn't locked, but Jamie had to force it open. When she finally stepped inside, she saw the reason for her difficulty as she shone her flashlight over the body of Pi Calendri. Her heart sank as she passed the light over the wound in his shoulder and the pool of blood on the concrete floor.

"Somebody help me," he moaned, and Jamie dropped to her knees beside him.

"Pi, what happened?" she asked, feeling for his pulse.

But she never heard his answer, as her head exploded in pain, and the world went black.

Chapter Twenty

Jamie came to in a fog of pain. Her head pounded and her arms ached, and the smell of dust and old wood smoke mingled with the haunting scent of her mother's perfume. As her head cleared, she realized she was lying on a bed, her hands bound beneath her back. Dusty wood beams stretched overhead and nothing looked familiar. She turned her head to the side and relief surged through when she saw a teary-eyed Donna staring back at her, and the memory of being with Pi in the garden shed returned. Someone must have attacked her and brought her to this place. "Are you all right?" Jamie whispered.

"I tore my tights," Donna said. "And I lost my flowers."

Before they could talk more, the door opened and a young man in a blue beanie and parka shuffled in. "Who are you and what are you doing with us?" Jamie asked.

"You don't know who I am?" He chuckled. "I'm the Ice Cold Killer."

Jamie recognized him now, from the flyer Travis had printed. Tim Dawson. "There are two of you," Jamie said. "Where's your friend?"

"So you figured that out, did you?" He stripped off his coat to reveal a faded red sweatshirt over jeans, then dropped into a straight-backed wooden chair. "He had some things he had to take care of."

"What are you going to do with us?" she asked.

"What do you think?" He clasped his hands behind his head. "The same thing we did to the others. My friend is out there now, looking for a good place to dump your bodies."

Donna began to cry. Though her hands were bound, Jamie shifted her body toward her sister, trying to comfort her. "Why are you doing this?" she asked.

"You haven't figured that out?" He leaned toward her. "Cops are so clueless. The Ice Cold Killer kills women, right? So killing a cop would be the ultimate. Your sister was just a way to get to you."

Jamie lay back on the bed, trying to memorize the details of her surroundings, searching for a way out. The room they were in wasn't very big, and seemed to be a combination kitchen, dining, living room and bedroom. A cabin, then. One of those Forest Service cabins where Alex and Tim had hidden before? Presumably when the second killer returned, they would kill Donna and Jamie, and transport them to the dump site. Or would they transport them first and kill them there? The latter provided more opportunities for escape, but she couldn't rely on that.

She would probably only have one chance to save her sister. She would have to be ready to take it, with no hesitation.

"WHERE'S JAMIE?" NATE ASKED, when he had finished searching the upstairs bedroom of the house, which had yielded no evidence that the two killers had ever been in there.

Dwight looked up from pulling books from the bookcase. "She went out to check the shed."

"You let her go out there alone?" Nate asked.

"I'd let you go out there alone," Dwight said.

Nate didn't bother answering but raced outside. The

door of the shed stood open, and as he approached, he heard moaning.

Pi Calendri lay in a pool of blood on the floor of the garden shed, his head resting on the deck of a lawnmower, his feet on a sack of mulch. Nate pulled out a phone and called for an ambulance, then knelt beside the young man and tried to rouse him.

Pi's eyes flickered open. "It hurts bad," he said, his voice faint.

"Hang in there, buddy," Nate said. "Help is on the way." He examined the injury to the boy's shoulder. Pi had lost a lot of blood and he might be in shock, but the wound was a clean one. "Tell me what happened, so I can find out who did this."

"Those two climbers? I saw one this morning and figured they were in the neighborhood. I knew you were looking for them. I figured maybe they were the Ice Cold Killers. I figured I'd find them—you know, be a hero." He closed his eyes. "Guess I was really stupid."

"Stay with me," Nate said. "The ambulance will be here soon."

Pi moaned.

"Pi!" Nate patted his cheek and the young man opened his eyes. "Did you see a woman come in here? Just a little while ago."

"No, I haven't seen anything. Just help me, man, I'm scared."

"I'll help you, I promise," Nate said. "What did you see before you were shot?"

"I found the house. I knew it was the right one because I saw the Jeep in the garage. I looked through the back window and saw one of the guys with this chubby girl dressed all in pink. I was looking for a way into the garage. I thought maybe I'd disable the Jeep so they couldn't leave, you know? But when I got back here, the other one stepped out from the shed and just shot me."

"Did you overhear any conversation? Did they say where they were headed from here?"

Pi shook his head and closed his eyes again. "I didn't hear anything. It really hurts. Where's that ambulance?"

"It will be here soon."

The light changed and Nate turned to see Dwight in the doorway. "What happened to him?" he asked.

"Gunshot wound. The ambulance is on its way."

"Where's Jamie?"

"I don't know." Nate rose. "Stay with Pi, will you? I've got to go look for her."

He found Travis in the living room, on the phone. The sheriff ended the call. "I put out a BOLO on the Jeep, and there's already an Amber Alert for Donna."

"With the roads closed, we know they can't go far," Nate said.

"It's still a big county," Travis said.

"I think they'll go somewhere familiar," Nate said. "Some place they don't think we'll look, because we've looked there before."

"You think they'll go back to the summer cabins?" Travis asked.

"It makes the most sense," Nate said. "It's easy to get to, but away from other houses and people."

"Which cabins?" Travis asked.

"Sundance," Nate said. "They stayed there at least a few days, and the back way to the road makes it easier for them to get away. And they burned the Toyota there. They keep coming back to that location."

"Then let's go."

JAMIE FOCUSED ON keeping Tim talking. As long as she was talking, she and Donna were still alive. "What made you come to Eagle Mountain?" she asked. "You'd have a lot more targets in a big city like Denver."

"More cops, too," Tim said. "But coming here was my partner's idea. Some woman he knew was here and he wanted to see her. Then he realized how easy it would be to fool a little sheriff's department like this one. It was kind of an experiment, I guess."

"And you just went along with the idea of killing a bunch of women?" Jamie wasn't sure she did a good job of masking her disgust.

"Yeah, well, I was a little freaked out with the first one, but then, it was kind of a thrill, you know? Getting away with something, right under the cops' noses." He stood and walked over to the bed. "And now there'll be one less cop to follow us around."

Donna whimpered and pressed closer against Jamie, who could feel her shaking. "Is this really your sister?" Tim asked. "She doesn't look like you. Must be a drag, having to look after her."

"It's not a drag," Jamie said. "Donna is the most wonderful sister in the world. I'm very lucky to have her."

"Well, you won't have anything much longer. As soon as my friend gets back—" He made a slashing motion across his throat.

Donna began to sob again.

A phone rang and Tim answered. "Yeah? Where are you, man? I'm waiting… What? You're gonna make me deal with both of them?… No, I'm not saying I can't do it, just that that's not how this works. We're a team, aren't we?… All right, all right. I'll bring them and we can do them there. Where are you?" He glanced toward the window. "It's really coming down out there, isn't it?… Yeah,

I know you like the snow 'cause it covers our tracks. It's still cold... All right. Be there in a few." He replaced the phone in his pocket. "Change of plans, ladies. We're gonna go for a little ride." He reached for Donna but as soon as he touched her, she screamed.

"Shut up!" He slapped her across the face, then pulled a bandanna from his pocket and stuffed it in her mouth. "You cooperate or I'll slit your throat right here." He shifted his gaze to Jamie. "And if you give me any trouble, I'll kill her first—slowly."

Jamie suppressed a shudder. For whatever reason, Alex had left Tim to deal with her and Donna on his own. That upped the odds in her favor. "Donna, honey, you do what he says," she said.

Tim hauled Donna to her feet. "That's better," he said. "Now I'm gonna put you in this chair by the door, then I'll get your sister. I'll tie the two of you together and cut loose your feet, then we'll all go out to the car. And remember, don't try anything." He pulled a small pistol from beneath his sweatshirt. "I can't miss from this close range."

Jamie's stomach clenched as she stared at the pistol, then she forced herself to look away. Even if he fired on her, he might not kill her. Some chance of staying alive was better than none. She braced herself and when he bent over to pull her to her feet, she resisted. "I'm caught on something," she said, pretending to try to raise up. "I think the tape on my wrists is hung up on a spring or something."

"What?" He bent over to take a closer look and she brought her knees up and hit him hard in the nose. A sickening crunch, and blood spurted across her. Tim screamed and dropped the pistol, clutching at his nose. He stumbled backward and Jamie struggled upright. She dived for the gun even as he reached for it, and then he was standing over her, kicking her and cursing. She dodged his blows and kicked out at the pistol, sending it skittering under the bed. Tim struck her hard on the side of the head. Her vision blurred and her stomach heaved. "Donna, run!" she shouted. "Hop or crawl if you have to, just leave."

Donna remained in her chair, tears streaming down her face. "Jamie, I can't leave you!"

"Donna, go!"

"Neither one of you are going anywhere." Tim had retrieved the gun and stood over her, the barrel of the pistol inches from her forehead. Jamie closed her eyes and thought of Nate—how she would never see him again, or get to tell him that she loved him. She'd been so foolish, wasting time being afraid of what might happen, instead of enjoying the time they had together.

The door to the cabin burst open and gunfire exploded. Jamie braced herself against the pain she was sure would come, but instead only felt hands reaching for her. She opened her eyes to find Nate beside her, slashing through the tape at her wrists and ankles. She threw her arms around him and he gathered her close. "Donna?" she asked.

"She's fine. Travis is helping her."

The tears she had been holding back for the last few hours burst forth. "I love you," she sobbed. "I'm sorry I didn't tell you before."

"Shhh." He patted her back, soothing her. "You didn't have to tell me," he said. "I knew."

"How did you know?" She stared at him through the tears.

"That day I saw you at the scavenger hunt on Travis's ranch, when you wouldn't even look at me. I knew I'd never stopped loving you—and that you wouldn't avoid me like that unless there were still some strong feelings buried somewhere."

"You were awfully sure of yourself," she said.

"I was sure you were the only woman for me," he said. "I had to go away to figure that out, but now I'm back to stay."

Jamie clutched his shoulder. "I come with a lot of baggage, you know."

He hugged her close. "Donna isn't baggage," he whispered. "She's an extra bonus. I never had a sister, you know."

"Am I gonna be your sister?" Donna knelt beside them.

"If you'll have me for a brother," Nate said.

"I think you'd better ask Jamie if she'll have you for a husband," Donna said. "That's the way it's supposed to work, you know. You propose to your girlfriend, not her sister."

Jamie almost laughed out loud at the expression on Nate's face, but he recovered quickly and took her hand. "What about it, Jamie?" he asked. "Will you marry me?"

"Yes." She kissed him.

"Yes!" Donna said and kissed him, too.

Someone cleared his throat, and Jamie looked up to see the sheriff standing over them. "Tim Dawson is dead," he said. "Do you know where Alex Woodruff is?"

"He called and told Tim to meet him somewhere, and to bring us with him," Jamie said. "But I don't know where." She looked at Nate. "Did you shoot Tim?"

"If I hadn't, he would have killed you," he said.

She nodded. "Yes."

"Maybe we can trace Alex through Tim's phone," Travis said. "We'll gather what evidence we can here. In the meantime, Nate, will you take Jamie and her sister home?"

"I should stay and help," Jamie said, trying to scramble to her feet.

"Take care of your sister first," Travis said. "That's an order, Deputy."

"Yes, sir." She would take care of Donna. She and Nate together. They would be a family. Amazing how wonderful that sounded.

Ice Cold Killer Claims Another Victim

A twenty-three-year-old local woman is the Ice Cold Killer's latest victim, after her body was found in her vehicle on County Road Seven early Tuesday morning. Her identity has not been released, pending notification of her next of kin.

Sheriff Travis Walker announced Monday evening that Timothy Dawson, 21, who was one of the chief suspects in the string of murders that have shocked Rayford County over the past few weeks, was killed during a confrontation with law enforcement officers. Dawson's accomplice remains at large and, as the latest murder seems to indicate, intends to continue his killing spree.

* * * * *

COMING SOON!

We really hope you enjoyed reading this book. If you're looking for more romance, be sure to head to the shops when new books are available on

Thursday 17th October

To see which titles are coming soon, please visit

millsandboon.co.uk/nextmonth

LET'S TALK
Romance

For exclusive extracts, competitions
and special offers, find us online:

f facebook.com/millsandboon

🐦 @MillsandBoon

📷 @MillsandBoonUK

Get in touch on 01413 063232

For all the latest titles coming soon, visit
millsandboon.co.uk/nextmonth

JOIN US ON SOCIAL MEDIA!

Stay up to date with our latest releases, author
news and gossip, special offers and discounts, and
all the behind-the-scenes action
from Mills & Boon...

 millsandboon

 millsandboonuk

 millsandboon

It might just be true love...

MILLS & BOON
Desire

Indulge in secrets and scandal, intense drama and plenty of sizzling hot action with powerful and passionate heroes who have it all: wealth, status, good looks… everything but the right woman.

MILLS & BOON
True Love
Romance from the Heart

Celebrate true love with tender stories of
heartfelt romance, from the rush of falling
in love to the joy a new baby can bring,
and a focus on the emotional
heart of a relationship.